Praise for the *Henrietta and In:*

T0013902

A Ring of Truth:
"An engaging and effective romp rich with historical details."
—*Kirkus*

"Set in the 1930s, this romantic mystery combines the teetering elegance of *Downton Abbey* and the staid traditions of *Pride and Prejudice* with a bit of spunk and determination that suggest Jacqueline Winspear's *Maisie Dobbs.*"
—*Booklist*

"Henrietta and Inspector Howard make a charming odd couple in *A Ring of Truth*, mixing mystery and romance in a fizzy 1930s cocktail."
—Hallie Ephron, *New York Times* bestselling author

For *A Girl Like You:*
"Michelle Cox masterfully recreates 1930s Chicago, bringing to life its diverse neighborhoods and eclectic residents, as well as its seedy side. Henrietta and Inspector Howard are the best pair of sleuths I've come across in ages—Cox makes us care not just about the case, but about her characters. A fantastic start to what is sure to be a long-running series."
—Tasha Alexander, *New York Times* bestselling author of *The Lady Emily Mysteries*

"Fans of spunky, historical heroines will love Henrietta Von Harmon."
—*Booklist* starred review

"Flavored with 1930s slang and fashion, this first volume in what one hopes will be a long series is absorbing. Henrietta and Clive are a sexy, endearing, and downright fun pair of sleuths. Readers will not see the final twist coming."
—*Library Journal* starred review

A Spying Eye

A Spying Eye

A HENRIETTA AND INSPECTOR HOWARD NOVEL

BOOK 6

MICHELLE COX

SHE WRITES PRESS

Published 2022
Printed in the United States of America
Print ISBN: 978-1-64742-500-5
E-ISBN: 978-1-64742-501-2
Library of Congress Control Number: 2019916053

For information, address:
She Writes Press
1569 Solano Ave #546
Berkeley, CA 94707

She Writes Press is a division of SparkPoint Studio, LLC.

To Sue Splinter Conlon, my very first friend and co-founder of The Spying Eyes Detective Agency

We spent endless summers roaming pastures and playgrounds looking for mysteries to solve, and though we never found one, I will not soon forget those happy, innocent days. Thank you for unceasing friendship; it has meant the world to me.

Chapter 1

"How do I look?" Henrietta asked as she entered the well-appointed drawing room of Lord and Lady Linley's London home.

"Darling, you know very well you look ravishing." Clive lowered the newspaper he was perusing to glance over at her. He was, of course, already dressed in white tie and was merely passing the time by reading the London business news, waiting for her to descend from their rooms, where Henrietta's maid, Edna, had spent the last hour dressing her mistress.

Unlike the first time the Howards had crossed the Atlantic, which had been on their honeymoon trip to visit Clive's ancestral home, Castle Linley, in Derbyshire, England, they had this time agreed to at least bring along a lady's maid to aid Henrietta in her dress, especially as they would be much more in society this time, at least while in London, it being the height of the season, and likewise considering that Clive was hopeless at buttons.

It still made Henrietta smile to think of the years she had spent dressing herself in any number of costumes she had worn for her various jobs not so very long ago, her stints as an usherette at a burlesque theater and as a Dutch girl at the Chicago World's Fair being foremost in her mind. Never in those days of extreme poverty had she imagined that she would one day be married to the dashing heir of the fabulously wealthy Howard family of Winnetka and would thus be required to dress in such elaborate gowns that she needed the aid of another person to not only arrange and fasten them but to likewise style her hair every evening.

Her personal maid, Edna, herself barely twenty, had been hesitant to accompany her mistress to foreign shores when the idea was first announced, having never gone beyond the Chicago environs in her whole life. She had come round to the idea with amazing alacrity, though, when Clive's mother, Antonia, suggested that perhaps Gertrude, one of the downstairs parlor maids, should go instead—if Edna was reluctant, that is. No, Edna had suddenly declared, she would go.

As it turned out, however, poor Edna had spent the majority of their voyage on the Queen Mary sick as a dog in the bowels of the ship, leaving Henrietta to fend for herself much of the time, anyway. Henrietta had not minded in the least, as it left her and Clive to be blissfully on their own, unencumbered by servants or any other persons, for that matter, which had been the point of getting away in the first place, Henrietta more than once reminded Clive, who worried that she was overexerting herself while her maid lay in bed below deck. "Clive, don't be silly. I'm perfectly well. If anything, the sea air is doing me good."

Clive had not responded to this but had continued to hover around her in the most annoying, albeit charming, way. He, for his part, had managed to successfully leave his valet behind, saying that he would not be stalked by the odious Carter while trying to enjoy this attempt at a resurrected honeymoon, the first one having been brought to an unfortunate halt by the untimely death of his father, which had sent them hurrying back to Chicago before they had barely even gotten started.

"I don't know what you have against the man," Antonia had sniffed as she sat across from Clive at dinner the night before he and Henrietta had left on their grand trip. "He served your father very well all those years, and being English himself, he would be quite a valuable asset while abroad, Clive."

"Mother, we've been through all of this before." Clive let out a sigh. "Carter's positively ancient. He'd barely survive the voyage, much less our travels through the continent. We plan to do a lot of walking. Hiking, I think they call it. Isn't that right, darling?" he said, throwing a wink at Henrietta.

"Hiking? Whatever for? Sounds monstrous." Antonia rang the little brass bell beside her, signaling the new footman, Albert, to clear and reset their places for dessert. "You must consider Henrietta's condition, Clive. She needs rest; isn't that what you told me? And why do you need to scurry away just now instead of waiting until after the garden party? It's rather cruel of you, you know."

Henrietta was of the mind that it *was* actually a little bit unfair to leave Antonia to herself for the Howards' annual gala in late July, but Clive, used to his mother's manipulations, was having none of it.

"We can't possibly wait until after that, Mother. I mean to take advantage of the weather. Besides, Julia will be here, and you two have always managed it on your own, so I don't see what it matters. If you take my advice, which I'm certain you won't, you'll cancel it this year. After all, it hasn't even been a year yet since Father died. No one expects it."

"Of course, they do, Clive. How ridiculous. It's more important than ever, I should imagine."

"I *am* sorry to miss it, Antonia," Henrietta said sincerely, finally deciding to speak for herself.

"I know it's not your fault, dear." Antonia let out a little sigh of her own. "You'll just have to make the most of the Season, never mind the weather." She shot Clive a little dagger. "Now, I've made some . . . inquiries, you might say, and, as I mentioned just before we came in to dinner, you're to attend the Duke of Buckingham's ball the first week you arrive."

"Ah, yes. This again. Mother, please; we're trying to get away from all of that. That's the point of a honeymoon, remember?"

Antonia looked affronted. "You speak as if it's a burden, Clive! Well, I'm sorry," she said before he could speak, "but duty is duty. You can't possibly pass up this chance. And," she paused, waiting for Albert to finish placing a small dish of sorbet in front of each of them, "as it turns out, I have a little surprise." She looked eagerly from one to the other. "It seems I've finally unearthed the Von Harmons! With some help from Lady Linley, of course," she added with a conceding little tilt of her head.

Henrietta looked quizzically at Clive, who responded with a small shrug. Von Harmon had been her maiden name, but she had no idea what her mother-in-law was talking about.

"Now, it's all arranged," Antonia hurried on, either not noticing or ignoring their confusion. "You're to stop in Strasbourg on your way to Lucerne and stay with Baron Von Harmon. He is *most* intrigued to meet you."

"Who's Baron Von Harmon?" Clive asked with only mild interest. "I've never heard of him."

Antonia's look of delight withered slightly. "Why, Baron Von Harmon is an uncle of some sort to Henrietta. On her father's side. Do you not remember?" she asked Henrietta.

Henrietta set down her sorbet spoon and tried to think. She did not have a good feeling about this. She should have never repeated to Antonia the silly tales her father had once told his large brood of children as they sat with their meager supper in a shabby apartment in the city. They were stories of the "old country," as he called it—a place called Alsace-Lorraine, where the Von Harmons had, once upon a time, been part of the landed class, or so he had bragged. None of them, however, particularly Henrietta's antagonistic mother, had ever really believed that their father's stories were anything more than that—just stories.

But, Henrietta remembered now, in her own defense, she had not volunteered this portion of her family history readily; Antonia had prodded her into extracting it upon their very first meeting. Flustered in that moment, Henrietta had eventually managed to unearth a small detail from one of her father's tales, which was that an errant Von Harmon—or so she seemed to remember—had run off to Chicago, thus beginning the lowly American branch of the Von Harmons. Flimsy though this reference was, it was enough for Antonia to later confirm that Henrietta must indeed be a descendant of this noble line.

"Do you not recall when you first came to us, and I wrote to Lady Linley about the possible connection?" Antonia looked at her expectantly, as if this was all the explanation Henrietta should need to piece together the puzzle.

In truth, so much had happened so quickly when Clive had initially brought home the impoverished Henrietta, proudly announcing her as his fiancée, that she must have forgotten this choice bit of information. What had been more distressing—for Henrietta, anyway—and more immediate in its effects, had not been the discovery of her father's supposed noble connections, but the revelation that her mother had in fact been an Exley, one of Antonia and Alcott's gilded set. Antonia, however, desperate as she was at the beginning to validate Clive's inappropriate choice of a wife in any way that she could, had made much of *both*, Henrietta seemed to remember now. At the time, Henrietta had judged the theory regarding her father's family to be a bit farfetched, but she was much too shy and confused in those early days to counter the formidable Antonia Howard.

"Antonia, I'm sure they are no relation." Henrietta traded her sorbet spoon for the etched wine glass to her right, sensing that a battle with her mother-in-law was just on the horizon. "Von Harmon is probably a very common name."

"Yes, and we can't possibly change our itinerary to stay in some crumbling château on the French border with these people you assume are Henrietta's relatives. It's absurd. And even if they are related in some distant way, what significance would it possibly serve for us to meet them, sparing perhaps a mild curiosity on the part of Henrietta?"

"Clive, honestly," Antonia said stiffly. "I know you cannot

possibly be this naïve. You're just being stubbornly obtuse, and it's very bad form, not to mention unfeeling. I've gone to considerable trouble, so do not thwart me in this. You must absolutely reconnect with Henrietta's family. If not for our sake, then surely for hers. The Von Harmons are a very old family. There is a Hapsburg connection somewhere there, and Louisa Von Harmon was a lady-in-waiting to Queen Mary. You have no idea how much this will elevate us, Clive."

"I wasn't aware we were in need of any further elevation, Mother. I'm quite breathless at this height as it is," Clive said crisply. "Isn't having Lord and Lady Linley as your in-laws a close enough connection to the peerage to be content?"

"Don't be impertinent, Clive. What I'm asking is not so very much, is it? You're going to be in London anyway. Why can't you attend the duke's ball? And why not stop in Strasbourg for a few days? It's a very beautiful city, you know."

"Mother, I—"

"Of course, we'll attend the ball, Antonia," Henrietta interrupted, giving Clive a look. "You'll have to help me choose which gown."

"But of course, my dear. See, Clive? She's being sensible."

"Sensible?" Clive laughed. "I suppose you're right to a certain extent. She's sensible enough to know when to change tactics."

"I *am* still in the room, you know," Henrietta said with raised eyebrows. "And as far as Strasbourg is concerned, I confess I *am* a little curious to meet this Baron Von Harmon. Aren't you, Clive? You never know, it might be entertaining."

"I can think of a better word for it," Clive grumbled, swirling his glass. "Let's discuss it later."

With that answer, Henrietta knew she would not get any more from him at that moment, but she also knew that, in the end, he would deny her nothing. What difference would it make if they had a diversion for a couple of days from their decided path? Isn't that what they had wanted? Spontaneity? But she knew that if she presented it this way, he would say that it wasn't spontaneous at all, apparently having been planned weeks in advance by his mother and his aunt, Lady Linley.

Antonia, also seeming to sense that she would not get anything more from Clive on the subject, abruptly rose from her place. The gangly Albert hurried over to pull her chair for her. "Shall we go through and leave poor Clive to his port, my dear?"

"Yes, of course, Antonia." Henrietta rose as well, though she knew that Clive was itching to do away with these old traditions, particularly since his father's death. He had suggested as much a few weeks prior, but Antonia would have none of it, insisting that nothing about their routine should change in the slightest. Clive had fumed about it in their private rooms, but Henrietta had advised him to wait it out.

"I say, you do look rather beautiful," Clive said now, folding his paper and looking at her appreciatively.

Henrietta made a show of turning this way and that, showing off the gold lamé Chanel gown with puffed sleeves and an exposed back that Antonia had insisted she wear, saying that it would be absolutely perfect for this evening's gala. "It's a shame Wallace and Amelie couldn't be here as well."

"Well, you know Wallace. He was never one for London." Clive stood up and adjusted his tie. "A drink before we go?"

Henrietta nodded. "Still, I would have liked to see Amelie again. And the boys, though no doubt they would have left them behind."

"There's a chance that Wallace might make it down before we're off." Clive lifted the heavy crystal decanter from the sideboard and poured out two sherries. "But no guarantees. He's always hated this place." Clive handed her a glass. "In fact, I'm pretty sure Wallace will sell it once Uncle passes."

"No! Really?" Henrietta took a sip of her sherry and looked around the old-fashioned room, papered in dark green flock and trimmed in mahogany. "What a shame!"

"He's said as much, anyway, in his last letter to me," Clive said, putting the large crystal stopper back into the decanter with a clink.

"Said we should 'live it up' before it goes up on the block. I think he was specifically referring to the wine cellar. Provided the servants haven't already drunk it dry," he said, shifting his gaze to the doorway, as if a servant might be standing just on the other side, which wasn't likely, Henrietta guessed, as there were precious few servants here at all—just a butler, a housekeeper, a cook, and one footman, who likewise doubled as the chauffeur. It was terribly understaffed, and Henrietta couldn't imagine how they operated such a big house on their own. A hired maid appeared every morning, but she did not live in, making Henrietta again grateful that she had followed Antonia's advice and brought along Edna.

"I can't say I blame Wallace," Clive went on. "It *is* horribly outdated, and I'm sure it costs a fortune to run. A fortune, we both know, that Wallace doesn't have."

Poor Wallace, Clive's sole cousin, had gone against Lord Linley's wishes—nay, his pleading, almost bullying—that he marry well, and had instead secretly married a penniless French woman who had nursed him back to health after he was injured in the war. It was assumed that this was one of the reasons Lord Linley still lay ill in bed, the discovery of his only remaining son's imprudent marriage nearly crippling him. Wallace's older brother, Linley, the heir, had not been quite so fortunate as Wallace during the war and had perished on the Somme, thereby passing the title and all of its heavy burdens onto Wallace, who had absolutely no desire to be "lord of the manor." Brought utterly low by Wallace's rash decision to marry for love, Lord Linley had declared that it meant certain financial ruin for the crumbling estate and had taken to his bed. Not even the revelation that Wallace and Amelie already had a son and future heir as well as another newly born could rouse Montague Howard for more than a few hours a day. And then, the tragic news of his brother's untimely death in Chicago had nearly finished him off completely.

"Maybe we should buy it," Henrietta suggested, taking another sip of her sherry.

Clive scoffed. "Darling, whatever for? It's positively ghastly. If we do someday return to England, we can always stay at The Savoy or travel up to Castle Linley, provided Wallace doesn't turn the whole thing into a home for shell-shocked soldiers, or some such damned thing, once Uncle dies."

"You don't really think he'll do that, do you?"

"Well, he's threatened it enough."

Henrietta looked around the room again. It would be a shame to lose something that had been in the family for so long, and she hated to see the end of things. "I thought you liked old-fashioned things," she said wistfully, running a finger along the ornate rococo clock on the mantle. "And what about sentiment?"

"Darling, there's a difference between old-fashioned and foolish. Especially when it involves a new slate roof, a new heating system, and tuck-pointing, to say the least." He took a large drink. "Besides, it's 1936. Sentiment, unfortunately, has died. We must move on. Be modern."

"Well, I rather like this place." She looked around again. "What will they do with all of this stuff?"

"Sell it probably. Or ship it to Castle Linley."

"What a shame."

"Yes, it is, darling, but it's not our concern. We have enough at Highbury to worry about, speaking of repairs. Another?" Clive asked, holding up his now-empty glass.

"We'd better not, Clive. We should go."

"All right," he sighed and gave the thick strap that hung beside the fireplace a tug.

Within moments, Evans appeared. "You rang, sir?"

"We're leaving now, Evans. Tell Farnsworth to bring the car around."

"Very good, sir," Evans said, swaying slightly in the doorway before withdrawing.

Clive took a step toward Henrietta and ran a finger down her arm. "Do we really have to go to this?"

Henrietta patted his cheek. "Clive, don't be such a child. Of course, we do. Antonia would be furious if we missed it."

Evans entered the room, then, balancing Henrietta's fur stole across his arms.

"Must you always bring my mother into it?" Clive sighed, stepping back as the elderly butler attempted to drape the stole across Henrietta's shoulders, his rheumatic hands letting it slip several times. Finally, Clive stepped forward. "Thank you, Evans, I've got it."

"As you wish, sir," Evans said, blinking his droopy, watery eyes several times as he stood back.

Clive arranged the stole, letting his hands linger on Henrietta's bare shoulders. She could see the all-too-familiar flicker of desire in his eyes.

"If we didn't have this damn ball to go to, I'd take you upstairs and—"

"Clive!" she said, putting a finger to his lips and rolling her eyes toward Evans, who was still sagging nearby.

Clive let out a little laugh. "I find it utterly charming that you're still shy in front of the servants," he whispered into her ear. "Very well," he said, standing up straight, "shall we go and get this over with? Evans, is the car ready?"

"I believe so, sir, yes."

Evans shuffled ahead of them and held open the front door, adjusting his wrinkled suit coat and attempting to stand as much at attention as his rounded shoulders would allow.

"Thank you, Evans. That will be all for tonight," Henrietta said gently.

Evans turned his viscous eyes to Clive, apparently seeking validation.

"Yes, yes, Evans," Clive said absently, stealing a grin at Henrietta as he took her arm. "You needn't wait up."

"Very good, sir."

Chapter 2

The drive to Grosvenor Square was not long at all, Lord and Lady Linley's home being, as it was, located in the only slightly less fashionable area of St. James's.

When they alighted from the ancient Rolls, Clive told Farnsworth not to wait, that they would either walk home if it was still warm, or hail a cab if it wasn't. Henrietta could visibly see the relief on the man's face as he tipped his hat to them and wished them a good evening.

Clive linked his arm through Henrietta's and led her up the few front stairs of the Duke of Buckingham's London home. From the outside, it resembled all the rest of the Regency mansions lining the square, several stories high and just as wide, with Corinthian pillars built into the red brick. It exuded power and elegance and stately tradition, but as the Howards stepped inside, Henrietta was stunned by how very modern the interior appeared.

The grand foyer was paneled halfway up in a sleek cherrywood, and art deco sconces lined the walls where once, Henrietta assumed, ornate fixtures of gilded brass or gold might have been. Also gone was any sign of the usual thick wallpaper, the walls instead being painted in a color that Henrietta could only describe as some shade of bluish-green—aqua, she thought it was called. Besides the servant who stepped forward to take her stole and Clive's top hat and the two perfectly uniformed footmen standing guard at the front door, there seemed to be absolutely no other vestige of formality, at least that Henrietta could see. Indeed, several guests in varying degrees of drunkenness were laughing and talking in the foyer, and one woman ran past them, giving a little screech of delight as a young man chased her.

"What were you saying about modern?" Henrietta murmured to Clive as they stepped past a fountain, of all things, that had actual running water cascading into a pool in the floor in the middle of the room. Clive responded with merely a little harrumph and guided her toward what she assumed was the ballroom, which, she soon found, had more the feel of a nightclub than what one would expect from a "ball" given by a peer of the realm. No servant stepped forward to announce them, not that he would have been heard anyway over the loud jazz that emanated from somewhere deep inside the room, so they merely stepped into the throng of people who were laughing, chatting, dancing wildly, and throwing back what looked to be martinis. If *this* is what passed for fashion and respectability amongst the London aristocracy, she thought, looking eagerly around, then they were woefully behind in Chicago, where their gilded North Shore set still primarily entertained with a string quartet and waltzes and old champagne.

Henrietta gripped Clive's arm and strained her ears to try to pick out what the band was playing. Her heart gave a little thrill when she realized it was "Lovely to Look At," which made her feel at once both a little homesick and nostalgic. It had been one of her favorites when she worked as a taxi dancer in a cheap dance hall in Chicago, which is where, coincidentally, she and Clive had surreptitiously met. At sixteen years her senior, Clive's musical tastes, she knew, ran closer to those of his parents', but he was wonderfully indulgent of her love for the latest big band sound and had even hired the famous Helen Forrest to sing at their wedding reception as a surprise. Likewise, he didn't mind when she wanted to listen to *Your Hit Parade* on the radio at night in their private wing at Highbury, and he had also bought her several jazz records for their Victrola.

A footman carrying a large tray of drinks passed very near them, and Clive managed to snag a martini and a flute of champagne before the man disappeared completely into the crowd, gingerly weaving his way through. Henrietta gratefully accepted the champagne Clive held out to her and looked around the room for the duke.

The duke, one Archibald Villiers, Clive had explained on the drive over, had only recently assumed the title and was quite young— barely twenty-two—and already had a reputation as being a bit of a scamp. Likewise, he was rumored to be close friends with the abdicated King Edward, which also implied much.

"Do you see him?" Henrietta shouted at Clive over the din.

"Who?" Clive asked, looking around himself.

"The duke, of course."

"Well, never having met him, I can't say for sure, but if I had to guess, I'd say that was him over there." Clive gestured with his martini in the direction of a young man surrounded by an eager group of hangers-on. He cut an elegant figure, his suit perfectly tailored and his short, very blond hair slicked back. Henrietta studied him. He was laughing, exuding an air of confident frivolity, as if he were just a schoolboy having pals over during the holidays and not entertaining London society as the Duke of Buckingham.

"And here I thought you knew all of the British aristocracy," Henrietta teased. "Is he married?"

"Heavens, no. But I think Mother mentioned that an arrangement has been made with Josephina Ridley, one of Viscount Ridley's daughters."

"An arrangement? Sounds like a business deal."

"It very probably is." Clive took a drink of his martini, which, Henrietta was surprised to see, was already almost gone. She knew he couldn't possibly be intimidated in this aristocratic setting, but, she also knew, neither did he enjoy it, or any such privileged event he had been born to. It was one of the reasons he had tried, after the war, to take up a new life in the city as a detective with the Chicago police before his parents had successfully reeled him back in to take his place at the helm of Highbury and his father's firm, Linley Standard. Also, she knew that crowds sometimes afflicted him—an aftereffect of the war. "Fits" he called them, though he was extremely ashamed to ever talk about them at length.

After studying Clive for several moments and deciding that he was not about to experience one of them now, Henrietta finally pulled her eyes from him to again look over at the duke and noticed that they seemed to have somehow caught his attention. It was only momentary, however, before he looked away, laughing at something someone near to him said. Henrietta continued to observe him, though, until he shot her another unexpected glance, catching her in the act of staring at him and causing her to flush a little with embarrassment. She looked away. He was dreadfully handsome. She forced herself to look around at the crowd, briefly trying to memorize the gowns, as she knew Antonia would expect her to write about them in her next letter home. But after only a few moments, she found her gaze ventured back to the duke, and she was surprised to see that he was now walking straight toward them, the crowd parting easily for him as he did so.

"I say, you must be the two Americans we've been expecting," he said once he stood before them, his voice light and boyish. "Mr. and Mrs. Howard, is that right?" He gripped a cigarette between two fingers of his right hand, the other resting lightly in the front pocket of his tuxedo.

"That is correct, Your Grace." Clive gave him a respectful nod. "I'm Clive Linley Howard, and may I present my wife, Henrietta Howard."

Henrietta held out her hand to the duke, who took it and brought it to his lips. "Delighted." He looked her up and down completely before releasing her hand.

Clive cleared his throat. "I must thank you for the invitation," he said stiffly, drawing the duke's attention back to himself. "I'm afraid that was my mother's doing, and I do apologize."

The duke chuckled. "Think nothing of it. What would we do

without meddling mothers, eh? Fortunately, mine has disappeared somewhere or other. She doesn't quite approve of my soirees," he said, gesturing widely with his cigarette.

"I was sorry to hear of your father's death," Clive said, trying not to shout over the music.

"Thank you. Thank you, indeed. Rotten luck," the duke said, his brow a little furrowed. "He was a great friend of your uncle, Lord Linley, I believe. Shame he couldn't attend tonight, but I daresay I'm very glad for the chance to meet the two of you," he said, his eyes flicking to Henrietta, where they hovered a few extra moments. "What brings you to London?" he asked, turning back to Clive now as he inhaled deeply. "Surely it's not to attend this gathering. If so, you're sure to be disappointed. Frightfully dull, really," he said, looking around ruefully.

"A bit of business. I'm here to meet with some of our London investors, and then off we go to the continent."

"Ah. Wise move. London during the season is positively beastly. I presume you're off to Italy?"

"Eventually," Clive said, draining his martini. "We'll spend some time in Switzerland before going on to Italy and then finishing in Paris."

The duke gave an approving nod. "Switzerland is beautiful this time of year, but I'd give Paris a miss. It's overrated, if you ask me."

"Well, I can't wait to see it," Henrietta said boldly and took a sip of her champagne. "Clive's promised to take me to the Eiffel Tower."

"Have you never been?" the duke asked, looking at her with incredulousness.

"No, I haven't. It will be my first time."

The duke studied her intently. "Well, then, you must forgive me. I forget that not everyone is as jaded as I am."

"You're awfully young to be jaded, Your Grace," Henrietta said and instantly blushed.

A wry smile erupted across the duke's face. "I say, Mrs. Howard, would you care to dance?"

Henrietta hesitated. She wasn't intimidated, exactly, by the man standing before her—hadn't she danced with hundreds of men at the Promenade? And hadn't she already danced with an assortment of the aristocracy at Castle Linley? But she felt a twinge of disappointment that her first dance would not be with Clive. She knew, however, that she couldn't very well refuse the Duke of Buckingham, especially as a guest in his home. She glanced at Clive, whose eyes, instead of expressing any sort of empathy or what was usually jealousy in these types of situations, was looking on with a maddening trace of amusement. Rascal!

"But of course, Your Grace," she said sweetly, making sure that Clive saw her bat her eyes at the duke as she accepted his arm. The duke proceeded to lead her across the floor, but Henrietta couldn't help but glance back over her shoulder and suppressed an urge to laugh at the sight of Clive's now-narrowed eyes.

"You really must call me Archie," the duke said languidly. "Everyone does. Heraldry is such a bore, don't you think?" He turned to face her now and took her hand in his.

"I . . . I wouldn't know, Your Grace. I mean . . . Archie."

"That's better." He smiled at her and placed his other hand on the small—the very small—of her back, expertly leading her into the rhythm. He smelled delightfully of expensive cologne and tobacco. There was silence between them for the first few moments of the dance, and Henrietta concentrated on watching all of the couples swirling around them.

"I must say, you dance beautifully, Mrs. Howard," the duke said, leaning close and speaking near her ear to be heard over the music.

"Thank you," she said, biting back a secret smile. "I've had a lot of practice."

"Chicago, is it? Where you're from? I think that's what my mother told me. I forget so much of what she says, if I'm being perfectly honest."

"Yes, Chicago. Though Clive and I live north. Highbury is the name of the Howard estate."

"I've never been to Chicago. New York a few times, of course, but not to the wilds."

Henrietta laughed. This was not the first time she had heard the English liken Chicago to some sort of frontier town. "You should try it sometime. You'll find us quite civilized. My husband and I would be happy to entertain you, though I think you might find Highbury rather dull, as you put it just now."

"Oh, I can't imagine any place being dull if *you're* there, Mrs. Howard," he said close to her ear again.

Henrietta pulled back slightly. She had begun attracting men's stares since she was a girl, and now, at just twenty years old, her beauty was unmatched. She was a woman whom men looked twice at, and, if truth be told, it had been what had sparked the attention of the cold, aloof Inspector Howard when he had shown up at the Promenade that night.

When she had eventually agreed to marry Clive, she naïvely thought that living amongst more genteel persons might finally eliminate this unwanted lasciviousness, but she found, to her disappointment, that there were just as many men in the landed class that stared at her full breasts and shapely legs as there had been bartenders and fry cooks who were guilty of the same.

"Am I to congratulate you, Your Grace?" she asked stiffly and enjoyed his momentary look of confusion.

"I don't know. *Are* you?" he asked, righting himself just as quickly. He twirled her. "But of course, you are referring to my impending engagement to the honorable Miss Ridley," he said once she was back in his arms. "How very informed you are, Mrs. Howard."

"I suppose you must call me Henrietta."

"Henrietta." He tilted his head approvingly. "I very much like the sound of that. And very cleverly done."

"Your Grace?"

"I'm sure it's not an accident that I'm granted the use of your Christian name only after my betrothed is mentioned. Very sensible."

Henrietta couldn't help but let a little laugh escape.

He instantly leaned closer. "How long did you say you would be in London?"

"*We* leave in two days' time."

"Ah." He was silent for a few moments. "And exactly why are you going abroad? Did you already mention it?"

"It's sort of a second honeymoon, I guess you might say." She contemplated mentioning Alcott's death, but before she could decide whether to bring all of that up, he spoke.

"A second honeymoon, eh? It begs several impertinent questions, but I'll refrain. It sounds dreadfully tedious, not to mention romantic. But, then again, you *are* American."

Henrietta wasn't sure what to say to that.

"Where are you staying in Switzerland?"

"Lucerne for a time, and then we go to Zurich. But first we're stopping in Strasbourg."

Henrietta felt his shoulder stiffen slightly under her gloved hand, as if she had said something wrong.

"Strasbourg? How terribly odd. Whatever for?" His brow wrinkled. "It's a charming little place, I'll grant you that, but there's really nothing there to see."

"Have you been?"

The duke shifted. "A few times, I believe. Nothing to signify."

"Oh, then you'll have to tell us where to go. I apparently have family there. We're going to stay with them at Château du Freudeneck."

"Château du Freudeneck?" He pulled back just a little to look more closely at her. "Can you possibly mean Baron Von Harmon?"

"Why, yes! Do you know him?"

"Not personally. He may be a distant cousin, I believe. You're related, you say?"

"Yes," Henrietta answered, noting the change in tone in the duke's voice, which had gone from flirtatious to suddenly serious and intrigued. "My maiden name is Von Harmon," Henrietta continued. "I haven't the faintest idea of how I'm related, but Clive's mother is convinced there is a connection, so we've agreed to stop."

"This is most interesting, Mrs. Howard."

"Oh, dear, I must have said something very wrong. Now I'm back to being Mrs. Howard." She tried giving him a sly smile, but it did not resonate the way she had hoped.

"Not at all," he said. "You've been the most charming of partners." The song ended, then, and the duke released her. "Thank you, Mrs. Howard. Henrietta," he said, giving her a slight bow. "It was a pleasure to meet you. I suspect we'll meet again very soon."

"Well, perhaps, but—"

Clive appeared at her elbow, surprising her.

"Ah. Mr. Howard. Perfectly timed." The duke tilted his head. "Enjoy your time in London. And abroad," he added, his eyes darting to Henrietta. "You'll excuse me now," he said with a forced smile. "I must greet my other guests." He turned, then, and wove his way into the crowd, just as the band began playing "You Are My Lucky Star."

"What happened?" Clive asked, over the music.

"I'm not sure. I've just had the strangest conversation."

"Well, I can't say I'm surprised. Come on," he said, putting an arm around her waist. "Let's dance. They're playing our song."

"I didn't think you noticed," Henrietta said, putting her hand in his.

"Well, I *am* a detective, you know. I tend to notice little things." He pulled her tight.

Henrietta let out a little laugh. "Clive! You'll crush my dress."

"I don't care," he said, twirling her now and then pulling her close again.

"Well, your mother will."

"Must you always bring up my mother?" His right eye twitched mischievously as he stared down at her.

"If necessary. Yes."

"Let's get out of here," he whispered in her ear, sending a little shiver of arousal cascading down her back.

"Already? We've only just arrived!" she said, trying to fight it.

"Darling, there's a wine cellar that needs attention."

"And here I thought it was me you wanted."

"That goes without saying," he said and bent to kiss her despite the fact that they were in so very public a place. She doubted, however, that anyone was paying the slightest bit of attention to them, which was wonderfully refreshing. She laced her fingers behind his neck and kissed him back.

"Oh, all right. But don't think you're always to get your way, you naughty thing."

"Understood," he mumbled through a grin and kissed her again.

Chapter 3

"Telegram for you, sir," Evans said quietly, creeping into the breakfast room with a silver salver, on top of which lay a crisp envelope.

Clive grimaced as he reached for it. They hadn't been in London for more than forty-eight hours and were already receiving a telegram. This could mean nothing good. "Thank you, Evans," he said curtly and waited for him to retreat before examining it. "Shall we wager on who this is from?" He held it up in the air.

Henrietta looked up briefly from her toast, to which she had been studiously applying jam.

Without waiting for her to answer, Clive went on. "My guess is that it's Elsie saying—" he paused to think, raising his eyes to the ceiling. "Saying that Anna's been kidnapped," he finished, referring to Henrietta's sister and the little girl she had recently become the protector of.

"Clive!"

"Well? Would it surprise you?" he asked, using a clean butter knife to open the envelope. Elsie was always getting herself in some sort of scrape, particularly of late. He pulled out the thin sheet of paper and quickly read the brief message. Thank God. It wasn't, after all, something to do with Elsie—or anyone back home, for that matter.

He tossed it to the side of his plate. "It's from Wallace. Apparently, he won't be traveling down today after all."

"That's too bad," Henrietta responded sincerely, "but I didn't think it was worth it anyway. We're leaving this afternoon." She very prettily took a bite of her toast. "Does he say why?"

"Apparently, Uncle Montague has taken another turn."

"Oh, no! Perhaps we change our plans. Go to Linley instead?"

Clive pushed his plate to the side, trying not to think of what his mother would say if she were here to see him do so. She would positively despair at the servants' inattentiveness. "No, I don't think so. He urges us not to, says that he will see us when we arrive back from Europe."

Henrietta reached for the pitcher of milk. "Speaking of, are you all packed? We leave in a couple of hours, you know."

"I'm aware of that, darling. And you needn't lord it over me," he said, picking up the newspaper, neatly ironed and folded at his right elbow. He knew that she was enjoying the fact that Edna had already arranged all of her things in her houndstooth cases, while he had been left to pack for himself. He opened the paper and gave it a little shake.

"All I'm saying is—" She was interrupted, however, by the entrance of Evans yet again.

"I'm sorry to disturb you, sir."

Clive let out an irritated sigh and put down his paper. "What is it now, Evans?"

"There is a gentleman here to see you, sir. Shall I say you're at home?"

"A gentleman?" His brow furrowed. "Who is it?"

"He says he is a Mr. John Hartle, sir."

Hartle? Clive had not spoken to Chief Inspector John Hartle since their original trip to Castle Linley where Clive—and Henrietta, as it had happened—had assisted him in solving the murder of a man in a local pub. But why on earth would he be in London? Dread filled Clive's chest as his mind immediately jumped to his uncle. Had he died? But that didn't make sense; wouldn't someone have tele-phoned? *Perhaps it's something to do with Wallace . . . or one of the children*, he worried.

"Show him into the study, Evans. I'll be there directly."

"Very good, sir," the elderly man answered and disappeared.

Clive stood up and shot a glance at Henrietta. "Coming, darling?"

"If you think I should," she said with a slight dip of her chin and a certain look, both of which suggested she was testing him.

"Darling, this is no time to quibble. Of course, I want you to come. I can't imagine what the man is doing here, but it can't be anything good."

"I agree," Henrietta said, quickly folding her napkin and setting it next to her plate. "I suppose it's too much to hope that it's a social call?"

"I doubt it," Clive said, adjusting his tie. "Come. Let's get it over with."

Though there had been various fits and starts in the early days of their relationship, Clive had finally promised Henrietta that she would be a real partner in their fledgling detective agency, such as it was. It was a promise, however, that he still privately had reserva-tions about and one which he found difficult to keep at times, as he was fiercely protective of her, despite her reminding him that she had grown up in poverty in Chicago and was not quite the china doll he imagined her to be. It was only after Henrietta's recent miscarriage and subsequent fall into depression that Clive had finally "come to his senses," fearing this sad change in his wife more than any exter-nal threat. For the first time, he found himself helpless to protect her, and upon the advice of Bennett, his father's right-hand man at the firm and now his, he had tentatively involved her in a case in a desperate attempt to cheer her, no matter that he had practically had to *invent* one. As it turned out, the case did prove successful in rous-ing Henrietta from her malaise, though, as usual, it had turned into something much more sinister than he could ever have predicted. Even after it was solved, he tried not to think about the danger she had been in and instead attempted to simply be grateful to have her back to her old self. But he had resolved that he wasn't about to take any more chances with their happiness. It was the reason he had proposed this trip in the first place.

"Inspector Hartle," Clive tried to say cheerfully as he and Henrietta entered the study. "What an unexpected surprise."

Hartle, looking out onto King Street, his hands in his pockets, turned from the window where he stood. His hair was grayer than Clive remembered, but otherwise he looked exactly the same—the same barreled chest and stocky figure.

"Ah, Mr. Howard. Thank you for seeing me." He stepped forward and shook Clive's outstretched hand.

"Certainly. You remember my wife, Henrietta," Clive said, gesturing toward her as she took up a stance beside him.

"Yes, of course." He smiled politely. "Mrs. Howard would indeed be difficult to forget."

"Hello, Chief Inspector," she said warmly.

"Is there something wrong, Hartle?" Clive asked, slipping into their old familiarity. "My uncle?" He gestured them toward the fireplace at the far end of the room.

"Your uncle?" Hartle's brow wrinkled. "Heavens, no. There's nothing amiss at Linley, as far as I know."

"Won't you sit down, Chief Inspector?" Henrietta suggested.

"I'm afraid this isn't a social call, Mrs. Howard. I was hoping I might have a word with your husband," he said awkwardly, flicking his eyes to Clive. "Maybe somewhere private. If you can spare the time, that is. It's a rather complicated matter."

Clive bit the inside of his cheek. He knew he couldn't ask Henrietta to step out—for one thing, he had no desire to start their trip on a sour note—and yet what was he to do?

"Of course, Chief Inspector," Henrietta acquiesced smoothly. "I'll leave the two of you. Shall I have some tea brought in?"

Clive reached for her hand. "Please stay," he said quietly, giving her the smallest of winks and thrilling to see her resultant smile. "There are no secrets between us, Hartle," he said, looking over at him now. "We're quite of one mind."

Hartle inclined his head and studied Clive with a raised eyebrow, skepticism writ large across his pock-marked face. "Very well, then. As you wish," he said with a sigh and sat down heavily on the red silk sofa.

"Tea, Inspector?" Henrietta asked.

"Not for me. Something stronger, perhaps," Hartle suggested gruffly.

Clive resisted the urge to check his wristwatch, but he was pretty sure it was not yet even eleven a.m. "Of course," he answered calmly as he walked to the old-fashioned drinks cart in the corner, though he began to worry afresh about what Hartle might have to relate. Obviously, it was of some weight. "Brandy?" he asked as he lifted the decanter. At Hartle's nod, he poured two brandies, as well as a sherry for Henrietta.

"What's this all about, Hartle?" Clive handed him a thick glass with an inch of amber liquid within. "What brings you to London? A case, perhaps?" he asked, hoping it was this and nothing else.

"I'm afraid you don't understand, Howard. I live in London now. I'm no longer with the Derbyshire constabulary. I left not long after you returned to America."

"Left? But why?"

"A position opened up in London, let's just say. So I took it."

Clive considered this information as he handed Henrietta her sherry and then took a seat in the leather wingback chair next to her. It was hard to believe that this rural detective was now a part of something as big and professional as Scotland Yard. He did not remotely look the part, sitting there in his outdated suit and scuffed shoes, and yet Clive knew that Hartle's criminal instincts, so to speak, would be appreciated wherever he served.

"Well, how do you find it?" Clive asked, crossing his legs neatly. "London, that is. Must be quite a change."

"Look, Howard, I don't have much time, so let's get straight to it," Hartle said, nervously glancing at the tall windows behind him.

"All right, then. Proceed." Clive eyed him coolly and took a long drink of his brandy, despite the early hour. Contrary to his initial impression that Hartle seemed as steady as ever, he perceived now that there *was* something a little different about the man. A slight disquiet, perhaps.

Hartle glanced at Henrietta before turning his gaze back to Clive. "I understand that you're traveling to Strasbourg."

"Strasbourg? Why, yes. How do you know that?" Clive's eyes narrowed.

"It is of no consequence."

"I strongly beg to differ."

Hartle took a drink, as if buying time while he weighed up his thoughts. "All right," he said slowly, "if you must know, it was the Duke of Buckingham."

"The duke?" Clive looked over at Henrietta.

"Yes, it must have been me," she said haltingly, as if trying to remember. "I mentioned it to him while we were dancing. He had a strange reaction to it, I seem to recall."

"What do you mean strange?" Clive asked.

"Just that he was . . . well, he was rather flirtatious before that," she said matter-of-factly, "but once I mentioned Strasbourg and the Von Harmons, his manner changed completely. As if I had disturbed him somehow."

Clive looked at Hartle. "I fail to see the connection. What do our travel plans have to do with the duke? Or you, for that matter?"

"What is your reason for going there?" Hartle's tone was oddly accusatory.

Clive merely stared at him, irritated by what was seeming more and more like an interrogation. "Do I have to have a reason?"

"The duke informs me that you will be staying at Château du Freudeneck," Hartle said, ignoring Clive's question. "Is that correct?" He shot another glance at Henrietta. "And that the Von Harmons are distant relatives of Henrietta?"

"Listen, what's this all about, Hartle? Be plain, man. Obviously, you think us involved in something underhand. Well, I'm sorry to disappoint you. There's absolutely not a shred of truth to whatever your theory happens to be. We're simply stopping in Strasbourg to fulfill some last-minute whim of my mother's before we travel on the Lucerne. That's it. Case closed."

Hartle studied him for several uncomfortable moments and then let out a deep breath. "No, I don't think you're involved, per se. Though you might *become* involved. And, yes, there is definitely something underhand going on, if you put it like that."

Clive was suddenly tempted to throw out a jest—suggesting art fraud, a boundary dispute, an illegitimate child—but he did not, a more rational part of him realizing that Hartle's very presence here implied something far more serious. Something big enough to catch the attention of the Duke of Buckingham and apparently of Scotland Yard.

Hartle stood and walked to the empty fireplace and leaned a hand on the mantle. "Have you ever heard of the Ghent Altarpiece?" He turned and looked at them.

"Can't say that I have. You, darling?" Clive looked over at Henrietta.

"No. Is it an altar cloth?"

"No, it's an artwork," Hartle answered. "A very valuable artwork, at that. It was painted by Jan van Eyck in 1432 and is considered a masterpiece of European art. One of the world's treasures, apparently, though I wouldn't know. As the name implies, it resided in Ghent at the Cathedral of St. Bavo." He paused to gauge their reactions thus far, which were nothing more than polite puzzlement. "Turns out," Hartle went on, "it has a very storied past. Not only has it survived several fires, but it's been stolen half a dozen times, including by Napoleon and even by Kaiser Wilhelm during the last war." He stopped to take a drink. "For a time, the kaiser had it displayed in Berlin, but when Germany fell, the altarpiece was forcibly repatriated to Belgium as part of the Treaty of Versailles. Now, it seems, it has come to the attention of the Nazis and Mr. Hitler, who considers the loss of it a national embarrassment and is determined to have it back. Some say he is obsessed by it."

"But it's safely back in St. Bavo's now?" Henrietta asked. "The painting, that is."

"Yes, for now. But there is talk of shipping it to the Vatican for safekeeping before the war breaks out."

"The war? It's not a certainty that there will be a war." Clive took a drink of his brandy.

"A war *is* coming, Howard, and if you don't believe that, you're more naïve than I thought you were. It's only a matter of time."

"So, the painting is safe, then," Henrietta suggested. Her brow was wrinkled up in that charming way it did when she was puzzled, and Clive felt a respondent little pull in his chest.

"Well, yes, but there's a bit of a snag." Hartle took a long drink.

"Of course, there is," Clive said wryly.

"The problem is that two years ago, one of the panels of the painting was stolen."

"A panel?"

"Yes, the altarpiece is composed of twelve panels, some of them over six feet tall."

"Oh!" Henrietta interjected. "I was imagining something small."

"No, the altarpiece is a massive work. It spans fifteen feet and is made up of hinged panels that fold in on themselves," Hartle explained, drawing it in the air with his hands. "Altogether, it weighs over two tons."

"Go on," Clive said, slightly more interested now.

"Each panel depicts a part of the larger scene. The missing panel is called 'The Just Judges.'"

"But why steal this one panel? I still don't understand the significance. Obviously, the thief wouldn't have been able to sell it," Clive reasoned.

"Indeed. But it's more complicated than that. The thief, one Arsène Goedertier, actually stole two of the panels and sent a series of thirteen letters, or ransom notes with clues to where the panels were hidden, to the bishop of Ghent, demanding one million Belgian francs for their return."

"One million francs!" Henrietta exclaimed.

"Apparently Goedertier returned one of the panels before the ransom was paid as a gesture of good faith but kept the Just Judges panel. When he was eventually caught, however, *without* the panel in his possession, it was discovered that he had more than the ransom amount already in his bank account." Hartle began to pace a little in front of the fireplace.

"So, he didn't need the money?"

"It would appear not. And it was obvious that he must have had help—"

"Why do you say that?" Clive interrupted.

"Because it would be almost impossible for one man to carry it alone."

"Yes, I see," Clive said, taking another drink.

"At any rate, the thief died under mysterious circumstances before he could reveal where he had hidden the panel."

"How unfortunate." Clive eyed Hartle carefully, suddenly guessing what was coming next and not liking it one bit.

"Yes, and we believe it's no coincidence that it was stolen barely a year after Adolf Hitler became chancellor of Germany."

"I'm afraid I don't understand," Henrietta said.

"Someone guessed—correctly, as it turned out—that with Hitler's continued rise to power, his eye would soon fall upon the Ghent Altarpiece, so a panel was taken and hidden somewhere, thereby devaluing the whole thing," Hartle explained.

"Suggesting that Goedertier was just a puppet of someone else, a government, perhaps—or a faction of a government?"

"Yes, exactly."

"Yours, perhaps?" Clive said, lifting his chin slightly as well as an eyebrow.

"Well, obviously not, or we wouldn't be so desperate to find it," he said, taking his place again on the sofa.

"We? Since when does Scotland Yard have anything to do with international affairs?"

"I never said I worked for Scotland Yard," Hartle said quietly and then took a drink.

Clive took several moments to digest what this meant. "MI5?" He was aware that his tone was one of incredulousness, but he couldn't help it. It had been hard enough to believe that Hartle was employed by Scotland Yard, but MI5 seemed almost impossible. "Jesus Christ, you're a spy?"

Hartle did not answer and instead just stared at him.

Clive groaned. "Let me guess. You suspect it's somewhere in Strasbourg."

"Very astute."

"Look, Hartle, you can stop right here. Send in one of your agents. It has nothing to do with us, and I'm not getting caught up in this."

"We did send in an agent. He's missing."

"Forget it, Hartle. I mean it." Clive stood up now and began to pace himself, trying to mitigate the turmoil that was brewing. If it were just him, he would jump at the chance to be involved in this case, but it *wasn't* just him. He had to think about Henrietta and the fragile state she was in. Dr. Ferrington had warned him that she needed rest and entertainment after her ordeal at Dunning Asylum in their search for Liesel Klinkhammer, and he was not about to jeopardize her sanity.

"Hear me out, Clive. Listen, we lost contact with our agent. It's been several weeks. We suspect the worst," he said, briefly flicking his eyes in Henrietta's direction.

"So, we're supposed to just step into his shoes?"

"We were just about to send in another agent when we heard of your proposed trip to Château du Freudeneck. It's a perfect ruse. An American and his wife on a honeymoon trip. No one will suspect. And it's our brilliant luck that you're such a fine detective. It's almost too good to be true."

"Yes, it *is* almost too good to be true," Clive said, eyeing him steadily. "Forget it, Hartle. We're not interested."

"Clive, listen. I wouldn't ask, but this is a matter of national security."

"National security? A painting? I find it very hard to believe that British Intelligence would care this much. If you really believe another war is inevitable, I suggest you put your resources into building more planes, not sending agents on wild goose chases through France in search of some work of art. Which is another thing—"

"It's not just a work of art, Clive," Hartle said, letting out a sigh.

"What do you mean?" Clive stopped in his pacing.

"Some believe, Hitler foremost among them, that the Ghent Altarpiece, when complete, contains a coded map."

"A map? Of what?"

"I'm not exactly sure. But something big enough to change the course of the war, something that will give Hitler unlimited power."

"Such as?"

"We don't know for sure, but we suspect it has something to do with the relics of power he seeks. A map to them, perhaps."

"Relics of power?" Clive's voice was suspicious. "What do you mean?"

"Things like the Ark of the Covenant, Thor's Hammer, the Holy Grail—that sort of stuff. Hitler is fascinated by the occult and believes that whoever possesses these ancient items will wield unstoppable power and rule the earth."

"Oh, for Christ's sake." Clive let out a deep breath of disgust and threw himself back into the armchair. "You can't be serious, Hartle. This is the stuff of fairy tales." He glanced over at Henrietta for agreement, but observed, uncomfortably, that she seemed wholly absorbed in what Hartle was saying. He hoped she wasn't falling for it the way she had back at home with that charlatan spiritualist, Madame Pavlovsky. Except that Madame Pavlovsky had proven to not really be a charlatan, he thought uneasily. But only he knew that.

"Think what you will," Hartle said, "but Hitler has already begun sending out teams to scour Europe, South America, and even northern Africa for these relics. But the biggest prize, of course, would be the panel itself, since he believes that will lead him to the rest."

Clive rested his elbow on the armchair and his chin on his fist, one finger braced against his cheek. "Well, let him, then. Let him attempt to collect all of these fantastical items. It will be a colossal waste of time and resources. And if he does somehow find these hidden relics somewhere in the frozen ice or in some moldy cave in Spain, he'll find out soon enough that he's been had, as it were. Let him pursue his silly scavenger hunt. Seems a perfect plan."

"Yes, it would seem, but the British Government doesn't see it that way."

Clive shifted. "Why Strasbourg?"

Hartle let out a deep breath. "Our sources tell us that Hitler is very much influenced by a sorceress by the name of Sárika Becskei, who claims to have 'seen' the panel in Alsace-Lorraine. Or course, we don't know the exact location, but we are guessing it could be near Strasbourg."

Clive laughed out loud. "And you believe this?"

Hartle's face soured. "It doesn't matter if I believe it. It's that Hitler believes it. And time is of the essence."

"Yes, it is, as a matter of fact. Look, Hartle, I'm sorry to be abrupt, but we really do have a train to catch. I thank you for the entertaining story."

"War *is* coming, Clive. We have to do what we can now. Do it for your country."

"This isn't my country."

"It was your father's. Do it for him."

"Maybe it wouldn't hurt to at least have a little bit of a search, Clive," Henrietta added tentatively. "Since we're going to be there anyway."

Clive sighed and brushed a stray thread from his wool trousers. As much as he outwardly scoffed, he didn't like the sound of this— relics of power, the occult, a sorceress? But even if he dismissed all of that as lunacy, the Nazis, he knew, were very much real. And there was the disturbing fact that a man was missing, presumably dead. He glanced across at Henrietta, who was looking at him in that pleading way of hers. It went without saying that she would see this as some sort of gay scavenger hunt. No, he couldn't chance it. He was on the brink of saying so when a random thought of his father came to mind, niggling him to "do it for Blighty, old boy." He could almost hear him asking him to do his duty. But he didn't want to! He had done his duty for Blighty in the first war and lost his wife and child in the process, returning home with a bum shoulder and a damaged heart. And he had done his duty again when, at his father's urging, he had reluctantly agreed to take the reins of Linley Standard and Highbury. But how could he just walk away from this now? Damn, Hartle! He had known exactly how to get to him.

"All right, Hartle," he said, exhaling deeply. "We'll have a look, but no promises. Our first honeymoon trip was already ruined by this type of malarky . . ."

"Your honeymoon wasn't ruined because of a case, it was ended because of your father's death," Hartle said stiffly. "But I'm very grateful. You'll likewise have the gratitude of the nation. And the Duke of Buckingham."

"What's his role in all of this?"

"Better that you don't know."

Clive rolled his eyes. "What did you say the agent's name was?" he asked with a long sigh. "And where do we look for him?"

"He goes by the name of Richard Stafford. You should go to an antiquities shop near the Strasbourg Cathedral. The street is Rue des Frères. The shopkeeper is a man by the name of Henri Bonnet. He was Stafford's contact. Start there."

"Got it."

"And you believe the panel to be hidden somewhere in the Von Harmons' château?" Henrietta asked. Clive could hear the unmistakable excitement in her voice.

"Yes, but you must be careful."

"Why is that, Inspector?" Henrietta asked, taking a sip of her sherry.

"Because," he said, keeping his eyes steadily on her, "we suspect the Von Harmons to be Nazi sympathizers. They must not know why you're really there."

"Which was to enjoy a holiday with my wife?" Clive said flippantly.

"Wait a minute," Henrietta put in. "If the Von Harmons are Nazi sympathizers, why would they not simply hand over the panel to Hitler? Surely, they would be handsomely rewarded for it, and what better way to prove their allegiance?"

"Ah-ha!" Clive said loudly, looking proudly across at her. "An excellent point." He folded his arms and turned his attention to Hartle.

"They might not yet realize that Hitler is searching for it. Or maybe it has been stored there without their knowledge. Or perhaps old Baron Von Harmon hid it and has since forgotten. He's reputed to be a bit touched."

"Well, of course, he is," Clive said, draining his glass. "This gets better by the moment."

"Again," Hartle said, standing up. "I caution you to tread lightly. Especially when you don't know exactly whom to trust."

Chapter 4

"Gunther, we must be very careful," Elsie said pleadingly. "Tread lightly, if just for a little while." The two of them were standing in the back garden of the Palmer Square house, watching Anna run about with Elsie's twin siblings, Doris and Donny, who appeared to be playing some version of tag. Nanny Kuntz sat at the other end of the garden on a white wrought-iron bench perched under a giant weeping willow, supposedly keeping an eye on them. From where Elsie stood, however, she could see through the long arching branches that the older woman appeared to be dozing.

Gunther glanced at Elsie, one eye squinted shut against the sun. "No, Elsie. I cannot continue to take advantage of your grandfather in this underhand way. Or your mother," he added, nodding toward the house. "It is wrong that we . . . I . . . am burdening her with another child."

"Anna is hardly a burden, Gunther, and Ma likes having her around."

This was not a lie, but it was an anomaly that did perplex Elsie. Ma had taken a strange liking to the orphaned little girl, which was odd, given the fact that Ma had never been particularly interested in her own eight children. Ever since Elsie's father had killed himself some five years ago, Ma had slipped deeper and deeper into depression, leaving Elsie and Henrietta to try to care for the large brood on their own. "And I think having Nurse Flanagan is good for Ma, too, not just Anna."

"This is also a problem," Gunther said, running his hand through his blond curls. "It is not right that your sister and Mr. Howard—"

"Clive."

"Clive. Should pay for a nurse to care for this child. It is *untragbar*—unacceptable."

"Gunther," Elsie said, laying a hand on his arm. His white shirt sleeves were rolled up to his elbows, and as her fingers brushed the thick, coarse hair on his arm, she felt a small stirring, but she pushed it down. "Don't think of that. Henrietta insisted on it. And it's good for Ma. You can see how patient Nurse Flanagan is with her. You have no idea how disagreeable Ma can be. *And* she's getting more and more forgetful. I'm sure you've noticed." She looked at him anxiously. "Like how she keeps calling you Stanley."

"Be that as it may, Elsie, it is wrong still for your sister to employ a nurse to watch over an epileptic child that is no relation to her. I should not have agreed to this."

"She and Clive are happy to do it," Elise said, her voice becoming more and more pleading. "Henrietta told me herself. She feels guilty that she cannot bring Anna to live at Highbury until . . . well, until things are arranged between us. Until we are married," she said softly.

Gunther turned his face from the children, then, and looked at her longingly.

It was enough to encourage her to go on. "Henrietta did ask Clive about having Anna stay at Highbury—"

"Ach!" Gunther pinched the bridge of his nose.

"But he said no."

"It is right that he should say no!"

"Not because he didn't want to help," she hurried on, "but because he thought it might not be the best with his father so recently passing. His mother is not in the best frame of mind, apparently . . ." Her voice died off.

"Elsie," he said, brushing her cheek with the back of his hand, "we must at least *tell* your grandfather. And I want to ask for your hand in proper way. It is not right that we should lie."

"But we're not exactly lying," Elsie urged. "We're just waiting a bit."

Gunther let out a little sigh. "It is the only way, *Liebling*. I already have explained this. Many times."

"Gunther. It won't do any good," she said, resting her hand on his, which now cupped her cheek. "He will never approve of my marriage to you, and it will only make things worse."

"Perhaps. But I will not steal you away, like thief in night. I will do the thing honorable and declare my intentions. You deserve at least that, Elsie."

"Gunther, let me try to think of something."

"Think of something? There is nothing of which to think." Gently, he lowered their hands, now locked together. "You ask me to be careful, but so must you be, too. You must be sure. Do you really wish to leave this?" His eyes darted around the exquisite garden, bursting on this July afternoon with blooms. The air was thick with perfume, and a faint haze hung just above the horizon. "It is not too late. Even now. We can end this before it even begins. Before we do something that will alter our lives forever and which we cannot call back. There is no shame in turning from the breaking of one's heart," he said softly. "It is a messy business."

Elsie swallowed hard, a lick of panic circling her heart. "Gunther, there is no turning back now. I . . . I love you. How can you speak so cavalierly about . . . about us? Do you not feel the same?"

He pulled her to him and wrapped his strong arms around her, and she easily rested her head on his chest. "Elsie," he said, his warm breath on her hair, "of course, I do. More than I thought I could ever love another." He drew back and looked into her eyes now. "But it is for this reason I am willing to let you go. It is because I love you so much. And I will never be able to provide this for you."

Despite the depth and comfort of his words, Elsie felt a tiny flame of irritation. Why did no one ever take her seriously?

"Gunther," she said, staring into his very blue eyes and returning his serious look. "I've told you before. I don't want all of this. This has been a place of sadness and loneliness for me. I wish only to be with you, even if it is in your little hut. Caring for you and Anna. And any others that might come along," she said with a blush, her gaze dropping from his eyes to his buttons.

Gently, Gunther placed a knuckle under her chin, lifting her eyes back to his. He leaned toward her and kissed her lips softly. He rested his forehead against hers. "But first you must finish school. You promised."

"Yes, I suppose so, but don't you see?" She paused, not wanting to ruin the moment, but she knew she had to try one last time to convince him. "This is why we must wait a while before telling Grandfather. We must let Anna settle. She's been through so much already. More than a little girl should. She barely speaks at all anymore. Give her time. And, as you say, I need time to finish my studies. Why can't we simply keep on this way? It's not forever. And if we wait a little, perhaps I can think of a way to get Aunt Agatha on our side—"

"Elsie," he interrupted, looking at her steadily, "the end never justifies the means." He reached out and tucked a stray strand of her hair behind her ear, which sent a shiver down her spine. "This you know, I am pretty sure."

Elsie stared at him, unable to speak. She knew he was right, of course, in a certain way, but she also knew he did not understand her grandfather's cruel wrath the way she did.

"No, my mind is made up. I will go to him tomorrow," he said sternly.

"Then take me with you."

He stared at her for several moments before letting out a deep breath. He released her hand and instead ran it along the top of the lavender nearby. A sudden breeze that had picked up further waved the flowers. "Very well," he said quietly. "If you so wish it."

The next morning, Elsie somewhat regretted her decision as she and Gunther walked up the long tree-lined lane to her Uncle Gerard's

Lake Forest home, an Italianate mansion set on an exquisitely mani-cured property of ten acres, where her grandfather, Oldrich Exley, also resided. They had taken a bus from the city and walked the rest of the way, despite the fact that Elsie could have easily paid for a hired car. In all situations, but especially in front of Gunther, she sought to veil her wealth. Having suddenly come into money was surprisingly unsettling to Elsie, though she thanked God repeatedly that at least she did not have to play the role Henrietta found herself in—the future mistress of the palatial Highbury.

Not knowing what to do with the allowance afforded her each week from her grandfather, she mainly gave it to any hobos she happened to see on the streets, or else she mailed it off to her brothers at board-ing school. She almost never used it on herself, much to the despair of Aunt Agatha, Oldrich's daughter-in-law, whom he had conscripted not only to educate Elsie on the finer points of being a lady of society but also to procure for her a suitable matrimonial match. This had proven to be more difficult than poor Agatha had initially realized, as Elsie, though extremely pliable and obedient, was what one would call frumpy and not a little bit robust about the middle. Likewise, the girl had not the slightest interest in being matched.

Nonetheless, never one to shirk her duty, Aunt Agatha had done her very best to beautify her young niece and had accordingly escorted her to an endless number of operas, ballets, garden par-ties, and balls until she had succeeded just this past spring in bring-ing about an acceptable proposal from one Lloyd Aston, a North Shore playboy whose father very desperately wanted the large dowry Oldrich had placed upon Elsie. Elsie herself had thwarted all of Aunt Agatha's clever machinations regarding Lloyd Aston, however, and heartbreakingly—for Aunt Agatha, anyway—rejected Aston out-right, claiming him to be a cad and a brute, though, in truth, there was another reason behind her shocking rebellion, which was simply that she had already fallen in love with an impoverished German immigrant.

Elsie had met Gunther Stockel at Mundelein College over the

Christmas break, when she wandered, lonely, through the deserted dormitories, eventually discovering through a series of mishaps that he was caring for a little epileptic girl that had been left in his care. Though both of them knew the extreme unsuitability of their love, they had in the end engaged themselves to each other, though no one yet knew about their plan, not even Henrietta or Ma, and certainly not Sister Bernard.

As Gunther and Elsie slowly made their way up the stone steps of the Exley mansion, her insides began to twist, and she took Gunther's hand, who squeezed hers in return. Elsie had only been here a handful of times, despite her grandfather's somewhat omnipotent presence in her life. It was usually Aunt Agatha who was the go-between, or else Henrietta, and thus Elsie herself had had very little actual interaction with Oldrich Exley.

Now it was Gunther who sought to speak for her, and as much as she thought him the perfection of manhood, she suspected he was no match for her grandfather. She gripped Gunther's hand tighter, and he looked over at her. She gave him a small smile of encouragement, but he did not return it, which told her much. His face was set like stone and grayish in hue as he took the gargoyle knocker in hand and banged it against the tarnished bronze plate.

The door was promptly opened by the Exleys' very dour butler, Morton.

"Miss Von Harmon." His tone was one of slight confusion as he stood aside to let them in. "We were not expecting you today. I'm afraid Mr. Exley is already engaged for the morning." His eyes darted disapprovingly at Gunther as the two stepped inside.

"This is Mr. Stockel," Elsie explained nervously.

"Mr. Gunther Stockel?" His brow furrowed. "I see. Mr. Exley is expecting *you*. I'm to show you through," he said to Gunther. "Would you care to wait in the drawing room, Miss Von Harmon?"

"No, I'm coming, too," she said, wrapping her arm through Gunther's.

"Elsie," Gunther said, gently extracting himself, "perhaps you should wait. It is better this way."

"No, it isn't. We agreed."

"I agreed that you should come along, but not that you would speak to your grandfather. That is my duty. Not yours. I will not have you beg."

"But I . . . I'm not here to beg," she stammered, though in truth she had considered it.

"*Liebling*, you must trust me," he said, his eyes mournful, as if he, too, had no hope, as if he knew he was walking into his execution.

"If you're *quite* ready, sir," Morton interrupted. "Mr. Exley has several other engagements this morning."

Gunther gave Elsie a last look and then followed the butler past the grand staircase to a set of double doors beyond. Morton knocked briefly and opened the door, quietly announcing, "A Mr. Gunther Stockel, sir."

Elsie strained to hear her grandfather's response, but Morton shut the door, blocking it out. He then returned to where she stood, twisting her hands.

"Are you quite sure you wouldn't care to wait in the drawing room, Miss Von Harmon?" Morton asked again. "I would be happy to bring tea."

Elsie looked around desperately, not wanting to leave the foyer. She spotted a small marble bench nearby, clearly for ornamentation only, and gingerly sat upon it, tucking her gray wool skirt under her. "I'll just wait here."

The butler's face wrinkled. "Are you sure, miss? That is very irregular."

"Yes, I'll be fine. Honestly."

Morton gave her yet another disapproving look and then bowed. "As you wish, miss," he said stiffly and turned to go.

Elsie watched as he disappeared deeper into the mansion, then she crept toward the study. Morton had closed the pocket doors, but not completely. Miraculously, there was a fraction of a space still open between them, and Elsie, barely daring to breathe, leaned toward it, turning her head so that her ear was almost on the crack.

"If you have some sort of grievance, you should have spoken to my agent, Mr. Bernstein," Grandfather said.

"No, this is not the nature of my visit." Gunther's voice was clear, surprising Elsie in its firmness. She would be terrified to face Grandfather.

"Well, what is it, then?"

"It is of a matter personal."

There was a pause, and Elsie bit her lip, imagining the irritation that was surely now on her grandfather's face.

"What do you mean?" Grandfather asked slowly.

"Mr. Exley, I am here to declare my wish to marry your grand-daughter, Elsie Von Harmon." Again, Elsie was impressed with the strength in his voice.

There was silence, and Elsie felt a pain in her stomach as she imagined her grandfather assessing Gunther. She guessed that he would appear little better than a tramp in her grandfather's eyes, due to the fact that even his best jacket was patched, and his bow tie fraying.

"Marry her?" Grandfather sputtered. "That's ridiculous. Is this some sort of jest, man? Is it money you seek? Well, you'll find none here. Get out."

"Mr. Exley, please. May I speak?" Gunther asked. "Please to hear me out."

There was silence for a moment, which Gunther must have taken for permission, or maybe Grandfather had gestured for him to continue.

"I know I am not worthy to marry Elsie. No one is. And yet, she has accepted me, which is no small thing. I will strive always to be worthy of her. More than her hand, she has given me her love, and, God help me, I love her, too. I give you my word that as her husband I will provide for her, love her, and . . ." he paused, as if searching for the right word, "*hegen*—cherish her until my dying day. As long as I am living, she will not have cold or hunger, and I will never raise my hand to her."

Tears filled Elsie's eyes as she waited, her heart in her throat, allowing herself to hope for just a moment that Grandfather might be moved by her lover's speech, if even a little bit. She was crushed, then, when she heard him instead bark out a short laugh.

"That's it? That she won't be hungry or cold and that you won't beat her? It's not my business how her husband chooses to keep her in line. I could care less. It doesn't further your case in the slightest. But simply out of curiosity, how exactly do you imagine you could provide for a wife and family? You don't even look to have a job."

"I am employed as custodian at Mundelein College. But in my country, I am professor. I hope to one day be so again. Here in Chicago."

"Mundelein College? Is that where you met her? I should have known." Elsie heard him toss something, like a pen. "I was assured that by attending an all-women's college run by nuns she would not be in any contact whatsoever with men, but I was obviously misinformed. Here, I thought the thorn in my side would be Eugene, but it turns out it is Elsie," he said disgustedly, referring to the oldest Von Harmon boy, whom Oldrich had sent away to military school after he had been caught in a series of embarrassing scrapes with the law. "She's a very wayward girl. The sooner she is married—to someone suitable—the better."

"She is not wayward," Gunther said quietly through what sounded like gritted teeth.

"You're not the first fortune hunter to appear, you know," Grandfather replied. "So, you can give up now. Her dowry is not for the likes of you, and she's no longer a maiden, so I am told, so that should silence your poetic nonsense rather quickly, I'm sure. Be off with you."

Elsie's face burned in mortification, and she longed to run out the front door. How could her own grandfather say such things aloud? It was too much to bear, yet she could not pull herself away.

"How dare you speak of her in this way?" Gunther demanded loudly, taking Elsie off guard. She had never heard him angry before.

"I beg your pardon?"

"How can a man speak of his granddaughter in this way? How dare you—"

"Stop right there. I have no use for your pretended hurt sensibilities. I know what you're after. But Elsie's to marry someone equal to her social standing. Period. Now get out. And you will not so much as lay a finger on her, if she hasn't allowed you to already—"

Elsie then thought she heard the sound of scuffling and, dismayed, took advantage of the added noise to wiggle her fingers into the crack between the doors and push them open a little farther. She was alarmed to see Gunther holding onto the lapels of her grandfather's suit and giving him a shake.

"Gunther!" she cried out and ran to the two of them. Startled, Gunther released the old man.

"Elsie?" Grandfather said, righting himself and smoothing the hair on the side of his head. "You're here as well? I might have known. Well, this should be extremely illustrative. You can see what kind of man you've been fooled by yet again." He gestured at Gunther. "His violent nature."

"Grandfather, please. You don't understand!"

"That will be all, Elsie! You've wasted quite enough of my time. First that reprobate Barnes-Smith and now a poor kraut? Frankly, I'm not sure which is worse. Your taste in men is abominable and not to be trusted. I still don't understand why you rejected Lloyd Aston." Heavily, he dropped into the chair behind the desk. "What I do know is that first thing next week, I'm calling Mundelein. You're finished there; that's for sure. I've allowed that indulgence long enough. You'll go and stay with Agatha and John indefinitely until you come to your senses."

Panic filled Elsie's chest, and she felt she couldn't breathe. "No, Grandfather," she sputtered. "You . . . you can't stop me from going to school. Henrietta is paying for it, so . . . so it's nothing to do with you. You . . . you can't control me. You can't just wall me up in a tower like in some sort of fairy tale and force me to marry someone I don't love!" Tears filled her eyes now against her will. "It's barbaric."

Oldrich let out a little snort of disgust. "You're behaving like a child, Elsie," he snapped. "Don't be like your mother. She had every advantage. We even sent her to finishing school in Switzerland. But she threw it all away for your father. A butcher's delivery boy. It was monstrous! And now, you're no better. Don't make the same mistake. Look how badly it turned out for her."

Elsie paused, considering how badly it really had turned out for Ma—the shabby apartment, her father's suicide, listening to Doris and Donny cry themselves to sleep at night from hunger . . . But hadn't Ma once been in love? Hadn't that been worth it?

"And," Grandfather continued, "if you proceed with some foolish idea of perhaps eloping, I will not only cut you off, my dear, but I will cut off the whole family and throw them all back into squalor where I found them. Do not think for a moment that I won't do it."

"Grandfather, I—" Elsie could barely get any words out, her throat aching from the tears she was fiercely trying to keep at bay.

"Think carefully, my dear. You may not think it such a hardship to live in squalor with this degenerate. You might even think it romantic in some silly, idealistic way. But think what it will mean for Eugene, finally doing so well at school, rising to the rank of sergeant already. Or Herbert and James and Edward, called home from Phillips. Little Doris and Donny stuck in some wretched garden apartment in the worst part of the city. And last but not least, your poor mother, Martha, whose original selfishness was the cause of all your suffering in the first place. Will you follow in her footsteps? You would be worse than your mother, actually, because, having tasted a life of privilege, your family's new life of want will be all the more painful. So. You choose. Either renounce this gutter snake immediately, here in my presence, or you are all doomed."

Elsie's face burned, and she tried to control the rapid pounding of her heart. She felt she might be sick at any moment. What was she to do? Her mind raced, trying to think of some way out of yet another trap, when she heard Gunther speak beside her.

"No," he said hoarsely, almost inaudibly. He looked at her tenderly, as if she were the only person in the room with him, his blue eyes swimming with love. "I will not cause you the pain of having to choose, Elsie. *I* will say it. I renounce you. It is finished."

Chapter 5

"Where are we?" Henrietta asked, groggily lifting her head from Clive's chest and looking out the window of their private train carriage at the French countryside rolling by.

"Nearly there. We should be arriving in Strasbourg in about a half an hour," Clive said, deftly flipping open his pocket watch. Though he now always wore the wristwatch Henrietta had given him for a wedding gift, he could not seem to part with his pocket watch, a predilection that Henrietta had at first been slightly offended by, but which she now found rather endearing.

"How long have I been asleep?" she asked, rubbing her eyes.

"Not too," Clive said, slipping the watch back into his vest pocket.

"You should have woken me! Now I've missed everything."

"I can assure you that you have not, darling. It's been just as you see now," he said, gesturing toward the window at the passing low hills of endless grapevines. "And, anyway, you need the rest. You know what Dr. Ferrington said." His face was grim.

"Clive," she said, leaning forward and patting his cheek. "I've had days and days of rest. You mustn't worry so much. Losing a baby is not an illness."

Clive did not respond but merely removed his pipe and a pouch of tobacco from his inner jacket pocket and began filling the one with the other. Henrietta watched him for a moment and then looked back out the window. She could see Strasbourg in the distance now. "What I *am* worried about, though, is that we're a whole day late in arriving. I hope we haven't disrupted their plans."

"I seriously doubt it," Clive said, striking a match. "I did wire them. And you know these old families shut up in their castles. One day is much the same as another, I suspect."

"Clive!"

"Well, it's true," he said, puffing deeply now. "Look at Aunt and Uncle. Montague probably doesn't even know what day it is."

"How cruel you are! And anyway, we don't know what the Von Harmons will be like. Maybe Château du Freudeneck is a bustling center of social activity in the heart of Strasbourg."

Clive looked at her wryly.

"Well, you don't know."

Clive exhaled a perfect ring of smoke above his head. "You're right, there, darling. We don't know, but it's probably quite safe to guess that we're on a wild goose chase, in more ways than one."

"Wild goose chase?" Henrietta adjusted her thick, olive-green traveling skirt and sat back against the plush red fabric headrest.

"Looking for a painting—or whatever it is—that was stolen two years ago, that no one has yet been able to recover, and that Hitler has all of his top men searching for across Europe doesn't sound remotely like a wild goose chase?" Clive took a deep puff. "And even if it *is* hidden somewhere in this remote château on the French border," he jabbed his pipe at the trees in the distance, "how are we to find it in three days' time before we go on to Lucerne? A feat, mind you, which a trained British agent was unable to achieve? Yes," he said, giving her a superior look, "I'd call that a wild goose chase."

Henrietta crossed her arms impatiently across her chest, irritated that he was making an awful lot of sense.

"*And*," Clive maddeningly continued, "we don't even know what this thing looks like. So, my guess is that we're not likely to find it. Just a hunch, though."

"Well, Inspector," Henrietta said, her voice matter-of-fact, "perhaps the British agent *did* find it and is spiriting it away even as we speak."

Clive raised one eyebrow. He looked dreadfully handsome in his tweeds. "Yes. *Perhaps*," he said, a smile about his lips.

"Well, if you think it's so hopeless, why did you tell Hartle we'd look for it?"

"What else could I say? He backed me into a corner, as it were." He glanced briefly out the window. "Look, darling, we'll have a poke around, but that's all we can really do. I don't expect much will come of it, and then we'll be off. It doesn't really concern us."

"Since when does theft not concern you? You're a detective, after all."

"*Was* a detective," he corrected her.

"No, you *are* a detective."

"Not while I'm on holiday with my bride. Now, let's forget about it." He picked up the folded newspaper beside him.

Henrietta was accordingly silent a moment as she looked around for where her hat had gone. "What did you mean by the other goose chase?" she asked, spotting it on the floor and reaching to pick it up.

"Sorry?" Clive looked up absently from the paper.

"You distinctly said that it was a wild goose chase in more ways than one. What did you mean?" She gave the hat a few brushes with her hand and placed it on her head.

"Oh." He gave her a rueful smile. "Something tells me that will soon be revealed."

"Whatever do you mean?" Henrietta thought for a moment as she pinned the hat into place. "Do you mean about the baron being 'touched,' as Inspector Hartle put it?"

"In a way. I just don't think reconnecting with your long-lost family will prove the advantage Mother thinks it will. Especially if they're Nazis. She would die if she knew. So yes, traveling here to gain their societal influence is a bit of a wild goose chase, don't you think?"

"Clive! You're positively curmudgeonly. Goodness knows what would have happened if I hadn't come along when I did."

"I'd probably have a few less strands of graying hair, for one thing," he said, tossing the paper aside.

"Inspector! How rude."

"It *was* rude of me, I beg your pardon," he said, taking her hand and kissing it while he shot her a wink. "You have been the savior of my heart."

"Now you're just teasing."

"Forgive me, darling," he said more seriously now and leaned over and kissed the side of her head. "You know I love you completely."

They arrived in Strasbourg exactly on time, and as Clive arranged with a porter to collect their baggage, not to mention a somewhat disheveled Edna from third class, Henrietta observed the sprawling town around her, or as much as she could see from where they stood on the station platform. It was a much bigger city than she had imagined, though it was positively charming with its wattle and daub buildings, high peaks and dark cross beams. Everywhere there were large pots of flowers outside the little shops—some of them hanging, others perched together in a jumbled but pleasing way. Several horses and carts wound their way down the streets among the motorcars that sped by them. It was like walking into a fairy-tale land.

"Come, darling," Clive said, taking her gently by the arm. "I've secured a car." Clive led her to a waiting cab, a large Citroën Traction. Edna was helping the porter to load the last of Henrietta's hat boxes.

"Thank you, Edna," Henrietta called to her. "How was the journey?"

"Fine, miss," Edna answered, though Henrietta thought her face looked rather pale.

Clive opened one of the passenger doors, and Henrietta slipped into the boxy interior. There was a fold-down seat across from her, which she thought Edna might sit in, but the girl climbed into the front seat next to the driver, as was more seemly. Henrietta thought about inviting her to sit with them, but then changed her mind as Clive slid in beside her. He would certainly not think it appropriate, and Edna would feel awkward and shy, Henrietta knew, if she had to sit across from her master the whole way.

The car lurched to a start, and Henrietta looked out the window, eager to see her first European city—besides London, that is, and Calais, she guessed she should include, where they had spent the last night in a quaint little inn not far from the Citadel, having unfortunately missed the last train to Strasbourg. Hartle's unexpected visit in London had caused them to subsequently miss *all* of their connections, initially a source of irritation to Clive, but one which magically dissipated once they were finally on French soil. He seemed to relax, then, charmed perhaps, as Henrietta was, by the slow pace around them. The porter who unloaded their bags from the ferry suggested taking the night train to Paris and connecting there, but Clive, after a few moments' consideration, decided against it. Despite Henrietta's protestations to the opposite, Clive insisted that she was weary and besides, he said more than once, he wanted to keep Paris, the crowning jewel, for the end of their trip.

They had accordingly dined at a quaint little restaurant near where they were staying, sharing several bottles of wine before finally stumbling back to the inn, which Henrietta adored. The old couple who ran it oddly reminded her of the Hennesseys, her surrogate parents back in the city when she had waited tables for Mr. Hennessey in his corner tap, Poor Pete's. The inn was nothing like Poor Pete's, of course, nor could she understand a word the couple said, but there was something about them, even so, that reminded her of them. She had been tempted to ask Clive if they might stay on for a few days and explore Calais, but she knew it was out of the question. They had a mission now, and they needed to get on with it. Still, she thought, they might stay there a few days upon their return.

Clive laced his hand in hers and squeezed it. "Tired, darling?"

"Not a bit," she said, giving him a smile and then looking back out the window. The buildings were thinning out now, and it seemed to Henrietta that they were headed out of town, not into it. "Are we going the right way?"

Clive bent his head to see out the front window. "Yes, the driver tells me that Château du Freudeneck is actually outside of Strasbourg. Nearer a little village called Wangenbourg."

"Oh! Well, how are we going to investigate Monsieur Bonnet?" Henrietta asked in a low voice.

Clive's brow furrowed in confusion.

"*You know*, the antiquities shop . . ." she whispered.

Clive smiled. "Ah. Well, I suspect we'll think of something."

Henrietta looked out the window again and saw that they were now back in the countryside, driving through the rolling hills of grapevines, which were broken up only by an occasional field of sheep. Before long, however, the terrain began to rise, and the driver shifted the chugging car into a lower gear. Slowly, the vines gave way to woods, and the road grew more uneven, Henrietta jostling once or twice against Clive.

"Goodness! Are you sure this is right? There doesn't seem to be anything up here, even a road!"

As if the driver could sense her unease, he looked over his shoulder briefly and said, "*Pas beaucoup plus loin maintenant. Attendez.*"

"He says it's not much further and to hold on," Clive interpreted, saying the last part with an elevated tone as they rounded a sharp bend. Henrietta slid toward Clive.

"*Attendez. C'est la crête du Schlossberg. Ne regarde pas en bas.*"

"He says that this is called the Schlossberg Ridge and not to look down," Clive repeated, which, of course, caused Henrietta to immediately look out the window. She gasped at the sight of the deep chasm to their left and slid closer to Clive. *How on earth had they gotten this high so quickly?* She gripped Clive's arm.

"*Ci-dessous se trouve la gorge de Freudeneck,*" the driver said, turning his scruffy face to them again.

"Keep your eyes on the road!" Clive snapped, pointing urgently toward the windscreen. Though the man could presumably not understand English, he obviously understood Clive's meaning and let out a wheezy chuckle.

"What did he say?" Henrietta asked nervously.

"That the ravine to the side is called the Freudeneck Gorge."

"Charming," Henrietta muttered.

"*Le voilà!*" the driver said now, pointing toward a castle-like structure poking through the trees ahead.

"Oh, my," Henrietta muttered, straining to get a better look at the château. The steep woods leveled off suddenly, giving way to a wide plateau, and as they got closer, the road appeared paved—if that was the accurate word—with giant pieces of flagstone. "I was expecting a sort of townhouse in Strasbourg, not a castle on a hilltop! Were you?"

Clive adjusted his tie. "Not exactly. Though names *can* be deceiving, darling."

"I suppose so," Henrietta mused, thinking about how surprised she had been when she discovered that *Castle* Linley, for example, was not a castle at all, but simply a large Georgian manor house. *Why did Europeans not say what they meant?*

The driver pulled to the front of the château and rolled the car to a stop. It was an imposing structure of gray stone flanked by two windowless towers. Flagstone steps led up to a set of thick, medieval-looking doors. Two miniature stone knights looked down at them from the stone lintel. The whole place had a sullen, somber feel, Henrietta observed as she slowly exited the car and stared up at it. There was no sign of life anywhere, and Henrietta, had she not known better, might have guessed it to be uninhabited. She suddenly had a very bad feeling about this place.

Edna slipped out the car as well, looking as fearful as Henrietta felt. Henrietta went to her and put her arm through hers, but before she could offer any words of comfort, the main doors opened, and a servant, presumably the butler, stepped forward.

"*Bienvenue, Monsieur et Madame Howard,*" he said stiffly, and almost as if by magic, several servants appeared from another doorway to the right, hurried toward them, and began to unburden the car of their many cases. "*Par ici, s'il vous plaît.*"

Clive gestured for Henrietta to precede him, but she was reluctant to leave poor Edna, who was positively trembling.

"Edna," Henrietta said quietly near the girl's ear. "Are you all right?"

Edna gave a slight nod. "Yes, miss," she croaked. "I mean, madame."

"You'll be okay, Edna. Just follow the others," she said, nodding toward the servants who were carrying luggage toward the service entrance. "Take my hat boxes, at least. I'll find you later."

"Yes, miss," Edna said forlornly and shuffled off toward the other servants.

"Ready, darling?" Clive asked.

Henrietta gave Edna a last look and then, almost reluctantly, took Clive's arm. Together, they climbed the ancient stairs and stepped through the thick oak doors studded with iron bolts. Henrietta could not help but notice the large iron knocker that hung in the center of one of the doors, the end of which was a gruesome sort of gargoyle, which oddly reminded her of the one on the front door of the Exley mansion in Lake Forest.

"*Bienvenue, par ici, s'il vous plaît,*" the butler repeated once they were inside.

"*Merci,*" Clive responded as they followed him into the château.

The interior was dim, lit only by massive circular candled chandeliers that hung from the vaulted ceiling by heavy chains. Henrietta blinked rapidly and looked around. They appeared to be in what she imagined a hunting lodge in Germany might look like, not an exquisite French château. The walls were of thick stone, as was the staircase leading to the floor above, which was open, save for a balustrade that ran the length of the landing and formed a sort of stone balcony. Over the banister, every few feet, hung various regional flags. Other than these, there was very little ornamentation.

"*Par ici, monsieur, madame,*" the servant said and led them across the room, pausing to open a tiny rounded door, which, upon stepping through, revealed what looked like a medieval great hall. A massive stone fireplace hulked in the middle of the wall to their right and had a small fire blazing despite the fact that it was July. Mounted into the stone were a variety of guns, most of which looked so old they could almost to be termed muskets, and an impressive assortment of swords. The walls here were paneled in thick dark wood, and several stuffed heads of deer and other animals hung around the room. The sconces appeared to be of pewter with antler bones woven through them. There were little groupings of chairs and sofas at both ends of the room, but the ones arranged in front of the fireplace looked to be the most comfortable and used.

"*Attendez ici, s'il vous plaît. Le baron sera avec vous sous peu. Puis-je vous offrir un rafraîchissement?*" the servant asked.

"*Deux sherries, s'il vous plaît,*" Clive answered.

"*Oui, monsieur.*"

"What did he say?" Henrietta asked as soon as he was gone.

"He said to wait here for the baron, and he's bringing us a sherry."

Henrietta wandered toward the leaded glass windows peppered along the far wall and looked out upon a terraced garden with a huge fountain in the middle. In the distance, she could see down into a valley where a tiny village lay huddled.

"That must be Wangenbourg," Clive said from behind her.

"It's beautiful, isn't it?" she said. "I wish Elsie could see this. It's like something out of one of those novels she loves—"

Henrietta was interrupted, however, by the sound of a door opening at the other end of the room. Both she and Clive turned to see a short, stout man wearing a riding outfit shuffle in. Except for his dress, Henrietta would have mistaken him for a servant with his rounded shoulders and shuffling gait. He seemed utterly unaware of their presence as he crept along the far wall.

Clive cleared his throat, and the man startled and stopped in his tracks. He peered at them suspiciously before his eyes opened wide.

"*Comtesse?*" His voice was hoarse, as if he hadn't spoken in some time. "*Comtesse,*" he said in a baffled tone, hurrying over to them. "*Je savais que vous reviendrez un jour. Vous nous honorez de votre présence.*" He bowed before her.

Henrietta looked questioningly at Clive.

"He is calling you 'Countess' and is saying that he knew you'd come back some day. That you grace him with your presence." Clive let out a deep sigh. "The words 'wild goose chase' do come to mind."

Henrietta bit back a laugh. "I'm sorry, but I don't understand French," she said loudly to the man in front of her, who was now taking hold of her hands. His small, sunken eyes stared at her in confusion.

"*Mais bien sûr tu parles Français, ma Dame,*" he said in a mystified tone. The man looked pleadingly at Clive, then, who absently scratched his chin.

"He says of course, you speak French."

"*Père,*" a voice called, and the man hurriedly dropped Henrietta's hands. Both she and Clive turned to see a trim young woman enter the room. Her pretty face wore a frown as she approached, and Henrietta observed that she was wearing the latest Parisian fashion, which looked decidedly out of place in this medieval great hall. "*Je t'ai dit de m'attendre,*" she gently scolded the man and then looked immediately at Henrietta and Clive. "*Pardonnez-moi*, you must be Mr. and Mrs. Howard, no?"

"Yes," Clive answered, holding out his hand to her. "We've only just arrived."

"Yes, I am sorry no one was here to greet you. I see you have met my father," she said in a light French accent. "Allow me to introduce you properly. May I present Baron Von Harmon? Father," she said, bending toward the baron as if she were explaining something to a child, "this is Mr. and Mrs. Howard. From America? Remember?"

Another look of confusion passed across the baron's face. The woman repeated the introduction in French.

"*Mais non, Claudette, c'est la comtesse! Vous ne voyez pas? Vous la reconnaissez sûrement?*—But no, Claudette, it is the countess! Can you not see? Surely you recognize her?" the old man sputtered.

"Father, speak in English," the woman instructed, but the baron remained silent, quietly studying them. Henrietta tried not to stare at the crusting age spots dotting his forehead and temples and the slight cloudiness in his eyes. He was obviously confused, and she felt instantly sorry for him.

"I am Claudette Von Harmon," the young woman said, holding out her hand to Henrietta and then to Clive.

"You speak beautiful English," Henrietta commented.

"Thank you. I lived for several years in London, so I am very well versed. I—"

"But it *is* the countess!" the baron interrupted in English now, looking at Claudette impatiently. "I knew you would come back some day," he said in a low tone to Henrietta, as he reached for her hand again and this time brought it to his thin lips.

Henrietta wasn't sure what to say, but she was saved from having to correct the baron by the convenient entrance of the butler, who approached carrying a silver tray with two sherries. Clive reached for them, and as he did so, Claudette addressed the baron. "Father, why don't you go upstairs and dress for dinner? We can talk with our guests later. François will escort you."

"Are we not riding today?" The baron looked confused.

Claudette kissed him on the cheek. "No, Father, not today. Go with François now, and Aldric will help you."

The baron's face was still one of confusion, but he gave a tiny nod and laid his hand on Claudette's arm. "*Ne dis pas à ta mère que la comtesse est ici*—Do not mention to your mother that the countess is here," he said conspiratorially. "*Cela ne fera que la perturber*—It will only upset her."

"Yes, Father," Claudette said with a sigh. "Now go. Have a rest before dinner. You'll feel more yourself."

"But I am myself!" he mumbled as François led him from the room.

"You must excuse him," Claudette said to Clive and Henrietta as soon as the baron was safely out of the room. "He has not been himself for quite some time. He has these—what would you call them?—spells. He becomes confused and forgets things."

"I'm very sorry," Henrietta said.

"Did I overhear the baron refer to your mother?" Clive asked. "We were told that the baroness had passed away some time ago."

A look of something crossed Claudette's face. "You understand French?"

"The war," he said grimly.

"Ah, yes. It changed many of us, did it not?" she said, studying him as if seeing him in a different light. "But *oui*, you are correct. My mother has been dead these past five years."

"I'm sorry," Clive said.

"It is better this way. She was ill for many years."

"May I ask who the countess is?" Henrietta asked.

Claudette smiled. "Forgive me. I think Father is mistaking you for the Countess of Koenig. You do look extraordinarily like her. Well, how she once looked. There is a painting of her in the library, but she is long since dead, of course."

"Who was she?"

"I cannot be certain, of course, but I believe she was Father's mistress."

"What?" Henrietta sputtered.

"*Mais, oui.* It was fairly common knowledge. Surely you are not that naïve?" she asked, shooting Clive a conspiratorial glance.

"Perhaps, given the circumstances, we should stay in town?" Clive asked. "My mother led us to believe she was in communication with the baron. I apologize."

Claudette gave a little laugh. "That was me. I take care of all of Father's correspondence now. I have done so for some time. No, you are quite welcome here, if you do not mind Father's—what would you call them?— *excentricités*. He is not always like this. It is *très* unfortunate that he is having one of his fits now, just as you have arrived."

"Of course, we don't mind," Henrietta said. "But, I hope we're not imposing."

"Not at all. It is nice to have visitors. We get very few these days.

Except for Valentin's occasional guest, but those are more business colleagues."

"Valentin?"

"Yes, Valentin is my brother. You will meet him tonight at dinner. He is not often here. Normally he stays in Berlin, where his work is. But, please. Stay. You are most welcome."

"Very well." Clive glanced over at Henrietta. "We'd be delighted," he said with false politeness.

"Splendid. I will have Fortier show you to your rooms."

"Rooms? Are we not sharing a room?" Henrietta asked.

Claudette laughed again. "I assumed you would want separate rooms. I forgot that you are not English. Would you like me to change them?"

"No, of course not. Whatever you've arranged is perfectly fine."

"All right, then, I will let you get settled. Just ring the servants if you need anything. Dinner is at eight."

Upon entering her private chamber, Henrietta was surprised by how quaint it was, given the rather spartan décor below. At one end of the room was a stone fireplace, a small replica of the one below, with a fire already crackling in it and a chaise lounge nearby. Opposite was a canopied bed with thick red velvet curtains tied to each of the posts with a gold braiding, and a thick Persian carpet covered the stone floor. Along the far wall was a set of leaded glass windows, some of the panes of which were colored glass. Henrietta found it utterly charming. There were no electric lights, just lamps and candles, all of them lit, presumably by Edna, whom Henrietta knew to be frightened of the dark and who was, at this moment, busily engaged in lifting the last of Henrietta's underthings out of one of the cases.

"Are you finding everything all right?" Henrietta asked, setting her handbag on a fragile-looking writing desk perched in one corner.

"Yes, miss," Edna said briskly, without looking up.

"What's the matter, Edna?" Henrietta moved closer and saw that the girl had been crying. "Are they not treating you well?" she asked, suddenly concerned.

"Oh, no, miss. It's nothing like that."

"Well, what is it?" she asked, removing her hat. "Are you homesick?"

"Perhaps a little, miss," Edna squeaked. "I'm sorry."

"You don't have to apologize. Everything will be all right."

Edna sniffed. "If you say so, miss . . . I mean madame. But how am I to get along here? Telling me this and that in French. I don't know what I'm doing or where I'm going. Only a couple of them know any English. And I'm way up on the fourth floor in some kind of scary attic room. I'm afraid it might be haunted, miss!" Edna broke down fully into tears now.

Henrietta bit her lip, wondering if Clive was right in his frequent declarations that bringing Edna had been a mistake. Henrietta had hoped that after being in London for a week after the turbulent voyage, Edna might have adjusted, but she was, in truth, still mopey and despondent.

Henrietta put her arm around the girl, though she knew such behavior was inappropriate—that she was not supposed to be familiar with the servants in any way. It was a lesson hard-learned during her early days at Highbury, but even so, Henrietta couldn't help but to sometimes make an exception for Edna, with whom she had been through so much. "Listen," she suggested softly, "why don't you take the day off tomorrow. Or even two days."

Edna sniffed. "That's kind of you, miss, but what on earth would I do?"

"Explore the grounds?"

Edna remained unmoved, her big brown eyes still sad and unsure.

Henrietta decided to try a different tactic. "Listen. Mr. Howard and I hope to return to Strasbourg tomorrow, if we can get away, that is," she added, silently despairing that they were so unexpectedly far from the town. "Why don't you ride along and explore? I'll give you some pocket money from your wages."

"On my own, miss?" Edna squeaked.

"Well . . ." Henrietta began, wondering if they could take her along on the investigation, but quickly dashing this as absurd. "Well, what if another servant went with you?" Henrietta offered, though she worried that this plan, too, would be difficult to orchestrate. Still, she couldn't bear the thought of Edna lying in her bed, miserable, while she and Clive gallivanted off on a case.

"I don't think so, miss," Edna said morosely. "I don't want to make trouble, and, like I said, not many of them speak English, so what good would that do?"

She had a point. It would be an awkward request to make of Claudette, especially as it involved the entertainment of her servant, of all things, and not her. And she was pretty sure Clive would also balk.

"Let me discuss it with Mr. Howard. I'm sure we can come to some arrangement."

"Oh, no, miss. That's okay. Just knowing that you even thought of the idea is enough for me. Honestly. Please don't go to any trouble on my account."

"Well, we'll see," she said, patting her arm. "Why don't you lay out tonight's gown?" she suggested, hoping a task might take her mind off her woes, at least for a little bit.

"Yes, miss," Edna said forlornly. "Will you be wanting the silver or the blue?"

Henrietta thought for a moment. "The blue, I think."

"Very good, miss," Edna said, picking up the empty case. "Sure you don't want me to unpack that one?" she said, nodding at the large trunk at the end of the bed.

"No, there's no need. We won't be here long enough."

Edna silently got to work laying out the requested gown but then suddenly stopped in her efforts after only a few moments. "You . . . you won't tell Mrs. Caldwell, will you?" Edna asked abruptly, referring to Highbury's housekeeper.

"Tell her what?" Henrietta asked from where she stood beside the fireplace, examining the ancient books on the mantle.

Edna blushed. "That I've been so foolish."

Henrietta turned to her and smiled. "Of course, I won't. And you haven't been foolish. All of us get homesick from time to time." She was about to include herself in that number, but before she could do so, there was a stiff knock on the thick oak door. Clive poked his head around. "Mind if I come in?" he asked with a grin.

"Of course not, darling. That will be all for now, Edna." Henrietta nodded at the door. "We'll discuss this later."

"Yes, madame," Edna said with a little curtsey. She hurried past Clive, giving him the most cursory of deferential nods, careful not to look at him as she squeezed past.

"Why does she always look terrified of me?" Clive asked when Edna had left, shutting the door quietly behind her.

"Oh, I don't know," Henrietta said, taking hold of one of the bed posts. "It could be the fact that you once threw her beau up against a wall. Or that you fired her fiancé?" she drawled. "Either of those might explain it."

Henrietta enjoyed Clive's momentary look of outrage before he broke down into a smile. "Darling, you know I had very good reason. Though I do regret the incident with Virgil—a fact which you are very much aware of, and, as such, you are most unkind to resurrect— James was another story. He was an actual criminal."

"Still," she said pertly, "you might at least speak to her from time to time."

"Speak to her? As in have a conversation? That's ridiculous."

"It pains me to say this, but you really are a snob, you know." She tapped his chest with a finger.

Clive let out a laugh. "A snob? Hardly."

"Well, she *is* a person."

"She's also my wife's maid and a young girl at that. Thoroughly inappropriate that I should take an interest, a fact which should, in truth, bring you a fair amount of comfort. But for the sake of argument, I'll ask what seems to be the trouble this time. Surely it can't be another love interest. All of the servants in the London house were positively elderly, and she was sick as a dog on the ship. And we've only just arrived here, so it can't be that. Or is this an attachment from Highbury?" he asked drolly. "At this rate, she'll soon outpace Elsie."

"Clive! How dare you!"

Clive laughed. "I'm only teasing," he said, crossing his arms. "Honestly, I'm sorry. I didn't mean that. Tell me. No—let me guess. In earnest this time. She's homesick?"

"Well, yes, actually. I was thinking of giving her the day off tomorrow. Maybe she could ride into town with us? Assuming we're going into Strasbourg to try to find this antiquities shop that Inspector Hartle mentioned?"

Clive sighed. "Darling, I'm not sure that's a good idea—"

"Which? To go into Strasbourg or to take Edna along?"

"Both, I suppose."

"Well, I outrank you, so . . ."

"Outrank me?" he asked, a grin creeping across his face.

"Yes, I'm a countess, in case you forgot. And since you're merely the son of the second son of an English lord, I think I have you beat."

Clive shot her a look of puzzled disbelief before letting out a loud laugh. "All right, Countess. You win," he said, taking her in his arms and bending to kiss her. He further surprised her, then, by scooping her up in his arms.

"Clive!" she squealed. "What are you doing? You'll wrinkle my dress!"

"I don't care," he said thickly as he carried her to the bed and laid her upon it, shrugging out of his jacket.

"Clive!" she laughed as she looked nervously at the door. "What are you doing? We can't make love now!"

"Why not?" he said, loosening his tie. "We are on our honeymoon, and I've always wanted to make love to a countess in a castle."

"No, you haven't!"

"Try me," he grunted and laid down beside her.

"But we have to dress for dinner . . ."

"Plenty of time," he said and then kissed her lips and then her neck.

Despite the precariousness of the situation, she felt a pulse of attraction course through her. He was the only man she had ever been with, and she still thrilled to his touch. He paused in his efforts now, and she reached over to hold his face in her hands, staring into his eyes, which held an intense look of love. She ran a finger along his lips, and he leaned his forehead against hers, pausing for a moment as if savoring what they were about to do. He kissed her again, slowly this time. She ran her hands down his back, and she felt him stiffen. He moved from her lips and then began planting tiny kisses on her forehead, her jawline, and in her hair. She felt a flush of pleasure when his hands wandered to her breasts. He rubbed his thumbs against her nipples through the fabric of her dress, and she felt a pull between her legs. His kisses were deeper now, and she began to return them in kind, her arousal growing.

They continued this way, rolling on top of the coverlet until Henrietta's hair had come undone and Clive began to fumble with the buttons of her dress. Knowing from experience that he would rip them if he couldn't get them open, she undid them for him and slipped out of her brassiere. He was breathing heavily now, pausing to take her all in, and then cupped her bare breasts in his hands. He kissed each of them, and she moaned, entwining her fingers through his hair.

"Clive," she muttered, as he ran his hand up the inside of her leg.

"Yes?" he grunted through his kisses.

"I love you," she whispered.

He did not answer but tugged at her underthings, pulling them down until she was just slightly exposed. When his fingers began to explore, and she let out another low moan. Her breath began to come in short pants, and he pulled his hand away to undo his trousers, not bothering to remove them as he rolled on top of her. He entered her, his hands again caressing her breasts, and she groaned as he began to thrust. Her hands gripped his back, and she arched into him, shuddering with him as he climaxed. Breathing heavily, he showered her with kisses—her lips, her cheeks, her neck—until he finally collapsed beside her.

For several moments, neither of them said anything as they lay on their backs, panting and staring at the canopy above them until Henrietta felt Clive wrap his fingers through hers. "Oh, Henrietta. I love you, too."

"That was lovely, Clive," she said, turning her face to him. She stared into his deep hazel eyes flecked with brown. "But very naughty."

He squeezed her hand and grinned.

"What if someone had walked in?"

Clive raised himself up on one elbow and ran a finger down her chest. "Well, what of it? You *are* the countess. I expect that means you can do whatever you want."

"You're enjoying this, aren't you?"

"Immensely. I can hardly wait for tonight's dinner conversation. It should prove most entertaining, if nothing else."

"Clive! We need to be serious."

"Oh, I'm very serious." He kissed her and rolled on top of her again.

"Clive!"

"I can be fast," he whispered as he kissed her neck.

Henrietta glanced at the closed door, wondering if they had time. She ran a finger along his stubbled cheek. "Maybe I don't want you to be fast," she murmured and wrapped her arms around him.

Chapter 6

"Mother, it's hardly a disaster if the Fields don't come," Julia said, looking up from the envelope she was addressing and wrapping her arms around herself. The air in the library at Highbury had grown chilly.

"But it *is*, my dear," Antonia said worriedly. "If word gets out that the Fields are not attending, then who knows what will happen? Very probably the Armours will drop as well."

"Mother," Julia continued patiently as she affixed a stamp, "the Fields have a perfectly good excuse, and you know it. No one will drop because of them, if nothing else out of sympathy for you after Father. Every year we go through the same thing. You worry and fret for nothing. An invitation to your garden party is the North Shore's highlight of the summer. You know this."

"You're beginning to sound like Clive now," Antonia sniffed.

Julia laughed and picked up another envelope. "Speaking of Clive, have you heard from them?"

Antonia sighed. "Clive telephoned when they arrived in London to say they had made it safely. And I've received only one short letter from Henrietta. Apparently, the Duke of Buckingham's ball was 'quite enlightening,' is how she described it and promised to give all the details upon their return."

"I wonder what she means by that?" Julia mused. She liked her sister-in-law very much. She reminded her of how she herself had once been—young and innocent, though no one had ever seemed to perceive her that way, even back then.

"With Henrietta, who knows?"

"Mother," Julia said warningly, knowing that, if encouraged, her mother would more than likely embark on a stinging critique of Henrietta's many—in her opinion, anyway—faults. "She's come a long way—you've said so yourself, and she's good for Clive. Remember that."

"Yes, yes, I know. You needn't scold. I'm very fond of Henrietta. She's exceedingly pliant, if nothing else. Eager to please."

Just as I once was, thought Julia. At thirty-seven, her carefree youth was long since over. As a young woman, she had been bubbly and gay, the life of any party, and though she still tried to at least pretend to have those qualities, they had, in truth, nearly been crushed out of her. Once she married the austere Randolph Cunningham, the reality of married life had obliterated the fantasy she had previously imagined: that it would be like something out of a fairy tale. Well, perhaps her life did resemble a sort of fairy tale, only instead of the prince she had thought she married, she had in fact married an ogre, from whom she had no escape. Randolph had been polite at first, if not a little cold, but as time had gone on, he had become more violent; careful, however, never to hit her in places that might show. He was, after all, a gentleman.

Several times, in the early days, especially, Julia had tried to broach with her mother the subject of Randolph's "behavior," as she called it, but it was always met with deaf ears. As far as Antonia was concerned, what happened behind closed doors should stay there, and, she sternly instructed Julia, marriage required sacrifice. "I've done my duty a thousand times over," she had told the tearful Julia. "And now you will, too. As it turned out, your father and I actually fell in love, so I'm sure it will be the same for you. Give it time."

Julia was confused by this answer, sure that her mother didn't really understand the extent of Randolph's brutality, but she was hesitant to elaborate. It was horribly shameful, and she was beginning to think it was somehow her fault that Randolph flew into rages. She rejoiced, then, when she found herself pregnant, thinking that he might be more gentle with her, but, alas, he was not. Nor was he after their second son was born. In fact, as the years went on, he had become more and more intolerant of not just her, but everyone around him, including the boys, which opened up an all-new—and deeper, if that were possible—source of sadness in her heart. There was nothing, she knew, that she could do about it, and while she at one time had despaired of Randolph's plan to send the boys away to Phillips as soon as they were old enough, she now practically counted down the days, wanting them to be as far from Randolph as possible.

Even now, on a lovely Saturday in July, when they could have been here with her, roaming the grounds of Highbury as she and Clive had been allowed to do as children, Randolph had them locked up in the study of their Glencoe mansion with a private tutor he had hired for the summer. She mourned for them, thinking that they grew paler by the day, but she had already paid the price for objecting and was still, in fact, nursing a bruised rib.

"I think this is the last one," she said, stretching with a wince to place the final envelope on the stack in front of Antonia.

"You'll stay for dinner, won't you?" Antonia asked, clearly unaware of Julia's pain. Julia could hear the eagerness in her mother's voice. "Since Randolph is out of town?"

"I should probably get back to the boys, Mother," Julia answered with a sigh, though she knew that by the time she got home, their nanny would have them bathed and dressed for bed. If she were lucky, she would be in time to kiss them good night, but that would be all. Randolph ruled the servants with an iron fist, and if they deviated at all from his instructions, they were instantly fired. Even when he was away on business, the servants strictly adhered to his orders, no matter how much Julia tried to redirect them. She was like a child herself in her own home. She was to appear beautiful and charming and poised, and that was all. The perfect hostess on the arm of her influential husband.

"Fiddlesticks!" Antonia quipped. "You can see them when you get home. Anyway, I need you here to make up the numbers."

"Make up the numbers?" Julia said, stiffly turning toward her now.

"Sidney is coming, and regrettably he's asked to bring his nephew along."

Julia paused, allowing herself a moment to absorb this statement. It was a little worrying how familiar Mr. Bennett had become in what seemed a very short period of time. He had never been a dinner guest while her father had been alive. For one thing, she knew that her father, however friendly he might have been with his right-hand man, would have never mixed business with his personal life, and, if he *had* been of a mind to invite him to dinner, it was a proposal that Julia was almost certain her mother would have shot down as being ridiculous, Sidney Bennett being so far beneath them on the social strata. Her mother, she knew, was the quintessential snob. Which made her current "involvement," for lack of a better word, with Mr. Bennett all the more baffling. He was at least a monthly dinner guest now, as far as Julia knew, anyway, and worse, her mother had taken to calling him by his Christian name, which she had never once used in all the years in which he had worked for Alcott.

"By Sidney, are you referring to Mr. Bennett?" Julia asked with just a hint of her old playfulness. It had a tendency to come out when she was back at Highbury, where she and Clive had run wild through the house as children.

"You know that I am, Julia. Don't be flippant."

Julia never ceased to be amazed by her mother's astonishing ability to always make everyone else seem in the wrong, the current conversation proving yet another excellent example.

"Mr. Bennett seems to be a rather frequent dinner guest of late, Mother," Julia countered gingerly. "If one didn't know otherwise, one might be inclined to think you've formed some sort of attachment."

"Really, Julia! I'll not be badgered by you, or anyone, for that matter, in my own home. I happen to like Sidney's company, if you must know. I've been very lonely." Julia's ears perked at the sound of genuine emotion in her mother's last statement.

"Forgive me, Mother," she said more gently, bitterly understanding, firsthand, how it felt to be lonely, especially in a house full of servants. It made the loneliness all the more acute. "Of course, you can spend your time as you wish."

"There are things you don't know, Julia. Things that . . . well, things that no one knows."

Julia's heart skipped a beat, wondering what her mother meant by this. Surely, her mother had not entertained an affair . . . had she?

Antonia looked across the desk at her. "The truth is that I was once in love with Sidney Bennett," she said plainly.

Julia's heart dropped into her stomach. "Mother!"

"Before you jump to conclusions," she said, holding up a hand. "It was before I knew your father."

"I . . . I never knew . . ." Julia was stunned.

"No one did," she said as she carefully set down the pen she was holding in front of her. "He was my father's protégé, and he was often at the house. It was the summer of my coming-out season. He was never invited to the balls or galas, of course," she said, glancing up at Julia now, "but somehow he managed to steal my heart."

Julia was tempted to say something, but she made herself be silent. Her mother rarely confided in her, and she had no wish to break the confession now.

Antonia's face relaxed into a small smile as she stared at a spot on the desk. "I was naïve enough to think that perhaps we had a future, but of course, that was not to be." She looked up at Julia now. "Father informed me one summer afternoon that I was to marry Alcott Howard. That he was arriving on the Queen Mary at the end of the week, in time for my coming-out ball, and that he was to be my first dance." She let out a little sigh. "I devised to hate him, of course, but, in truth, he was every bit the English gentleman. He was courteous, polite, kind, handsome in a certain way, and I could find no objection to marrying him besides the obvious, which is that I didn't love him." Antonia stood up now and walked toward the window.

"Oh, Mother, how . . . how awful for you," Julia said, though she felt strangely sympathetic toward her father in this story as well.

"I cried, of course, and carried on, but my mother scolded me and asked, 'whatever does love have to do with marriage?'" Julia shifted uncomfortably, recalling Antonia's early advice to her. "My father was keen to have ties to the British aristocracy," Antonia continued, turning away from the window. "So much so that he was willing to sacrifice his oldest daughter for a chance that his grandchildren would be part of the peerage. In exchange, a full third of my fortune, which was considerable," Antonia said with a tilt of her head, "was transferred to the Howard's ancestral estate, Linley, which was purportedly in dire need of ready cash. Alcott, I later discovered, also played the part of the sacrificial lamb and did his duty, which was to marry for money, while his older brother inherited the title. Likewise, after we had both been talked into this marriage of convenience by our respective parents, we later learned that we were to take up life in Chicago, where my father hoped to strengthen his business accounts. It came as a shock to both of us. I had no intention of leaving New York and the Newport society I had grown up in, and Alcott was likewise under the delusion that we would live on British soil," she said and let out a deep breath.

"Well, according to Clive and Henrietta, you got the better of the two houses," she tried to say, partly as a jest, but Antonia did not smile.

"That is according to opinion," Antonia said stiffly. "I know your father didn't think so."

"How does Bennett figure into all of this?" Julia asked, not wanting Antonia to lose the thread.

"Well, my father insisted not only that we move to Chicago but that Alcott head up a new firm my father had created, Linley Standard. Poor Alcott of course tried to protest, explaining that he had absolutely no knowledge of business, having read Greek at Cambridge, of all things, and that he was thoroughly unsuited for the job. My father was one step ahead, however, and had already arranged for Sidney Bennett, his brilliant protégé, to accompany us in our move to Chicago to be Alcott's right-hand man."

"Oh!"

"Yes, I could hardly say anything, could I? But the prospect of having Sidney Bennett, the man I was actually in love with—or thought I was in love with, anyway—so close at hand filled me with dread. I wasn't sure I could endure the temptation, so I made it plain from the very beginning that Mr. Bennett was never allowed to be a guest in our home, declaring it to be unsuitable. Alcott balked, of course, but he went along with my wishes, as he usually did, the poor thing. Sidney appeared now and again over the years with documents for Alcott to sign, but I always made sure I was never in the vicinity."

Julia sat, stunned, unable for once to think of a single thing to say. She wondered if her poor father had ever suspected. She missed him terribly; no one knew how much. She had always found so much comfort in his presence. Often, he had told her that she was the brightest spot in his life and that the day she had been born was his happiest ever.

"Don't think I didn't love your father," Antonia went on, as if she could read her thoughts. "I did. And after so many years passed, and you and Clive came along, my passion for Sidney cooled. I think I could have endured Sidney's presence then without being tempted into a scandal, but by then we had established boundaries and there seemed to be no need to change it. I asked little about him over the years, but I did glean that he never married and never had a family. I could only imagine it was because of his unrequited love, though I sincerely hoped, for his sake, that it was not."

"Oh, Mother."

"So, when your father died so unexpectedly, and with Sidney being involved as he was in that tragedy, he was suddenly brought back into my life with full force. It took me completely off guard."

"Yes, I can imagine," Julia offered.

"I tried to object to him coming to see Clive on various matters, but, of course, no one listened, particularly Clive. That is why I kept urging Clive to go downtown to the office and take up his duties there; it was to prevent Sidney from having to come here. But you know Clive and his pigheadedness and his infuriating obsession with detective work. So," she gestured weakly, "I had no choice but to face Sidney. He was at the funeral, of course, but we barely spoke to each other. One night he came here looking for Clive, and I was forced to at least greet him. I admit, I was curious about how I would feel after all these years, and I found that, while not exactly in the throes of love, I still . . . well, care for him in a certain way. As a friend, perhaps. I could never betray your father, even now, and yet I find Sidney's presence very comforting. Almost as if a little part of your father is still here." She uncharacteristically twisted her hands. "I know this probably doesn't make any sense. It barely does to me."

Julia's head was swirling. "No, it does, Mother. I understand."

"I don't regret my decision to marry Alcott," she continued stiffly. "It was the right thing to do; I see that now. But I don't see any reason why I shouldn't enjoy Sidney's company from time to time."

Julia did not respond. She couldn't possibly criticize her mother's choice of companion after all that she had been through. And there was something about their long-unrealized love that touched Julia deeply. But, she knew, if it went beyond simple companionship, there would be others of their set who would not be so understanding, Victoria Braithewaite, for example, being one of them, despite claiming to be one of Antonia's bosom friends. She wondered if anyone suspected. Probably not.

"Does Clive know?" she asked tentatively.

"Heavens, no. And I don't want him to. You know what he's like. And, anyway, what does it matter? It's not up to him, though I daresay he thinks otherwise."

Julia pondered this. Clive could be damnably obtuse at times, but surely Henrietta would have noticed . . .

"So, will you stay, then?" Antonia asked again, disrupting Julia's musings.

"Stay?" she asked.

"For dinner, dearest. So, you can help me entertain his nephew. He's a young lawyer, I believe, so I'm sure he'll be dreadfully dull. I find those types exceedingly hard to make conversation with."

"And I don't?" Julia almost laughed.

"You're so much better at all of that, Julia. You know you are. For once put it to good use to help me."

Julia felt that a rather unfair statement, given that she had helped her mother on too many occasions to count over the years, but she knew she hadn't really meant it. "I thought Bennett didn't have any family," Julia said.

"Nor did I, but one way or another, a nephew has now materialized and is staying with him for several weeks. I hope he doesn't plan on offering him a position at the firm. That would be highly irregular. I mean, what if he isn't qualified?"

"Oh, you mean like the grandson of the founder of the company being named the chairman of the board though he has not one ounce of business acumen?" Julia said in a teasing voice, referring, of course, to Clive.

"That's different, and you know it!" snapped Antonia.

"Very well," Julia exhaled, giving in. "I'll stay for dinner." She was, in truth, a little curious to see how her mother would interact with Sidney. This was a whole new side to her mother that she hadn't known existed, and she was still struggling to understand it all. "But I'm not exactly dressed," she said, looking down at her mint-green shirtwaist dress with tiny white polka dots.

"There are still some of your things up in your old room, I'm sure. Put on one of those."

"I'm sure they're horribly outdated, Mother. And they probably don't fit."

"Well, Andrews can help you," Antonia snapped, referring to her personal maid. "And I'm sure they won't notice if you're not in the latest fashion. You know how men are."

Julia *did* know how men were—generally unobservant—except Randolph, who was somehow keenly aware of every little detail and who criticized Julia if she did not present herself in the latest styles, as if it were somehow a slight to him if she did not.

"Well, I'd better go see what I can find," she said with a sigh and thought that she should probably telephone home to let the servants know she would be dining out and home late, not that anyone would care.

"Do hurry," Antonia called out after her. "They'll be here in an hour or so."

Sidney Bennett and his nephew arrived promptly at seven, both dressed smartly in tails and white tie. Julia had managed to unearth a peach crepe evening dress from her old armoire, and Andrews had helped her with her hair. How a Worth gown had been left behind, Julia wasn't sure. It was about ten years out of date, but, still, it looked lovely on her, contrasting perfectly with her dark hair. Julia felt a flush of nostalgia, and not a little wrenching of the heart, to be back in her old rooms, dressing for dinner, just as she used to before so many of life's tragedies had befallen her.

Julia had of course seen Bennett at her father's funeral, but he struck her now, as the two men entered the drawing room, as being almost elegant. He was almost exactly her mother's height and had frosted gray hair that had once been dark, she could see. He held himself very upright, and Julia could see what attracted her mother, or had once upon a time. He had a sort of quiet dignity to him, and his soft brown eyes were exceedingly kind and gentle.

His nephew, a Mr. Glenn Forbes, as he was introduced, did not appear young or awkward at all, which is how Julia had somehow imagined he would be. From her mother's brief mention of him, she had expected him to be fresh out of college, but instead, he appeared to be in his thirties, if Julia wasn't mistaken. He was tall and broad, with a ruddy complexion and thick dirty-blond hair. She would never have guessed he was a lawyer, who—in Julia's experience

anyway—were usually tiny, tight-lipped men who possessed a certain shrewdness about the eyes. Mr. Forbes, on the other hand, had
an easy, relaxed demeanor to him as he took the proffered drink
from the tray Billings held in front of him now; it was as if he knew
them all intimately and indeed felt at home here. He had yet to stop
smiling, and, Julia mused, as she took a sip of her sherry, if he was
acting, he was very good.

"I must thank you for the invitation, Mrs. Howard," he said,
addressing her mother now. His voice held a slight drawl, which Julia
couldn't place. "Uncle Sid speaks very highly of you."

Julia watched with amusement as Antonia's eyes fluttered slightly
at this gross address. Bennett's face, Julia noted, meanwhile remained
bland, though he did shift slightly from one foot to the other.

"Not at all," Antonia answered, her lips drawn into a tight smile.
"We're happy you could join us, Mr. Forbes. How long have you
been in town?" She was dressed elegantly, if not modestly, in a black
tapered silk.

"Just about a week now." He threw Bennett a glance. "I was hoping
to meet your son, but it seems I just missed him."

"Yes, he's touring the continent with his wife. A sort of honeymoon trip, as it were."

"Yes, Uncle Sid informed me. I'm right sorry for your loss."

"Thank you," Antonia said stiffly. There was a bit of a silence, then,
which Julia felt was her cue to step in.

"And where are you from, Mr. Forbes? Do I detect a southern
accent?"

"I hail from Austin, Texas, ma'am."

"Texas! So far. I've never been. What's it like?"

"Big," he said, his gray-green eyes twinkling, as he took a drink.
"My family owns a ranch just outside of Austin."

"A ranch!" Antonia exclaimed, as if she had just sampled something distasteful.

"Only a little one, Mrs. Howard," he said, throwing Julia a wink. *A
wink!* "Just about a thousand acres."

"Goodness, Mr. Forbes! A thousand acres is hardly small," Julia laughed, deciding to ignore the wink.

"It is by Texas standards."

"How extraordinary," Antonia commented.

"May I ask you a question, Mr. Forbes? I hope you won't think me forward," Julia said.

"By all means, Mrs. Cunningham. I doubt there's anything you could ask me that I would consider forward."

"What was your interest in going into the law?"

Mr. Forbes surprised her by letting out a loud laugh. "*That's* the forward question?" He seemed to enjoy saying this word, as if it were new to him, and yet he obviously understood its meaning. "Why, that's an easy one. My dad has five sons, you see, so he thought he'd put them all to good use. The oldest brother is the business man; he'll take over the ranch someday, but the rest of us were told what we were to study. So, there's a doctor, a lawyer," he gestured at himself and then went back to ticking off his fingers, "a banker, and an army officer. Dad wanted Teddy to enter the seminary when he finished college, but instead he ran off and joined the Texas Rangers. Dad was mad for a while, but he soon got over it. Especially when Teddy made captain. I always thought that the army sounded just as strict as being in the priesthood, but Teddy seems to like it all right."

"I see," Julia mused. "But what about you, Mr. Forbes? Do *you* like your chosen profession?"

Mr. Forbes let out another deep laugh. "Liking don't have much to do with it, Mrs. Cunningham, but, in point of fact, I don't mind it. There are parts that are interesting. Isn't that right, Uncle Sid? I guess I'm lucky in that I find many things interesting."

"Why lucky?"

Mr. Forbes shot her a puzzled look. "Because if you can find something interesting in whatever happens to be in front of you, you're never bored, are you? Never down in the mouth. You can always find something entertaining, something worthy of study, or something just downright beautiful, even in the ordinary. I call that lucky."

"My, Mr. Forbes, you're quite a philosopher," Julia said with a teasing smile, though, in truth, his words had struck a chord with her. He was an extremely interesting specimen of a man. He was dressed properly, had perfect manners, and knew how to properly converse, yet everything he said seemed to be in defiance of the confines of society. It was as if he were secretly laughing at it all while still following all the rules. It reminded her of herself, she realized, when she had been much younger. Laughing at society and all of Mother's instructions and admonishments and expectations but participating just enough to still be deemed acceptable. Barely. She had begun running with a fast set, girls she knew from school who went to nightclubs with young men and smoked and drank and danced to all the latest jazz in short dresses and bobbed hair. "Debutantes do not go to nightclubs," Antonia had scolded, and before Julia knew it, she had somehow found herself engaged to Randolph, whose older, wiser hand, it was hoped, would steady the wild Julia. Well, his hand *had* in fact steadied Julia, particularly when clenched in a fist.

"Can't say that I know anything about philosophy, but if you want to call it that, I sure won't stop you."

"And what is it that you find interesting?" she asked, going back to his original statement. "In particular."

Glenn put one hand in his jacket pocket. "Why, a good many things, as I've said. Horses. Thoroughbreds, to be exact. Whiskey. Art. In fact, this is probably as good a time as any to confess that I'm here under false pretenses."

"Glenn," Bennett warned from across the room.

"False pretenses?" Antonia asked from where she sat on the sofa, close—but not too close—to Bennett, her brow creased.

"My, my," Julia clucked. "This sounds deliciously intriguing, Mr. Forbes. Whatever can you mean?"

"Just that Uncle Sid has told me about your father's private collection, and I'd very much like to see it. If I may, that is. It is the reason I begged him to bring me along tonight."

"Is that all?" Julia laughed, though she could tell by her mother's stony face that she didn't share her amusement. "We seem to be equal now."

"Equal?" His face was one of delighted curiosity.

"I surprised you with my question earlier, and now you've surprised us with the true nature of your supposed false pretense. Wanting to see our collection is hardly a crime, is it, Mother?"

Antonia did not say anything.

"Well, I suppose we shouldn't deny you any longer," Julia said with a smile as she turned back to him. "Shall I take you upstairs to the gallery?"

"I would be indebted to you if you would."

"Do we have time, Mother?"

"Yes, I suppose so, but listen for the gong," she chirped, as if Julia were still a child. "You know what Mary's like if her sauces go cold."

"Indeed, yes. She'll be upset for a week. Come along, Mr. Forbes. It's this way."

Chapter 7

Dinner at Château du Freudeneck was held in a cavernous room adjacent to the main hall, though it was not of stone as most of the rest of the château was. Instead, it had thick plaster walls painted a deep red and covered by what looked to be very ancient tapestries. The table itself was the largest Henrietta had ever seen, its thickly carved mahogany legs being wider that her waist. The china, too, looked to be very old with a faded blue pattern of the Orient. Upon the table itself sat several exquisite crystal bowls filled with rose heads floating in water, but on the sideboard stood two gigantic vases filled with a vast array of flowers, and Henrietta wondered if they had been plucked from the gardens or delivered from town.

The baron, dressed now in white tie, sat at one end of the table, while Claudette graced the other. She was again wearing a lovely gown, which Henrietta guessed was probably a Schiaparelli. Henrietta, herself dressed in a powder-blue Vionnet gown with a matching lace cape, sat to the right of the baron, and next to her was the illustrious son of the house, Valentin-Marie. Unlike the baron, both Valentin and Claudette were very tall, causing Henrietta to conclude that the baroness must have been a lady of stature. While Claudette had a kind, generous manner to her, Valentin-Marie Von Harmon seemed

unusually stiff and formal and not at all entertained by the Howards'
presence. In fact, he seemed a little put out by them, or very possibly
bored. Even Henrietta's usual charms seemed to have little effect on
him.

Across from them sat Clive on his own.

"You must forgive our small number," Claudette said now, glancing at him. "We thought it best to have just a family affair for the first
night."

"Not at all," Clive answered, a polite smile about his face as he
raised his glass slightly.

"Valentin," the baron suddenly spoke, "do you not think Mrs.
Howard has the look of the Countess of Koenig to her?"

Henrietta was amazed at the baron's current lucidity. It was as
if the man they had met earlier today had been a different person
entirely. Did these strange spells that Claudette had described
really alter him so dramatically? Henrietta watched him carefully
and noticed that he now seemed to need no reminders to speak in
English. In fact, he seemed rather fluent, as did Valentin, who, for his
part, claimed to know English only because it was the language of
business and of money.

"Certainly not," Valentin said, barely glancing at Henrietta. "Do
not be ridiculous, Father. You embarrass yourself and Mrs. Howard."

"Well, I suppose there is a small *ressemblance*," Claudette said,
taking a bite of beef.

"*Exactement!*" the baron said, tilting his head appreciatively in her
direction.

"Father, really. It is obviously a coincidence. And what is the difference? All of this heraldry is very much nonsense. It is a thing of the
past," he scoffed, reminding Henrietta of something very similar the
Duke of Buckingham had said to her, or maybe it had been Wallace.

"It matters certainly," the baron bristled.

"Father, you forget a little thing called the French Revolution."

"*Oui*, but that was Paris and the aristocracy. Not the noble lines of
Alsace and Lorraine."

Valentin sighed tiredly. "You must forgive my father," he said directly to Clive. "He is a relic of another age."

"I'm not so old that I cannot hear you," the baron nearly shouted.

"Valentin," Claudette warned, "not tonight. Let it be."

"All I am saying is that we need to look ahead to the future. Leave behind these little fiefdoms with their lands and their flags and their titles. Become more modern. I thought that would naturally happen after the war, which it did, to a certain extent, in places like Paris and Nice, but here in this backwater, we are still miserably clinging to an outdated century. It is *ridicule*! Only a twenty-five years ago, we were German. Now we are French," he said with a shrug. "The fact that we are continually re-relegated to one country or another should prove that all this heraldry is utterly without meaning."

"*Mais, non*, it proves the opposite," the baron retorted. "That no matter what nationality is thrust upon us by the rulers of the day, we must cling to our true roots." He pounded his chest with one fist. "The Von Harmons are a very ancient family, as you know, Valentin. Why is that so hard for you to accept?"

"I do acknowledge that, Father. But we must change with the times. Reinvent ourselves. Like what Heir Hitler is doing right now in Germany."

"You're a follower of Hitler, then?" Clive interjected.

"Not a follower, per se, but an admirer, let us say. It is impressive the way he is uniting the country for the greater good, is it not?"

"But how do you know it is for the greater good?" the baron demanded. "I have heard *choses terribles* about this man and his party, the Nazis. And, no, it is never a good thing to give up one's familial allegiance."

"Let us speak of other things," Claudette suggested quietly.

Silence then fell over the table for several moments, and all that could be heard was the clanking of silverware against the china.

Finally, Valentin spoke. "Since we were speaking of familial allegiance," he said, picking up his wine glass, "perhaps this would be a good opportunity for Mrs. Howard to enlighten us as to her particular connection to the Von Harmon family, besides her maiden name and her uncanny resemblance to the Countess de Koenig, that is. It was never fully explained to me."

"Valentin!" Claudette scolded.

"I mean no offense. I am merely curious," he said, examining his glass as he swirled it and then looking at Henrietta. "Please do elaborate."

Claudette looked about to say something more, but Henrietta spoke first. "I don't mind answering, though I'm afraid there's not much to tell. And, please, you must call me Henrietta. I insist." She looked directly at Valentin. "As I said before, I really don't know very many details. My father was Leslie Von Harmon, and I believe that it was his grandfather who came to America. Apparently, he fell in love with an American woman traveling through the Alps with her family. I don't know what he was doing in the Alps to have met her, but they did somehow meet." She looked unsteadily around the table and tried to offer a smile, but no one responded. "The match must not have been approved of on one or both sides, however," she went on, "because they ended up running off together and getting married. They fled to Chicago. Again, I have no idea why, but they settled down there. I know very little else, just that my father used to tell us that the Von Harmons were, once upon a time, 'barons in the old country,' as he used to say." She let out a deep breath and reached for her wine.

"*Extraordinaire*," the baron exclaimed, drumming his fingers on the cloth. "That must have been Otto Von Harmon. He was my great uncle, I believe. He was one of five. Let me see. There was Manfred." He paused, thinking. "Then there was Louisa. Another girl whose name escapes me. Jean-Claude, who was my grandfather. And then, of course, there was Otto. He was the youngest, so probably not missed when he ran off. That was right around the time of the Napoleonic Wars. Or one of them, anyway. At any rate," he said, looking up at Henrietta now, "it is *extraordinaire* to have one of Otto's descendants sitting right here with us. Do you not think, Claudette?"

"What did they do when they got to Chicago? Do you know?" Claudette asked, after giving the baron the most cursory of nods.

"I'm afraid I don't. I think *my* grandfather might have been a butcher. I guess that would have been Otto's son." She felt a bit of heat creep up her face and, embarrassed, looked over at Clive, who gave her a steadying wink. "My father was his delivery boy before he got a job at Schwinn," she added, lifting her chin just a little.

"Schwinn?"

"It's a factory that makes bicycles."

"Oh, very good," Valentin said drolly, a rare smile illuminating his face now as he made a show of clapping his hands together. "You see, Father? Where all of this ends? The noble house of Von Harmon descended to a factory floor in America."

"I wouldn't say that," Clive put in in a surprisingly icy tone. "You forget that Henrietta is my wife. And, as my uncle is twelfth in line to the throne of England, I would say she has more than sufficiently restored the Otto Von Harmon branch of the family to its place of nobility."

"Ah! Rescued by the English, is that what you mean?" Valentin scoffed, no amusement whatsoever in his tone.

"Yes, and it isn't the first time." Clive stared at him coolly.

"That depends on whether we are talking about the French or the Germans."

"Exactly." Clive did not alter his gaze. "Which are you?"

"A little of both, as I just said before. It matters not."

"I think it matters very much whose allegiance you hold, especially at this particular moment in time."

"Valentin! Is this any way to treat our guests?" Claudette finally interjected. "You are *impossible* tonight. Why?"

"Yes, Valentin," the baron grumbled. "You shame me. It is not often that I entertain guests of my own."

"I apologize," Valentin said somewhat flippantly. "I mean nothing by it."

Clive gave a curt nod.

Valentin cleared his throat. "Well, now that you *are* here," he said, gesturing widely, "what do you plan to do? There is very little to occupy oneself, I can assure you."

"How do you spend *your* days?" Henrietta asked pertly. She was beginning to tire of this particular relative.

"I spend most of my time in Paris and Berlin. You just happened to catch me at home. I have a bit of business in Strasbourg over the next day or two."

"Why don't you take Clive shooting?" Claudette suggested. "Do you hunt?" She looked pointedly at Clive.

"Yes, a little."

"In July, Claudette? It is not the season for it. However, you can always go riding, if you would like. One of the grooms can act as your guide."

"Actually, we were hoping to go into Strasbourg ourselves. Have a look around. See the cathedral and all of that. Play the tourists," explained Clive.

"Yes, that would be most enjoyable for you!" the baron said eagerly.

"It is too bad I have various previous engagements tomorrow, or I would be glad to give you a tour of the cathedral. I am what you might call an expert on cathedral architecture," Valentin offered. "Why do you not wait a day?"

"That's kind of you, Valentin, but I'm afraid we don't have much time in Strasbourg. We're happy to just wander about; aren't we, Clive?" Henrietta took a drink of her wine.

"Yes," Clive answered quickly, throwing her a grateful glance. "Might we borrow a car, Baron?"

"Borrow a car? *Ridicule!* Gaspard will drive you. The roads are quite dangerous, you know. And French cars are very different from American cars," he warned.

Henrietta observed Clive's jaw clench slightly and could tell that his patience was waning.

"That may be so, but my father was a bit of a collector. His prize was an Isotta Fraschini Tipo. So, you see, I *am* familiar with foreign cars," he said tightly.

"An Isotta? That is impressive, I do agree. But, no, Gaspard will drive you. I would not think of it."

"Thank you, Baron. That would be lovely," Henrietta said, attempting to smooth Clive's clearly ruffled feathers as a servant deposited a plate of cheese before her, while another placed a glass of port. Cheese? She didn't think she could eat another bite after the massive meal they had just consumed. She wasn't used to eating so much in one sitting. Dutifully, however, she began to sample a fair portion of it before looking to Claudette for some sort of signal to excuse themselves. Mercifully, it wasn't long before Claudette caught her eye and accordingly stood.

"Come, *chérie*; we will leave the men, no?"

Grateful, Henrietta stood and followed, Claudette intimately wrapping her arm through hers in a way that an English hostess would never have done.

The rest of the evening passed uneventfully. The men eventually joined them for one final drink, but the conversation lagged. The baron looked to be asleep in an armchair in the corner, and Clive, Henrietta could see, was fighting to disguise his yawns as well. Finally, Claudette rang for a servant to help the baron to bed, and Valentin took the opportunity to also excuse himself, bidding them a curt good-night and expressing his regret that he probably wouldn't see them until dinner the following day, if at all.

Henrietta and Clive took that as their cue to retire as well, Claudette reminding them to ring for the servants if they needed anything. Heavily, they climbed the stairs, Henrietta distinctly feeling as if they were somehow in another century. She tried to imagine what it must have been like living here hundreds of years ago. She shivered a little when they reached the top and looked down the darkened hallway, lit only by an occasional candled sconce, and hoped it wasn't haunted.

Clive kissed her and rubbed his hand down her arm. "Good night, darling," he said, kissing her on the forehead now. "I'll see you soon."

"Good night," she said wistfully, assuming he meant in the morning and somewhat surprised that he wasn't insisting that they sleep together. The beds *were* rather small, however. He kissed her again, not as deeply as she thought he might, and clipped off down the hall, giving her a final look and an unexpected wink before entering his room.

Henrietta entered her own room and found everything perfectly laid out. Likewise, the fire had been built up and several candles had been lit, indicating that Edna must have just been there. Henrietta went to the armoire, hulking in the corner, and began to undress. She slipped into her nightdress and robe and wandered to the bedside, where she saw that Edna had even remembered to place her book for her, *A Room of One's Own,* which she had purchased while in London. She picked it up, wondering if she had the mental capacity to continue with it just now, after such a large meal, not to mention a few too many glasses of wine. She had started Miss Woolf's essays on the train and, while she found them rather intriguing in their somewhat startling content, they were, she had to admit, just a little difficult to completely comprehend and absorb. At any rate, she was sure they would not make for light bedtime reading, though she was grateful to Edna for this extra effort and resolved to try to cheer the girl up.

She set the book down and was just about to climb into bed when she jumped at the sound of a sharp rap on her door.

"Who is it?" she cried, tightening the belt of her robe. No one answered, however, and she crept closer to the door. Perhaps it was Edna?

"Who is it?" she called again and opened the door a tiny crack. Instantly, she let out a sigh of relief to see that it was only Clive. He was dressed in his navy-blue dressing gown and leather slippers.

"Oh, it's you!" she exclaimed, opening the door wider. "What's wrong?" She looked up and down the hallway.

"Darling, you don't really think I'm going to sleep alone, do you?" He stepped inside. "There has only been one such night, and it is not one I plan to ever repeat," Clive said, referring to the night they had argued at Castle Linley.

"Well, why didn't you say so?"

"Funny, I thought I did," he answered, his forehead creased in mock puzzlement.

"Oh, all right," she said, feigning indifference as she shut the door behind him, this time locking it. "But only if you behave yourself. I'm very tired. Not to mention uncomfortable after all that cheese."

Clive pulled her close. "All right. You win. I'll only ravage you a little bit."

"No, you naughty thing! None at all."

"How about a bit of kissing?" he said, brushing his lips against hers. Henrietta felt herself respond, her chest fluttering as she returned his kiss, and breathed in the delightful smell of his lingering cologne.

"No!" She pulled herself away from him. "We must be sensible."

"Whatever for?" he said, putting his hands into the pockets of his silk dressing gown.

"Well, for one thing, we have to discuss the case, now that you're here." She climbed into bed and eased herself back on the thick goose-down pillows and pulled her knees up, wrapping her arms around them.

Clive groaned. "Darling, as far as I can tell, there is no case. I can't imagine that any of them has ever heard of the Ghent Altarpiece, much less be hiding it. I think Hartle got his theory wrong. It could be in any number of châteaux in this region. Not to mention none at all."

"Well, what about Valentin? He seems like he could be in league with the Nazis. He practically admitted it."

"Maybe," Clive said, easing himself onto the bed. "But he seems harmless enough to me. A bit of a pompous ass, but not a Nazi."

"I'm not so sure."

"Regardless, this seems a fool's errand, Henrietta. We can't possibly search this whole place in only a few days' time. Even if it is here, it could be anywhere! Valentin might sleep with it under his pillow, for all we know."

"Clive! Really." Henrietta laughed. "We have to at least try."

Clive let out a sigh. "Very well, we'll have a poke around. Tell Hartle we tried, and then go on."

"But what about the agent?"

"Yes, yes," Clive said, running his hand through his hair. "We'll investigate this shop tomorrow and see what we can find out. I admit that that is the only solid part of this case. Perhaps the missing agent is alive and well and simply holed up somewhere with a French tart and has missed his communiqué from headquarters."

"I don't believe that for one minute, and neither do you."

"You're right. I don't," he said, turning toward her.

"Clive!"

"Must we bring Edna with us tomorrow?" he said, kissing her neck now.

"Yes. She's terribly homesick, Clive, and she won't tag along. She'll sit in the front with the chauffeur."

"Do you really think it wise to let a young girl wander the streets of a foreign city not even speaking the language?"

"Yes, I've thought of that. I'm going to speak to Claudette about it. Maybe they can spare someone to go with her."

"Are we destined to never ever truly be alone?" he asked, running a finger across the silk material thinly covering her breast.

"We're alone *now*."

"Yes, but any moment we're sure to get a telegram from my mother announcing some disaster or a desperate letter from Elsie alerting us to some danger she's fallen into at home."

"Clive!" His pajama top had fallen open, and she gave his chest hair a playful tug. "You know that's not true! Must you always be so pessimistic?"

"Ow! And I'm not being pessimistic, darling. I'm just being realistic," he said and kissed her deeply. "Which is a different thing altogether."

Chapter 8

Elsie dearly wished she could talk to Henrietta. Her sister would know exactly what to do. It had been just over a week since her and Gunther's disastrous visit to her grandfather, and she was still just as rudderless as when it had happened. Worse was the fact that Gunther was now avoiding her, telling her when they parted that day that it was for the best.

They had initially said very little to each other on the bus ride home, Elsie crying silent tears, and Gunther sitting stiffly and staring out the grimy window, his hands folded loosely in his lap.

Finally, Elsie had made herself speak. "Gunther," she said quietly, "you didn't mean what you said back there, did you?" She waited for him to reply, but he did not, continuing instead to stare out the window. "How can you . . . how can you just turn your back on me?" she went on. "Go back on what you said? You . . . you told me you were in love with me. Did you not mean it?"

Gunther shifted his gaze to the back of the seat in front of them, but still remained silent for so long that Elsie assumed he did not mean to answer her, causing a fresh wave of despair to overwhelm her.

"Gunther, please! Say something!"

"Elsie," he finally said, thickly. "It is *because* I love you that I must let you go. Sometimes . . . sometimes these things are not meant to be."

"How can you—"

"That does not mean there is not love," he said, looking sideways at her now. "It just means it cannot be . . . *aktualisiert*—actualized. That we cannot be together. It is as if one of us is in prison or exiled in another country, perhaps. Or shipwrecked. Yes, that is it. We are shipwrecked, you and I. That does not mean I do not love you. Never that. It is just that we must live apart."

Elsie took hold of one of his hands. "Gunther, please. Just listen. I—"

"Elsie, what sort of man would I be if I reduced your whole family to poverty simply because I chose to follow my heart?" he responded, gently pulling his hand from hers.

Elsie paused, trying desperately to think of a counter to this. "But isn't that what you're always talking about?" she finally sputtered. "All the poems you've read and written . . . about following one's heart . . . true love?"

"Yes, but there are some sacrifices that are just too great. As I once said to you, the end does not justify the means."

"But what about Anna? You forgot to mention her to Grandfather."

Gunther closed his eyes. "I did not forget, but I saw that it was hopeless that I should also plead her cause. Elsie, if we marry, then your own siblings will lose their home. Is that right? Would you have me trade one child for another? No. I will find a way. Whatever we do, there is no place for Anna with your family, as I said from beginning. We need to go. Start over somewhere else. A farm somewhere perhaps, where Anna can live with me in peace."

"A farm!" Panic shot through Elsie's heart. "Where?"

"There are many farms in need of laborers. This you know, Elsie. Do not make it harder than it is."

"Gunther, no. Wait," Elsie pleaded. "We'll call off our engagement, as you say. But let Anna stay at Palmer Square with Ma. After all, it is

Henrietta and Clive who are paying for Nurse Flanagan. Let her stay there. Please."

"That was meant only to be temporary, Elsie. I found it difficult to accept your brother-in-law's charity in the first place, but I cannot accept it any longer, especially now. It is only matter of time before your grandfather discovers her."

"But what difference does that make?" Elsie said fiercely, dangerously close to tears. "Why are you being so stubborn? It's infuriating!"

"It is his house, Elsie," he said, looking at her gently. "No, this is the only way."

All through the next week, Elsie had tried valiantly to carry on as if nothing had changed, determined to find a way through this . . . complication—her new word for their current dilemma—but as the week had rolled along and Gunther had made himself more and more scarce, she began to lose hope. Just this morning, she had accidentally come upon him in one of the skyscraper corridors and accordingly rushed to him.

"Gunther! I've been looking everywhere for you! I must speak to you!"

He did not answer her, however, merely giving her a sad smile before turning and walking back down the hallway from which he had just come.

"Gunther!" she had called after him, but he had not looked back. Tears filled her eyes, and she felt on the verge of sobbing, the realization that he might truly be serious about their separation finally overpowering her, despite the thin armor she had been frantically trying to construct all week against this exact eventuality. Trembling, she knew she couldn't possibly face her morning English class and had instead turned and practically run back to Philomena Hall, knowing that Melody would have already left for her own set of classes by now.

Elsie was indeed relieved to find the room dark and immediately threw herself on her bed, finally allowing herself to succumb to the tears that had been threatening all week. At first she cried for the loss of Gunther, of course, but eventually all of her old sadnesses began to bubble to the surface, adding to her despair.

Oh, what was she to do? She couldn't possibly give up Gunther. Not now. But she couldn't reduce her family to poverty, either. She suspected that Ma would claim she didn't care and that she hadn't wanted to accept her father's charity in the first place. But Elsie knew that, having been restored to, if not exactly the luxurious lifestyle of her childhood, at least a very comfortable one, Ma would suffer greatly in returning to their old life of struggle and want. Grandfather had been correct in that. And what about the boys? They had all complained about being sent away, and yet, what would happen if they were all called home and made to get jobs in the streets or a factory? Furthering their schooling would be out of the question, of course, except for Jimmy, who was only seven.

But how could she possibly give up Gunther? She had never met anyone like him, and her heart beat a little faster every time she thought of him. Not just his thick blond hair and blue eyes, but his goodness. The word "purity" kept coming to mind, and yet that didn't seem to fit. It was more than that. She had tried to explain it all once to Henrietta—how she felt differently about Gunther than the other men in her life—but she could tell that Henrietta didn't believe her.

But she *did* love Gunther. She knew it for a certainty.

What she had felt for Stanley and even for Harrison had been just a silly schoolgirl attachment, just as Gunther had once called them. She had been hurt by his initial assessment of her past loves, but when she thought it over later, more carefully, she had had to admit that he was right. They *were* silly and immature, and she bemoaned the fact that she had ever thought of them as something more, especially her dalliance with Harrison Barnes-Smith. How could she have thought herself in love with someone who had taken, forcibly, her virginity? It was something that still caused her to be fearful—almost nauseous—especially in the dead of night, when the memory of what he had done invaded her dreams and tormented her.

Gunther, on the other hand, was the most noble a man she could ever imagine. He was humble and honest. Gentle. Kind. And not only was he a scholar and a teacher, sharing his love of books with her and encouraging her to think for herself, but he had sacrificed all of it, his very life, to help a little girl find her mother in a strange country. And when they had finally discovered the mother, poor Liesel Klinkhammer, to be dead, he was determined to care for the girl himself rather than have her committed to an insane asylum or an epileptic colony. No, Gunther was a man she loved with her entire being, her very soul, and even despite her young years, she knew that she would never meet another man like this.

The problem, she thought as she rolled onto her side, the tiny bed creaking under her, was that the very things she loved him for, his lofty ideals and beliefs, were the things that were holding them apart. He was so stubbornly committed to his ideals that he refused to bend, even if it meant that those around him would suffer. It was utterly maddening. Why couldn't he see sense!

She fingered a stray thread on the quilt she lay upon, her eyes examining it closely. If he refused to marry her, then, she decided with a deep exhale of breath, she saw no choice but to revert to her earlier plan to enter the convent. If she couldn't have him, she wanted no one. She lay there, turning it over in her mind, relaxing into the comfort the thought of it momentarily provided. Not only would it solve her problems, she convinced herself, but it would ultimately thwart her grandfather, though she knew this was not a good reason to proceed down this path. Plus, she knew that Sr. Bernard might not really believe that she had a vocation. Elsie had already spoken to her once before about becoming a nun, and she had advised Elsie to proceed with caution, to give it time. Well, hadn't she already given it time?

Elsie pulled on the thread, but it would not come loose. She knew that Sr. Bernard had meant to wait at least a year, not months, and wondered how she could get around this. Before she got any further in this line of thought, however, her musings were unexpectedly cut short when Melody, of all people, burst into the room and scooped up her mathematics book from where it sat forgotten upon her desk.

"Oh!" she exclaimed upon seeing Elise curled up in a ball on her bed. "What are you doing here? Are you ill?" Melody tiptoed closer.

"No, I'm not ill, Mel. You go on. I just need a bit of a rest," Elsie mumbled, trying to hide her face in her damp pillow, which was certainly disagreeable, but better than having to discuss her woes with the likes of Melody Merriweather.

Melody Merriweather was the most popular girl on campus, but even with her wealth of friends, she included Elsie in her inner sanctum, declaring not five minutes upon meeting the new girl that they were sure to be the "very best" of friends. Elsie was not convinced that that would actually be the case, but she enjoyed Melody's generosity, at least in the beginning when everything was strange and new. Melody seemed to know everyone, and Elsie could see why. She was light and bubbly and happy all of the time and seemed to fill every room with light whenever she entered. Elsie found herself wishing she could be more like Melody Merriweather, but, alas, she could never seem to shake her heavy worries and her serious, shy demeanor. While Elsie tried her hardest to concentrate on her schoolwork during her first semester at Mundelein, Melody, it seemed, thought of nothing but romance. She constantly begged Elsie to reveal any "secrets of the heart" she might be keeping, and, when Elsie had fibbed, saying she had no secret love, Melody had promptly begun to badger her to go on various dates with boys she rounded up for Elsie to try. Poor Elsie, already the subject of a similar scheme with Aunt Agatha, had finally confessed to Melody that she was in truth affianced to Gunther Stockel, the school's custodian, which had thoroughly shocked and delighted her friend.

"You can't be serious!" Melody had twittered. "But you *are* a dark horse. I always said so! Wait till I tell Cynthia! It's a scream. No wonder you never took to Clarence Frazier. And what's all this talk about you being a nun? Was that simply to throw me off the scent?"

"No!" Elsie had exclaimed. "It was a serious consideration. But it doesn't matter now. I really am in love with Gunther, Melody, but I don't know what to do."

"Oh, yes! It's a scandal to be sure! Your grandfather's sure to be furious. Have you told anyone else yet, or am I the first? Did he get you a ring?"

It had been impossible in that moment of her past confession to get Melody to discuss the more serious implications of accepting Gunther's proposal, as Melody had been more concerned with the more romantic aspects of the happy event—how he had done it, what he had said, when the wedding was to be. In the end, Elsie had simply given up and allowed herself to be questioned by Melody, though she found it hard to answer, as she and Gunther, she had nervously realized at the time, had not discussed the more practical aspects of their union or how it was to come about. In light of last week's developments, however, it sadly no longer mattered.

"Fiddlesticks!" Melody exclaimed now. "You don't need a rest. Why . . . you've been crying! Oh, dearest," she had said, happily tossing her mathematics text onto her bed and hurrying over. "Have you and Gunther been quarreling? No! Don't answer that! I'll be right back." Melody then disappeared out the door and, in a remarkably short amount of time, returned with two cups of cocoa from Philomena's ancient Victorian kitchen below.

"Here, take this," she commanded. "Come on, sit up!"

Elsie looked at her blearily and knew that she could not escape. "You're missing class, Melody. Go on," she attempted, even so. "I'll be all right."

"Class? How could I possibly go to class when there's an affair of the heart to be discussed!" she declared, fishing her handkerchief out of her pocket and handing this to Elsie as well. Elsie sighed and pushed herself up on one arm, trying to simultaneously scoot herself back upon the pillows, a feat that was difficult to do in a lady-like manner.

"Don't mind the stitches," Melody said with a nod at the handkerchief, which Elsie was now wiping her tear-stained face with. "My kid sister, Bunny, gave it to me for my last birthday. It's horribly uneven."

Elsie peered at the faint pink roses and felt guilty for dirtying it. *Must she always feel guilty about everything?* She let out a little moan.

"It's Gunther, isn't it?" Melody asked, her eyes bright with curiosity as she planted herself on her own bed, kicking off her red Oxfords and letting them clunk to the floor.

Red Oxfords? Who bought such a thing? Elsie couldn't help but contemplate, despite the situation.

"Come on! Don't keep me in suspense!" Melody cried, drawing her knees up now and wrapping her arms around them.

Elsie took a small sip of the cocoa, which subsequently burnt her tongue, and related as best she could what had happened between Gunther and her grandfather, which had not only resulted in Gunther withdrawing his proposal but in him refusing now to speak to her at all.

"Oh, Melody, what am I going to do?" Elsie moaned once she had finished.

"Well, that's easy." Melody calmly blew on her own cup of cocoa.

"Easy?" Elsie wiped her eyes again, trying to use just the corner of the handkerchief.

"Well, he obviously didn't mean it."

Elsie's brow furrowed. "Who do you mean by *he*?"

"Both of them, I suppose." She took a sip.

"Yes, they're both horribly stubborn," Elsie groaned, crumpling the handkerchief into a ball in her hand.

"Listen, Els. Your grandfather is calling your bluff."

"Calling my bluff?"

"Haven't you ever played poker?"

"No! Have you?

"Course I have. Me and Freddy and Bunny used to play all the time for peanuts until Mums found us out," she said with a little laugh.

"Oh." Elsie was confused, not for the first time, about Melody's strange, privileged upbringing in Merriweather, Wisconsin, a town which had apparently been named for Melody's grandfather.

"Anyway, that's beside the point. Think about it logically, Els. Your grandfather, after finding his long-lost daughter and setting her and all your siblings up in a mansion in Palmer Square to save the embarrassment of her living in a hovel in the city—no offense, like—is not going to so easily revoke all of that, is he? And what about getting Eugene into Fishburne and—"

"Yes, because he stole from a rectory," Elsie moaned.

"Well, no one knows that, do they? And anyway, it's still a prestigious academy. And the other boys at Phillips . . . would he really call them home?"

Elsie thought this through. Melody did have a point. She knew her grandfather had gone through considerable trouble to get the boys, including the troubled Eugene, enrolled in their East Coast boarding schools; would he really order them home because she refused to marry as he wished?

"And best of all is the fact that Henrietta is now married into the Howards. That's the ultimate feather in his cap. You've practically said so yourself. His greed and his pride have backed him into a corner. He's like one of those attack dogs—more bark than bite. Can you imagine his shame, if nothing else in front of the Howards, if he revoked everything? It doesn't make sense, Elsie. Think about it. He's just trying to scare you."

Elsie took a moment to consider her friend's words and admitted that there was some truth to them. A tiny flicker of hope flamed in her chest, but it was quickly extinguished by thoughts of Gunther himself.

"That may be true, Melody, but what about Gunther?" Elsie said. "I can't force him to marry me . . ."

"Well, Gunther's a harder nut to crack, I admit. Are you absolutely sure you love him?"

"Yes, of course, I do. More than anything," she said morosely.

"I envy you, you know," Melody said abruptly. "True love." She squeezed her knees tighter. "I so desperately want to have it, but I can't seem to find it. Still. I suppose I'm young, as Mums says."

"What about Douglas?" Elsie asked hesitantly, though she was more than happy to turn the conversation away from herself. "I thought you loved *him*."

"Well, of course, I love him in a certain way. But is it *true* love? I'm not so sure . . . Anyway," she broke off, "if you really love Gunther, then you have nothing whatsoever to worry about. As I always say, true love wins in the end."

Elsie didn't say anything in response to her friend's naïve declaration, knowing as she did that that wasn't always the case. She had only to look at her own parents' failed relationship, for a start. She wished she could see life through Melody's rose-colored glasses, but it was too late. She had seen too much already.

"I'm not so sure, Melody. He's very determined. And now he's talking about moving to a farm and—"

She was interrupted by a sharp rap on the door.

"Who is it?" Melody called.

The door opened and a girl, Rosalind Chambers from down the hall, poked her head in. "Sister Joseph says to tell you that there's a telephone call for you," she said to Elsie.

"A telephone call?" Elsie shot a fresh look of worry at Melody. Clearly, God did not want her to lie in bed and cry. This was the second interruption in less than an hour. "Did she say who it is?" Elsie said, standing up now and trying to pat her hair into place. Her first thought was that it might be Ma, but Ma, she knew, would never telephone her, as she had a fear of the "contraption," as she called it, and anyway didn't even know how to operate it.

"I suppose this will be Grandfather," she said morosely to Melody. "Or maybe Aunt Agatha, which might even be worse." She slipped on her shoes.

"Be strong!" Melody advised.

Elsie crept down the stairs and nodded her thanks to Sr. Joseph as she gingerly picked up the heavy black receiver from where it lay next to the telephone at the far end of the counter. She took a deep breath and tried to steady herself.

"Hello?" she said tentatively.

"Miss Von Harmon?"

It was a voice Elsie didn't immediately recognize.

"This is Nurse Flanagan."

Elsie's mind instantly shifted from one of dread to one of sheer panic, guessing that perhaps Anna had had another fit or that something had happened to Ma.

"Yes? Is something wrong?" she asked, her voice suddenly strained and high.

"Well, that depends, I suppose," she said in her thick Irish brogue. "There's a man here. Says his name is Heinrich Meyer. Says he's Anna's father. That right?"

Anna's father? Elsie could barely understand the words. *Anna's father?* Desperately, Elsie tried to remember what Gunther had told her about Anna's father, which, she realized in a panic, was little. Something about him running away to America and Liesel following, abandoning her newly born baby with Gunther and his mother . . .

"Miss Von Harmon?"

Elsie snapped back to attention. "Yes? Yes, I'm here. I'm sorry."

"He says he wants to take her. What should I do?" Her voice was remarkably calm. *How could she be this calm?*

"Don't . . . don't let him take her! I'll be there as soon as I can."

"Well, I'll try, like, but I don't know whether I can stop him . . ."

"What about Karl? Ask him to help you."

"Begging your pardon, miss, but you and me both know that Karl is hardly up to fisticuffs, if it comes to that, that is."

"Yes, I suppose you're right. I . . . just try your best. If . . . if nothing else," she faltered, "telephone the police."

"The police?"

"Yes, just . . . just do it."

"But if this is her Pa? Her real Pa, that is?"

"I have no idea who he is! He . . . he could be anybody," Elsie exclaimed, her voice frantic now. "Just . . . just keep him there."

"I'll try me best, like, Miss Von Harmon, but—oh, dear! I must go!" she said abruptly and hung up, leaving Elsie standing with the receiver in her hand and hearing nothing but dead air.

"Well, what did he say?" Melody flitted down the stairs. "I hope he wasn't too beastly," she added as Elsie heavily replaced the receiver, rattling the muffled bell within.

"Oh, Melody," she said, putting her arms around her friend, "something terrible has happened."

Chapter 9

Clive put his arm through Henrietta's as they walked down the cobbled Rue du Chapon, not far from the Strasbourg Cathedral, and hoped they weren't making a terrible mistake. Though he was playing the whole thing off to Henrietta as being a silly waste of time, he was, in truth, quite concerned about the case and had been from the first moment Hartle had told them about it. The missing agent was the thing that alarmed him most, not the loss of some painting that purportedly revealed an ancient treasure map. That was obviously nonsense. And, having been stolen over two years ago with no leads, Clive considered it to be a cold case. More than likely, it was holed up in some Italian villa or had found its way into the hands of an eccentric American collector in New York or Los Angeles. Whatever the case, he did not see the harm in allowing the Nazis to scurry around the globe searching for it. As he had said to Hartle, it seemed to him to be a good distraction from the actual business of war.

But the missing agent was a different matter, and thus the most concerning part of the case. More than likely, he had been captured or killed, which made this whole thing seriously dangerous. And that was another thing. While it was true that he didn't suspect the Von Harmons to be hiding the missing painting, as he had said to

Henrietta, he felt there was definitely something amiss at Château du Freudeneck, but he couldn't put his finger on what. Valentin's angry demeanor and his admiration of the Nazis did worry him, but it was the baron who struck him as being the most odd. Did he really have strange spells in which he seemed to forget everything? But if they were fabricated, what would be the point? And what about this "countess" business? The whole thing was absurd.

He looked over at Henrietta, dressed in a plain tweed skirt and matching jacket, which is what she always wore when they were on a case, or what she believed was a case, and smiled. She never ceased to amaze him, never ceased to arouse him, a thing she seemed delightfully unaware of, which attracted him even more. His heart positively swelled at the fact that she so willingly gave her love to him, that she had agreed to be his wife. It was the greatest blessing of his life, but it made the fear of losing her never far from his mind.

"This is charming, Clive!" she said, peering around. Strasbourg was indeed a beautiful old medieval town, thankfully untouched by the war, though the fact that it so resembled a German town and that so much of the population spoke German as easily as they did French made Clive jumpy. He kept expecting a German regiment to round various corners, and at times he had to close his eyes and try to breathe deeply. When he had proposed a European tour, he hadn't expected so many memories to flood back.

"Yes, it is," he said grimly and looked over his shoulder. The cathedral towered in the background now.

The baron's chauffeur had dropped them off just in front of it, as that was their excuse for wanting to come into town, but once he had driven off, they had proceeded on their search for the antiquities shop.

Henrietta looked back over her should now, too. "Do you think Edna will be all right?"

At Henrietta's request, Claudette had happily arranged for one of the junior servants, a young man by the name of Pascal, to escort Edna. "This is *très généreux*," Claudette said to Henrietta when she had explained the situation. "The English, nor the French, would be so considerate of a servant," she said approvingly, a small smile about her lips. "It is usually this way in America?" Henrietta wasn't sure how to answer this, knowing that what she was asking was unconventional, even by American standards, but before she could explain, Claudette had rushed on. "But, of course, your poor maid will have an escort. Leave it to me, *chérie*."

Henrietta had been surprised, then, when Claudette had produced not the older, wiser woman Henrietta had been hoping for, but instead a *young man* to accompany Edna, saying that of all the servants, he spoke the best English. Edna, herself, seemed initially mortified at the sight of him, but rather than make any more of a fuss, reluctantly agreed to go, though she had sat tight-lipped and stiff for the entire ride into Strasbourg.

"I expect so," Clive answered. "Did you not hear the stern warning I gave him when we separated?"

"Well, I heard it," Henrietta said, stepping over a puddle. "I couldn't understand it, of course, but from your expression, I guessed your meaning. You were quite severe."

In truth, Clive had not liked the excited gleam in the young man's eye, and had therefore threatened him, in French, warning him that he would break his arm if he was anything less than honorable. This was not something, however, that he thought behooved him to relate to Henrietta.

"I'm sure he'll be a perfect gentleman," he grunted. "It's this way, I think." Clive abruptly turned down a little walkway between two white stone buildings that was barely wide enough for them to walk abreast, so Henrietta followed behind. This little passageway opened up into a bigger square, La Place du Marché Gayot, which was filled with quaint shops and merchants selling their wares from old-fashioned carts. Clive was tempted to buy some flowers for Henrietta, but he wanted to be unencumbered when they arrived at the antiquities shop. Perhaps on their way back. They continued on, passing several cafés with outdoor tables occupied by either groups of people drinking wine and laughing, or solitary men drinking espresso and reading the newspaper. In the middle of the square was a stone statue of a man on horseback that looked to be riding into battle.

Henrietta's pace had slowed as she observed all around her, and once again, Clive bemoaned the fact that they could not just simply be tourists.

"This way, darling," he said, pulling her gently toward the Rue des Frères, a small side street off the square.

"How do you know where you're going? And what's the rush?"

"I have a map. And I just want to get this over with. For one thing, the chauffeur will be back in just a few hours, and I'd like to have time alone with my wife. Perhaps sit at one of those cafés we just passed."

"So you are a romantic!" she called from behind him, as they had turned down yet another street, which had again narrowed. Shops lined both sides, but the street itself was so narrow that only one wagon or motorcar would be able to squeeze down it at a time. Many of the shops were of white plaster with heavy black crossbeams, except one or two at the end, which were of brick.

"I think this is it," he said, standing in front of a tiny shop with a big bay window, in which sat various pieces of antiquated furniture, one miserable-looking painting, several pieces of china prettily arranged on a Napoleonic-era table, an old-fashioned Victorian lady's hat, and many thick books, their spines trimmed in gold leaf.

Clive pushed open the heavy door, and a shop bell tinkled. They stepped across the stone lintel, which had a deep groove in the middle, worn down from hundreds of years of people coming or going. The musty interior was dim and seemingly devoid of any customers, at least as far as they could see, the only creature being a black cat stretched out leisurely across a row of books on a table. He looked up curiously when they entered, the tip of his tail following, before he lazily blinked and then lay his head back down, clearly unimpressed.

"*Bonjour!*" Clive called out loudly, picking up an old bugle from one of the shelves and examining it. He set it back down, waiting for an answer, but none came. He glanced at Henrietta, his eyebrows raised. *"Bonjour?"* he called again, taking a few steps forward.

"Je suis à l'arrière!" called a gravelly voice.

Henrietta looked at Clive expectantly, and he nodded his head toward the back of the shop.

They wound their way through several rows of bookshelves, each of them towering all the way to the ceiling and absolutely stuffed with books, some upright and some stacked on their sides, until they squeezed into a little room at the back. Two whole walls of this little chamber were also lined with bookshelves, but on one wall hung a very old painting, its paint cracked in several spots. In the far corner sat an ancient desk, it, too, nearly covered in books and strange objects from the past, their original use Clive could only guess at.

"Comment puis-je vous aider?" asked an elderly man from where he sat dwarfed behind the desk. He had patches of white wispy hair and wore a flowing white shirt, tied at the top and conscripted at the arms with old-fashioned cloth bands. Indeed, he resembled something out of the Old Curiosity Shop. He peered at them over the tops of his spectacles, examining them carefully as if assessing whether they were carrying anything of value.

"Qu'est-ce que vous voulez?—What do you want?"

"Monsieur Bonnet?"

"Oui?" His voice rattled, as if he had something viscous stuck in his throat.

"Do you speak English?"

"Un peu." His eyes narrowed.

"We're looking for a man by the name of Richard Stafford," Clive said slowly in English, deciding to test him. He was encouraged when he thought he saw a flicker of something in the man's eyes.

"Je ne comprends pas," M. Bonnet wheezed with a shrug.

"Look, we've been sent here by British Intelligence."

M. Bonnet said nothing. He merely blinked and then adjusted his spectacles, pushing them farther up his nose.

Clive sighed. "Your roses are beautiful this time of year," he recited, hating that he had to resort to the code Hartle had given him. There was a reason he hadn't gone into this line of service. He did not enjoy subterfuge.

The shopkeeper did not react except to again narrow his eyes. "Yes, they are an unusual color, are they not?" he asked, now in thickly accented English.

"Except for the thorns," Clive answered back, trying to hide his surprise that the code was actually working.

"Who are you?" M. Bonnet asked in a low, raspy voice, glancing beyond them.

"My name is Clive Howard. This is my wife, Henrietta."

"You are *Américain*?"

"Yes, but we have a connection to Inspector Hartle in London. He sent us."

"I do not know the name of the English source." M. Bonnet stood up now and brushed past them, making his way through the maze to the front of the shop. He turned the key hanging in the lock and pulled down the window shade, causing the room to dim further.

"Do you know anything of Stafford?" Clive asked, following him.

"*Oui*, he came here." M. Bonnet rubbed his hands together, studying the stone floor.

"Do you know where he is now? Where we can find him? British Intelligence has lost contact."

The man shrugged. "*Oui*, that would make sense."

"Why is that?"

"Because he is dead."

Clive looked over at Henrietta, who's cheeks immediately flushed. She raised her eyebrows at him.

"What happened?" Clive asked, turning his attention back to the man.

"Not here," he wheezed softly and gestured for them to follow him back to his inner sanctum. "You know what he was seeking, *oui*?" M. Bonnet asked once they were back in the little room.

"Yes, the Just Judges panel."

The man nodded, looking relieved.

"Did he uncover it?" Henrietta asked eagerly.

M. Bonnet studied both of them for several more moments and then exhaled deeply. "I do not know."

Clive put his hands on his hips and looked away. "What do you mean you don't know?"

"Just that I do not. He came here asking about the panel. I told him all I knew, and he went away. The next day he was found with a knife in his back in the river Ill."

"Was there an investigation?"

"*Bien sûr que non*—Of course, there was not. Asking that means you do not fully realize who you are dealing with."

Clive decided to ignore this. "Why was he sent here?" he asked, his brow furrowed. "Do you know where the panel is?"

"I would not be here if I did." He shuffled behind his desk and sat down heavily.

Clive sighed. "Well, how *do* you fit into all of this? Are you connected in some way with MI5?"

"I did not say I was connected to MI5." He paused to cough. "And it is of no importance to know how I am involved," he said, his voice hoarse now. "Let us just say that I know of a great many things, especially things people want to sell, things that turn up on the black market, valuable things."

"What can you tell us about this piece, Monsieur Bonnet?" Henrietta asked. "We know very little about it. We don't even know what it looks like."

"How can you be looking for something you know nothing about?" he wheezed.

"There wasn't time before we left," Clive answered. "And, anyway, our main inquiry was to the whereabouts of Stafford. Secondary was the finding of this artwork."

"You have your priority mixed up, *mon ami*."

"I beg your pardon. I think a man's life is of more consequence than a bloody painting."

"*Je ne veux pas vous offenser, monsieur* . . . I mean no offense. But many men have already died because of this painting, and many still could."

"Not this again." Clive rolled his eyes.

"Tell us about it, Monsieur Bonnet," Henrietta urged.

The man paused, as if trying to think of a way to describe it.

"We know that it is very large," Henrietta suggested.

"Here. I will show you." He stood up again, one knee cracking in the process, and sidled past them, making his way down one of the aisles to the right. The cat appeared, then, and went right for Henrietta's leg, rubbing himself against her. She bent down to pet his head, and his back arched in response.

"This doesn't sound good," Clive whispered to her.

"No, it doesn't," she whispered back, taking the cat in her arms. Clive could hear his loud purr even from where he stood. M. Bonnet reentered the room, then, carrying a large book, and the cat startled and jumped out of Henrietta's arms.

M. Bonnet inched his way past them and, after shoving several items out of the way, set the volume down heavily on the desk. He cracked open the frayed cover, and some dust motes began their ascent, illuminated by the weak light shining in through a tiny window cut high into one of the stone walls. M. Bonnet began to carefully turn the gold-trimmed pages, which were so thin they were almost translucent, like tracing paper. "It is here somewhere," he said impatiently turning the brittle pages. "Ah. Here." He pointed to a beautifully colored illustration and turned the book sideways for them to see it better. "The Ghent Altarpiece," he proclaimed, brushing the back of his hand across it.

Both Henrietta and Clive stepped forward to examine it more closely. The illustration was made up of twelve panels, just as Hartle had described, most of them being filled with various figures and angels.

"Do you know anything about art?" M. Bonnet asked, looking from one to the other.

"Well, *I* don't," Henrietta answered, still staring at the book. "But this is quite magnificent."

"It is considered to be one of the world's masterpieces," M. Bonnet explained. "There are over one hundred figures in the whole piece. This is Christ the King, or some say it's God the Father," he said, pointing to the enthroned image at the top of the panel. "This is Mary and John the Baptist. Adam and Eve," he continued quickly, pointing to each. "This main panel, *ici*," he said, touching the image in the center of the piece, "is called 'The Adoration of the Mystic Lamb.'" It depicted a grassy field in which a lamb stood on an altar, surrounded by various figures and angels. From its side spewed a stream of blood, which collected in a chalice. "That is, of course, Christ, the sacrificial lamb, bleeding into the Holy Grail."

"Which part is the missing part?" Henrietta asked.

"*Ici*," M. Bonnet said, pointing to the panel in the lower left corner. "This is the panel of the Just Judges."

Clive peered at it closer. It depicted ten men, most on horseback, with what looked like three castles in the distance. *JUSTI JUDICES— Righteous Judges* was written across the bottom frame. Across the bottom frame of the panel next to it was written, *CHRISTI MILITES— Warriors of Christ*. "It doesn't look all that significant," he said.

"*Non*, it does not."

"Who are they supposed to be?" Henrietta asked.

"No one in the art world is sure. Some think they are . . . how do you say . . . aldermen of Ghent, painted by Jan van Eyck to appease them. Some say they are wisemen of the Bible. Most historians, however, think that this one is Jan himself, and that this is his brother, Hubert, who also had a hand in creating the whole piece."

"It's really quite extraordinary," Henrietta said, bending to study it more closely.

"*Oui,* and the panels fold in on themselves, depicting an outer set of panels that you see here," he said, turning the page briefly to reveal what the piece looked like when folded. "It is thought that the original frame might have included . . . *mécanismes d'horlogerie* . . .

clockwork mechanisms for moving the shutters and even playing music, but it was damaged by Cromwell during *la Restauration*."

"What can you tell us about this supposed coded map?" Clive asked. "Something about relics of power. We were told that is why the Nazis are particularly intrigued."

"You know of this?" M. Bonnet asked, looking furtively from one to the other.

"A bit. But surely this is nonsense."

"That is a matter of opinion," he said cryptically. "Depends on whom you ask."

"What do you mean?" Henrietta asked.

"There is a theory about it," M. Bonnet said wearily, "but I am an old man, and my legs grow tired of standing. *Venez, c'est une histoire qui demande du vin*—Come, this is a story that requires wine." He padded over to one of the bookcases and reached his arm up as far as his rounded back would allow, his fingers lightly tapping along the uppermost shelf until he retrieved a large skeleton key. He then pulled out two books from a middle shelf to expose a keyhole, into which he inserted the key, and the whole bookshelf swung open. The old man pulled on the door, opening it wider to reveal yet another little room, which, from first glance, appeared to be his living space.

"*Venez*, come, come," he said, holding on to the whitewashed stone wall as he stepped down into the little room. Clive followed, half expecting by the lock and the secrecy for the room to be filled with the shop's most precious treasures, but instead it appeared to be incredibly spartan. There was only a tiny round table pushed up against one wall with a few mismatched chairs and what appeared to be a bed along the far wall, partially hidden behind a thick gray curtain. There was a small sink and a tiny woodstove in one corner. He gestured for them to sit while he shuffled to a cabinet in the corner and extracted three glasses and a bottle of red wine.

"*Nous voilà*," he said after he had poured it out. "Much more civilized."

Clive took a drink, surreptitiously glancing at his wristwatch as he did so and resisting the urge to tell him to get on with the story.

"You were saying?" Henrietta asked charmingly whilst quickly shooting Clive a disapproving glance. Clive bit back a smile. "About the map?"

M. Bonnet took a long drink and stared at the wall beyond, as if deep in thought or perhaps trying to decide where to begin. "*Oui*, there is a theory that the Ghent Altarpiece contains a coded map. Or at least, this is what Hitler and the top Nazi officials believe."

"A map to what? The location of these relics of power we've heard about?" Henrietta asked, further encouraging him.

"*Oui*, that is it," he said, nodding.

"But what would Hitler do if he did find the Ark of the Covenant and—what was it?" she asked, turning to Clive. "Thor's hammer?"

"*Non*, it is not those that he seeks," M. Bonnet wheezed. "Well, yes, I suppose they are, but it is something even greater than these that he is after. He is searching for the Arma Christi."

"The Arma Christi?"

"The instruments of Christ's passion."

Clive took a deep breath. This was terribly tedious. "Which would be what?" he asked, crossing his legs.

"The Crown of Thorns, the Holy Grail, and the Spear of Destiny, to be exact. You know of these, *oui*?" The old man took a drink of his wine.

"What's the Spear of Destiny?" Henrietta asked, clearly much more intrigued by this story than Clive was. "I've never heard of it." She glanced at Clive, who shrugged.

"It is the tip of the spear that the Roman soldier used to pierce the side of Christ during *la Crucifixion*."

"Ah." Clive said, casually folding his arms.

"It is said by some that the Arma Christi have mystical, supernatural powers. And that whoever possesses them can unleash unlimited power over the world."

"This is absolute nonsense," Clive interrupted, unable to hold back any longer.

M. Bonnet shrugged. "*Peut-être. Peut-être pas.*—Perhaps. Perhaps no." He swirled his glass slowly and sniffed it. "Let me go back farther," he said and took a sip. "Have you ever heard of the Ahnenerbe?"

"The Ahnenerbe? No," Clive answered, glancing at Henrietta, who also shook her head, one eyebrow raised. "What is it?"

"It's not really an *it*, it is a group. A Nazi intelligence propaganda group run by an SS officer by the name of Heinrich Himmler." He turned to look at them as if to see if any of this registered.

"I'm not sure what you mean by SS," Henrietta said.

"Hmmm," M. Bonnet muttered. "How to explain? The SS are the *Schutzstaffel*. An elite group of soldiers that Hitler has created and surrounds himself with. They are like his . . . how do you say? Guard of the body?"

"Bodyguard?"

"*Oui.* That is it. The SS are hand-selected for their . . . well, for their pure 'Germanness.' Tall, blond hair, blue eyes. In order to be chosen for the SS, a man must be a perfect example of the Aryan race."

"Forgive me," Henrietta interrupted. "What do you mean by Aryan?"

M. Bonnet pushed his wispy white hair back with one hand, clearly getting more agitated. "The Aryans are supposedly an ancient Nordic race of peoples," he began. "Hitler believes all true Germans are descendants of these Nordic peoples, whom he claims are biologically superior to all other people and are therefore *une race de maître*—a master race."

"A master race?" Henrietta scoffed.

"And this Ahnenerbe group? How do they fit in?" Clive asked, rubbing his chin, a tad intrigued, finally, despite himself.

"They are a group of scientists and scholars . . . archeologists, but not serious. They are—what is the word? *Amateur?* Not professional."

"Yes, amateur," Henrietta encouraged.

M. Bonnet nodded his thanks. "Their mission, as far as we know, is to provide proof that the Aryans are this master race, that they are indeed the founders of all civilization and culture. Even now, Heir Himmler is sending out expeditions to various points on the globe in search of proof."

"Proof? What kind of proof could they possibly find?" Clive asked.

M. Bonnet shrugged. "You would be surprised. Already eight years ago, an expedition set out for *les Andes* to study ruins that Himmler now claims were designed by the Aryans millions of years ago. Last year, a group traveled to Sweden to study rock art that they are saying reveals the beginning of a Proto-Germanic language. Another group was sent to Finland to seek out a soothsayer by the name of Miron-Aku to record her pagan chants about the creation of the earth and a master race."

"How bizarre," Henrietta mumbled, glancing over at Clive.

He wished he could gauge whether she was falling for all of this or just humoring the old man. "Well, what does any of this matter? So what if he uses this Ahnenerbe group to rewrite German history?"

"You do not see the threat in one man rewriting history to suit his own agenda? One in which he claims there is a master race? Do you not see how dangerous that is?"

Clive took a drink. "Yes, I suppose you have a point."

"Very recently," M. Bonnet continued in a lower voice, his wheeze almost as loud and rhythmic as the cat's purring, "Himmler sent a team to Iceland to try to find the entrance to a magical land called Thule, which is supposed to be the home of telepathic giants and faeries and also the Aryans. Hitler believes that if they can find the lost entrance to Thule, then they can recover the Aryans' supernatural powers of flight, telepathy, and telekinesis, which were lost when they began interbreeding with 'lesser' races."

"My God!" Clive snorted. "And this man is the Chancellor of Germany?"

"*Oui*, and he gains power by the week."

Clive ran a hand through his hair. "Look, what does any of this have to do with the Ghent Altarpiece?"

"Ah, yes." M. Bonnet look a long drink. "Hitler believes that van

Eyck was a direct descendant of the Aryans, and thus that his masterpiece has mystical powers and contains a map to the—"

"Relics of power?"

"*Oui*, the Arma Christi."

"But since those don't really exist," Clive said slowly, as if explaining something to a child, "then why the worry if he finds this missing
panel? I've said this before. Let him waste his time . . ."

"Well, we know not for certain that it is a waste of time."

"Come on, man. Be sensible."

"Do you not see? If Hitler has the complete Ghent Altarpiece in
his possession, he can use it to instill fear and obedience in all those
around him. This is the way of such men, is it not?"

Clive drained his glass. How did he manage to always get caught
up in this sort of thing? His cases in Chicago had all been *real* cases.
Murder, rape, theft, prostitution, bootlegging. Not mystical paintings linked to the occult and a madman.

"It is very important that we find the panel before he does," M.
Bonnet croaked.

"Who's we?"

"*Je ne peux pas vous dire ça.*—I cannot tell you that."

"Of course not," Clive said, disgusted. "Look. Let's get back to
Stafford. When did you last see him?"

"Just last week, as I said."

"Do you know if he went to Château du Freudeneck? Did he
search it?"

"I do not know. It was his plan, of course, but I have no idea if he
succeeded before he was killed." He reached for the bottle of wine
and topped up Clive's glass and was about to fill Henrietta's but she
held up her hand.

"But how can you be so certain that it's hidden in Château du
Freudeneck?" Henrietta asked, as he instead filled his own. "It could
be anywhere in Europe. Or beyond, for that matter."

M. Bonnet inclined his head. "*Oui, vrai.* But there is a source who
has whispered that it is here in Alsace."

"You mean Hitler's sorceress?" Henrietta asked before Clive could head her off. He was hoping to test Bonnet to see if he would reveal this, too.

"You know of her?" M. Bonnet asked incredulously over the top of his spectacles. "Then you are very well informed. *J'ai sous-estimé les Britanniques.*—I underestimated the British," he said, looking at Clive now.

"Well?" Clive asked impatiently. "Is that the source? Or do you have an actual reason to suspect it's hidden somewhere in this vicinity?"

"Perhaps," M. Bonnet answered cagily. "But even without this sorceress, it would make sense. There are many old Germanic and French nobles still in this region. Families that are centuries old that even predate the Hapsburgs and the de Medicis, who can trace their roots to the Cathars."

"The Cathars?"

"The Cathars were a sect of the ancient church," he said with an absent wave of his hand. "They were exterminated for what were called their 'heretical ideologies,' but some believe that not all of them were killed, that they were instead absorbed into the Knights Templar."

Henrietta broke her gaze with the old man and looked over at Clive. "Goodness, we're receiving quite the history lesson today, aren't we? I suppose the next question would be to ask who are the Knights Templar?"

"They were a company of knights who defended the Church during the crusades and were said to possess the Holy Grail themselves. Some believe that it is the example of the Knights Templar that Hitler is using to form his elite SS troops."

"Oh, my. This is very circular, indeed," Henrietta commented.

"Again. Exactly what does this have to do with anything?" Clive asked.

"Why, *n'est-ce pas évident?*—is it not obvious?" M. Bonnet looked from one to the other. "Some believe that it is the Cathars who are hiding the missing panel of the Ghent Altarpiece."

"Ah. I had forgotten where we were going with this. Let me guess. The Von Harmons are an old Cathar family?"

"It would seem," M. Bonnet answered with a tilt of his head. "No one knows for sure, of course."

"I very much doubt it, from what we've seen," Henrietta put in. "They're rather eccentric. Don't you agree, Clive?"

"Entirely," he agreed quickly, but his mind did wander to all of the heraldic banners on display. The Von Harmons did seem very rooted in tradition—at least the baron was, if last night's dinner conversation was anything to go by. "Even if the panel *is* somehow hidden in Château du Freudeneck," Clive mused, "I doubt Baron Von Harmon is even aware of its existence."

"What about his son, Valentin-Marie?" asked M. Bonnet. "We are pretty sure he has ties to the Reich. He does a lot of business with them in Berlin. And sometimes in Munich."

"What type of business?"

"He is an importer and exporter of goods, as far as we can tell. He is very secretive."

"Well, as Henrietta pointed out back in London, if Valentin really is a Nazi sympathizer, why wouldn't he simply hand over the panel? Surely, it would be to his extreme advantage."

"Perhaps he doesn't know it's there?" Henrietta suggested. "If it *is* hidden there, that is. Perhaps someone else hid it."

"Like who? The baron?" Clive scoffed. "You've seen him. Hartle was right. He's a bit touched. I don't think he would be capable. Or capable of keeping a secret, more importantly."

"Perhaps a servant? Or someone posing as a servant?" she suggested, reminding Clive of the Jack Fletcher incident back home.

"Listen," M. Bonnet wheezed, leaning forward slightly. "I have a theory—"

A loud banging was heard, then, coming from the front of the shop.

"What was that?" Henrietta asked, jumping slightly.

The banging repeated.

"Someone's knocking at the door," Clive said, standing up.

M. Bonnet stood as well, his face crumpled with worry. "I am certain that I put the closed sign in the window," he muttered. Placing a hand against the whitewashed stone wall, he gingerly stepped up and out of the little chamber, Clive and Henrietta following.

The banging repeated. "*Bonjour?*" called a man on the other side of the door. "*Es-tu là-dedans?*—Are you in there?"

"*À venir!*—Coming!" wheezed M. Bonnet. "*J'arrive!*" He reached the door and lifted the shade a fraction, before quickly dropping it. "It is Valentin!" M. Bonnet whispered hoarsely over his shoulder and gestured for Clive and Henrietta to step back between a row of books.

There was another sharp rap just as M. Bonnet turned the lock and opened the door of the shop, the bell tinkling wildly.

"*Ah! Alors vous êtes là*—Ah! So you *are* here." Clive heard Valentin's unmistakable voice from where they stood huddled between the stacks.

"*Oui, j'ai eu une petite urgence. Qu'est-ce que vous voulez?*—Yes, I had a small emergency. What is it that you want?" M. Bonnet asked, his voice, Clive observed, betraying his nerves.

Clive heard Valentin step into the shop. "*Excusez-moi, monsieur,*" he said, "*Je cherche deux touristes américains. Un Monsieur et Madame Howard. On m'a dit qu'ils étaient là. Est-ce que je les ai manqués?*—I'm looking for two American tourists. A Mr. and Mrs. Howard. I was told they were here. Have I missed them?"

"*Oui, monsieur,*" M. Bonnet said cautiously.

Clive bit the inside of his cheek. It was useless to continue hiding. Valentin obviously knew they were here. But how? Had the chauffeur secretly followed them? Or maybe someone was watching this place... his throat tightened. "Ready?" he mouthed to Henrietta, who gave him an understanding nod.

Clive accordingly marched out from between the stacks, trying to appear as nonchalant as he possibly could. "Ah! Valentin! I thought I heard you. How odd!"

"Yes, I was just saying that," M. Bonnet wheezed and picked up the cat that was hovering about his feet.

"Hello, Valentin," Henrietta said sweetly as she stepped around Clive and sauntered toward the man. Clive watched as Henrietta batted her eyes at Valentin and was, not for the first time, amazed at how deftly she could turn on the charm. "How extraordinary that we should bump into you. I thought you had engagements all day."

"I finished early," he said gruffly, looking around the room as if assessing it. When his eyes re-alighted on Clive, he gave him a stiff nod.

"Well, how fortunate for us," Henrietta continued. "You might show us the cathedral now. If you have time, that is."

Valentin looked flustered, but only for a moment. "Certainly," he said slowly. "That is why I came back into town."

"Ah. Well, lucky that you found us in such a big city."

"Yes, is it not? I happened to bump into Pascal, and your maid said you might be here. I could hardly believe such a story, since you declared that your express reason to come into town was to view the cathedral. And yet, here you are," he said, gesturing around the dusty shop.

"Yes, we decided to take advantage of the fine weather and poke about the shops," Clive said, wondering if Valentin had *really* bumped into Pascal, or if he had perhaps arranged to meet him ahead of time.

"But how odd to find the shop locked and closed in the middle of the day," he said, turning his gaze on M. Bonnet now.

M. Bonnet gave a false little laugh. "Yes, well, as they are American, I wanted them all to myself, you see. No interruptions," he wheezed and dropped the cat to the ground.

"Well, in that case, I apologize." Valentin gave a slight tilt of his head.

"No, no, monsieur," M. Bonnet said hurriedly. "I believe Mr. and Mrs. Howard were just leaving, *oui*?" he asked Clive.

"Yes," Clive said gruffly. "Are you quite ready, my dear?"

"Quite." Henrietta flashed a smile at Valentin.

"But wait a moment," M. Bonnet interrupted. "Do not forget your purchase. I will just get it."

Confused, Clive was about to respond, when Henrietta jumped in. "Yes, thank you, monsieur," she called. "That would be lovely."

Without responding further, M. Bonnet shuffled as fast as his stiff legs would take him toward the back room. Henrietta then turned to Valentin, who was assessing them carefully.

"Thank you for taking the time to come find us, Valentin," she said amiably. "It's really very kind of you."

"But, of course," he said stiffly.

M. Bonnet appeared, then, carrying the book with the illustration of the Ghent Altarpiece. "Here it is," he wheezed, holding it up slightly. He was so winded, he could barely speak. Valentin arched his neck slightly to try to see the cover as M. Bonnet squeezed behind a counter and began wrapping it brown paper.

"You read French?" he asked Henrietta.

"No, but I like the pictures," she said, a grin about her lips. "It's a book of art."

"Ah. I didn't realize you were an admirer."

"Yes, I am, actually."

"You should have said. I could show you our collection. It is rather extensive."

"That would be lovely," Henrietta said so convincingly that for a moment Clive was jealous. She was utterly amazing. But, then again, hadn't she fooled even him, all that time ago at the Promenade when he had come in and bought a ticket to dance with her? She had seemed so much more experienced than she turned out to be . . .

"Thank you, monsieur," she said smoothly to M. Bonnet as he handed her the wrapped book. "I shall enjoy this very much. Shall we?" she said to Valentin and looped her free arm around his. "Coming, darling?" she said over her shoulder to Clive and allowed Valentin to lead her from the shop.

Chapter 10

"Ma? Nurse Flanagan?" Elsie didn't even bother knocking on the door of the Palmer Square house and instead barged in, Gunther following closely behind. After receiving Nurse Flanagan's alarming call, Elsie was desperate to find Gunther and had therefore gone directly to Sr. Bernard to discover his whereabouts. Sr. Bernard had suggested she look in the gardens behind Piper Hall, where she thought he might be fixing a fence, which turned out to be blessedly true. After quickly relating to him Nurse Flanagan's alarming message, they had hailed a taxi, neither of them having any qualms this time about using the plentiful stash of money in Elsie's handbag.

"They are in the drawing room, miss," said the ancient Karl, hobbling forward from whatever corner he kept himself in.

Elsie rushed down the hallway, praying they weren't too late, and let out a deep breath of relief when she saw Anna, her fingers in her mouth as was her habit, wedged protectively between Ma and Nurse Flanagan on the sofa. Elsie's relief was short-lived, however, upon noticing not only a man, whom she guessed to be the one claiming to be Anna's father, but a woman as well, sitting on one of the armchairs and looking highly pleased with herself. The man stood behind her, his hat in his hands as he shifted from foot to foot, his trousers wrinkled and stained.

"Papa!" Anna wailed, running to Gunther wrapping her arms about his legs. Elsie could see that her own little legs were trembling.

Gunther picked her up and kissed her softly on the side of the head. "Hello, *Kleiner* . . ."

"Papa? You ain't her Pa!" the strange woman snipped.

"I'm Elsie Von Harmon," Elsie said tightly, trying desperately to imagine what Aunt Agatha would advise a lady to do in this situation. "This is my—" Elsie hesitated to announce him as her affianced— "friend, Gunther Stockel. And you are?"

Elsie had addressed the question to both of them, but it was the woman who spoke. "I've already told these." She nodded at Ma and Nurse Flanagan. "I'm Rita Meyer, and this here's my husband, Heinrich. *He's* Anna's Pa. We come to collect her."

"Collect her?" Elsie could only stare, trying to think of something to say to this. It seemed unthinkable that the two people before her were a married couple, much less that they wanted to take on the responsibility of caring for a child. The woman was excessively plump, a thick roll of fat hanging over her tightly tied collar, while the man, Heinrich, was as scrawny and tremulous as a willow branch. They seemed grossly mismatched.

"Yes, collect her. You hard a hearing?"

The man moved slightly from behind the chair. "Please," he gave the woman a worried glance, "let me say. My name is Heinrich Meyer. I am from Heidelberg, like you," he said, nodding toward Gunther. "*Ich erkenne dich. Sie und Ihre Mutter führten die Pension, in der Liesel wohnte.*"

Elsie looked expectantly at Gunther.

"He says that he recognizes me from my mother's boarding house. I don't remember you," Gunther said to the man. "I am sorry."

Heinrich rubbed his hand roughly through his hair. "*Nein, das würde ich nicht glauben. Liesel und ich haben eine sehr kurze—*"

"Speak English!" Ma barked.

Heinrich looked at her as if he forgot she was in the room and began again. "I am sorry," he said with a slight nod of his head. "I forget . . ." He looked nervously at Rita and then turned his attention back to Gunther. "Liesel and I had very short . . . how do you say it? Romance?"

"What he means is that they did the business," Rita said sharply, followed by a high-pitched little laugh.

Heinrich's cheeks flushed. "I . . . I did not know Liesel was with child when I left for America," he said to the floor. "She did not tell me." He looked back up at them now. "She finds me here." He paused as if trying to think of the words. "*Ich arbeitete in einer Fabrik auf Damen, und sie war Putzfrau in einer Schule in einer Stadt, die sehr weit von der Stadt entfernt war. Irgendwie fand sie mich aber und erzählte mir von unserem Kind noch in Deutschland.* I am sorry. I do not know words."

"He says that Liesel found him working in factory on Damen and told him about Anna, still back in Germany," Gunther translated.

"Why didn't you take Liesel in, if you were in love?" Elsie asked.

"I did not say I was in love with her," Heinrich said uneasily. "And, besides, I . . . I was already married here to Rita."

Rita shot her a smug look.

"I was . . . how you say? . . . *Besorgt*?"

"Worried?" Gunther translated.

"Yeah, that's right," Rita put in. The buttons on her dress were pulled so tight across her large bosom that Elsie could see her dirty brassiere through the gaps. "He was real worried about Anna. A real loving father, he is."

"I go to this . . . this school to look for Liesel, but she is not there. She was in hospital, her friend tell me. I go to find, but she not there either. She was in . . . ?" he looked at Rita for help.

"In the looney bin, she was. Stark raving mad."

"She wasn't mad!" Elsie blurted out, surprising herself. "That was a mistake."

Rita ignored her. "Poor Heinrich even went to see her in the looney bin. Didn't get much outta her except her beggin' him to get her out, but not much he could do. He went back one other time, but she was already dead. Think how surprised he was when they tell him that his and Leisel's little girl had turned up there as well. But she got lucky, they told him. That she was rescued by a bunch of swells and was bein' takin' care of by them. Well, didn't take too long to figure it all out, and here we are. Ready to take her off yer hands."

"You can't just come in and take her! She doesn't even know you!" Elsie declared.

"Well, she'll learn. There's a whole pack of little ones back in the apartment for her to play with. It ain't nothin' like this, but I reckon she'll get used to livin' a little more rough. She'll have to share a bed with Caroline and Fanny, but it'll do. You'd like someone to play with, wouldn't ya, girlie?" Mrs. Meyer cackled at Anna, whose response was to turn her head and wrap her arms tighter around Gunther's neck.

"You have other children?" Elsie asked, incredulously.

"Seven. Three is ours, and the other four are mine from my first marriage. Mr. Gilroy died, God rest his soul."

Elsie could hardly believe what she was hearing. "Why on earth would you want to take in another, then? Can't you see she's well provided for here?"

"Well, I do see that, missy, but Heinrich here won't hear of it. He's been pining all this time for his missing child. Just like the missing sheep in the Bible. Ain't that right? That shepherd had ninety-nine good sheep in the pen, safe and sound—didn't stop him none from going and findin' the lost one. Ain't that right? I been to Sunday school, and I knows my Bible."

"Is this true?" Gunther finally spoke, addressing Heinrich directly. "You so badly want this child back?"

"Course he does. He's near dying of a broken heart," Rita answered for him.

Gunther's face remained calm, but Elsie caught the look of fear in his eyes.

"But she is ill . . . she has fits," Elsie pleaded.

"I reckon that's 'cause she's had too much rich food. Good hard work will cure that." Rita stood up. "Come on, Anna," she said sharply. "Tell yer maid, or whatever she's called, to go git yer things. It's time for us to let these people get back to what they were doing, which looks to be about nothing, but there you have it." She walked around Gunther so that she could see Anna's face. She leaned close to her and poked her on the arm. "Go on!" she said thumbing the stairs. "Get goin'!"

"Now you listen, here," Ma said, suddenly coming to life from where she had been sitting, silent, listening. She slowly got to her feet. "You're not walking out of here with that girl any more than you're walking out with me."

"I beg yer pardon?"

"You have no proof that he's the father. You can't just come in here and take this child."

"We've got the law on our side."

"The law?" Ma scoffed. "Well, then I suggest you bring the law. Karl!" she shouted. "Show them out!"

"Not so fast," Rita said smoothly as she held up her hands. "We're not unreasonable. We can see that Anna's settled here and that you all are attached. And we do have hearts, don't we, Heinie?" She shot a quick glance at Heinrich, who looked utterly wretched, nervously twisting his cap in his hands. "We might be persuaded to let little Anna here stay," Rita continued, "but we think we should get something for our pain and trouble. Our suffering, as it were. And how we might suffer in the future without our little girl—"

"That's ridiculous!" Ma blurted. "You're nothing more than fortune hunters!"

"You wish to be paid?" Gunther asked quietly, looking straight at Heinrich. "You would stoop to selling a child?"

Heinrich looked at the ground.

"Now, now. Ain't no one sellin' a child. We're just sayin' that we should get something for our time and trouble," Rita inserted, roughly crossing her arms in front of her. "It ain't as if you can't afford it," she said, looking around the room.

"Time and trouble?" Elsie mumbled. "Time and trouble?" she repeated, louder now. "Do you have any idea what Gunther has been through with this child? Him and his mother caring for her when Liesel just ran off? The threat of her being sterilized if the Nazis found out about her epilepsy, the long journey here to find Liesel—his mother dying on the way, giving up his career as a professor and taking a job as a janitor, hunting day and night for Liesel?" she asked furiously, her speech growing louder and louder as she went along. "And then having to put Anna in an orphanage that sent her to *an insane asylum* for having one too many fits? And *you* demand payment for time and trouble?" She was shouting now. "How dare you—"

"Elsie," Gunther said gently, laying a hand on her arm. "It is okay. Do not fret. It will be okay."

Elsie looked into his calm blue eyes and managed to rein in the rest of the torrent that was building within her. Her chest heaving, she put her hands over her eyes, trying desperately not to break down into tears.

"How much do you want?" Ma asked stiffly.

Rita eyed her carefully. "Well, we hadn't thought, had we, Heinie? Seein' as we were expectin' to leave with little Anna today. But since yer askin' . . ." She looked up at the ceiling, one eye squinted shut, as if trying to add up how much their "suffering" had been worth. "How about something along the lines of three thousand?" she suggested, focusing her eyes back on Ma.

"Three thousand dollars!" Elsie exclaimed. "We don't have three thousand dollars!"

"Well, from what we've been able to discover, you have a grandfather that does, don't you? Maybe he could help out," Rita suggested, a sly grin on her face.

"Get out!" Ma shouted and gestured to Karl, who had answered her previous summons and was hovering nearby.

"We were just leavin' anyway, weren't we, Heinie? Seems you have a lot to think over, and we got to get back to the kids. Fanny has lice, you see, and we need to give her a wash. You decide."

"There isn't a decision. You can't extort from us."

"Well, we'll be back, then, with a lawyer. We have an appointment with a bona fide lawyer on Monday, don't we Heinie? You haven't heard the last from us. Bye, girlie," Rita said, giving Anna's hair a little tug as she walked by. "Be seein' you real soon."

Anna began to cry, then, and continued long after Rita and Heinrich were shown out, reflecting how Elsie herself felt. She wished she could simply burst into tears, too. Anna kept crying and periodically saying "no!" such that she was in danger of working herself up into either a tantrum or a potential fit, and Gunther was obliged to take her out of the room, Nurse Flanagan hurriedly following.

"Oh, Ma!" Elsie said, alone with her mother now. "What are we going to do?"

Ma remained silent and sank into her armchair. "I don't know," she said heavily. "I reckon I'm going to have to talk to your grandfather."

"Oh, no, Ma. Not that!" Elsie said, knowing that a plea to help the little girl would fall on deaf ears, just as Gunther's proposal had, and might, in fact, make things worse. Already things were spinning out of control. It was becoming more and more clear, however, that she needed to distance herself from Gunther, not only as a way to save her family, but Anna, too. As long as she was connected to him, this Rita and Heinrich would seek the Exley money. It required a very great sacrifice on her part, she knew that. And yet, she just couldn't see herself marrying some North Shore dandy of her grandfather's choosing. She rubbed her temples. There was only one other way, and she resolved to seek out Sr. Bernard the very next day.

Chapter 11

"Oh, no, Edna!" Henrietta called from bathtub. "Not my dressing gown. Bring out something else. The Lanvin, maybe."

"Are you sure, madame?" Edna asking, peeking around the door. "I thought you weren't getting up today."

"Yes. I've changed my mind." She gave the rose-scented bathwater a final little splash and stood up. She was eager to get on with her assigned task of the day, which was to search the château as best she could for the panel while Clive was out riding with Valentin. It was a plan they had concocted late last night in bed. Claudette had suggested at dinner that they go and tour the Videk Gardens and Waterfall, or *cascade*, as she had put it, but Valentin had strongly urged them to go riding instead, that he had rearranged his diary specifically to accommodate them. Both Clive and Henrietta thought Valentin's new interest in being the perfect host to be a bit strange, considering how aloof and almost rude he had been upon first meeting them. Something had changed, and Henrietta could not help but wonder if it had something to do with finding them in the antiquities shop. Did he somehow suspect that they were here under false pretenses?

Valentin had led them from the shop and given them a rather exhausting tour of the cathedral, condescendingly lecturing them and revealing endless minutia about every little statue and stained-glass window, essentially holding them captive for hours. It was almost as if he were trying to either bore them to death or keep them from returning to the château. Henrietta suggested as much to Clive, wondering if Valentin did indeed have a reason to keep them in town, but Clive had discounted it, of course, still refusing to admit that Valentin was the obvious villain. She had never been so relieved as when the chauffeur was finally called, poor Edna and Pascal already perched in the front seat, waiting for Valentin's tour to be over.

Regardless of whether or not Valentin had an ulterior motive in keeping them from the château, Clive and Henrietta had no time at all to search for the panel upon their return, having to almost immediately dress for dinner, which was much the same as the previous night, only instead of beef daube, they were served filet of cod and pickled beef tongue. The baron, Henrietta noted, had not much to say, but Valentin entertained them with long monologues about art until Claudette had interrupted and managed to change the subject, asking Henrietta about the gardens at Highbury. Following this discussion came her suggestion about the Videk Gardens, an idea which was dashed by Valentin's insistence that they go riding.

"Don't you think that's suspicious, Clive?" Henrietta asked as they lay in bed later that night, her head on his chest.

"I'm not sure, darling. It's hard to know what is in that man's mind."

"Well, we don't have much time here before we're scheduled to leave. Why don't you go riding, and I'll stay back. I'll say I have a headache."

She could tell by the way his chest muscles tensed that he did not like this proposal.

"Clive, don't be tiresome. I know what you're thinking, and it won't be dangerous in the least. What could happen? Valentin will be out with you. It's the perfect plan."

Clive, however, did not immediately answer and instead ran his finger along her arm as she lay cradled against him. "It's not a bad plan, I suppose," he said with a sigh. "But, darling, be careful. Stick to the main rooms. No going in the attic or the cellar or any other strange place. Wait for me for all of that. I won't have you trudging through those alone."

"But, Clive, the panel is surely not hanging in one of the rooms in plain sight," she argued, raising herself up on her elbow.

"Well, who knows? Maybe they're all innocent and don't really know what is in their possession."

"Valentin, the art expert?"

"Henrietta, please. You can poke your head into closets and wardrobes and the like, but be careful. I'm begging you."

"Is that a command, Inspector?" she said, running her hand across his chest.

"Yes," he said huskily as he rolled toward her and kissed her. "And I expect to be obeyed."

"But what about your headache, miss?" Edna asked, the pale-green Lanvin day dress in her arms.

"The bath must have cured it," Henrietta answered lightly and felt a tinge of guilt at having earlier lied to her about feeling ill. "Yes, that will do," Henrietta said, nodding at the dress. "Help me, would you, Edna? I'm in a bit of a hurry, as it turns out."

Henrietta allowed herself to be helped out of the bath and wrapped in a towel by Edna, though she still found it ridiculous in the extreme. She had originally balked when Antonia had insisted on assigning Edna to be her personal maid upon her marriage to Clive, saying that she was not in need of any maid's help, having basically been one herself for most of her life. But Antonia would not hear her protests, and Henrietta had eventually given in, especially when she realized that Edna's life would be considerably easier as a lady's maid, arranging her jewelry and laying out gowns rather than scrubbing floors and making beds. Still uneasy, however, Henrietta at one point had attempted to make Edna into a sort of personal secretary, much to Clive's bemusement, rather than allow the girl to toil as something so horribly outdated as a lady's maid, but Edna had proven to have atrocious handwriting and was likewise very shy at answering a telephone. This, plus the fact that, as of yet, no secretarial work had actually arisen, meant they had gone on as they had started. Edna, for her part, seeming quite content to go on brushing her mistress's hair and bringing her cups of tea, and enjoyed, Henrietta could tell, her new exalted position among her fellow servants, at least back at Highbury, at any rate.

"Did you enjoy your day out?" Henrietta asked as she sat down now at her little vanity.

"Oh, yes, miss! Thank you ever so much!" She picked up a hairbrush and began brushing Henrietta's long amber locks.

"I hope Pascal did not take advantage," she said, studying Edna's face in the mirror.

"No, of course not, miss," Edna said, her eyes remaining on her mistress's tresses, but Henrietta thought she detected a slight pinkishness about the girl's cheeks. "He was the perfect gentleman, he was. Showed me all sorts."

"Did he now? Well, how is it that he can speak English?" Henrietta asked, reaching for a small jar of cream.

"I asked him that, too, miss. Seems one of the grooms that used to work here was English, so he taught him some."

"A groom? Is Pascal a *stable* boy?" Even as she said it, she could hear the disapproval in her voice and reflected that if Clive were here, he would not pass up the opportunity to call her a snob.

"He was, miss, but he got moved up to boot boy."

"Ah." She fought back a smile.

"He's terribly keen on America, miss. Asked me ever so many questions. He's seen more films than even I have. Isn't that something?" She began to twist Henrietta's hair up now into a pretty sort of bun.

Henrietta merely raised her eyebrows in the mirror, and Edna smiled. "There you are, miss. Perfect as ever. Will you be needing me today? Just that I have some postcards to write to everyone back home. Bought them in town, like."

"No, thank you, Edna," Henrietta said, turning around to look at her. "I'll be fine. Has Mr. Howard left?"

"Hours ago, I believe, miss."

Henrietta bit her lip. It must be later than she thought, and she would have to hurry.

Henrietta made her way carefully down the main staircase, thrilled that Clive had entrusted her with an actual task, and crept into the main hall. She half expected to find the baron or Claudette, but neither were there. She had a quick look around, but there were no paintings in this room, nor were there any cabinets or closets or antechambers into which she might peek. She tiptoed into the dining room, then, which was empty, too, and had a thought to look behind the giant tapestries. She pulled at their corners, but they were surprisingly very heavy, and she could see nothing.

Henrietta continued through several more rooms, the purposes of which she could only guess at, before she reached a rather large drawing room, long and formal, which looked to be rarely used. On one wall were floor-to-ceiling doors that opened out unto a private terrace, which led down, Henrietta could see, to the gardens below. On the far wall was a fireplace with built-in cases on either side of it. They began midway up the wall and were rounded at the top, and they held, on thick glass shelves, a perfectly magnificent collection of jade and ivory carvings.

Henrietta crept closer and observed that there were tiny figures, animals, and even an immense jade pagoda, which took up one whole shelf entirely. It was exquisitely carved down to the last detail, including tiny links of a chain fence that ran around the perimeter. Henrietta was utterly mesmerized by it, and stood staring for several minutes before finally pulling herself away, noting with a quick final glance of the room that there were few paintings on the walls, nor anything which might be hiding a large panel.

She passed into the next room, which appeared to be a cross between a study and a library, as two of the walls were covered with bookshelves, upon which sat rows and rows of very proper book sets, all with gold lettering and edges, none of them looking as though they had ever been opened. It was a very manly sort of room with dark wallpaper, upon which hung more stuffed animal heads. There was even a complete stuffed fox, posed in a running stance, sitting on a little table in the corner. Henrietta steered clear of it and instead observed the paintings on the remaining walls, which were mostly portraits, done in what she thought would be called a Jacobean style. Not for the first time, especially on this particular trip, she lamented the fact that she did not know more about art and promised to take more seriously Clive's attempts to instruct her, using the rather significant collection at Highbury, as soon as they got back. After all, as the mistress of Highbury someday, wouldn't she be expected to know such things? A few stray old demons about her inadequacy to fill Antonia's shoes began to rise up, then, but she quickly pushed them away. She would worry about that later.

She spotted a tall cabinet in the corner—maybe a gun cabinet, she suspected—and crossed the room. She didn't think it looked quite big enough to house the panel, but she decided to look anyway, it being the first possible hiding place she had yet found. She pulled on one of the two knobs and opened the door, relieved when it didn't make a noise. Eagerly, she peered inside but was disappointed that it was filled with shelves, most of them littered with various papers and journals—

"Countess?" sounded a gravelly voice behind her.

Henrietta jumped and turned to see the baron, of all people, standing in the doorway. He was staring at her, a confused expression on his face, which rapidly evolved into one of excitement, as if he had suddenly come upon an unexpected treasure, which was ironically what she herself was searching for.

"*Comtesse, ça fait si longtemps*—Countess, it has been so long . . ."

Henrietta sighed. This was not expected. "Baron," she said pertly. "I'm not the countess. I'm Henrietta Howard, remember?"

"*Pourquoi jouez-vous à ces jeux?*"

"Baron, please speak in English."

The baron again looked perplexed and twirled the end of his mustache. "But why, *chérie*? Why do you play these games with me?"

Henrietta sighed again. "Forgive me, I must return to my room." She attempted to brush past him, but the baron stopped her by laying a hand on her arm.

"Do not run away, little bird. You seem frightened of me. You never used to be. What has changed?" he asked, his voice oddly raspy now.

"Baron," Henrietta said, pulling away from his grasp. "I'm not who you think I am."

"Yes, yes, I know. And I know all about the spy."

Goosebumps suddenly appeared across the back of her neck. *Spy?*

"What do you mean?" she asked in a low voice.

"About Yves, slinking about here and there. You remember, don't you? But that shouldn't change how we feel about each other. It did not in the past." He took her hand and brought it to his lips. She was tempted to pull it away, but upon consideration, allowed him to continue holding it.

"I thought you were lost to me," the baron continued, speaking faster now. "I have been in torment ever since. Why did you wait so long to return? Was it because of Yves? Was he a brute?" He kissed the inside of her wrist now.

"Baron, we must be sensible," she said sternly, but not without a hint of tease in her voice as she pulled her arm from him.

"Why do you call me 'Baron'? Call me Gustave, as you used to do when we wandered the meadows undetected." He grasped her hand again. "I will kill him, you know. Just as I did Richard. Why won't you let me, *chérie*?" he begged, again bringing her hand to his lips.

At the mention of Richard, Henrietta felt her skin prickle, remembering the name of the murdered British agent, Richard Stafford. "Who do you mean by Richard?" she tried to ask calmly, as he began planting little kisses up her arm.

"The informant, *chérie*. The one who ruined everything for us with his spying eye," he whispered.

Henrietta's heart beat a little faster. "You didn't really kill him, did you?" she asked tentatively.

"*Chérie*, why do you tease me? You know the answer to this."

Henrietta's mind was racing, trying to decide what to say next. It seemed unlikely that the baron was speaking sensibly, but how could she not at least investigate further? But what could she say?

"*Chérie*," he repeated, more urgently now, as he wrapped his arms awkwardly around her.

"Baron, please!" she said, wriggling from him. "I really must go!"

"Go?" The baron looked confused and then a big smile broke out across his face. "Ah! *Oui!* I remember. Our game." He looked around the room. "But why begin it here, *chérie*? This room is so dismal. Usually we began somewhere sunny," he said, twirling his mustache again and looking at her hungrily. Henrietta could see that his desire was rising, but she wasn't sure how to get past him. She wondered if she should simply call for help; surely one of the servants would hear her . . .

"As a matter of fact," she said, suddenly thinking of a different plan. "I was admiring the paintings," she said briskly, walking over to one of the portraits, hoping he would follow.

"The paintings?" the baron scoffed. "You were never interested before, *chérie*."

"Yes, I know," she said coyly. "But I'm looking for a particular one, you see. Perhaps you could help me," she said laying her hand on his arm. A part of her did feel guilty that she was toying with someone who was clearly ill. But, if nothing else, she needed to get him further away from the door.

"But of course, *chérie*. Which one? I know them all."

Henrietta was about to mention the portrait of the Countess de Koenig, as she could think of nothing else, when another idea occurred to her. Perhaps she should directly ask the baron about the panel, seeing as he was, in the moment, suffering from one of his spells and probably wouldn't remember any of this later, anyway. It seemed too good an opportunity to pass up. "I . . . I'm interested in something very old," she began tentatively. "It is a panel of a bigger piece. It is called 'The Just Judges.' Do you know it?" She watched his face eagerly and observed that his right eye twitched slightly.

"Yes, in fact. I do know where that is," he whispered. "It is hidden away in a special place."

"You do?" Her heart began to race. "Can you take me to it?" she asked eagerly, wrapping her arm around his in a quaint, intimate sort of way. "I'd dearly love to see it," she said, smiling at him so that her dimples showed. "I'd be ever so grateful."

The baron let out a loud grunt and patted her hand, resting on his arm. He was all smiles. "But of course, *chérie*. This way." He let out a little chuckle. "I will show you, if that is what you wish."

Henrietta allowed herself to be led out of the room and all the way up the stairs to what was apparently the baron's private chambers. He was slightly winded and coughed several times as he led her into his inner sitting room. "Here we are, *chérie*. Just as before," he gestured widely.

Henrietta looked around eagerly for any sign of the panel but did not see it. In fact, there seemed to be no paintings hanging anywhere that she could see.

"The painting, Gustave," she urged, remembering to call him by his Christian name.

"You are so eager, my love. Allow me one moment to catch my breath. I am an old man, but not unskilled, as you know, in the art of lovemaking." He sat down heavily in one of his leather armchairs and closed his eyes.

Henrietta watched him for several moments, her impatience growing, until she finally worried that perhaps he had fallen asleep. "Baron?" she called, worried that if he fell asleep, his current spell might be broken upon his waking and her chance at finding the panel would be over. "Baron?" she called again.

The baron's eyes fluttered open, and he let out a little chuckle at the sight of her. "You are so eager, *chérie*. Come, come; I will show you now. I can see you cannot wait."

Henrietta breathed a sigh of relief that he was still in his disordered state of mind. He pushed himself up out of the deep chair and took her arm, leading her across the room and through another doorway into what appeared to be his bedchamber. Again, Henrietta looked eagerly around the room but saw no sign of the panel. The baron released her and moved toward a hulking armoire. "It is here, just as it has always been."

Henrietta quickly tried to size up the armoire, wondering if it was tall enough to house the panel. It very well could be, she decided excitedly, a thrill running through her. With a tug, the baron opened the doors, Henrietta peering over his shoulder as he did so. Upon first glance, she saw nothing. Inside hung his various jackets and waistcoats, shoes lined up on a little shelf that ran across the bottom. *Oh, why had she thought this would lead to anything?*

"Here we are, my naughty little bird," the baron said now, giving her a glance before he pushed the jackets to one side to reveal what looked to be short black velveteen curtains hanging in the back, like those hanging across the Punch and Judy booths she and Clive had passed in London. With both hands, the baron tugged the curtains, thrusting them open with a flourish to reveal a painting! But it was *not* the Just Judges panel, Henrietta immediately observed, but a painting of a naked couple in the act of sexual union with all of their parts exposed and engorged. It was grotesque!

"Oh, my!" Henrietta exclaimed, taking a step back and averting her eyes.

"*Oui, chérie,*" the baron said, unbuttoning his cravat now. "Remember how instructional it was when I first took you? You were so innocent then. Barely a woman. I am touched that you want to return to it. Come, come. Undress, dearest, so that I might ravage you, as I used to." He removed his jacket.

Henrietta stared at him, incredulous. "Baron, no! This isn't what I meant!"

"*Oui, chérie!* I love it when you pretend to be so shy and innocent. It inflames me! *Je veux te faire l'amour passionnément!*"

"There's been a mistake!" Henrietta said, irritated, and tried to move past him. How did she always get herself into these situations?

"The only mistake has been the time that has elapsed since our last encounter, *chérie*," he said, grasping her upper arms with both hands and leaning in to kiss her.

His grip on her was surprisingly strong, but Henrietta instinctively knew she was stronger. She had no wish to hurt him, however, and tried to merely pull back. Still, he managed to hold onto her. He was rather unsteady, however, and Henrietta wondered if she somehow unbalanced him, he would simply fall over. His lips missed the mark, grazing her cheek instead, and in that moment, she resorted to stomping on his foot.

"*Chérie!*" he howled, lifting his foot in dismay.

Henrietta pushed past him and walked quickly through to the sitting room.

"*Chérie!*" the baron called, following closely.

"Baron! I must ask you to stop!" she shouted, her chest heaving with emotion. She wasn't frightened in the slightest, just angry at herself for being so stupid. She looked behind her to gauge his progress after her. He was not even remotely close. She turned around again to escape the rooms and was surprised to run straight into Claudette. She nearly fell but managed to right herself before she did so.

"Oh, Claudette!" she cried, flustered.

"What's happened?" Claudette asked, concerned, but when she saw the baron appear now, in a state of undress, she let out a deep moan. "Oh, Father! What have you done? Mrs. Howard, I can only guess," she said, turning to her as she wrung her hands. "I am so sorry!" Claudette's face was a scarlet red as she took hold of her father and led him back to his rooms. "Aldric!" she called, and the baron's valet came running. The door wasn't closed, however, and Henrietta, from where she still stood in the hallway, could hear Claudette speaking rapidly in French to the valet. Within moments, Claudette appeared again in the stone hallway, closing the door to her father's rooms behind her. "Come, Mrs. Howard," she said, taking her by the arm. "I cannot apologize enough. I am terribly sorry."

"Please. Call me Henrietta. And don't trouble yourself over it. It doesn't signify in the least," she said, still breathing a little heavily. In truth, however, she *was* a bit distraught.

"My father insulting you in so violent a way? I beg to differ."

"If anything, it was my fault. Clearly he's ill. I should never have allowed him to lead me up here."

Claudette considered. "Yes, why did you follow him? What did he promise you? He had quite a reputation as a rogue in his day, I am sorry to say. It drove my mother to distraction. Until she found her own . . . interests . . . shall we say."

Henrietta paused, wondering if she should confide in Claudette. She probably shouldn't, and yet perhaps it was a good idea. Maybe Claudette could shed some light on this whole affair.

"I was looking for a painting," Henrietta began uneasily.

"A painting?" Claudette paused in her descent of the main stone staircase.

"I was . . . I was looking for something in particular," Henrietta chanced.

Claudette's brow furrowed. "Well, if that is the case, you should have taken Valentin up on his offer last night to show you the collection. Father does not remember it all anymore."

"Yes, I'm sure you're right. I didn't think."

"You were not to know." Claudette leaned against the iron railing and put her hands over her face. "What a terrible day this has been."

"I'm sorry to be the cause of such distress, Claudette," Henrietta said, her heart suddenly softening further to the woman.

"No, it is not you. Sometimes, though . . ." She glanced back toward her father's rooms.

"Perhaps we should have a drink, shall we?" Henrietta asked. "Before the men return?"

Claudette stared at her with weary eyes for a moment and then broke into a smile. "*Oui.* An idea perfect. Come."

Claudette led her to a small sitting room that was much more feminine than any other Henrietta had yet seen in the château, with walls papered in a deep rose and cherrywood furniture. On a sideboard was an enormous bouquet of flowers. It reminded Henrietta a little of the morning room back at Highbury, except that the morning room at Highbury was light and bright, while this room, though attractive, was darker.

Claudette gestured for Henrietta to have seat on the red velvet settee before the fire while she poured from a large crystal decanter. For a moment, the gold cross around her neck glimmered from an errant ray of sun that shone in through the leaded windows.

"What a charming room," Henrietta commented as she looked around.

"Yes, it is my refuge," Claudette said, handing her a large cognac glass. "No one ever comes here but me. I hope you do not mind cognac. I despise sherry."

Henrietta *was* a little surprised by Claudette's choice, but she didn't say so. "Of course not. Thank you," she said, taking a little sip.

Claudette did not say anything in return but sat in a matching velvet wingback chair and looked at the fire.

"It must be difficult for you. Here alone without any other women to talk to, that is," Henrietta commented, not knowing what else to say.

"It is, *oui.*"

"Did you . . . did you never think to marry?" Henrietta asked tentatively, broaching a subject she had wondered about since they arrived. Claudette, while not exactly beautiful, was certainly attractive. She had a kind of confident elegance to her.

Claudette gave a sad little laugh, her face partially illuminated by a small fringed lamp on the side table next to her chair. "But of course. I have had . . . what would you say . . . affairs of the heart, but not marriage. I was engaged as a very young woman, barely eighteen, but he was killed in the war."

"I'm sorry."

Claudette waved absently. "It was a very long time ago. I am not sad anymore. As I have said, there have been others since." Claudette reached for a silver box on the side table. "Cigarette?" she asked, opening it and offering it to Henrietta.

"No, thank you," Henrietta answered and instead took another sip of her cognac.

Claudette took one and lit it. "I have a lover, of course, but he is in Paris. Also, he is married. So, a further complication."

Henrietta was a little shocked at her cavalier confession, but then quickly realized it was not a confession. Claudette, she observed, did not appear even remotely remorseful, as if this was the normal course of things.

"Do you . . . do you love him?"

Claudette laughed. "You Americans are so naïve. Olivier is good for me right now. Sometimes I need to get away, you know?" she said, blowing out a large cloud of smoke.

"Yes, I can imagine."

"Father is getting worse these days, and Valentin is never here. So." She shrugged.

"Have you thought about hiring a nurse?" Henrietta suggested, taking another drink. It was going down surprisingly well.

Claudette laughed. "*Oui*, but of course. No one will stay for long, though. Eventually Father attempts to seduce them, and then that is the end of it."

"Maybe someone . . . older?"

Claudette laughed again. "I have tried that as well. It does not seem to matter to him. But if they are *too* old, well, they can hardly do the job, can they?"

"Yes, I see what you mean. How unfortunate." She wondered how Valentin fit into the equation—

"And what about you, *chérie*?" she said, inhaling deeply. "Are you happy in love with your inspector? He's quite dashing, I must say, for an American."

"Yes, very much," Henrietta said and was surprised by the slight heat on her cheeks. She didn't know what to say next.

"I am afraid we are a rather dull stop on your honeymoon trip. I suppose there is a certain sentimentality to your wanting to unearth family, as it were, but as you have discovered, there is nothing much left."

"What about Valentin?"

"What about him?"

"Well, does he not want to marry and carry on the name? The line, as it were?"

"Ah," she said, exhaling a large cloud of smoke. "Valentin is a hard one to figure out. He tells me very little. I suspect he has a wife in Berlin, though his real passion is politics."

"A wife?" Henrietta exclaimed, though an errant guilty thought of Clive's cousin, Wallace, popped into her mind.

"Yes, he is *très* secretive."

"But why not bring her here?"

"I do not know. Perhaps he thinks father will disapprove."

"Forgive me, but Valentin hardly seems the type to care."

"He is terrified of being left out of father's will. That is probably the only reason he still comes back periodically. To stay in his good graces. Marrying a German, after all we went through in the war, would be unforgivable in Father's mind."

"But hasn't Alsace sometimes been a German territory? I wouldn't think the baron would care."

"*Oui, c'est ça.* It makes little sense."

Henrietta thought for a moment, wondering if she should broach the far-fetched subject Monsieur Bonnet had brought up. "This is an odd question, Claudette," she said hesitantly, impulsively deciding that she would. "Forgive me. But I was wondering if the Von Harmons are . . . well, if they're descendants of the Cathars?"

"The Cathars?" Claudette said, her eyes flickering now with sudden interest as she drained her cognac. "Wherever did you hear that?"

"In . . . in that old antiquities shop in town. Remember? We mentioned it at dinner. The one where Valentin found us yesterday? We were . . . we were browsing you see, and the topic somehow came up. The owner, Monsieur Bonnet, was giving us a fascinating lesson."

"Really?" she asked, taking another drag of her cigarette. "In regard to what?"

Henrietta's heart was in her throat. Instinctively, she felt she was deliciously close to finding out additional information, but she dared not reveal their mission. And yet, she felt certain that Claudette knew more than she had thus far revealed. It was just a matter of asking in the right way, Henrietta concluded, though she guessed that Clive would not agree. Well, Clive was not here, and she was.

"Actually," she began, "it's odd that you would ask, because we . . . Monsieur Bonnet, that is," she fumbled, "happened to be telling us about an extraordinary work of art—the Ghent Altarpiece. Have you . . . have you heard of it?" she tried to ask in as innocent a way as she could.

Claudette did not answer but instead blew out a cloud of smoke through her nostrils.

"There's a panel missing, you see," Henrietta hurried on. "It's . . . well, it's fascinating. Monsieur Bonnet was explaining how it might be in the hands of an old family with ties to the Cathars, so I was just wondering . . . I just thought I would ask. Out of curiosity," she added, and then took a long drink, trying to will the burn that followed to burn away her now-heightened anxiety. She suddenly felt she had made a terrible mistake.

Claudette surprised her, however, by letting out a loud laugh, as she shifted in her chair. "That? Oh, *chérie*, you will not find that here, though every fortune hunter in Europe is looking for it. Oh, but I see! You and the inspector are looking for it, too, are you not? It all makes sense now. You are not interested in us!" She laughed again.

"No! Claudette, you've got it all wrong, we—"

"And you suspect it is hidden here? You are not the first, you know. Perhaps we should be charging a fee of admission?"

"Honestly, Claudette—"

"Poor, poor Henrietta and her inspector. Disappointed on two fronts. No infamous painting, and no grand family. My, but you *were* keen," she said, snuffing out her cigarette. "Even enduring father's advances." Her eyes were bright with merriment.

Henrietta, accepting defeat, let out a little sigh. "I'm sorry, Claudette. We should have been more direct."

"I do not blame you," she said with a small smile. "But it is for the best, I think, that you have not found it. Trouble seems to follow this thing."

"What do you mean?"

"Just that a young man, English, I believe, turned up not but a few weeks ago, asking much the same questions. And since, I have heard, he is dead."

"Oh." Henrietta's heart began to pick up speed again at the mention of Richard Stafford. She was about to corroborate what she knew, but then suddenly realized that if she did, it would further implicate them in their deception. "That's awful," she said simply instead.

"Yes, a terrible shame. And I would not want something so tragic to happen to you, *chérie. Non*, it is best that this thing, whatever it is, remains lost."

Chapter 12

"What's a terrible shame?" Julia asked, entering her father's former study. It was now Clive's, of course, but he rarely occupied it.

Antonia stood behind the desk, rubbing her forehead with one hand while she let the telephone receiver bang into place with the other. "The Armours have canceled. Along with the Wrigleys and the Rosenwalds. Oh, Julia, this is turning into a bit of a disaster."

"No, it's not, Mother." Julia walked closer. "There are still over a hundred people coming. No one will even notice if the Armours aren't here. Believe me."

"Oh, yes they will. Believe *me*! And on top of it, Albert has quit! Today, of all days! Billings assures me they will manage, but I don't see how." She let out a groan. "These are the times I miss your father the most," she muttered, looking forlornly around the study.

Julia put her arm about her mother, but was careful not to crush her lemon organdy gown. "It will be all right, Mother. Don't worry. You go dress, and I'll speak to Billings again."

Antonia looked at her gratefully and then gently patted her cheek. "Are you sure, dearest?"

"Yes. Go on. I'll see to it."

"But when is Randolph arriving?"

"A little later. And here's a bit of good news: he's had a change of heart. He's allowing the boys to come after all."

"Oh, splendid!" Antonia's face lit up with momentary delight before it changed to one of worry. "But I don't have anything for them . . ."

"Mother! Go on. They don't need anything. They will be happy just to see you. And anyway, there'll be plenty at the party."

Antonia gave her a weary smile and then withdrew, leaving Julia to hope that the boys would behave, lest Randolph punish them severely. Their nanny would, of course, be in attendance, but Miss Brookes was getting up in years and was having trouble, Julia had noticed recently, in keeping up with the two boys. She made a mental note to try to help the older woman keep an eye on them today, but it would be hard, seeing as most of her attention would be required in the role of co-hostess.

Several guests had already arrived when Julia eventually made her way to the grounds behind Highbury, which magnificently butted up to Lake Michigan itself. The quartet was already playing in the gazebo, and only a mild breeze batted the linen tablecloths under the white tents. True to his word, Billings had somehow managed to produce another junior footman from a neighboring estate, and the staff had begun to competently weave amongst the guests, offering champagne and hors d'oeuvres, while Billings stood off to the side, overseeing the production.

Julia took a glass of champagne and surveyed the crowd from her vantage point near one of the trellises bursting with white Lamarque roses and filling the air with a heady perfume. Despite her insistence to Antonia that the party would be a success, she couldn't help but feel, as she stood in the beautiful grounds, the sunlight casting a thousand diamonds on the lake beyond, that in fact it wasn't the same without her father here.

She missed Alcott terribly, more than she thought she would, but there was no one in whom she could confide. A few times, she had mentioned her grief to Clive, but he had not said much except to pat her arm. More than likely, he had shared his sadness with Henrietta, Julia guessed, and she envied them, not for the first time, for their closeness. As soon as these disparaging thoughts filled her mind, however, she tried to push them away, scolding herself in the process. She was, in truth, happy—*more* than happy, thrilled—that Clive had finally found happiness after brooding for so many years over Catherine's death. He, of anyone, poor thing, deserved the love he had found.

Julia took a sip of her champagne and again surveyed the crowd. She recognized Victoria Braithewaite and the rest of her mother's bridge club standing near the fountain and decided they would be her first conquests. Before she could move in their direction, however, she was accosted by her boys, who had suddenly run up to her.

"There you are, Mama," Howard said breathlessly, a big smile on his face.

"Hello, my loves!" she said, her heart melting a little at the sight of them. She had not seen them yet this morning, having left the house early to help Antonia, more in the arena of moral support than anything else, as the servants were the ones doing all of the actual work. She gave Howard's head a little pat. "Don't you both look smart," she said, observing with approval that Miss Brookes had dressed them in short-panted sailor suits of white linen, with short white socks and white Mary Jane shoes.

"Thank you, Mama," Randolph, Jr. said politely. He was only ten, but he already acted like a little man, careful and exact in his words, always worried he would make a mistake. With his dark hair and dark eyes, he was a miniature of Randolph, though he was, of course, much more innocent and tender-hearted.

"Mama, can we go see the ponies?" Howard asked, scratching his freckled nose, which she was tempted to correct him for, not to mention his use of the word "can," but she did not, knowing how much they were already corrected constantly. She rubbed his curls again. He looked so much like Clive had as a boy—chestnut curls and chubby cheeks.

"Where is Miss Brookes?" she asked, looking anxiously around the crowd.

"She's over there," Randolph, Jr. said, pointing to one of the tents where an elderly woman sat fanning herself, a glass of lemonade at her elbow.

"Well, you'll have to ask her."

"She'll say no!" Howard complained.

"Why don't you go say hello to Grandmother. She's anxious to see you both."

"Father said we weren't to bother her today," Randolph, Jr. said.

Julia sighed. Of course, he would have said that. "Well, why don't—"

"Hello," said a deep voice beside her. She turned and was surprised to see Glenn Forbes, of all people. She had forgotten that Mother had invited both him and Sidney Bennett during dinner the other evening. At the time, they had thanked Antonia for the invitation but had not committed, and Julia had not thought about it again. Yet here was Glenn Forbes standing casually in front of her, dressed appropriately in a white Palm Beach suit with a bright-green bow tie that matched his eyes perfectly. He was, she had to admit, a very handsome man.

Glenn pushed his panama hat back to the crown of his head and looked at the boys. "And who might you two be?"

"I'm Randolph Cunningham, and this is my brother, Howard, sir," Randolph, Jr. said stiffly, standing slightly at attention as he said it.

"Well, pleased to meet you. I've heard a lot about you two," he said, throwing Julia a quick smile. "Did I hear someone mention ponies?"

"I did!" Howard said. "We want to go see them. But Mama said we have to ask Miss Brookes."

"Did she, now? And who is Miss Brookes?"

"She's our nanny, but she's very old. And very crabby. She's over there," Howard said, pointing.

"Howard!" Julia scolded.

Mr. Forbes's gaze alighted on the tents and then came quickly back, a small smile still hovering about his lips. "Well, it would be ungentlemanly of us to ask poor Miss Brookes to move from her chair, wouldn't it? So why don't I accompany you?"

"Oh, no, Mr. Forbes! Please. That's not necessary. Boys, go and play," Julia commanded.

"Now, not so fast," Mr. Forbes said, his hands on his hips now. "I've a mind to see these ponies myself, being a ranch man."

"Mr. Forbes, that's very kind of you, but completely unnecessary—"

"Do you really have a ranch?" Howard asked, one eye squinted shut against the sun, his head tilted, just as Clive used to do.

"I sure do, my good man. Now, you look like you know what's what," he said to Randolph, Jr., "so you lead the way."

Randolph, Jr. hesitated and looked to Julia for confirmation, which she gave in the form of a slight nod. Randolph, Jr.'s face lit up with a rare smile, and he turned to hurry off with Howard, both of them walking fast in the direction of the stables and trying not to run, lest they be scolded.

Glenn lingered for a moment, looking at Julia with a rueful smile.

"Thank you, Mr. Forbes," she felt inclined to say. "You're most kind."

"Won't you call me Glenn?"

"That's hardly appropriate."

"It's 1936, Mrs. Cunningham . . . Julia . . ." he said slowly, as if testing the waters. "Isn't it time to give up some of these niceties?"

"Shouldn't you go after the boys?" she countered smoothly, though she felt suddenly at sea.

"In a minute," he said with a grin. "I reckon they're old enough to find their own way to the stables and look at some ponies on their own. Hell, I was up on a full-grown horse on a cattle drive at their age."

"Really, Mr. Forbes!"

"You still not going to call me Glenn?"

"All right, then," she acquiesced and felt her face maddeningly flush. "Glenn."

"That's better," he said with a wink. *Another wink!* "I'll be back soon."

Julia watched him go and considered what an enigma he was. Tall and broad-shouldered, she could almost imagine him on horseback, riding across his ranch, and yet he seemed equally polished and well-mannered here at a garden party on the North Shore. There was something different about him, though . . . something that almost reminded her of Henrietta, actually. A spark of something that had yet to be crushed by the grind of the society in which they lived, and Julia found herself naturally drawn to it, even on that first night she had met him and had shown him the gallery at Highbury.

He had been most intrigued by her father's collection and seemed to know much more about the paintings that hung there than she did, which was saying much. Her father had indeed had two passions in life: automobiles and art, and he had been an avid collector of both. He had even gone so far as to have some of pieces from Castle Linley shipped over, which his brother, Montague, had approved of, seeing as he was—early on, anyway—of the opinion that poor Alcott had gotten the short end of the stick, as it were, having to go and live in Chicago, which both of them, at the time, essentially viewed as little more than a frontier town. These old masterpieces had given the collection a decidedly European feel, though in later years, Alcott's taste had shifted more toward American painters, and he had avidly bought pieces by Parrish, Homer, and Bogert.

"Does your ranch have a name, Mr. Forbes?" Julia had asked, as they lingered in front of a particularly dark landscape by Bristol.

"Course it does. Nothing so grand as 'Highbury,'" he said with a smile. "It's called The Liberty."

"The Liberty? How unusual."

"It is, really. My grandfather was schooled out east. Philadelphia, I believe. Hence the name, if you get my meaning. Made his way west and started a ranch. Now we have one thousand acres and six hundred head of cattle."

"Goodness, what a classic American success story," she said, unable to keep the sarcasm from her voice.

"It is, isn't it?" he said, without even a trace of self-consciousness.

They had moved on, then, to the next painting, which was a Constable.

"This is a mighty fine private collection. Nearly as good as ours."

Julia laughed. "Nearly?"

He shot her a sly grin. "Your father's collection is very European, a lot of the old masters. A lot of Renaissance. Ours is more American. Ah. Here it is," he said excitedly, stopping in front of what looked like a South American vista entitled *El Rio de Luz*. "This is Church's last landscape. We have several others by him."

"Yes, I've always liked this one," Julia said, studying it again. She had often paused in front of it as a child, drawn by the hypnotic pull of the moon on the water and the lush greenery framing it.

"Did you know that he was a friend of Mark Twain?"

"No, I didn't. I didn't realize you were such an expert, Mr. Forbes."

"I'm not really. It's my father that is the expert. I'm just here as his emissary."

"Ah. I see," she said, moving to the next painting, but Glenn remained stationary in front of *El Rio*.

"How much?" he asked, still staring at it.

"How much?"

"Yes, how much would you sell it for?" He looked over at her then.

Julia was taken aback. "I'm quite sure it's not for sale, Mr. Forbes," she said with an incredulous little laugh.

"Everything's for sale, Mrs. Cunningham." He looked at the painting again and then back at her. "How does five thousand sound?"

"Five thousand?" She blinked. "It's a very generous offer, Mr. Forbes," she faltered, "but I'm rather certain that my mother won't part with it, if only for sentimentality's sake. She's become extremely rigid in refusing to change even the slightest thing since my father's death. Clive had to practically beg to even have the servants' quarters painted and patched. Selling a painting would surely be out of the question."

"I see," he said, scratching his chin and thinking.

"I'll ask her," Julia offered, hating the look of disappointment on his face, as if the sun had suddenly dipped behind an errant cloud in an otherwise bright blue sky. "But I can't offer you any hope."

Glenn's face relaxed into a smile. "Any assistance you might offer me would be greatly appreciated, ma'am. You'll find that I usually get my way," he said, disturbingly reminding her for a moment of Randolph.

They had continued down the gallery, then, Glenn making comments about various pieces as they passed until a thought occurred to Julia. "How did you know we had this painting?" she asked.

"That's a mighty good question, Mrs. Cunningham. You'd make one fine detective."

Julia laughed. "I'll leave that to my brother."

"The truth is that my father is an expert on Frederic Church. He's made a study of all of Church's works and where they are all located around the world. He's writing a book, actually."

"How intriguing! How many of his paintings do you own, did you say?"

"I didn't," he said with a grin. "But of the oils, we have eighteen. And we have some sketches, too."

"I didn't realize he was so prolific. I'd love to see them."

"Perhaps someday you will."

Julia had smiled to herself, then, thinking how impossible a notion that was, as she led Mr. Forbes through the rest of the gallery. Randolph would never take a trip to any city west of the Mississippi, excepting perhaps Los Angeles, as he, like most of their set, considered only the East Coast worthy of their attention.

"Julia! Can I have some little bit of your attention, please!"

Julia shook her head from her reverie and found Agatha Exley, one of Antonia's bosom friends, standing in front of her, waving a pink gloved hand. "You're a million miles away today."

"I'm sorry, Agatha. I was thinking of something else. Are you . . . are you enjoying yourself?" she asked with forced enthusiasm.

"Oh, indeed! Yes, indeed," she said, looking around at the crowd, her buck teeth sticking out slightly. "However, I cannot seem to locate your mother. It's very peculiar, is it not?"

"She's around here somewhere," Julia answered, not wanting to tell Agatha Exley that the last time she had seen her mother, she had been very engaged in a rather close conversation with Sidney Bennett. "But how are you? I haven't seen you at the club in ages!"

Agatha looked unsettled, almost guilty. "Oh, I know! Everything's been topsy-turvy these past months," she whined. "I hardly know if I'm coming or going!"

"The last I heard, you and John were traveling to Miami for several weeks," Julia commented smoothly, finding her feet again. "And taking your protégé, too. Is that not right?"

"Oh, dear no!" Agatha said, throwing her hands up slightly in disgust. "That was all thwarted. Elsie refused to go in the end! Something about studying for final exams. As if that mattered in the least. In my day, that was unheard of." She sniffed. "You must admit it, don't you, Julia? A woman attending college? Whatever for? When I agreed to take Elsie under my wing, I assumed it would be easy. But I've had nothing but trouble with that girl. I know you and Antonia are fond of Henrietta, and well you should be, but her sister is quite impossible. Honestly."

Julia was about to try to defend poor Elsie, whom she had a real soft spot for, but before she could, Agatha went on—

"Of course, I got the blame. Father Exley is furious with me, as if everything that happens with Elsie is my fault! I've a mind to go and visit Ernest and Marie in Boston. They've just had a new baby, and it's time I visited my own grandchildren. I've said as much to John."

"Yes, perhaps that would be for the best," Julia tried to say encouragingly.

"I feel certain Elsie is hiding something from me," Agatha continued on with an unmatched pace now that her train of woe had been fired up. "Which I feel is cruel in the extreme after all I've done for her. God forbid it is a love affair. I still don't understand why she refused Lloyd Aston. After all the trouble I went through for that match—"

"I think I see Mother," Julia interrupted and made a point of looking beyond Agatha.

"Oh?" Agatha muttered, turning to see.

"There she is—in the rose garden. Do you see her?"

"Oh, my, yes. Thank you, my dear. But why is your father's lawyer talking with her? How very disagreeable for her! Who invited him? The nerve!" she said, beginning to walk away. "Thank you, my dear," she called over her shoulder. "I won't be a moment. I must rescue your mother, if no one else will!"

Julia watched her go and began looking for someone else to engage, as, after all, that was her particular role here today, to glide from group to group making pleasant conversation. It was what Randolph expected of her as well—to be a beautiful, charming accessory to his home, capable of throwing exquisite parties and inviting all the right sort. She let out a little sigh as she surveyed the crowd and was surprised to see Glenn Forbes heading right toward her.

"Where are the boys?" she asked, concerned.

"Miss Brookes is perhaps not so sleepy as she appears," he said with a grin. "She headed us off at the pass and gave us all a good scolding." He raised his eyebrows in such a comical way she almost laughed. "So here I am." He had somehow procured two glasses of champagne, of which he now handed her one. "I thought you might need another one of these."

Julia was about to protest, saying that she already had one, and was surprised to see that the glass she had been holding was already empty. She would have to slow down, she warned herself as she took the proffered glass with a smile.

Gallantly, he took her empty and smoothly slipped it into his jacket pocket, as if it were the most natural thing in the world. Julia could not help but to laugh.

"Are you in the habit of stuffing empty champagne glasses in your pockets, Mr. Forbes?"

"Not usually, no, but I'm most resourceful. There aren't too many problems I can't solve."

"You have a very high opinion of yourself," she said over the rim of her glass.

"I suppose I do. Nothing wrong with that, I don't think. Not where I come from anyway."

"No, I imagine not."

Neither of them said anything then, and Julia looked away, though she could tell that his eyes were still on her. If he kept on, she worried that she might begin to perspire, which would be dangerous in a yellow organdy dress.

"Well, thank you for at least trying to entertain the boys," she eventually managed, turning toward him slightly.

"You needn't thank me." He removed his hat and began fanning himself. "I was looking for an escape. This isn't really my cup of tea, pardon the pun."

"Why did you come, then? Merely to appease your uncle?"

"I thought you might have guessed," he said slyly.

She stared at him, unable to look away. *Was he flirting with her?* How dare he! She felt she should scold him, but she found it impossible and instead had to bite back a smile at the sheer absurdity of such a thing. "You must forgive me," she said finally. "I'm quite at a loss as to your meaning, Mr. Forbes."

"Glenn." He took a sip of champagne. "Why, I've come about the painting, of course." A mischievous grin erupted across his face, as he adjusted his hat back on his head. "Have you spoken to your mother about my offer?"

"Oh," Julia muttered, peeved that he was clearly toying with her. "I did, as a matter of fact," she said tartly. "It's as I expected, I'm afraid. She won't hear of selling it."

"Well, that puts us in a bit of a pickle. I'm instructed not to leave Chicago until I have that painting."

"I'm sorry to hear that, Mr. Forbes. I do hope your uncle has sufficient accommodation to house you permanently."

Glenn laughed. "It's Glenn, remember?" He took a large drink of his champagne. "Listen, I'll double my offer."

"Double?" she exclaimed, her eyes wide. It was an extremely generous offer, but one which she was sure would be met with the same outrage as the first had been. Antonia had reacted as if she had been personally affronted. "Buy one of your father's paintings? How dare he suggest such a thing?" Antonia had snapped after Julia had related Glenn's offer.

"Mother," Julia had countered. "It's not unheard of for collectors to buy and sell paintings. Mr. Forbes is simply trying to acquire a piece for his collection. I advise caution before a decision is absolutely made. Perhaps we should wait and consult Clive."

"*You?* Advising caution?" Antonia snipped. "Will wonders ever cease?"

"That is grossly unfair, Mother, and you know it," Julia muttered, surprised by how deeply her mother's acerbic comment hurt her. How long would she have to pay the price for her wild youth, which was not even remotely wild by today's standards? "All I'm saying is that five thousand dollars is a lot of money," she said, determined to ignore her mother's jibe. You should at least consider it."

"Money has nothing to do with it, Julia! Your father's collection is complete, and it shall remain that way."

"Mother," Julia continued calmly, "I know Father's death has been . . . difficult for you; of course, it has. But, in this particular case, I think we should perhaps set aside the past."

"Don't be ridiculous, Julia," Antonia had quipped and called for Billings to bring tea, thereby ending the conversation.

"Yes, double," Glenn said now. "Ten thousand dollars."

Julia bit her lip. She knew the increased amount would probably have no effect whatsoever on her mother's decision, and yet, Julia could hardly reject the offer out of hand. Perhaps she should try to contact Clive herself? "Have you spoken to Mr. Bennett about this?" she thought to ask. After all, he was Clive's business associate and also Glenn's uncle. Shouldn't he be the go-between in this transaction? Whatever did it have to do with her, or Antonia, really, for that matter?

"Spoken to Mr. Bennett about what?" Randolph asked, startling her. He had suddenly appeared at her side and was staring now at Glenn.

Julia felt her insides immediately clench. "Hello, Randolph," she said, turning slightly toward him. "Allow me to introduce you to Mr. Glenn Forbes. Mr. Forbes, my husband, Randolph Cunningham."

Glenn held out his hand. "Pleased to meet you, Mr. Cunningham."

"Mr. Forbes is Mr. Bennett's nephew," Julia explained. "He's up from Texas on some business."

"Ah. And what business would that be?" Randolph said, seeming more intrigued.

"I'm consulting with my uncle regarding some railroad contracts. Union Pacific is wanting to buy some of our land, you see."

"Seems straight forward enough. Hardly worth a trip to Chicago."

"Well, it's a little more complicated than that. But, I must admit, I'm also here with the intent of purchasing one of your late father-in-law's paintings."

Randolph's brow furrowed. "I wasn't aware any were for sale." He looked accusatorily at Julia, as if it were her idea.

"Well, turns out they're not, as your wife informs me. Still, I don't usually take no for an answer," he said with a smile.

"Nor do I."

Glenn shifted slightly, though he seemed utterly unthreatened by Randolph. "I was impressed by Mr. Howard's collection," he said, finishing his champagne. "It's very complete."

"Oh? When did you see it?" He looked again at Julia as if for an explanation.

"Last week, I believe it was," Glenn answered. "Your wife was kind enough to give me a tour, which I very much enjoyed."

"A tour? You didn't mention this." He glared at Julia.

"I hardly thought it worth mentioning, Randolph," she tried to say casually. "It was one night when I stayed to help Mother with the arrangements. I had no idea Mr. Bennett and Mr. Forbes had been invited to dinner."

"I see," he said with what she knew was forced calm. She could almost predict what he would say later—that it was highly inappropriate for her mother, a widow, and so recent a one, at that, to be entertaining two men for dinner, and not even those of her set. And he would somehow blame *her*, she knew, for her mother's behavior.

"Well, if it's a tour of the collection you wanted, you should have picked someone more astute," he said with a quick tilt of his head. "I daresay Julia would be of little help."

Julia felt herself blush, her alarm growing. Usually, Randolph reserved his verbal cruelty for private moments, but he seemed to have no restraint now. He was in one of his moods, she could tell, and if she wasn't careful, she would pay the price later.

"I beg to differ," Glenn said, slowly. "Mrs. Cunningham was most knowledgeable. Likewise, entertaining. The perfect hostess. I couldn't have asked for more." His eyes held hers, and she could read the concern there.

Julia looked away and tried to mentally will him to stop, knowing that whatever he said from this point forward would make it worse.

"Ah, Julia. Always entertaining aren't you?" Randolph said with a sneer.

"I did study art in Switzerland, Randolph," she said defiantly, unable to stand his criticisms any longer, especially in front of Glenn.

"And a great many other things, I was told. Drinking and jazz music being two."

Glenn cleared his throat. "Well, I should be off. Mrs. Cunningham, a pleasure," he said, lifting his hat and studying her with those deep green eyes of his. "I hope we'll meet again."

"I daresay not," she said and forced herself to look away.

"Mr. Cunningham," he said and gave Randolph a curt nod and then retreated.

"What were you doing?" Randolph hissed, once Glenn was out of earshot.

"Making conversation, Randolph. Like I'm supposed to be doing."

"It certainly looked like more than that to me. I saw how you looked at him," he snarled.

"Don't be ridiculous!" Julia hissed back, her cheeks burning with humiliation.

"I won't have it, you know. I've warned you about this before!" Roughly, he grabbed her arm.

"Ow! You're hurting me."

"Be quiet and do as your told. I'll deal with you later," he said, pulling her along now. Julia was used to such treatment, but never in public. She felt tears in the corner of her eyes. She prayed that Glenn was not watching and willed herself not to look back at him. After another pull from Randolph, however, she couldn't help it and chanced a quick glance over her shoulder. She was mortified to see that Glenn was indeed watching, his eyes sad and pitying.

Chapter 13

"It's such a pity," Henrietta said as she plucked a rose from one of the bushes circling the great fountain and put her nose to it. Its perfume was heavy in the humid air, and she gazed coyly over the top of it at Clive, who stood across the fountain from her. The sky behind him was cloudy and dark, making him oddly resemble some sort of Heathcliff character, standing there still in his riding clothes, moody and upset. The threat of rain had cut his ride with Valentin short, and he had only just now found her out back, after inquiring of various servants as to her whereabouts. His initial jovial mood, however, had been dashed after Henrietta related her odd tête-à-tête with the baron.

"What's a pity?" Clive picked up a stone and threw it into the fountain. He was clearly upset.

"About the baron, of course." She put the rose in the buttonhole of her white cardigan, walking toward him as she did so. "Such an elegant man reduced to senility."

Clive grunted. "Is that what you call it?"

"Well, he is, Clive," she said, putting her arms around him now.

"That's funny, I have a very different name for that type of behavior."

"Clive, honestly. We've been through all of this before."

Clive glanced angrily up at the château and then back at her.

"Darling, you have to admit how foolish it was for you to go into his rooms." He pulled out of her embrace and rubbed a hand through his hair, the other on his hip. "What were you thinking? Anything could have happened."

"But it didn't, Clive," she scolded. "And, anyway, I considered the danger before I went in and determined that there wasn't any." She began walking on the little path that led away from the fountain. "Come on, let's walk." She led him away from the fountain into a low maze of boxwoods, perfectly trimmed and symmetrical. It was easy to observe the pattern when viewed from the great hall above, but it was less obvious from within. "I could easily have toppled him at any moment," she said over her shoulder. "He's quite frail, in case you haven't noticed."

"That's hardly the point," Clive responded from behind her. "Thank God Claudette came along when she did before it came to anything."

"Darling, you must stop being so melodramatic." Henrietta turned off the main path and entered a row of tall arborvitae that led to another fountain, albeit smaller. They were out of sight now of any spying eyes from the château, she knew, and accordingly stopped and turned to Clive. "Though I admit it *was* good that Claudette came along so that I could ask her about the panel." She saw his jaw clench. "I know you don't agree, but my talking with her has proven to be very helpful. Now we know that the painting isn't here."

"According to her. Maybe she doesn't know. Or maybe she's lying." He angrily pulled at the nearest bush, ripping off some of the soft, flat needles.

"Lying? Why would she? She practically laughed in my face, as if this was some sort of wild goose chase, as you've been so fond of calling it."

"Suppose she informs Valentin of our search?" he asked, tossing the foliage in his hand to the ground.

"Well, what if she does?"

Clive let out a deep breath. "Darling, there's something about

Valentin. He's up to something; I'm just not sure what. He reminds me of Randolph, to tell you the truth. A stuck-up prig."

"What are you suggesting? That he killed Richard Stafford?"

"I don't think so. But it *is* more than a little suspicious that, according to Claudette, Stafford did turn up here and was shortly after killed—"

"We don't know that for sure," Henrietta interrupted, crossing her arms.

"What do you mean?"

"Just that we don't know that it was really Richard Stafford. All she said is that he was English."

"All right," he said deliberately, though he was clearly suppressing a smile. "You're right. The man we *assume* was Stafford showed up here looking for the panel and was not long after killed."

"Yes, but that doesn't mean it was Valentin. Maybe it was the baron?"

"The baron? You just said that he's completely frail and claimed you could . . . what was it? 'Topple him' I think are the words you used."

"Yes, but what about his claiming to have killed Richard? I think that's pretty damning, don't you?"

Clive sighed. "I don't know. You also just claimed that he was senile, so I wouldn't put much stock in what he whispered to you as he was trying to seduce you."

Henrietta could not help but laugh. She wrapped her arms around him again. "Jealous, Inspector?" she said, lacing her fingers behind his neck.

"Very," he grunted and kissed her. For a moment, she allowed herself to kiss him back, reveling in the scent of his faded cologne mixed with perspiration and tobacco. His hands strayed down her back and began to caress her buttocks.

"Clive," she murmured, pulling away. "Not here."

"Let's go inside, then," he whispered into her hair and bestowed her head with tiny kisses.

"No, we don't have time for that right now."

"Darling, we do. Dinner isn't for hours." He kissed her neck.

"No, we need to go back into town."

"Town?" He paused in his attentions.

"Yes, we need to revisit Monsieur Bonnet."

Clive rolled his eyes.

"Remember what Monsieur Bonnet said before Valentin barged in?" she asked eagerly. "That he had a theory? I think we should go back and find out what it is."

Clive slowly released her with a sigh. "Hmmm. I do remember that, now that you say it. He could have meant anything, though. A theory about the Cathars, or the mystical powers of the painting, or who the killer is or—"

"Exactly," she interrupted. "That's why we need to go back." She took his hand and began to pull him back toward the château.

"What? Now?" Clive exclaimed. "But I haven't even bathed yet from the ride," he said, gesturing at his breeches. "And dinner is in just a few hours."

"You were keen enough just now," she said, turning to him with one eyebrow raised, a smile lurking.

"Minx!"

"Come, come, Inspector. The game is afoot!" They were already back to the boxwoods.

"Henrietta! This is a very serious case," he said from behind her.

"Yes, I'm aware," she said, turning and crossing her arms across her chest. "Are you coming or not?"

"But why right now? We probably can't even get a car."

"Because we don't have very many days left here, as you very well know, and because it's the perfect time. Didn't you say that Valentin was planning to attend to various correspondences in his study for the afternoon? This is the perfect time to sneak away."

"Why is this somehow making sense?" Clive mused.

"Because it does. You go change. Don't take the time to bathe."

"Don't bathe?"

"We don't have time. Just freshen up. Doubtless, Monsieur Bonnet won't notice, or, if he does, he more than likely won't care."

He grabbed her about the waist again. "Are you really my wife?"

"Yes, I really am. Now get going," she said, kissing his stubbled cheek. "I'll go ask Claudette about using the chauffeur. Or maybe *she'll* let us take a car on our own."

Not an hour later, they were walking down *Rue des Écrivains* in the heart of Strasbourg. As it turned out, Claudette had not been available to ask about using a car, as, according to M. Renard, the butler, she was resting and was not to be disturbed. Renard, however, had been more than helpful and himself had arranged for Gaspard, the chauffeur, to bring a car around, a beautiful old Bugatti Royale. Clive had instructed Gaspard to again drop them off at the cathedral, but, not trusting him to not report back to Valentin, had led Henrietta into the ancient church and then exited through a side door. He then proceeded to lead them down a much more circuitous route to the antiquities shop.

Henrietta gripped Clive's arm now and stepped carefully on the wet cobblestones. It was a gray afternoon, the sky suddenly threatening more rain. She was glad that Clive was navigating, as she was hopelessly lost and privately judged his efforts at subterfuge to be somewhat unnecessary.

"Are you sure you know where you're going?" she asked as he turned down yet another small alleyway. It was strewn with old wooden boxes and trash, and a mangy dog lay curled up in a doorway.

"Yes, we're almost there."

They rounded a corner, then, and Henrietta was surprised to find that they were back in the little square they had been in just two days ago. The antiquities shop looked dark and deserted.

"Oh, no!" Henrietta said, just as big drops of rain began to hit the already wet pavement. "Perhaps he has closed it."

The shade was up, however, and as Clive pushed on the door, they were surprised that it opened, the little bell jangling. They hurried inside, just as the rain began to fall in force.

Clive shook the water off his hat, and the black cat that greeted them the last time from his perch atop a row of books appeared suddenly, meowing furiously as he frantically rubbed himself along Henrietta's ankles, twisting this way and that.

Clive peered toward the back where a light was burning. "Monsieur Bonnet?" he called. He inclined his head, and Henrietta followed him through the maze of aisles, the cat following closely. "Monsieur Bonnet?" Clive called again.

"Maybe he's asleep?" Henrietta whispered.

"Not likely," Clive muttered.

The little back room that contained M. Bonnet's desk was lit but deserted. Likewise, the door to his inner chamber was closed, indicating that he was not there, as there was no way to close the door tightly from the inside. "He must be in another part of the shop," Henrietta suggested. "Or maybe he stepped out for a moment?" She made a movement to retrace their steps.

"No, you stay here," Clive commanded. "I'll go. Something doesn't feel right."

"Monsieur Bonnet?" Clive shouted as he retreated back into the shop. "Monsieur Bonnet!"

Henrietta stepped behind the desk to see if there was anything to indicate why he was absent, but beyond a receipt book, a pipe that was filled with fresh tobacco but not yet smoked, and some stray books, there was nothing obvious that stood out. The cat jumped up, stepped gingerly across the books, and meowed again. Henrietta petted him, and he immediately began to purr, his back arching.

"He's not here," Clive said, stepping back into the room.

"Maybe you should try his room," Henrietta suggested, nodding at the bookcase that hid M. Bonnet's private chamber and taking the cat in her arms. "There might be something there?"

Clive did not answer but raised his arm and felt along the top shelf for the key. Retrieving it, he began to randomly pull on books until he found the hidden keyhole. He inserted the skeleton key, turning it once, and the door swung open with a creak. Clive peered inside and then immediately jumped back.

"Jesus Christ," he muttered, looking at Henrietta now.

"What is it?" Henrietta dropped the cat and hurried to him, but he caught her in his arms, stopping her from entering the room. Despite these efforts, however, she managed to peer around him and then let out a little scream at the sight of a crumpled Monsieur Bonnet, lying in a pool of blood, a knife in his back.

Chapter 14

"**H**ow very shocking!" Julia exclaimed.

"Shocking, yes, but it's not uncommon," Sidney Bennett said frankly as he half-sat on the front edge of his desk. "It's called extortion, plain and simple."

"But is there nothing to be done?" Julia gave Elsie Von Harmon's hand a little squeeze. They were sitting next to each other on a small Chesterfield sofa in Bennett's study in Logan Square. Elsie's male friend, Mr. Stockel, paced nearby.

Julia had been surprised when, not a few days ago, she had received a call from a rather tearful Elsie, who had begun the exchange with a profusion of apologies, saying that she didn't know to whom else to turn. Julia was immediately concerned. Not just because Elsie was Henrietta's sister, but because she was such a sweet, innocent creature. Like a little cat in need of a cuddle. She had helped Elsie once before by thwarting Lieutenant Harrison Barnes-Smith in his attempts to lure her off to a hasty elopement, but that had been at the request of Henrietta, who had swiftly written to Julia from Castle Linley whilst on her honeymoon trip, begging for her intercession. This time, however, the request for help was coming directly from Elsie herself, and it warmed Julia's heart to think that perhaps Elsie really did think of her as a sister, as the three of them had pledged to be on the morning of Henrietta's wedding.

Likewise, Julia was glad of a distraction from her woes at home, happy to be of service to someone without it being in the form of witty banter at a cocktail party. With peculiar interest, then, she had listened as Elsie related her current dilemma and concluded, after hearing it all, that they should appeal to the opinion of Sidney Bennett, who was the only lawyer she knew personally, excepting Randolph, of course, and consulting *him* was certainly out of the question. And only briefly did Julia remember, with a twinge of sadness, that the last time she had needed help for Elsie, it had been her father she had gone to, and she despaired a little that Bennett had seemed to so easily step into that role—in more ways than one, perhaps. But she couldn't allow herself to think of that now.

Elsie had surprisingly requested to be present during the consultation, and Julia had agreed, though she had not anticipated that Bennett would suggest they meet at his home to discuss these "troubles." She had assumed that he would suggest they meet at Highbury, but she supposed that did not make much sense, given that Elsie would then have to travel all the way to Winnetka instead of merely across town to Logan Square, nor did it make sense to meet in the offices of Linley Standard.

This meant, however, that Julia would instead have to travel down to the city, but she didn't mind. For one thing, it would give her a chance to see the interior of Sidney Bennett's home, which she was more than mildly curious to see given the fact that he had become her mother's new . . . companion. (She could think of no other word to use in reference to him.) Eagerly, she wondered if the interior of his home would reveal anything about the interior of the man himself. And secondly, she was certain there would be no danger of running into Glenn Forbes, who had, according to her mother, anyway, safely returned to Texas.

Though she wouldn't admit it, Julia had been avoiding Highbury ever since the disastrous garden party on the off-chance that she would see Glenn Forbes. Normally, she was quite adept at hiding any evidence of Randolph's brutality, and the fact that Glenn, with his worried eyes and pitying smile, had inadvertently witnessed Randolph's rough treatment of her still shamed and vexed her. According to Antonia, he had written directly to her after the party, asking again to buy the Church painting and offering ten thousand dollars, but she had again rejected him. As far as she knew, Antonia had told a silent Julia on the telephone, he had finally accepted defeat and returned home, at least that was what Bennett had told her.

Nothing could have prepared Julia, then, when, upon arriving a few minutes early to Bennett's home, hoping to have a private word before Elsie turned up, the front door had been opened by none other than Glenn himself.

Flushed by the sight of him, Julia stood silent and staring before she finally uttered, "What are you doing here?"

Glenn, who had annoyingly returned her stare with an amused look on his face, now broke into a real grin. "Well, that's a fine how-do-you-do."

"I thought you had returned to Texas."

"I changed my mind."

The two continued to stare at each other before Glenn finally spoke again. "Won't you come in?" he said, stepping aside.

"I've some business with your uncle," she said feebly, as she stepped into the house.

"Yes, he's told me. Here, let me take your things," he said, holding out his hands for her hat and duster. "Uncle Sid doesn't keep any servants, except some woman that comes in the mornings, so it's up to me to be butler today. You can call me Billings. Or else Forbes has a nice ring to it."

Julia, still flustered, did not smile, however, and simply handed him her things as she looked around the hall. It was papered simply in a mustard yellow with blue stripes, and beyond the rather handsome hat and coat rack in the corner, there was not much else.

"Ah, Mrs. Cunningham, come through please." Bennett had

appeared in the doorway of a room off the main hall and was gesturing to her now with two raised fingers. Julia hurried toward him with Glenn following silently behind.

"I hope you don't mind that I've asked Glenn to sit in," Bennett said, gesturing at the Chesterfield as he took up a position in front of her on the edge of a small oak desk. "His experience with the law is much broader than mine. I thought he might be able to help."

"No, of course not." Julia did not look over at Glenn, however, and instead tried to preoccupy herself with the details of the room, which, she reminded herself severely, had been one of her original objectives. Besides noting that the décor was simple and orderly and in no way ostentatious, she was maddeningly unable to concentrate further on it, as she could feel Glenn's steady gaze upon her all the while. She was just about to turn and ask him about his health, for lack of a better idea, but before she could, a knock was heard, and he thankfully rose to answer it.

Within moments, Elsie had entered the room, followed by Glenn and another man, who, Julia quickly guessed, must be her friend and the cause of Elsie's current troubles. Julia rose to embrace Elsie and gave her a quick kiss on the cheek, after which Elise, very red about the face, introduced the man beside her as Mr. Gunther Stockel. Julia indicated that Elsie should sit beside her on the little sofa, and Gunther, his hat twisting in his hands, took up a position along the wall. Julia was surprised that Elsie had brought her friend, though she supposed it made sense, as this was really *his* dilemma, not hers. Surreptitiously, she had snuck a look at Gunther and was relieved to find that, at first glance, anyway, he seemed steady and genuine. He carried himself well, though he was dressed simply in woolen trousers and a plain white shirt with no jacket, and Julia found herself approving. He reminded her, in some strange way, of Dennis Braithewaite. It was a shame, she had thought, that this man and Elsie were of a different class; they seemed to suit one another.

"Well," Bennett had murmured, followed by a slight cough,

"now that we're all assembled, why doesn't someone start from the beginning."

It was Elsie, surprisingly, who had spoken up first and related the incident with Heinrich and Rita, with Gunther merely nodding at various points, causing Julia to wonder if it was because he couldn't speak English. Glenn, she had noted, for once didn't look amused and seemed wholly absorbed in listening to Elsie's tale from where he sat in a corner in a small leather chair, his two forefingers steepled against his lips.

"But surely there is *something* we can do," Elsie urged now, echoing Julia and returning the gentle squeeze of her hand.

"Unfortunately," Bennett answered, "if this Heinrich *is* her father, he has every legal right to the girl. I don't see a way around it."

"Yes, but is he?" Glenn asked. He cleared his throat and stood up. "What proof can he offer?" He looked at Gunther.

"None that I know of," Gunther said hoarsely, surprising Julia. So he *could* speak English! "Except that he knows Liesel's story very well and mine, too. I do not know how else he would know of such things."

"I see," Glenn said, crossing his arms. "It's still not proof, though."

"Shouldn't the fact that Gunther has acted as a surrogate father to Anna from the moment of her birth count for anything?" Elsie suggested timidly.

"It should," Bennett said, standing up now, too. "But if they follow through on their threat to take the case to court, it would be risky. We could certainly appeal to the judge's better nature, but there would be no guarantee that he would side with you." He walked behind the desk and sat heavily in the desk chair. "Better to settle out of court, if we can, wouldn't you say, Glenn?"

"You can't really mean that these two should be paid the sum they're asking, do you?" Julia asked.

"No, of course not."

"Perhaps you could meet with him man to man, as two fellow countrymen," Glenn suggested. "Appeal to his better nature?"

Gunther shrugged. "I can try, but I do not think this will do much good."

"Isn't asking for money proof of their underhandedness?" Elsie asked. "The fact that they expect to be paid for their . . . their 'suffering,' I think is what they said?"

"It's a good point, Miss Von Harmon," Glenn answered. "But a judge might not see it that way. And if it comes to that, he will still look more favorably on Heinrich and Rita, a married couple with children, wanting to give the girl a home. By comparison, Mr. Stockel has little to offer, I'm sorry to say. It would look better if you were married, too, for a start," he said now to Gunther, who blushed slightly.

"Do we know for certain that this Heinrich and Rita are actually married?" Julia asked, finally daring to look at Glenn, who caught her gaze and smiled.

"No, but it would be easy enough to find out." Bennett reached for a piece of paper from the top drawer of his desk and wrote several notes.

"Could I not . . ." Elsie faltered, her hands twisting in her lap. "Could we not appeal to Henrietta and Clive?"

Bennett looked up at her, his brow creased. "In what regard?"

"Well. Henrietta has . . . has paid my tuition at Mundelein. Maybe instead of paying for that, she could—"

"No." Gunther said, loudly. "I will not have that."

Bennett cleared his throat. "I would have to agree. In the first place, it would be difficult to precisely locate them in order to send a wire, though I think they are currently in France. And secondly, in the case that Mr. Howard cannot be reached, all business and monetary decisions revert to me, and, I have to say, if I were acting in that capacity, I would not approve of forwarding funds for this purpose. I'm sorry."

"Why not?" Elsie asked with the slightest bit of irritation.

"No, Elsie, he is right," Gunther said sternly. "It is extortion, as he has said. If we give this money to them, even if we had this money, they will only ask for more. And then more and more. It is the way of such people."

"Yes," Bennett said, leaning back in his chair, "and after the investigation into his father's death, extortion is something Mr. Howard is particularly sensitive to."

"But . . . but what about Henrietta?" Elsie asked quietly. "Do you control her money, too?" She did not ask it unkindly, but more as a genuine question. Still, Julia was shocked by her boldness. Gone was the shy kitten she had known previously.

"Elsie!" Gunther's face was again flushed.

"It is a fair question," Bennett said, nodding toward Gunther. "You may not realize this, Elsie," he said, turning his attention to her, "but Henrietta has no money of her own. She has only what Clive allows her," he added quietly. "So, you see the problem. I don't wish to be cruel, but Clive would never agree to this."

Elsie stared at him for a moment, her mouth slightly open, before she looked away.

"Isn't there *anything* that can be done?" Julia asked, looking only at Bennett this time.

Bennett thought for a moment. "Have you thought about discussing this with your grandfather?" he asked Elsie. "You might appeal to him. Perhaps he could use his legal might and connections to thwart these two scoundrels."

"No, that's not an option," Elsie said quickly. "He doesn't care who gets Anna, and he certainly isn't going to do anything to help Gunther."

"How can you be so sure? Granted, there is a lot of prejudice against Germans after the war—please excuse me, Mr. Stockel—but Oldrich Exley is not completely unfeeling. He is charitable to a certain degree. I know this for a fact."

"I have already seen Mr. Exley once before." Gunther said quietly. He had been staring at his shoes, but now he looked at Elsie. "To ask for Elsie's hand in marriage."

Julia let out a little gasp. "Marriage?" she exclaimed and took

Elsie's hand again. "When did this happen?" she whispered, searching the girl's eyes for she knew not what . . . coercion? Sympathy? Surely not love . . . ?

"A short time ago," Elsie answered, her face oddly resolute. Julia watched as Elsie's gaze traveled to Gunther, who held it tenderly. The love between them was palpable, and Julia's stomach clenched at the sight of it. How had she not known?

"Dearest, does anyone know?" Julia asked tentatively. "Henrietta, perhaps?"

"No one except Grandfather. Gunther went to see him, as he said, to ask permission to marry me."

"I see," Julia muttered, stunned that Gunther had not only been so honorable, but so brave. She could only guess, however, at how badly that must have gone. "And?"

"He forbids it," Gunther answered. "He has made it very clear that if Elsie and I proceed to marry against his wishes, he will not only cut her off, but the entire family. So, you see, it is useless to ask him to help in this matter of Anna."

"I see. Well, this is grave indeed." Bennett glanced at Glenn and then drummed his fingers on the desk, thinking. "Have you considered whether Anna might actually be better off with them?" He let out a deep breath. "I know it must seem like anathema to you right now, but I suggest you consider it honestly."

"Better off with them?" Elsie asked loudly, again surprising Julia. "The poor little thing has lost her mother and her grandmother. Gunther is all she has. And she has fits! She was already sent to Dunning for it, until Clive and Henrietta were able to get her out, thank God. Next, she'll be sent to the epileptic colony in Dixon."

"Elsie—" Gunther began.

"This Heinrich and Rita don't really want her. They don't care about her! They just want money."

"Why don't we call their bluff?" Glenn suggested. "Refuse to pay them and hand over the child. As soon as she has a fit, they'll be more than willing to give her back."

Bennett rubbed his chin. "It's not a bad plan—"

"No!" Gunther said steadily. "I will not use Anna as a—what do you call it?—a pawn. She has already been through too much. I will not hand her over to these strangers for even one night."

"All right, then," Glenn said, stuffing his hands in his pockets. "Any other ideas?"

Bennett rubbed his brow. "I need to think more about this. Do nothing for now," he said to Gunther and Elsie. "Give me a few days."

Elsie nodded sadly and rose. Julia could tell she was fighting back tears. "Thank you, Mr. Bennett," she mumbled. She was suddenly back to her old deferential self. The flame of fight that Julia had momentarily witnessed as she challenged Mr. Bennett just now was all but extinguished. She seemed utterly defeated, as did Gunther.

"I'm sorry we don't have much to offer," Bennett said, standing as well. "But don't fret. Let me do a little investigating."

"I am most grateful," Gunther said, extending his had to Bennett and then to Glenn. "You have been very helpful, and I thank you both."

Julia gave Elsie a long embrace.

"Thank you, Julia," Elsie whispered. "I don't know what I would have done."

Julia released her and grasped her hands, trying to quell the hurt she felt at not knowing about Elsie's secret engagement. "I'll telephone you. We have much to discuss it would seem," she said.

Elsie gave her a sad nod.

"I'll show you out," Bennett said. "Don't lose hope." He ushered the two of them into the main hall, gently closing the study door behind him.

Alarmed by the fact that she was suddenly alone with Glenn now, Julia made a show of looking for her gloves inside her handbag and then stood up. "I should be going, too," she said briskly. "Thank you for your help."

"Julia, are you . . . are you quite well?" Gone was his usual jovial tone, which somehow made it difficult for Julia to breathe properly.

"Well? Of course, I'm well!" she snapped in her best version of Antonia. "Why would you suggest otherwise?"

"Have I done something to offend you?" he asked, true concern in his voice.

She closed her eyes briefly and then forced herself to look at him. "No, of course not. I spoke harshly. Think nothing of it."

"If I've been insensitive, I beg your forgiveness."

"I should go." She moved quickly toward the door. "Randolph doesn't even realize I'm gone."

Glenn did not follow her, but stood his ground by the desk. "Now that you mention him, he's the one I can't seem to get out of my mind."

"Randolph?" She turned back to look at him.

"Forgive me for remarking, but your husband seemed . . . upset at the garden party. I hope I wasn't the cause of something."

"Not at all!" She tried to utter a little laugh, but it failed. "Randolph is just a bit strict."

"That what you call it?" He walked slowly across the room. "He's what we call a fear-biter," he said, looking at her steadily.

"A fear-biter?" she muttered, her heart beating hard.

"A fear-biter is a type of dog that's got himself backed into a corner, afraid his bone's going to be taken away, so he lashes out before anyone can try."

Julia swallowed and looked away. "Really, Mr. Forbes. What an extraordinary comparison. I can't imagine what you mean."

"Oh, I think you can, Julia. I'm sorry for you."

"Well, you needn't be, Mr. Forbes," she said, something suddenly snapping inside of her. "I'm perfectly happy and content." She yanked open the study door, then, trying desperately not to cry.

"Julia, wait—" he called, but she didn't stop. She glided through the front hall, and without another word to anyone, opened the door and let herself out.

Chapter 15

"How perfectly awful!" Claudette exclaimed after Clive and Henrietta had relayed, over dinner, the story of poor Monsieur Bonnet's murder. "But, then again, I suppose you are used to such things, being detectives."

Henrietta was tempted to say that she had not as yet witnessed an actual dead body—besides Neptune, that is—but she did not. In truth, the sight of M. Bonnet lying in a pool of his own blood had sickened her, but she dared not tell Clive this lest he fret unnecessarily and urge her to return to bed, as if that would help.

"What did the police say?" Valentin asked, taking a bite of beef.

"Not much. No leads or clear motive. They believe we were not too far behind the killer. There was a broken window in the back where they assume he got in."

"Must have been a robbery. Shops like that are easy targets."

"Yes, Inspector Neuville thought the same, but it will take some time to determine what, if anything, has been taken unless they can find an inventory list. Which seems unlikely."

"Why unlikely?" Claudette asked.

"Because the shop is rather a disorganized mess. Doubtless, Monsieur Bonnet had a system, but the devil if anyone else can make heads or tails of it. The police made a rather thorough search, but no inventory of any sort was found. Maybe something will turn up later."

"It did seem quite dusty and shabby inside. I am not surprised." Valentin set his knife down next to his plate. "In fact, it is peculiar that you wanted to return." His eyes narrowed. "Especially as you already made one purchase. A book, was it not?"

Valentin's voice was oddly chilling, and Henrietta felt the hair on the back of her neck rise. "Yes," she said quickly. "I . . . I had spotted a broach the other day. I thought my mother might like it. So we went back."

Valentin did not respond, but took a drink of his wine, his eyes fixed on Clive now. "Ah, yes. You are leaving soon. When is this, exactly? Tomorrow, I think?"

"Valentin!" Claudette exclaimed from the other end of the table.

"Oh, but I am not being rude. You are very welcome to stay as long as you like." He inclined his head. "I only inquire because I leave for Munich soon. For some time."

"Must you go, Valentin?" Claudette asked, her tone oddly pleading now.

"Yes, my dear. I must. Urgent business." He wiped the corner of his mouth with his thick white napkin.

"Father will be disappointed."

"All the same." He tossed the napkin onto the table.

"Where *is* the baron?" Clive asked casually, studying his wine glass as he swirled it. "I haven't seen him all day."

"He went into town earlier today," Claudette answered. "Some business he said, though that's preposterous. He hasn't had any business dealings in his whole life. Still. We cannot exactly stop him."

"But are you not afraid to let him go when he's in one of his . . . well, when he's not quite himself?" Henrietta asked. "What if he got lost?"

Claudette gave a little laugh. "That is most unlikely. He strays usually to l'Epicerie, where he sits for the afternoon. And in any case, Gaspard is not far behind."

"But Gaspard drove *us*," Clive pointed out.

"So he did. It was one of the other servants who drove him today. Pascal. The one who showed your maid around, I believe."

"You seem rather concerned with my father's movements today," Valentin said. "Why?"

"Simple curiosity." Clive flicked his eyes at him. "Making polite conservation."

"Ah. The mind of a detective is a very curious one, is it not? You are sure to be on your toes always, *chérie*," Claudette said to Henrietta. "How difficult for you."

Henrietta laughed. "Not at all."

"In answer to your previous question," Clive said, emptying his glass, "we will stay an extra day; if you can accommodate us, that is. In light of Monsieur Bonnet's death, I think it is important we stay a little longer. Help with the investigation any way we can."

"Help with the investigation?" Valentin scoffed. "I am very sure the French police can handle it. The death of a random shopkeeper seems hardly worth your notice. Is there something you are not saying?"

"Of course not," Clive said smoothly. "Though I hardly think any man is random."

"*Je ne le crois pas!*—I don't believe that. Stop being so sanctimonious. You are a detective in Chicago and you have lived through war. You must be used to death by now."

"Yes, exactly," Clive said evenly. "It makes each life all the more precious."

"You do not fool me for a second."

"Valentin!" Claudette scolded. "Do not listen to him, *chéris*. He is always this way before he leaves. He claims to hate this place, and yet he acts like a sullen schoolboy when he has to go. It is *très étrange*, is it not? Anyway, I am delighted you are staying. It keeps me from being lonely. Now. I will plan a little soiree for tomorrow night. A sending-off party, as it were."

"Oh, no, Claudette! Please don't go to any trouble on our account," Henrietta begged.

"Nonsense! I have been wanting to give a dinner for quite some time now, have I not, Valentin?"

"No, Claudette. This is out of the question," Valentin snapped. "I have already asked some business associates to come down tomorrow night. You must forgive me," he said to Clive. "I understood you would have already left when I made these arrangements."

"Valentin! You ruin everything!" She rose from her place. "I insist we have a gathering. Your stuffy business associates can attend if they wish. What difference would it make? For once they will be greeted by something more than your long face and these stone walls!" Majestically, she crossed the room. "It is settled. Leave it to me. Shall we go through, my dear?" she said to Henrietta.

"Yes, of course," Henrietta rose and gave Clive a look. She desperately wanted to speak with him alone before following Claudette into the drawing room, but she knew it would have to wait.

"We can't possibly leave in two days' time, Clive!" Henrietta said several hours later, as she removed her earrings and tossed them on the vanity. The evening's after-dinner conversations had not yielded any new information and, indeed, had seemed rather tired and forced until finally Henrietta had begged exhaustion from the horrible events of the day as an excuse to retire early, Clive eagerly taking up the cue and following.

"Well, we are," Clive said gruffly and loosened his tie.

"What about the investigation? You told Valentin you wished to be a part of it . . ."

"I just said that. The police have it in hand, though I'm sure they don't suspect the real motive, which we cannot reveal, so all we would be doing is attempting to confuse them, which probably wouldn't be all that difficult."

"Snob!"

"I'm only waiting for a return telegram from Hartle. Doubtless, he'll be upended by the news of Monsieur Bonnet's death. Unless he knew of it somehow from some other source . . ." he mused. "Either way, it has nothing to do with us anymore. I'm taking us off this case." Clive tossed his jacket onto the end of the bed.

"But how can you say that, Clive? We're obviously getting close, or Monsieur Bonnet would not have been killed. Now we know for sure he was going to tell us something extremely valuable. We can't just give up now!"

"We don't know that for sure, Henrietta. His death could have been a coincidence."

"I know you don't believe that for one minute, Clive," she said, putting her hands on her hips.

Clive rubbed his eyes. "Darling, this is getting altogether too dangerous. This is really a case of international politics and espionage. We are in way over our heads. We told Hartle we'd look for the painting, which we did," he said, holding up a thumb.

"Not really. We—"

"We made an attempt," Clive said firmly. "And we spoke with Monsieur Bonnet," he said, holding up another finger. "And we confirmed the death of Stafford," he said, holding up a third finger. "That's it. We've fulfilled our mission."

"But you *must* suspect Valentin now, don't you?" she asked, trying to draw him.

"Of possessing the panel? Or of killing Monsieur Bonnet?"

"Either one! Or both!"

"I don't think so. For one thing, he was here all day."

"So he says. Can anyone corroborate that?"

"Darling, we are not getting involved in this any further than we already have."

"Clive, it's so obvious that it was him!"

"I wouldn't say obvious."

"You're being obtuse on purpose to vex me. The very same thing your mother complains about. For once, I sympathize with her."

"Darling, listen. I agree there's something underhand about the man, but he strikes me as the type whose primary motive is making money. Not secret paintings and killing people connected to them. Tends to be bad for business."

"But if he has the painting, he could sell it for a lot of money."

"Not something that famous. That's where most art thieves go wrong. A jewel can be cut and sold as pieces in the black market, but it would be pretty easy to trace a Renaissance painting that is considered a world masterpiece."

"Well, what about him giving it to the Nazis for favor?"

"I don't think he's a Nazi."

"He is! I heard him say 'Heil Hitler' on the phone just yesterday when I passed his study," she added with renewed urgency. "I forgot to tell you!"

"Just because he says 'Heil, Hitler,' doesn't make him a Nazi."

"Ugh! What else could it possibly mean? Honestly, Clive, you can be so stubborn, sometimes! It's not in the least bit attractive."

Clive let out a little laugh and scratched the back of his neck and gave her that look that suggested he wanted to take her to bed. "Perhaps it was the baron?" he suggested with a grin. "After all, he was in town all day."

"Don't be ridiculous, Clive." She removed her heels. "He hasn't the strength to swat a fly, much less stab a man in the back."

"So you keep saying. But isn't it odd that he wasn't at dinner?"

"Not really. Though what if he's dead, too, and they're not telling us!"

Clive laughed out loud. "Darling, now you're getting ridiculous."

"Well, did Valentin say anything unusual over your port?"

"Not particularly. He's not exactly a conversationalist, as you know. I tried asking him more about his business, but he was elusive. Something about importing goods. Said he stood to make a lot of money if there was another war." He shrugged. "See what I mean?"

Henrietta sighed and sat down on the chaise lounge and began unhooking her stockings, which she knew usually aroused him, but it couldn't be helped. She couldn't stay in her evening dress all night.

As predicted, it caught his attention. "Darling, allow me to assist you since Edna seems determinedly absent." He knelt on the floor in front of her.

"That's because you're in here. She's probably hovering somewhere in the hallway waiting to undress me."

"Allow me," he said, as he began rolling her stockings down her leg.

"Clive. Be serious."

"I am being serious," he said, kissing the inside of her knee.

"Clive!" she said, twisting her legs to the side.

"All right, I'll try," he said, standing up with a groan and rubbed the back of his neck with one hand. "Did Claudette say anything when you went into the drawing room?"

"Not really," she said, pleased that he was so far appeasing her. "She told me a few stories of her time in London. Sounds as if she was a little bit wild."

"Somehow that doesn't surprise me," he said, pulling her up.

"She reminds me somehow of Julia, don't you think? I could see them being very great friends." She turned so that he could unfasten her dress. Clive undid a few buttons and then gave up, kissing her neck instead.

"Darling, I hadn't given it a thought," he mumbled. "But must we discuss my sister while I'm trying to make love to you?"

"You're very naughty, Inspector," she chirped as he kissed her shoulder. "I'm peeved with you right now."

"Darling, don't be. I'll make it up to you in Switzerland," he murmured, nuzzling her hair.

"I don't see how. Doubtless the rest of the trip will seem rather dull in comparison, don't you think?"

"Not if I can help it," he grunted, and in one swift movement, rose and scooped her up in his arms as he did so.

"Clive!" she squealed and threw her arms around his neck to keep from falling.

"Come, Countess. I must have you in the castle one last time," he said, tossing her lightly on the bed, which elicited yet another little squeal. Panting slightly, he lay down on the bed beside her, propping his head up on his hand. Henrietta stared into his eyes and saw in them the love she was still sometimes utterly overwhelmed by. She could not deny that she adored him.

"All right, squire," she said softly, running a finger down his chest.

"Squire?" His lips curled in amusement.

"Yes, and you'll have to do as I say."

"If I must," he said with a grin and kissed her lightly. "What would you have me do?"

"Remember our last night on the ship?" She put her hand on his stubbled cheek. "Do that," she whispered.

"Oh, God, yes," he murmured, his voice thick.

"I love you, Clive," she said, as his hand began to wander lower and he kissed her neck. "I'll always love you. No matter what happens."

"Yes, of course," he said, breaking his kisses. "But don't talk that way, darling. Nothing's going to happen. I promise."

"If you say so," she murmured, and tried to push to the back of her mind the foreboding that had suddenly presented itself and instead allowed herself to enjoy her husband's attentions.

Chapter 16

Gunther pushed down his feeling of foreboding as he hurried down Ravenswood. At the sound of the shrieking whistle coming from the tower of the Molson Shoe Factory, he quickened his steps all the more. This was his third time slipping away from Mundelein to search for Heinrich Meyer, and he hoped he would be successful this time. He needed to be. Already, Sr. Bernard had once before noticed his absence. She had not said much when he made his excuse, but he knew that she was displeased.

The Meyers had left an address at which they could deliver either Anna or a lump sum of money, but Gunther didn't dare go there. That shrew of a woman would most certainly be there, and, besides, he needed to talk to Heinrich alone. Man to man, German to German, as Mr. Forbes had suggested.

Gunther was pretty sure it was Molson's that Heinrich had said was his place of work, but on his previous two ventures here, Gunther had failed to find him in the crowd of men that poured out after each shift. Concluding that Heinrich must work the night shift, if he worked here at all, Gunther had thus risen earlier than usual today and had made it to the main gate just as the sun was coming up over the horizon.

He perched himself off to the side and watched as the first men began shuffling out. Soon more and more appeared, and Gunther observed that the night-shift men were certainly more subdued upon being released than their day-shift counterparts. These were mostly silent as they trudged into weak sunlight, their dark shapes silhouetted against the pink and orange sky.

Thankfully, Gunther did not have long to wait before he spotted Heinrich, walking with his head down and a quick step on the far side of the yard. He seemed eager to either get away from the factory or to get back home, though Gunther couldn't imagine wanting to hurry home to the likes of Rita and a house full of lice.

"Heinrich!" he called, but the man didn't hear him. The herd of men was funneling through the narrow gate now, pulling Heinrich toward them. "Heinrich!" Gunther called again.

Heinrich heard him this time and looked in Gunther's direction. Heinrich's face immediately transformed from one of curiosity to one of surprise. He paused for a moment, as if caught in a trap, and then began to wriggle faster through the men.

"Heinrich, wait!" Gunther plunged into the crowd himself. By the time he broke free on the other side, however, Heinrich was already walking quickly down Bryn Mawr. "Heinrich!" Gunther called, but the man ignored him, hunching his shoulders forward and picking up his pace. Gunther followed him, jogging to keep up.

"Heinrich, please!"

Heinrich stopped finally and turned, looking nervously around, as if worried that someone would see him talking. "What are you doing here?" He spoke to him in German.

"Heinrich, I must speak to you," Gunther answered in kind.

"I have nothing to say to you. I must get home." Heinrich turned away and began walking briskly again.

"Let me walk with you," Gunther suggested, keeping pace.

"It will do no good. Go away."

"Heinrich, listen. Are you really Anna's father?"

Heinrich paused again in his walking and searched Gunther's eyes as if trying to decide how to answer. Finally, he dropped his gaze and let out a deep breath. "Yes, God forgive me. I am almost certain of it. Liesel had . . . had never been with a man before me. Nor after, I am fairly sure."

"Why did you leave, then? Why did you run off to America? Have you no honor?"

Heinrich sighed. "I—" he began and then stopped himself. "I didn't know she was with child. I . . . I had a friend who had bought a passage, but he grew ill and could not go. He offered it to me, and I took it." His eyes, weary and sunken, searched Gunther's again. "My father was a cruel man. The truth was that I wasn't thinking of Liesel. I saw my chance to leave, and I took it." He began walking again.

"And now you are married to this Rita and have other children. A different life." Gunther pulled his arm to keep him from walking farther. "You do not really want Anna, do you? What drives you to be a part of this?"

Heinrich angrily pulled his arm away but didn't answer.

"It is this Rita, is it not?"

Heinrich twisted his lips and looked away. "We need the money. Very badly, as it turns out."

"But why? Do you not provide for her and your children?" He nodded toward the factory.

"I try," Heinrich said bitterly. "I work constantly. Sometimes double shifts. But there is never enough money. Besides ours, we have her other children. Also, her brother and her mother that live with us. And Rita has certain . . . habits, shall we say."

Gunther closed his eyes and tried to think, silently despairing for this man who had gotten himself in so deep.

"Now that she knows about Anna and her connection to these . . . these people of wealth," Heinrich continued, "she will—"

"How did she find out?"

"Find out what?"

"About Elsie? Her family? About the Exleys?"

"I don't know." He shook his head. "But now that she does know, she will be relentless."

Gunther felt a rare surge of rage. "God damn it, man! Are you not her husband?"

Heinrich let out a strangled little laugh. "In name only. She is . . . You don't understand. She is cruel as well. In a different way than my father was. In a way that would make an ordinary man ashamed."

"Ashamed? And are you not ordinary, then?

"No, I am very ordinary, Heir Stockel. And very much ashamed. My advice is to not try to fight her. She will win in the end. She always does. Now that she has concocted this scheme, you cannot escape her."

"What can she do? Will she really seek the law?"

"Yes. It is not a bluff. Her cousin knows a lawyer who is . . . who is not quite honorable, to use your word."

"But if she brings it before a judge, there is a good chance you will be awarded Anna. And that is surely not what you want. What will happen then?"

Heinrich looked away. "Only God knows. If Anna really has these fits, as you claim she does, Rita will not endure that for a minute. She will more than likely have her put away somewhere. Declared insane."

"My God," Gunther muttered. "How can you live with her? With yourself?"

"Do not ask me this." Heinrich said bitterly. "Rita is counting on it never coming to this. She hopes to scare the money out of you. She will try to take advantage of your kind heart for her own gain."

"But I could say that you tried to bribe us. In court. I could say that."

"You could. But they will probably not believe you. Remember, she has a cousin in the law. They will fix the court."

Gunther felt as though he wanted to scream. "Is there nothing that can be done?" he asked desperately. "Can you not . . . could you expose her? Tell the truth?"

Heinrich shook his head sadly. "No, there is nothing. I have done . . . other things for which I am ashamed. Not quite lawful things. She found me after I had just arrived, when I was weak and alone with no money and no job. And now I am in her power. If she chose to expose me, I would very likely go to jail for all the things I have done."

Gunther rubbed his brow.

"The easiest, best thing for everyone is to just pay the money, Heir Stockel. Believe me, it is not for my gain. I will see little of it."

"But she will only ask for more," Gunther tested.

"No. That is not the way with her. She sees that as too risky. That is why she asks for one big sum." Heinrich shrugged. "Heir Stockel, I have been to the house in Palmer Square. I have seen the money these people have. Three thousand dollars would be nothing to them, but it would be a fortune for us. Enough to ease certain burdens, as it were."

"Heinrich, you don't understand. That is not my money."

"But you can get it. You know you can. You claim to love Anna, yes? Do you not see this is the best way for her? Then you can keep her, we go away, and nothing has to change. It really is the best option, Heir Stockel."

"But this is wrong!"

Heinrich gave a sad shrug. "No, it is not right, but this is the way of the world. Everyone has to survive somehow. You need to give up your high morals and your stubbornness." He shot him a look of disdain. "Now, let me go. I cannot be home any later than I already will be. Just go. Go back and decide what you will do." Heinrich turned, then, and hurried down the street.

Gunther did not go after him but stood, stunned, watching this broken man disappear down the first side street, his words still racing through Gunther's mind. Was paying them the money the only option? But where could he get that sum of money? It was impossible!

Gunther thrust his hands in his pockets and began walking back down Bryn Mawr toward the trolley stop on Broadway. He pulled out his father's pocket watch, the only thing he still had of his, and wished he could walk all the way back, but he couldn't spare the time. Sr. Bernard would be looking for him soon. He slipped the watch back into his pocket and hurried along, his mind wandering back to his father as he did so. Gunther had few memories of him. He, too, had been a professor at the University in Heidelberg. When the war broke out, he declared himself a pacifist, which had fallen upon deaf ears. He had been forced to fight for the kaiser, and though he marched in step with his comrades, he refused to fire his gun. Predictably, he was one of the first killed.

Gunther had grown up hearing his mother's stories about his father, about how stupid he had been not to fire while in battle. Surely, being attacked by another human warranted murder, did it not? she had often complained. Look where his ideals had gotten them! she would often say, as she wrapped a sweater around her shoulders in their cold house, all of it rented out to students except the few rooms they kept for themselves. But Gunther had taken these stories and woven them into his own narrative, making his father out to be a hero, the epitome of honor and justice and morality.

It had been so very easy as a boy to model his life on his mythic father, but now that he was a man of twenty-eight, he was finding it much more difficult to know what was right and what was wrong. He had been so sure of his black and white absolutes, but after Anna was left on their doorstep, everything had begun to smear into gray. He was unsure of everything now, as if he had lost his moral compass. More than at any point in his life did he wish he could speak to his father. He desperately needed guidance.

He watched the trolley approach, its headlights still on despite the early morning light, rendering their illumination useless. The trolley squealed to a stop, and he climbed on, rifling his pocket for the fare and made his way to the back, flinging himself down on one of the hard benches there. He needed to think. What the hell was he to do? He was in an impossible situation. Short of finding three thousand dollars, Anna seemed doomed.

He had told everyone that she was not his child, which was true, but he loved her fiercely, as though she *were* his child. He had sacrificed everything for her. Admittedly, he and his mother had cared for her at first out of necessity, keeping her alive while they waited for Liesel, one of their borders, to return for her as she had promised. But after a year and still no Liesel, they made the difficult decision to deliver Anna to an orphanage. Just before they did so, however, Anna began having epileptic fits, and they feared what would happen to her in an institution under the new Nazi laws. They heard mutterings that the "mentally feeble" would be sterilized, and some even predicted that these undesirables would be put to death so that they would no longer be a burden on society.

Unable to abandon the little baby to this fate, Gunther rescinded his professorship and their rambling old house in Heidelberg to travel to America in an effort to escape Hitler and the spying eyes of the neighbors, who whispered about the little girl next door who was possessed by a devil. Unfortunately, nothing had turned out as planned—his mother had died enroute; Liesel had been traced to an insane asylum, specifically to the cemetery behind it; and he had been forced, in the end, to take poor Anna to an orphanage, anyway, while he worked as the lowly custodian of an all-women's college. It had nearly killed him to take her to The Bohemian Home for the Aged and Orphans, but Sr. Bernard had insisted that not only was it inappropriate for a little girl to live with a man who was not her father, but that it was dangerous and negligent, too, to keep her locked in a hut while he worked. His only solace had been that the Lasiks, the couple who ran the orphanage, were kind and that they sometimes allowed her to visit him on weekends.

He didn't know if other fathers felt this way, but there was a tender, fragile place in his heart for Anna that he couldn't explain. Perhaps it had been born of all of their shared trials. Only in poetry could he express how he felt. He had dared to read a few of these poems to Elsie, and she had cried, the only person who seemed to understand the depths of his feelings.

He sighed and looked out the window at the buildings passing by on Broadway. Elsie Von Harmon. What was he to do with *her*? She was unlike any girl—woman—he had ever met, and his heart, in truth, was full of love for her, so much so that he felt in danger that it might burst. For this reason, he found it difficult at times to even be in her presence, and yet it was all that he longed for daily, nay, hourly. It made him wretched most of the time, but that was the way of love, was it not? At least, that is how the poets described it, and, upon tasting it now for the first time, he found their account of love to be tragically accurate.

There had been young women in Heidelberg, students, who had fancied him, he was pretty sure, but he had never allowed himself to toy with them, knowing as he did that he was not, at that time, in a position to marry. But here in Chicago, as an even poorer custodian, caring for an epileptic child, his situation was all the more desperate and untenable. He had certainly not been thinking of love when Elsie had appeared at Mundelein at Christmastime, when all the other girls had gone home to their families. She had been so frightened and unsure, and he instantly understood her feelings of loneliness and even despair—hadn't he felt them often enough himself?

Almost immediately upon meeting her, he had become aware of a dangerous fluttering in his heart, but he had squelched it, knowing that he was in no position to kindle love. But when he had injured his hand, and she had lavished her attentions on him with no thought for herself, his guard had been brought so low that he lost control of his heart anyway. He had managed to hide his feelings, for a time, or so he had convinced himself, but then Lloyd Aston had appeared on the scene and tried to force Elsie's hand, causing all of Gunther's noble resolve to wither almost entirely. So it was that, in a rare moment of weakness, he had asked Elsie to be his wife, and she had accepted!

His obvious initial feelings of joy, however, had almost immediately, cruelly, given way to ones of regret. Not because he didn't love her. No, he could barely breathe for love of her, but because it was such a foolish match. Not in the way her grandfather saw it, the inequality of their stations or their wealth, but because she had her whole young life before her and he didn't wish her to be tied to him the way that Masha was to Sergey in *Family Happiness*, the book he had stupidly given Elsie to read as a way of trying to test her.

When he had first met Elsie, she had barely the ability to think for herself or to have any dreams of her own. Over time, he had watched her blossom and had thrilled when she even began to imagine a life of study, of perhaps one day becoming a teacher herself. How could he ask her to give that up to care for Anna—and any others that would surely come along—in their miserable hut? They couldn't just pack off their children to Palmer Square and hope that Mr. Exley or the Howards would pay for their care. She had told him that she *wanted* to be a wife and a mother, but how could he ask her to give up her other dream? And how could he ask her to return to a state of poverty with him, having tasted the luxuries she was now used to? She said that she didn't mind, that she would welcome such a life, but he had his doubts. Regardless, this was not the life she deserved, and she was too selfless to see it. Therefore, it was his duty to see it for her, to predict the troubles that lie ahead and avoid useless heartache.

Thus, he decided manfully, he must call it off, for her sake. Time and again, then, he had resolved to tell Elsie that the marriage was impossible, that he had changed his mind, but as each day slid into another, he had lost his courage in the face of her tender concern and her obvious love, which she was too naïve to even attempt to hide from him. She was completely trusting, and the thought of breaking her heart was breaking his, though this was the very thing he had sought to avoid!

And then he had come up with the idea of asking her grandfather for her hand, insisting that it was born of a noble intent, which it was, but he suspected, deep in his heart, that it was for another reason, a more cowardly one. A part of him knew, as Elsie had tried to tell him so many times, that her grandfather would never approve and thus it would make it easier to dissolve the hasty engagement. For the most part, he was able to convince himself that it was the only honorable thing to do, but in the darkest part of the night, the truth niggled at him, and he began to despise himself for the obvious coward that he was.

As it turned out, he had been shocked by the extent of her grandfather's brutality, and the look of utter betrayal in Elsie's eyes as they stood in the Exley mansion. Her pleading all the way home had been terrible. He had since done his best to keep out of her way, but she had a way of finding him, of popping up when he least expected it, wanting to discuss a topic which, in his mind, anyway, was not up for discussion. The decision had been made, and it was the best for all. The words of his beloved Rilke came back to him frequently: "We need, in love, to practice only this: letting each other go. For holding on comes easily; we do not need to learn it."

God in Heaven! Nightly he prayed for the strength to let her go. She deserved someone better than him, a better life than what he could give her. He would not saddle her with his burdens and his woes. He would return to his old life and try to be happy in it, but he did worry about what was to be done with Anna. He couldn't keep her in the hut, and he was hesitant to return her to The Bohemian Home, if they would even agree to take her. Already, she had had several fits there, the last one causing her to be sent to Dunning, the asylum where her mother, Liesel, had died.

He had not had sufficient time to fully consider what he should do with Anna before this new threat had presented itself in the form of Heinrich and Rita. He buried his face in his hands. What *was* he to do? Even though he had severed his relationship with Elsie and thus the Von Harmons and the Exleys, he feared, as Heinrich warned, that Rita would not give up, convinced that she could somehow still squeeze the money from Elsie's family. He was in an even worse position than before, he realized miserably. Marrying Elsie was out of the question, for his own and her grandfather's reasons, and he had no way of procuring three thousand dollars, at least in some honest fashion. And yet, he refused to hand Anna over to them, merely to be sent to an epileptic colony or to be labeled insane.

Gunther pulled his face from his hands and was startled to see that they were already at Broadway and Sheridan. He pulled the overhead cord and stood up, holding onto the pole nearest him until the trolley slowed. Without waiting for it to fully stop, however, he jumped off and walked quickly down Sheridan toward Mundelein. Well, he thought bitterly, he would have to think of something. Perhaps his mother had been right all those years ago when she criticized his father's misguided sense of morality. There was a time and place for honorable actions, certainly, but this, he was now convinced, was not it.

Chapter 17

Henrietta twisted this way and that, wondering if she should have chosen the salmon silk Patou instead of the silver Schiaparelli. It was times like this that she wished she could have Antonia's advice. Still, she had Edna, and that was nearly as good. Edna had convinced her to wear the silver, and she decided finally, with one last turn, that it was perfect.

"Almost ready, darling?" Clive asked, poking his head into the room and startling her.

"There you are!" she exclaimed, rushing to him. "I was worried you wouldn't get back in time." She draped her arms loosely around his neck. "What did you find? Tell me everything."

"There's precious little to tell," he drawled. "Just as I suspected." He was already dressed for dinner in his black tails and white tie, his hair slicked back neatly, and Henrietta could not but admire how handsome a picture he cut. "The police have managed to take some poor chap into custody. Some vagrant that they're sure to pin it on. Seems they have everything already conveniently wrapped up."

"Like every other police force, seems to me," she countered mischievously.

Clive tilted his head in acknowledgement. "I suppose. I could use a drink," he said, kissing her on the cheek and simultaneously extracting himself from her embrace. "Anything here?" He looked around the room.

"There's the bottle of cognac you brought up last night, naughty thing. See it? It's there on the mantle where you left it."

He moved swiftly toward it.

"Well?" she asked impatiently. "What about Hartle? Did you manage to get through to him?"

"Yes, thank God. He was most upset by the news of Monsieur Bonnet's death. Asked me if we had made any progress with the panel."

"Was that it?"

"In a nutshell. He's requesting that we remain just a little while longer, but I told him 'rotten luck, old boy, we're leaving.' Didn't like that so very much. But. That's the way it is. We tried."

He pulled the crystal stopper from the decanter with a clink and poured himself a tall glass. "Want one?" he asked, looking over his shoulder.

"Not right now. I haven't finished getting ready."

"What do you mean, you're not ready? You look lovely," Clive said, studying her appreciatively.

"Don't be silly, Clive. Edna still has to do my hair."

"Do your hair? It looks perfect."

Henrietta laughed. "Honestly, Clive. Are you really a detective? How could you not notice the state it's in?"

Clive rubbed his chin. "Well, where is Edna, then? Hiding under the bed? Cocktails begin in half an hour," he said, examining his pocket watch quickly before closing it deftly with a click and returning it to his pocket.

"Well, you've already started, so I shouldn't worry." She bit back a smile. "And, anyway, she went to get my jewels." She gestured at her bare neck. "Or did you not notice that, either?"

"Minx," he said with narrowed eyebrows as he took a drink.

"Aren't you going to ask me about *my* search?" she asked peevishly. "That *was* my mission, remember? Or did you presume at the outset that I would not be successful?"

"Darling, I wisely deduced that should you have indeed found the missing panel of the Ghent Altarpiece, it would have been the first thing you announced. But since you did not, I assume that the search was, yes, unsuccessful."

"Well, not entirely. Claudette has instructed the groundsman at Videk to ship some rose saplings to Mr. McCreanney," she said with a small sigh, referring to Highbury's gardener.

"Very amusing, darling, but did you get anywhere with the search?"

"No, I did not," she sighed. "After the tour, I did try to poke around as many rooms as I could, but I found nothing. I still think I would have been more useful in town with you."

"Well, I can't say that."

They had decided early this morning to separate, much to Henrietta's displeasure. But not only did Clive suspect that the investigation into M. Bonnet's death would yield little, but it seemed only appropriate, given the fact that they were leaving the next day, for one of them at least to give in to Claudette's appeal to tour the Videk Gardens. Besides, Clive had suggested, perhaps when she returned, she could have one last look around for the panel or any remnant of Stafford's supposed visit. Any little clue. Henrietta had agreed, albeit a little reluctantly, knowing as she did that Clive didn't *really* believe the panel was here, which gave his suggestion on how she should employ her time a rather patronizing flavor, which she did not appreciate. She said as much at the time, but Clive cleverly responded that it was, after all, *her* family, so it made sense she should spend her last day here with them whilst he pursued the investigation on his own, especially seeing as how the French police were unlikely to take seriously a woman acting in the role of detective.

"I'll be glad to see the back of this place," Clive said and took a long drink.

"Yes, I'd have to agree. I do feel sorry for Claudette, however. She keeps apologizing for the baron's behavior the other day. I hate to leave her."

"Well, we have to leave sometime. Maybe she could come visit us."

"Oh, that would be lovely! I'll mention it."

"Have you and Edna finished packing?"

"For the most part. Except for this," Henrietta answered, walking to her desk and picking up the heavy volume of art that M. Bonnet had given her. "What should I do with it?"

Clive shrugged. "It's a magnificent book. Perhaps keep it as a souvenir?"

"Or maybe as a reminder of the one that got away?" she teased.

"If you're attempting to wound me, darling, it won't work. As my old chief in the city used to say, 'Every once in a while, one gets away. You try your best and move on. Catch the next one.'"

"Did he really say all that?" she asked, one eyebrow arched.

"More or less. Now get going; we're going to be late for this bloody dinner."

"You're really turning into a curmudgeon, you know. Soon you and Valentin will have more in common than you think."

"Now that did wound me. I'd hardly say I'm a curmudgeon simply because I fail to be excited about spending the evening with a bunch of stuffy French nobles."

"Think of your mother."

Clive rolled his eyes.

"Well, isn't it better than dining with just Valentin and Claudette and having to listen to Valentin drone on or to hear the baron refer to me as 'the countess' throughout?"

"Hmmm. You do have a point. I—"

He was interrupted, then, by the entrance of Edna, who, upon seeing him, immediately curtsied. "Oh, Mr. Howard! I'm very sorry, sir," she squeaked.

"Not at all." He gave her a false smile and set his glass on the desk. "Darling," he said, giving Henrietta a quick kiss, "why don't I meet you downstairs?"

"Yes, good idea." Henrietta gave his cheek several quick pats, which caused his eyes to crease in amusement.

"Minx," he silently mouthed and then stepped out.

"I'm sorry to have interrupted, miss," Edna said, hurrying to the vanity and laying down the velvet pouches she carried.

Henrietta, still holding the book, absently sat down on the little chair in front of her. Edna proceeded to carefully arrange the pouches while Henrietta flipped open the book to the page she had bookmarked with a postcard and laid it awkwardly on the vanity on top of her mother-of-pearl hairbrush and matching hand mirror. She stared at the illustration of the Ghent Altarpiece, as she had done so many other times since acquiring the book, trying to see if she could detect some sort of coded map, but she could see nothing but the imagery that was there.

"I brought both the diamonds and the pearls, miss. Which ones, do you think?"

Henrietta didn't answer and tilted her head both ways in an attempt to see the illustration from different angles. Perhaps she should turn the book upside down?

"Miss?" Edna asked, twisting her head around Henrietta's shoulder to catch her gaze. "You okay?"

"Yes," Henrietta said, looking up finally at Edna's image in the vanity mirror. "I suppose I'm just a little downcast."

"Why's that, miss? You homesick, too?"

Henrietta smiled. "No, not that. It's just that Mr. Howard and I were hoping to find a painting here, a particular painting, but we haven't had any luck."

"Oh, I thought we were here for you to see your family."

"Well, that, too."

"Sure it ain't here? There's an awful lot of paintings around. Even more than at home. And I would know, 'cause I used to have to dust them all."

"Yes, I'm pretty sure," Henrietta said with a sigh. "I suppose I'll have the diamonds," she said, trying to smile. "But perhaps you should do my hair first."

"That it?" Edna asked from over her shoulder, picking up a comb and jabbing it at the illustration. "The painting you're looking for?"

"Yes. Beautiful, isn't it?"

"Well, I wouldn't go that far," Edna said with a sniff and began brushing. "It's too bad they don't have the whole thing," she mused after a few moments. "I suppose that was what you were hoping to see."

"Yes," Henrietta agreed absently as Edna began twisting the ends of her auburn locks. "Wait just a moment," she said, the meaning of Edna's words suddenly sinking in, causing goosebumps to run down her arms. She turned slowly in her seat to face Edna. "What do you mean, *the whole thing*?"

"Just that they have only a part of it," Edna mumbled, several hair pins in her mouth. "At least as far as I could see."

Henrietta's heart quickened just a little. "You saw it? A part of it?" she asked breathlessly. "Which part?"

Edna pointed to the Just Judges panel and removed the pins. "That one there, I'm pretty sure. Unless I was mistaken, like," she said, looking nervous now. "Looks to be the boring bit."

"Oh, Edna! Where is it?" Henrietta stood up.

"Why, it's out in the stables, miss. Guess it ain't worth all that much if it's out there. Sure that's the one you're looking for?" Edna's face was scrunched up skeptically.

"The stables?" Henrietta's mind was racing. "What were you doing out there?"

Edna blushed deeply. "Don't be angry, miss. Please don't be angry. Nothing happened."

"What do you mean nothing happened?"

"Just that . . . just that after our trip into town, Pascal was kind enough to show me all around the estate. Well, parts of it, anyway. He wanted to show me the stables where he used to work, and, well, one thing sort of led to another, and we ended up having a bit of a kiss and a cuddle, as he called it." Edna's face was beet red.

"Where in the stable?" Henrietta demanded.

"Way up in the loft where the extra hay is stored." Edna was twisting the brush around and around in her hands. "He has a little place hollowed out, you see, and as we . . . as we sat there . . . I happened to look up and that's where I saw it. In the rafters. I thought at the time it was a strange place for a painting, but, well, I suppose I *was* a little distracted."

"Oh, my God!" Henrietta glanced at the clock on the mantel, trying to calculate if she could make it to the stables and back before dinner. *She couldn't possibly make it!* Well, she would have to. She would make some excuse.

"Edna, give me the diamonds! Hurry!" She slipped on her shoes, as she clipped on the earrings Edna handed to her. "Here," Henrietta said, sitting on the vanity stool again, "help me with the necklace." Flustered, Edna's fingers slipped a few times before she finally secured the diamond necklace around Henrietta's neck. "There. That's good. Let's go!" Henrietta said, clutching the silver stole from the end of the bed and hurrying toward the door.

"Go? Go where, miss? I haven't done your hair yet!"

"It looks fine. Come on, Edna, you've got to show me this painting before I go in to dinner."

"Right now?" Edna asked, trailing after her. "It's quite a distance, miss."

"Yes," Henrietta whispered once they were in the hallway. She put a finger to her lips. "Let's use the servants' staircase. You lead the way."

"Oh, miss," Edna said, scurrying in front of her. "Mr. Clive won't like this."

"Yes, he will. This is very important, Edna. But we must hurry."

Edna led her mistress down the servant staircase into the bowels of the château and hurried through the dull, thickly plastered hallways, all of which had extremely low ceilings. Along the way, they met several servants, who, though they looked surprised to see Henrietta, thankfully said nothing, merely bowing slightly as she and Edna raced past.

Once outside, Henrietta wrapped the stole around her shoulders and followed Edna, as she led her down the drive toward the stables. Edna had been correct when she said it was a distance, and after walking a good five minutes, Henrietta began to reconsider the wisdom of this plan. Perhaps she should have found a way to extract Clive first? That or worn different shoes. Well, it was too late now. And, anyway, it would have been difficult to get Clive away without attracting suspicion. Surely the other guests had arrived by now.

At first glance, the yard in front of the stone barn, clearly centuries old, looked to be deserted as Edna and Henrietta finally reached the main double doors, only the tops of which were tied open. There was no activity in the vicinity and no noise save the sound of horses neighing and snorting within.

"Where is everyone?" Henrietta asked.

"They're probably all up at the other garage. That's where they park the automobiles. This part's just for the carriages."

"So where is it?" Henrietta asked, poking her head inside. "The painting I mean."

"You sure about this, miss? It's awfully dirty inside."

"Well, we're here now," Henrietta responded, though she did think, again, that it had perhaps been a mistake to rush out here in her silver heels. "And we need to hurry, Edna."

"All right, miss," she said, forlornly. "Watch your step."

Henrietta followed the girl inside, the oddly combined smell of manure and fragrant hay hitting her immediately. Although the sun had already begun its slow summer descent, it was still blindingly bright outside compared to the dark interior of the stables. Henrietta blinked, waiting for her eyes to adjust.

"It's back here, miss," Edna said, leading her past a row of abandoned milking stalls and through a low stone doorway in the back. "At least, I think this is where it was."

Henrietta tried to hold her dress up as she gingerly trod across the stone floor strewn with bits of hay and crusted with what she hoped was simply dirt and not manure. She followed Edna through the stone archway, both of them ducking, and down a short passageway, which opened up to a bigger room with haymows along the far wall filled to the ceiling with hay. Eagerly, Henrietta brushed past Edna to peer into the room, hoping to spot the panel from where she stood.

"It's not in there, miss," Edna said. "It's this way."

"But we've just come from there," Henrietta said, peering back into the passageway.

"It's up there," Edna pointed to the slats of a wooden ladder cut into the stone itself and leading to a completely black hole far above them.

"What's up there?" Henrietta asked, suddenly feeling dizzy as memories flooded her mind of jumping down a laundry chute at Dunning Asylum to escape a deranged nurse.

"It's another hayloft, miss. It looks scary, but it's nice and cozy up there."

"Edna! What were you thinking? Going up into a dark, deserted hayloft with a strange man?" Henrietta hissed.

Edna immediately looked as though she had been struck. "Well, I guess I didn't think, miss. But he's not really a strange man. He's awfully nice. He bought me a coffee in town, and we went up here to find a litter of kittens. Just born they were, and he wanted to show me, and he didn't take advantage. Well, not much, like . . ."

"We'll discuss it later. For now, I need to get up there," Henrietta said, observing the stone-and-wood ladder, wondering how she was going to climb it while wearing a long, hip-hugging gown.

"Here, I'll go first, miss." Edna grabbed hold of the first slat and put her foot up. "See? It's not so hard."

Henrietta slipped off her shoes and pulled her dress up so that it was nearly around her waist.

"Miss!"

"No one's here to see me. Just keep going, Edna," Henrietta commanded and concentrated on the slats in front of her, not daring to look up again at the yawning black hole lest the nauseousness that had suddenly come over her at the memory of Dunning got worse. Instead, she continued to climb slowly, struggling a bit to find her footing on the uneven stone. She was sure her stockings were tearing.

"Almost there, miss," Edna cried from somewhere above. Henrietta chanced a glance up, but the girl was gone now, disappeared into the blackness.

"Here, take my hand."

Henrietta saw a small white hand poke through the blackness. She reached for it, holding onto the top slat with her other hand. Edna clasped her hand and gingerly pulled until Henrietta was able to finally step onto the wooden floor of the loft. She let her dress fall back down to her ankles. The air was very close and thick up here, and Henrietta had a hard time catching her breath. She peered around and was surprised that it wasn't entirely dark, as it appeared to be from below. There were small round windows at the two opposite peaks, through which dusty light filtered in. Beside them were squares, slatted, which looked to be some sort of air vent, though one of them was almost completely clogged with a bird's nest. In fact, the rafters were full of nests, Henrietta observed, her head titled back. Surely Edna had made a mistake. One of the world's masterpieces could not possibly be stored up here, barely covered from the elements . . .

"It's over here, miss." Edna made her way, Henrietta following, through what seemed like a maze of hay bales stacked nearly to the ceiling until they came to a little "room," where the bales weren't stacked quite so high and where one had obviously been untied and strewn about on the floor and covered with a plaid blanket. "This is it, miss." Edna gestured awkwardly at what was obviously Pascal's nest, which caused Henrietta to feel a fresh lick of irritation. The rogue!

"There, miss." Edna pointed to the rafters above the hay nest. "Stand here; you'll see it."

Henrietta carefully stepped on top of the blanket and looked directly up. At first, she saw nothing but the rafters, but as she stood staring, she began to perceive that there was indeed something wedged up between them. She stepped to the side and saw, very clearly now, an image of the now-recognizable three horsemen, the rocky cliff behind them, and beyond that, the castle. Her heart began to beat a little faster as she made a complete circle, observing it from every angle.

Could this really be the Just Judges panel of the Ghent Altarpiece? Her mind was racing at the prospect. *Yes,* she decided. *It must be!*

"That it, miss? The one you were looking for?"

"Yes! Yes, I believe so." She looked excitedly at the girl. "Oh, Edna! We've got to get back to the château. I must find Mr. Howard." She gave the panel one last glance before charging back through the maze until she reached the hole in the floor. She was grateful that she could at least see the bottom from this vantage point and went down on her knees, edging herself backwards until her foot was in the hole and grappling for the first slat. When her foot finally connected, she eased herself into the hole and began climbing down.

"Oh, miss! You won't tell him, will you?" Edna squeaked from above her.

"Of course, I'm going to tell him. This is the painting we've been searching for!"

"No, I mean about . . . about how I found it," she called, herself climbing down now. "About Pascal, I mean . . ."

"Edna," Henrietta said as she stepped onto the stone floor, a worrisome thought suddenly flooding her mind, "does Pascal know you saw the painting? Did you point it out?"

"Well, I'm not certain, miss," Edna muttered, midway down the ladder. "He might have noticed me looking at it."

"But you didn't discuss it?"

Edna jumped from the last rung and shook her head.

"Good," Henrietta mused. "Don't mention it to him. Or to any of the servants. No one can know."

"But why, miss?" Edna asked, nervously looking over her shoulder.

"Because it's a stolen painting. A very valuable one, and some people who are not very nice are looking for it. So mum's the word," she said, looking directly into Edna's eyes and clutching her forearms. "Understand?" she said sternly.

"Yes, miss," Edna squeaked.

"Come on, then. We've got to hurry."

Chapter 18

Henrietta managed to get her breathing under control by the time she walked into the main hall, filled now with what looked like some twenty-five people, if she guessed correctly. It surprised her that the Von Harmons actually knew this many people, as they seemed rather reclusive, not to mention eccentric. Before she could even locate Clive, however, her stomach clenched at the sight of Valentin making his way toward her.

Henrietta looked around quickly, trying to find anyone else she might begin a conversation with, but there was no one in the immediate vicinity, so she instead braced herself for what she assumed would be an unpleasant exchange.

"Henrietta," Valentin said in an annoyed tone, as if she were a recalcitrant schoolgirl. "Here you are. We were getting rather worried."

"Yes, I . . . I . . ." Henrietta's eyes darted around the room. "I needed some air. So I just stepped out for a moment." She gave him a false smile.

Valentin, however, merely stared at her, as if he didn't believe her in the slightest. He surprised her, then, by slowly reaching out a hand toward her. It was all she could do not to flinch, and she stifled a little cry in her throat that threatened to escape. He did not touch her, however, but instead pulled a piece of hay from her hair. His brow was furrowed as he held it up.

"Now, how did that get there, I wonder," he said coolly, flicking it to the floor.

Henrietta gave a little laugh. "I have no idea!" She made a show of looking around. "Have you seen my husband?" she tried to ask as casually as she could.

"As a matter of fact, I believe he went back upstairs to fetch you. Most concerned, he was. It is quaint the way he is so attentive to your well-being, is it not?" His tone was light, but his face was still stony.

"Thank you, Valentin," she said stiffly and was just about to make an excuse to powder her nose when a man—*dressed in a full Nazi uniform!*—approached them. Henrietta bit her lip, hard, and tried to control her panic. *Where was Clive?*

"Are you not going to introduce us, Valentin?" the man asked, a mischievous smile hovering about his lips. He had dark hair and a thin mustache and was oddly very attractive. He could easily have been a movie star with his bright blue eyes. It was most unsettling.

"Of course. Major Wirnhier, may I present Mrs. Howard. Mrs. Howard, Major Wirnhier."

Major Wirnhier took Henrietta's outstretched hand and kissed it. "Charmed, madame," he said with only a slight German accent.

"Mrs. Howard and her husband are visiting from Chicago," Valentin explained in a bored tone. "Mrs. Howard is a long-lost relative, you see. A Von Harmon."

"How intriguing," Major Wirnhier said, looking her up and down and making no attempt to hide it. "It is a shame you are married."

Henrietta was spared from having to respond to this impertinence by a booming voice behind her.

"Countess!" called the baron, who quickly appeared by her side now. He was dressed in an old-fashioned suit, complete with a scarlet banner across his chest that had several medals dangling from it. Ignoring both the major and Valentin, he looped his arm conspiratorially through Henrietta's. "I've been looking everywhere for you, *chérie*. You look exquisite."

"Countess?" Major Wirnhier asked and looked questioningly at Valentin.

Henrietta could see Valentin bristle. "A pet name," he said quickly. "It means nothing." He shifted his body slightly, then, so that he partially blocked the baron and Henrietta from the major's view. "Come, Major. Let me introduce you to Monsieur Leroux. You'll find him most resourceful." He held out his arm, gesturing for the major to proceed him.

"Very well," the major said. He stretched slightly to see around Valentin and tilted his head deferentially. "Mrs. Howard. Baron. Perhaps we will have time later." He clicked his heels together, then, and turned in the direction Valentin had indicated. Valentin began to follow, but then unexpectedly stopped and retraced his steps so that he was standing very close to Henrietta. "Should you need any more air, Mrs. Howard," he said in a low growl, "please allow me to escort you. The estate can be dangerous at night."

He must know! Henrietta's heart was pounding in her chest, and she could think of nothing to say to him. Finally, however, she managed to utter her thanks and turned away.

"*Chérie*, you are trembling," the baron said, putting his lips close to her ear. She jumped accordingly. She had almost forgotten he was still by her side, her arm wrapped through his. "Are you chilled, or is it fear?" he asked in a low voice. "The enemy is near, *oui*, but I will protect you as I did last time. I will not fail you. Come to my rooms tonight, or shall I come to you?"

"Baron, please! I must find my husband!"

"Yves is here?" The baron looked around nervously. "No wonder you tremble, my little bird. Perhaps tonight is the night we flee, *oui*? I have it all planned. Please say yes this time, *chérie*. Do not deny me any further. No longer will you have to endure his loathsome touch." Henrietta followed the baron's gaze, which oddly followed Valentin.

Did he think Valentin was her husband, this Yves, as he kept referring to?

"Baron, please, I must . . . I must powder my nose," she said, trying
to pull her arm from his grasp, but he held her tight. After several
tugs, however, she succeeded.

"You are so strong, *chérie*. It excites me!" he whispered, twirling
his mustache.

Henrietta looked desperately around the room and finally spotted Clive, who had just entered at the other end. His eyes found
hers immediately, and he began to make his way through the crowd.
Relief flooded through her. "Excuse me for a moment, Baron. I'll just
be a moment." She hurried away from him and rushed to Clive, who
gently grasped her upper arms.

"Darling, where have you been?" His eyes were wide with worry.
"I've looked everywhere."

"Clive, I found the panel!" she whispered.

"What?"

"Yes, I've found the panel. It's in the stables," she said, taking his
arm and leading him away from where the baron stood hovering,
watching them intently.

"The stables?" Clive hissed. "Is that where you've been? But why?"

"Yes," Henrietta said, retreating further into a relatively isolated
corner. "It was Edna, actually. I'll explain it all later."

"Are you sure it's the panel?"

"Yes, of course, I'm sure! I'm the one that's been looking at the
book every night trying to puzzle it out."

A servant appeared in front of them, then, with a tray of champagne, but Clive waved him away.

"Where in the stables?" Clive asked in a low voice.

"Up in the rafters of the hayloft. It's cleverly tucked away. Do you
think—"

"*Messieurs et Mesdames*," boomed out Renard from where he
stood at the entrance of the hall. "Dinner is served. Please follow me."

Henrietta looked nervously at Clive. "I was going to suggest I show you."

"Not now." His eyes darted around the room. "How unfortunate that we find it the night before we're leaving *and* the night the house is full of Nazis. Just our luck."

"Yes? What are they doing here?"

"I've no idea. I assume they are the business associates Valentin was referring to."

People were brushing past them, heading for the dining room. Henrietta could see Valentin's eye on them from across the room where he was standing with a group of officers. "I think Valentin knows I know," she whispered to Clive.

"How?"

"He found a bit of hay in my hair when I came in. And it's the way he is not taking his eyes off me."

"Jesus."

"What should we do?"

"Let me think. I'll—" She stopped talking when she saw that Major Wirnhier was now approaching. He stopped in front of them and bowed slightly.

"Mrs. Howard," he said with a thin smile. "I'm your escort, I believe." He held out his arm to Henrietta, who, after a quick glance at Clive, took it, surprised that the Von Harmons were following the formal English system of dinner etiquette. "You must be Mr. Howard," the major said, holding out his other hand to Clive, who grasped it firmly. "I'm Major Wirnhier. I believe you're with Mademoiselle Guillot," he said with a slight nod of his head toward a group standing not far off.

"Ah. I see. I was not informed," Clive said stiffly. "Thank you, Major." He gave the man the smallest of deferential nods. "I'll see you inside," he said quietly to Henrietta, who watched him then approach the group near them and extract a young brunette.

"You seem distracted, Mrs. Howard," Major Wirnhier commented, as he led her toward the dining room. "Might I even suggest agitated.

Are you quite well?" His startlingly blue eyes looked at her with what seemed real concern.

"No, I'm fine, Major. Just a little tired, perhaps."

The major was silent, then, as he led her toward their assigned seats and pulled her chair out for her. Henrietta despaired that she had not been placed at the other end of the table, closer to where Clive and Claudette were arranged. The two of them, she observed, were already engaged in conversation, and Henrietta saw Claudette lean toward Clive and whisper something to him, which caused him to actually laugh, a feat that was nearly impossible, Henrietta knew. It must have been something terribly funny, she assumed, but pushed down her curiosity to look around the rest of the table. The baron, she quickly noticed, was nowhere to be seen. Had Valentin had him whisked up to his rooms in case he said something embarrassing, or was he somehow indisposed?

Either way, Valentin had taken the baron's place at the head of the table. On his right was a bullish looking man who wore the German uniform of a captain, if Henrietta was not mistaken. He had shorn blond hair and small, cruel eyes. His neck was the size of Henrietta's thigh, and he was deep in conversation with Valentin, their heads slightly bent toward each other.

Major Wirnhier seated himself in the chair beside her, signaling that not only had he been her dinner escort, but he was apparently to be her table companion as well, at least on her right. On her left was a Madame Faucheux, who, Henrietta sadly soon discovered, did not speak a word of English.

"Are you sure you're quite well, Mrs. Howard?" Major Wirnhier asked in a low voice as the servants began pouring the wine.

"Yes, perfectly, Major," she said, forcing herself to examine him more carefully, trying to control her fear. If she was to be seated next to him for the entirety of the dinner, she quickly decided, she might as well try to extract some information from him. She sat up straighter and studied his face. His jaw was firm and angular, and a thick Adam's apple could be seen above the stiff black collar of his uniform, the silver SS insignia shining in the flickering candlelight.

All in all, his looks would be deemed severe had it not been for his long lashes and bright-blue eyes, which were studying her intently. In fact, had she not known him for the enemy, she might very well have been charmed by his polite, concerned manner. There was something about his voice, however, that chilled her.

"I suppose I'm worried about the baron," she said, taking a sip from her glass.

"The baron?"

"Yes, the baron. He's not here at dinner," she said, gesturing slightly, "though we saw him just a few moments ago. I hope he's not unwell."

"Do not worry, madame. He is fine, I can assure you. He rarely attends these dinners."

"You . . . you've been here before?"

Major Wirnhier laughed. "But of course. Though they are rarely this elaborate. This is for your benefit, I am sure." He took a sip of his wine. "The Von Harmons and I are not exactly friends, but we are what one would call associates."

"I see. Do . . . do army officers often have business dealings with private citizens?" she dared to ask.

The major let out a little laugh. "Sometimes, as it happens. But who said anything about business?"

Henrietta's mind raced, wondering what this answer meant, while a servant placed a small plate of goose pâté and pickled onion slices before her. Her stomach roiled. She could definitely not eat at a time like this, but she worried that not doing so would draw unwanted attention. Uneasily, she picked up her fork.

"You must not be put off by my uniform," the major said, eagerly taking a bite of his pâté and spearing an onion alongside of it. "I'm not so very different, you know. And as a Von Harmon, surely you must be not quite so hostile to us Germans."

"You speak remarkably good English. Does everyone here?" she deflected.

"Thank you for that compliment, madame. But, no. Not everyone. Captain Steuben," he said nodding his head, "for example, does not."

Henrietta glanced down the table at Valentin and the bulldog beside him. Unfortunately, Captain Steuben happened to look up at that moment and, catching her eye, would not let go until Henrietta looked away.

"Many see the Führer as aggressive," Major Wirnhier continued. "Power hungry, but he is uniting Germany. Making us strong again," he said proudly.

"Is that what you call it?" Henrietta dared asked.

"Many see his edicts as barbarous, but I am not so sure. He seeks to relieve society of the burden of its weak and feeble. The insane, the cripples, so that we might be stronger. Less encumbered." He took another bite of pâté. "What is wrong with housing them together where they can be cared for by the state and not left to reproduce?" His voice was calm and deliberate, as if explaining, say, how an automobile worked. "It is the way of nature, is it not, to eliminate the malignant? The Führer is simply aiding that process. Speeding it up, as it were. Some say it is more humane."

Henrietta thought of little Anna and felt sick.

"You have barely touched your food, madame. Is it not to your liking?"

"I . . . I suppose I'm not hungry."

"This food is too heavy for you. Too rich. Not what one would be served in America, I am sure."

"No, it's not that."

"You seem disturbed, Mrs. Howard. Unsettled. You need more wine." He signaled a servant to fill her glass.

"No, I—" she said, trying to wave off the servant, but she was too late to stop him.

"You must not mistake me, madame. I am a loyal soldier of the Reich, it is true," he said, his eyes darting toward Captain Steuben, "but I am also merely trying to survive, like everyone else. This seemed the easiest way," he said, gesturing toward his uniform.

"To join the army as a way of surviving a war?" she asked, intrigued. "Forgive me, but that seems counterintuitive."

"Some might say. But the Reich will soon bleed across Europe, and it is far better to be a part of it than to oppose it."

"I'm not so sure."

"It is a luxury to be able to make that statement. To be able to take the moral high ground. Not everyone has that privilege." Again, he said it matter-of-factly, without any bitterness. "I am merely a banker's son. I joined early in hopes of getting a good position."

A servant removed her untouched food, then, and replaced it with a plate of roast pork, potatoes, and sauerkraut. She wasn't sure she could eat any of this, either.

"And did you?" she asked, taking her wine glass in hand instead. "Find a good position, that is?"

"Yes, I believe so. I am what you would call a supply officer."

"A supply officer?" She took a sip. "I imagine that would be quite difficult. Finding supplies for a whole army?"

Major Wirnhier laughed. "I am sure it is, but that is not my province. I am charged with procuring special items. Items that are difficult to locate." His eyes were bright with a secret.

Henrietta's skin prickled. "I see. And what sort of things would those be?" She said it casually, almost playfully, forcing herself to use her charms on even such a one as him.

"Many things," he said, looking at her appreciatively. "Things that interest the Führer or the Reich. As a matter of fact, that is why you find me here this night. I have been told that the Von Harmons have come into possession of something of great value that might interest the Führer," he added in a low tone.

Henrietta's heart began to beat a little faster. "How extraordinary, Major. How did you discover this?"

Major Wirnhier laughed again. "The Führer has many spying eyes, madame. You would be surprised."

"And what is this item you are hunting for?" she asked, concentrating on keeping her voice steady as she batted her eyelashes twice— not too much, just enough to intrigue him.

"You are a most beautiful woman, Mrs. Howard," he said, his eyes resting briefly on her breasts. "But of course, you already know that." He leaned toward her.

"Thank you, Major," she answered sweetly. "But I am so very curious. Perhaps we should play a guessing game." She made a show of looking around the room. "Is it the jade pagoda in the drawing room?"

"No, but that is fine indeed."

"Perhaps a sword?" she dared asked, thinking of the Arma Christi.

"A sword?" The major's lip curled into a smile, and his eyes held amusement. "No, not a sword."

"Hmmm. Perhaps a painting, then" she said coyly, gesturing at the ones on the walls around them while taking a sip of her wine.

Major Wirnhier tilted his head ever so slightly, the fraction of an inch, and gave her a small smile. "Perhaps."

She felt sure she had guessed it!

"Your husband seems much older than you," he said, taking a bite of his pork. "Perhaps he retires early?" He looked at her.

"Sometimes." She felt her leg tremble. She knew she was entering dangerous waters. "Might you show me this wonderous item before you leave with it?" she asked demurely.

"In the morning, perhaps?"

"We leave in the morning, I am afraid. So it would have to be tonight." His gaze flicked to her breasts again. "If you are really that interested. There is much I could show you, in fact."

"By all means. I'll see if I can get away."

"Later, then," he said, laying a hand on her thigh, causing her to stiffen, though she responded with what she hoped was a convincing smile. She looked down the table at Clive, but, alas, he did not notice how far out to sea she had drifted.

Chapter 19

Elsie hesitated for a few seconds, looking at the envelope she had neatly addressed to *Mr. Oldrich Exley* one more time before dropping it in the mailbox outside of Mundelein's skyscraper building and then breathed a deep sigh.

It was finally finished. No going back now.

She stared at the mailbox, not really seeing it, and then turned away. There was nothing more to be done. She had composed the final version of the letter to her grandfather in the wee hours of the morning before succumbing to a fitful sleep at her desk. She awoke with a start early this morning, the sun's rays hitting her square in the face, and read it all through again before hastily addressing the envelope and marching it down the street before she could change her mind.

It was not a very long letter, just enough to inform her grandfather that she was renouncing his money and his authority over her. That she had already spoken to Sr. Bernard, who had agreed that she might join the novitiate in the fall semester with the goal of eventually taking Holy Orders. She hoped, she had written, that he would not punish the rest of the family because she was answering the call of God, but if he did, it was his decision and one which he would someday have to reconcile with God himself. She further hoped, she had added, that she might still call him Grandfather, but if he chose to deny her even this, then she would simply have to accept it as God's will. Either way, she promised to faithfully pray for his soul daily for the rest of her life and hoped that his heart might be filled with peace.

It was an honest letter in that Elsie believed everything she had written, though it did contain one small fib. In truth, Sr. Bernard had *not* agreed that she could join the novitiate in the fall, but had instead told Elsie that she would consider it. But Elsie, ever hopeful, had decided to view it as a certainty.

After the disappointing interview with Julia and Mr. Bennett, Elsie had taken matters into her own hands and had sought out Sr. Bernard as soon as she could, creeping up to her office on the second floor of the skyscraper building and requesting an appointment. Mercifully, Sr. Bernard had been free at that particular moment and had taken the girl into her sanctuary.

"My daughter, what troubles you so?" Sr. Bernard had asked soothingly as she gestured to the two cane chairs opposite the large mahogany desk where she herself sat, her back ramrod straight and her habit perfectly starched.

Elsie gratefully took a seat and felt herself immediately relax, despite her woes. She loved Sr. Bernard's quiet wood-paneled office for the peace it exuded, its only ornamentation being a large crucifix on one wall and one tiny stained-glass window. There were no candles anywhere, but the office smelled faintly of beeswax all the same. Elsie sat staring at Sr. Bernard, whom, in truth, she loved dearly. A part of her longed to be attached to Sr. Bernard always, living this life of quiet simplicity and peace, with no worries, no wrinkles in the habit of life to disturb her. There was only one niggling snag, which was the fact that she was in love with Gunther, but surely that would fade over time, she prayed. She would work hard to transfer her love for him to a love of God and the church.

"Elsie," Sr. Bernard had said after Elsie had again asked—nay, pleaded—to be allowed to join the convent, "remember what I told you earlier when you came to me asking the same thing? That the veil is not to be donned in fear but is to be put on with great love? Forsaking all others. Can you really do that in light of your . . . romantic attachment to Gunther?"

Elsie had broken down into tears, then, wondering how Sr. Bernard knew about her feelings for Gunther, and had hastily explained that Gunther now refused to marry her.

Sr. Bernard seemed surprised by this and asked her gently if there was anything she wished to tell her. Anything at all, without judgement.

"No, nothing like that," Elsie sniffed, sensing what Sr. Bernard feared. For a moment, she contemplated telling her the whole story but then quickly decided against it. It sounded ridiculous, she sadly realized, like the plot of a cheap melodrama. Besides, she knew it would not sit well with Sr. Bernard if she explained that if she could not have Gunther, she would have no one. And also that joining the convent was her only way to remove herself not only from her grandfather's grasp, but to release Gunther and Anna from the grasp of Heinrich and Rita. If she cut herself off from her grandfather's money and influence, then it naturally followed, she hoped, that Heinrich and Rita would lose interest in Anna, as there would be no money to be gained.

She did not reveal all of this to Sr. Bernard, of course, but she *did* inform her that either way, she would have to drop out of her classes, as she felt she could no longer accept the Howards' money for her education.

Elsie supposed that there had always been a part of her that knew that Henrietta's bold declaration to fund her education had been dubious, misguided at best, as obviously, the money had come from Clive, but Elsie hadn't wanted to face it. Now, however, after Sidney Bennett's blunt explanation, she had no choice but to acknowledge that it was money wrongfully taken, money that was not Henrietta's to give.

Of all the things that Elsie said to Sr. Bernard that day, it was this declaration that seemed to cause the most alarm in her mentor. "Oh, no, Elsie, you mustn't stop your education. You have a gift."

"Well, that may be," Elsie had said uncomfortably, not enjoying the compliment, "but I . . . I can no longer pay for my classes."

"But I thought your sister was your financier," Sr. Bernard said calmly, her hands perfectly folded.

Elsie wasn't sure how to explain the situation. "Well, all that's changed."

"Have you quarreled?"

"No, but I . . . I no longer wish to accept anyone's money, Sister. I—" She broke off here, flustered.

"I see."

"Surely I don't have to go to college to become a nun?" Elsie blurted, her hands twisting in her lap now. "Can't I just be an ordinary nun? One who cleans the convent or something? I wouldn't mind, Sister," she pleaded.

Sr. Bernard had merely laughed. "No, my child. That's what the novitiates are for. No, we cannot waste the gift you have been given. Do you not remember your desire to become a teacher for the poor? Or has that changed, too?"

"No, but, I—"

"If you have a true vocation, Elsie, the church will provide you with the education you need to become a teacher, though you will have to work for it."

Elsie's eyes widened. She hadn't considered this. She quickly thought it through and decided that she would gladly work to earn her way. "Are you sure, Sister?"

Sr. Bernard majestically stood up now and gazed at the large crucifix for a few seconds before looking back at Elsie. "There is one condition, however," she said quietly.

Elsie looked at her expectantly from where she sat, crumpled and upset.

"You will be allowed to begin your postulancy here, but I must insist that you work toward your novitiate at our sister college, Clark, in Dubuque."

"Dubuque? Where's Dubuque?" Elsie felt a sudden burst of panic.

"It is in Iowa. It is a beautiful campus, just like this one, and a fine place for you to work and study and pray about your decision. If you agree, I will write to Sister Theodore and make the arrangements."

"But I . . . I can't just leave!" Elsie cried.

"But why not, my child? This is the life you say you desire. To leave behind home and loved ones to become a bride of Christ and willingly go wherever you are needed, to be His hands and feet on Earth. Remember that your final vows will include obedience." She gazed lovingly at Elsie. "Can you do this?" she asked gently.

"I . . ." Elsie began and then stopped.

Could she? Somehow, she hadn't fully thought this through. She imagined that in becoming a nun she would remain here at Mundelein, close to her family and to . . . to Gunther, of course, devoting her life to prayer and teaching. But, she hastily considered now, what it would mean to take irrevocable vows of poverty, chastity, and obedience?

Poverty, she knew, would be easy, as she had spent her entire life— until recently, that is—being poor. Being forced by Grandfather to live in the Palmer Square house with a staff of servants had always made her squeamish and uncomfortable. In fact, so self-conscious was she in this role that she had never once asked a servant to do a single thing for her, insisting on making her own bed and doing her own laundry. The only thing she was not allowed to do was to cook. Though she had, once upon a time, cooked all of the meals in their shabby apartment on Armitage, she was now never allowed anywhere near the kitchen by the domineering chef who resided there.

Chastity also would not be difficult, she blushingly decided. While it was true that she was no longer a virgin, she had not enjoyed Harrison's intimacies. And though she had felt odd stirrings—ones that had, in truth, left her breathless—the few times Gunther had kissed her, she felt sure that she could successfully push away any resultant current or future carnal desires with the right amount of prayer.

That only left obedience, and before this conversation with Sr. Bernard, Elsie had assumed that obedience would be the easiest of all. Hadn't she ever been dutiful and compliant to any authority for all of her young life? But now, she suddenly realized as she sat in the chair before Sr. Bernard, she was not so sure. She had refused to obey Aunt Agatha and Grandfather, and now she was finding it hard to blindly agree to go to Dubuque to study and then to wherever the Mother Superior of the Order of the Blessed Virgin Mary might wish to send her. What if she was sent to teach in Africa, for example? Africa? *Oh, God . . . perhaps she was making a mistake!* And could she really leave her family forever?

Well, she considered, trying to control her rapid breathing, Sr. Bernard's eyes upon her, she supposed she could.

The boys were gone, Doris and Donny were wrapped up in Nanny's world now, Henrietta in Clive's world, and even Julia, her adopted sister, had her own cares and life. That just left Ma. There was a slight pull on her heart when she thought about her mother, but, deep down, Elsie knew she was not her mother's favorite; perhaps she was too much like her in too many ways. No, Elsie was sure, Ma would not miss her.

And what about Gunther? Could she really leave him behind? Well, she would have to. Wasn't that the whole point of becoming a nun? She couldn't expect to just live and work beside him, loving him from the top floor of the skyscraper like some sort of Rapunzel while he toiled away below as the custodian. It would be torturous for them both. No, she quickly concluded, it would be better if she left, if she were sent far, far away. Then at least he and Anna might continue to live here in peace, safe from fortune hunters or anyone else that sought them harm, she rationalized, thinking about Dunning and even the orphanage in Germany. It was a sacrifice she was quite willing to make.

"Yes, Sister," Elsie finally said, standing now. "Yes, of course, I will."

"Very well, then," Sr. Bernard said with a kind smile. "I will make the arrangements. Can you be ready in one week's time? Clark begins their term in early August, and there is not much time for you to get settled."

"One week?" Elsie asked, her stomach twisting.

"Do you need longer to consider?" Sr. Bernard asked gently.

"No . . . I . . . no, of course, I can go. There is nothing for me here."

"Are you quite sure?"

"Yes," Elsie mumbled, unbidden tears welling up in her eyes.

"My child, what is wrong?" Sr. Bernard asked, stepping closer.

Elsie quickly wiped her eyes. "Nothing, Sister. I'm . . . it's just that . . ."

"Just that what?" she asked gently, as if she were hoping she would confess something.

"Just that I'll miss you."

Sr. Bernard had enveloped her in her arms, then. "Ah. Well, we'll see each other from time to time, God willing, that is." She pulled back and searched Elsie's bleary eyes and then kissed her on her forehead.

Elsie turned from the mailbox now and walked dejectedly back to Philomena, rethinking her decision for the hundredth time since her interview with Sr. Bernard just yesterday. She felt emotionally drained, not only from the conversation but from writing her confession to Grandfather, and she longed to lie down on her bed and sleep. She didn't dare skip her classes, however. They seemed more important than ever, now that she was going to take up her studies at a brand new school.

She supposed that she should go tell Ma the news as soon as possible. To say good-bye and to warn her that her life might be changing in the very near future if Grandfather followed through on his threats. She could only imagine the choice words that would fly from Ma's mouth. Perhaps she should not actually go but merely write her a letter, she considered, but she knew that was the cowardly way out. Henrietta, too, would have to be told, but she would wait and write to her later. She had already caused her enough trouble while on her first honeymoon, and there was no need to trouble her now while she was on her exciting trip through Europe. Telling Gunther would be harder, she knew, and tried to think about how best to go about it. He, too, would be upset with her decision to become a nun, as he had been the first time she had brought it up.

She had reached Philomena now, and she went around to the back, slowly opening the kitchen door to avoid having to face whoever was on duty, probably Sr. Joseph again, in the front lobby. She had no desire to explain why she had been out on the city streets even before the sun had fully risen. She peered around the kitchen and saw that the breakfast things had all been set out, but Sr. Alphonse, who could normally be found here in the early mornings, was thankfully nowhere to be seen. Elsie quickly crossed the room where she had spent so many happy evenings with Gunther during the Christmas holidays and proceeded up the back staircase, her fingers running along the black metal railing. *Could she really leave Mundelein?* She swallowed hard. *Of course, she could.* She would do it for him.

She quickly wiped the few tears from her eyes and then pushed open her bedroom door as quietly as she could. Her stealth, however, was unnecessary, as Melody was already awake and dressed and let out a little cry of delight upon seeing her.

"There you are! I've been terribly worried!" she exclaimed. "Your bed doesn't look slept in and I thought, gracious! What's happened? I seem to remember you sitting at your desk when I went to sleep at night, but I didn't hear you leave. If I didn't know you better, I might have thought you were out paying a visit to a certain custodian's residence," she said with a little smile, "but just as I was contemplating such a situation, Sister Joseph surprised me by knocking to say that there was a telephone call for you. Did she not tell you?"

"No, I . . . I came up the back. A telephone call?" she asked nervously and for a moment imagined it had been from Grandfather, reacting to her letter, but that was obviously impossible. She had just now mailed it. She rubbed her brow. She must try to get more sleep. Things were beginning to blur in her mind. "Did she say who it was?"

"Yes, it was that nurse you have at the house. You're supposed to ring her back."

"Nurse Flanagan? Again?" Elsie's heart immediately began to race, imagining that Heinrich and Rita had reappeared. In a panic, she contemplated simply running out of Philomena to catch a cab, but she stopped herself. Maybe it wasn't that at all, she counseled herself. Maybe it was something simple, though Elsie couldn't think what that would be.

"Thanks, Melody," she said, her brow furrowed, and retreated back into the hall. Hurriedly, she made her way down the main staircase.

"Elsie! There you are. Where were you so early this morning?" Sr. Joseph chided.

"I . . . I was walking, Sister."

"Well, you have a telephone message," she said, handing her a piece of paper.

"May I use the telephone, Sister?"

"You may," she said stiffly, lifting the big black telephone from where it normally sat on the back desk and placing it on the counter where Elsie stood.

"Thank you, Sister," Elsie said and quickly dialed the operator. "PA 91452," she requested and waited for the connection to be made.

"But, remember, Elsie, you have to sign out, otherwise we don't know where to find you—"

Elsie nodded, not really listening, instead straining to hear the ringing at the other end of the receiver. No one picked up. As the seconds ticked by, Elsie's panic increased, and she considered hanging up and just going over there. Finally, someone answered.

"Von Harmon residence." It was Karl's unmistakable sleepy tone.

"Karl, this is Elsie. May I speak with Nurse Flanagan? I'm returning her call to me."

"Yes, miss. But, things are all topsy-turvy here this morning, I can tell you that. First, Nellie dropped the ash pail, and then—"

"Karl! Please!"

"Yes, miss."

Elsie heard a clunk, then, which she guessed was Karl putting down the receiver. She twirled the cotton cord, waiting for what seemed forever for someone to come back on the line. She glanced over at Sr. Joseph, who had retreated to her desk, but, Elsie was certain, was also listening.

"Elsie?" came the now-familiar voice of Nurse Flanagan.

"Oh, Nurse Flanagan! What is it? Is it that Heinrich again? Is it Ma? Or is it Anna? Has she had a fit?"

"No, it ain't anything like that. Yer ma's fine, and that git hasn't been back. Though I do think I saw him slinking around one night just after dark. Can't be certain though—"

"What is it, then?"

"Well, it does have to do with little Anna. Thought I should inform you that she's gone."

"Gone?" Elsie felt all the air leave her lungs. "What happened?"

"Now, before you get all hysterical on me, it was Gunther himself who took her."

"Gunther?"

"He showed up early this morning, said he wanted to take her for a bit. I wouldn't a thought anything odd about it, seeing as he takes her back with him from time to time, as you know. I asked him if I should pack her a bag, and he said no, that he would do it. But when I went upstairs just a bit ago, I noticed that *all* of her things are gone, not that there was much to start with, like. But that seemed strange, don't you think?"

Elsie breathed a little sigh of relief. "I think I understand," she said calmly. "I think he's bringing her back to Mundelein to stay with him."

"But I thought that nun over there said he couldn't do that."

"Yes, I know, but he's somehow got it into his head to try again. I'll . . . I'll go talk with him."

"Well, that's not all, though. Seems Nanny Kuntz overheard him talking to Anna in German, and she swears he told her they were going on a train. On an adventure."

Elsie could feel all the blood draining from her face. "Did he say where?"

"No. Except to tell her that they were going to live on a farm and that she could have her very own kitten."

"Oh, my God," Elsie said hoarsely, panic utterly filling her. He was fleeing. Just as he said he would.

"Thank you, Nurse Flanagan. I . . . I'm going to the train station now."

"Want me to meet you there? Or call the police?"

"No, there's nothing you can do. Stay there with Ma."

"Oh, yeah. She's in a right state, she is."

"Yes, I can imagine. See what you can do for her, and I'll let you know."

She hung up, then, and tried not to succumb to the panic that was overwhelming her. There was no need for him to leave because of her! She had already resolved the situation; it was she that should leave!

She turned to hurry up the stairs for her handbag and nearly ran into Melody coming down.

"What's happening?" she asked, full of intrigue.

"Oh, Melody! I've got to get to the train station. Gunther's taken Anna and is trying to flee."

"Oh, my! Oh, do let me come, too!"

Elsie considered. As much as she didn't want to ask for help, it might be easier to find Gunther if there were two of them. "Yes," she said quickly. "If you don't mind."

"Mind? Of course, I don't! This is just like the movie picture, *It Happened One Night*, only it's reversed a bit . . ."

Elsie groaned. Did Melody ever take anything seriously? "No, it's not! This is real life, Mel!"

"Well, I know *that*," she said, following her back up the stairs. "But what is it they say—art imitates life? Or is it the other way around?"

"Come on, Melody! We don't have time for all that. We have to go!"

Chapter 20

As soon as the ladies rose from the dinner table to adjourn to the drawing room, Henrietta breathed a sigh of relief, grateful to finally be free of Major Wirnhier's company. Normally, she could play a flirtatious hand easily, but there was something about the German that made the hair on the back of her neck stand up. Likewise, she sensed that he would not be so easy to escape from as had been the baron. He was certainly more serious, and, she guessed, deadly, if need be. He reminded her in an odd way of Neptune, and her stomach clenched at the memory of what that madman had nearly done to her.

The men stood now as well, waiting for the ladies to absent themselves. Wirnhier offered Henrietta a grim smile, which she barely acknowledged before turning away. She made a point of walking very near Clive and whispered, "I must speak to you. In the hallway. Whenever you can." Clive did not look at her but responded with a slight nod.

Henrietta followed the other ladies to the drawing room and, after a just few minutes of milling about, excused herself, saying she had to powder her nose. Claudette, thankfully, barely seemed to notice, so preoccupied was she in conversing with Madame Dupuis, the woman who had been seated to her left at dinner.

Henrietta crept out into the hallway and stood, shivering slightly, waiting for Clive. She did not have to wait long before he appeared, his face creased with concern. Hurriedly, she pulled him into a little alcove, which seemed to be an additional butler's pantry, if the extra napkins, serving dishes, wine glasses, and candles were any indication.

"What is it?" Clive asked in a low tone.

"I think the Germans are here to collect the panel tonight!" she whispered frantically. "We have to do something."

"I've been picking up on that, too. I was trying to listen in on Valentin and Captain Steuben's conversation, but I was too far away. Also, from the little I could hear, they spoke only in German."

"What should we do?"

"We need to get to the stables."

"Now?"

"No, later somehow." He looked around the room and, spotting the box of candles, stuck one in his jacket pocket. "We can't stay in here much longer, though; they'll be wondering where we are."

"Yes, all right. But when the men join us, don't leave me alone with Wirnhier."

Clive's face contorted. "Jesus." He rubbed his hand through his hair. "That bad?"

"Yes, there's something about him. I'm supposed to be meeting him later."

"Meeting him? You agreed to this?" Clive hissed.

Henrietta bit her lip, knowing she might have gone too far this time. "Well, in a way. He said he would show me the 'valuable item' they've come to collect. What could I say?"

"I'll just bet he wanted to show you a 'valuable item.'"

Henrietta suddenly laughed despite the situation. "He asked if you retire early."

"This is not a laughing matter, Henrietta. We need to think!"

"Well, I feel a headache coming on," she said with a sly smile.

Clive gave her a puzzled look. "Yes! That's it." He grinned at her. "You retire early, then I'll—"

"Henrietta?" called a voice from the hallway. Henrietta spun around to see Claudette in the doorway. "I thought I saw you go the wrong way. The *toilette* is that way," she said pointing down the hallway. "Ah, but I see now," she said, smiling at Clive. "A romantic tête-à-tête! I forget that you are still newlyweds. Or is it a lovers' quarrel?" she drawled, looking from one to the other and giving Clive a little wink. "You both look much too grave to be making love. Either way, *chéris*, there will be time enough for lovemaking later! Come," she said, stepping in and looping her arm through Henrietta's. "The ladies are asking for you. They are all intrigued to meet an American."

Henrietta blushed. "As a matter of fact, I was . . . I was just feeling a little tired. A slight headache, you see." She glanced at Clive. "Perhaps I should lie down for a little while."

"Nonsense! On your last night? Come. Champagne will cure any headache! Or better yet, Pastis. I will ring for some."

"But I . . ."

"Come along. I must savor every moment with you, *chérie*! I will be lonely once you leave."

"Well, all right, then," Henrietta said with a weak smile. "I'll see you later, darling," she said over her shoulder to Clive and shot him a look of despair as Claudette led her to the drawing room.

True to her word, Claudette had Renard bring Henrietta a glass of Pastis, which she hesitantly took a sip of. The thick yellow liquid tasted of licorice—or was it anise? Whatever it was, it was utterly horrible, but she could not refuse it. Instead, she sipped it occasionally and allowed herself to be led around the room by Claudette, who seemed eager, for lack of a better explanation, to make up for her previous inattentiveness. Indeed, she rarely left Henrietta's side and took great pleasure introducing her to all of the more eminent ladies of Strasbourg and beyond. Henrietta was surprised by what a conversationalist Claudette was, much more so than when she was in the presence of Valentin. But, then again, he had a way of sucking all the joy out of any room. Without him, she positively shone.

Thankfully, the men did not remain at their port long before making their way into the drawing room, at which point Claudette released her, finally, to join an older man to whom Henrietta had yet to be introduced. Henrietta watched as Claudette laughed and flirted with him and wondered, suddenly, if this might be Olivier? No, it couldn't be, she decided. It would be much too risky to invite her married lover to a house party, wouldn't it? And yet, they seemed so very familiar. Perhaps he was an old friend?

Clive had caught her eye when he entered the room, but he had not approached and was now somehow engaged in a conversation with another man, who Henrietta thought might be Madame Dupuis's husband. Henrietta took another distasteful sip of her Pastis and considered giving it to a passing footman when her eyes landed unfortunately upon Major Wirnhier, who was gazing at her from across the room where he stood next to a group of chattering German officers. He appeared to be only half-listening to what was being said, casually sipping his cognac as he watched her, as if willing to bide his time indefinitely. She looked away.

Claudette was now seated at the piano beside her male friend, who was picking out a tune or two, much to Claudette's amusement. She seemed almost drunk. Henrietta looked around for Valentin, curious as to what his reaction would be to his sister's antics, and spotted him finally near the now-lighted shelves of jade figurines, the glow from which unnaturally illuminated half his face, while the other was in shadow. He seemed oblivious to Claudette's behavior and was instead, Henrietta noticed uncomfortably, staring at her, just as Major Wirnhier was. They were like two wolves waiting to attack. Henrietta shivered and walked toward a group of ladies standing near the doors to the terrace. They were closed and curtained, however, so that it was impossible to see outside, which

Henrietta thought odd, considering that it was a beautiful summer night.

Henrietta pretended to be interested in the ladies' conversation, which she couldn't possibly follow, and tried to think of a plan. The room seemed dreadfully close, and she wished she could step outside. Claudette must have thought the same, because two footmen entered the room, then, and began drawing back the thick gold damask curtains, tying them securely with gold cords and then carefully began folding the doors open, letting in a delightfully cool summer breeze. Henrietta excitedly looked around the room for Clive, who caught her eye and tilted his head toward the terrace.

Henrietta excused herself from the ladies as best she could in broken French and weaved her way outside, the lovely breeze hitting her warm face and sending the auburn tendrils that framed it aloft. The terrace overlooked the gardens, though it was impossible to see anything at night except the illuminated fountain. Henrietta positioned herself in a dark corner, away from the stone steps that led down into the gardens, trying her best to avoid any of the other guests who had wandered outside as she waited for Clive to extract himself. After only a few moments, he thankfully appeared.

"Thank goodness!" she whispered to him. "I thought I might faint in there. Especially with both Valentin and the major staring at me. I'm sure they know, Clive."

"Well, let's go then." His face was grim as he held out his arm to her.

"Now? It's too risky! Maybe we should wait until everyone's asleep."

"I have a feeling no one is going to sleep tonight," he said in a low tone. "We should go now while everyone is preoccupied and before it's moved. Who knows? Maybe the servants have already been instructed to take it down and start packing it up."

"I hadn't thought of that."

"Come on," he said, holding out his arm again. "Just pretend we're

strolling the gardens under the moonlight. See? There are other couples down by the fountain as well. We'll just slip away."

"Okay, but we'll have to be fast," she said, gripping his arm.

The stables were completely dark and abandoned when they finally
reached the old stone building. It had an eerie, almost haunted feel to
it at night. Henrietta shivered and gripped Clive's arm tighter.

Clive pulled out the candle he had stolen from the butler's pantry
and handed it to Henrietta. "I wish we had a flashlight, but this will
have to do." He fished in his other pocket for the little box of matches
he always carried and lit it. He tossed the burnt match to the ground
and then drew out his revolver, cocking it. "Here, give me the candle,
and you try the door."

Unlike earlier today, the big double doors had now been fastened
shut, and when Henrietta pulled on them, they held fast.

"Let's look for a side door," Clive suggested, leading the way. "Here,
take this," he said, handing her the candle and roughly pulling on the
old black iron handle of a tiny rounded door cut into the stone. With
a heavy creak, it swung open. He gave her a little wink and reached
for the candle again. "I'll go first. Stick close."

Carefully, they stepped over the stone lintel into utter darkness.
Clive held the candle high, long shadows dancing along the walls.
Henrietta tried to get her bearings. It all looked so different and men-
acing in the pitch black.

"That way, I think," she said, pointing toward the back of the barn.
"See that little archway? Through there."

Clive began walking toward it. "What did Wirnhier say to you at
dinner?" he asked over his shoulder.

"He's a type of supply officer, I think he said. He obtains valuable
objects that the Führer might be interested in," she said in a low voice,
though there was obviously no need to be quiet.

"Did he specifically mention the panel?" Clive asked, his voice
subdued as well.

"No, but when I suggested that the object he was here to collect was a painting, he just gave me a strange smile. I'm sure that's what they're here for. Wait," she whispered, pulling on his jacket to stop him from going into the back room. "It's up there." She pointed up at the black hole above them.

"You went up there?" he asked incredulously, his face distorted by the light of the candle.

"Yes. Dressed in this, too, I might add."

Clive grinned. "Darling, you amaze me at every turn. I—"

Something rustled behind them, and Henrietta jumped. "Shh!" she hissed, putting her fingers to his lips. "Did you hear that?"

Clive shook his head.

Henrietta turned and peered into the darkness, goosebumps traveling down her neck. "Someone's there," she whispered.

Clive strained to hear, both of them frozen in place.

"Who's there?" Clive shouted, holding the candle high again, but they could see nothing outside of the circle of light they stood in. "Show yourself."

No sound was heard, however.

"Come on," Clive said in a low voice. "Let's hurry."

Henrietta was still uneasy, certain that someone or something was lurking in the darkness, but she knew they couldn't just stand there. "All right," she said, turning her back. "You go first with the candle." She slipped off her shoes. "It's not so bad once you get started."

Clive stuck his revolver back into his inner breast pocket and heaved himself up the stone-and-wood ladder, which was difficult to do with a burning candle in one hand.

Henrietta took one last look over her shoulder and followed.

This time, upon reaching the hayloft, it was completely dark, as the moon had not yet risen and thus no light shone in through the high windows.

"Now where?" Clive asked, looking up at the pitch-black rafters.

"Here, give that to me," she said, taking the candle and looking for the path through the maze. "I think this is it," she called, carefully making her way, sure that her stockings were well and truly in shreds by now. Without too much trouble, she managed to locate Pascal's nest and hurriedly checked the rafters above to make sure the panel was still there. It was terribly hard to see, and for a moment, she feared it was somehow gone.

"It's here somewhere," she said, almost to herself, as she moved from side to side. "There! There it is! See?"

Clive stood beside her and took back the candle. He lifted it high, enough so that the images of the horsemen could be seen. "My God. I don't believe it."

"Do you think it's damaged, stored out here?"

"I have no idea. Surely if it is, an art restorer can have a look."

"But why hide it out here?"

"I'm not sure. Perhaps it's not the original hiding place. Maybe when Stafford turned up, Valentin realized things were getting too close for comfort. Certainly no one would think to look out here."

"What should we do?"

"I need to try to telephone Hartle. Maybe I can sneak into Valentin's study. I think I saw a telephone in there."

"What good will that do? He has yet to act on your other call. And anyway, he's miles away."

"Well, what choice do we have?" he asked, holding the candle up high again to take another look at the panel.

"Clive, we need to *do* something! The Germans are planning to leave with it in the morning, and I'm pretty sure Valentin knows that I know."

"Yes, that's unfortunate," he said grimly, lowering the candle and looking at her.

"Maybe we should telephone the French authorities?"

"Like who?"

"The police?"

"I thought about it, but who knows who is loyal to who? Remember when I asked Monsieur Bonnet if there had been an investigation into Stafford's death? There wasn't. And then he went on to say that in asking that question, I clearly had no idea who I was dealing with.

Which I don't. Next, Monsieur Bonnet is murdered, and the police pin it on a vagrant? It stinks of rot."

Clive began to pace a little now. "I suppose you're right, though. Even if I do get through to Hartle, what can he do from London? We only have a few hours before the panel falls into the hands of the Germans." He groaned. "We can't risk waiting. It's foolhardy, but we're going to have to act on our own."

"What are you suggesting?"

"I don't see what else we can do but steal it ourselves. Leave in the middle of the night when everyone's asleep."

"Clive! Are you sure?"

"Yes. I think it's our only option. That or let the Germans take it. I'll try to telephone Hartle, but if I don't get through, I'll leave a message as to where we can meet. Maybe Paris."

"But how are we going to get there?"

"We'll have to 'borrow' one of the baron's cars. Do you think Edna can be ready?"

"Yes, I think so," she said hesitantly, knowing how badly Edna would fret. She gazed up at the painting again. "How are we going to get it down?"

Clive sighed. "I'm not sure. We'd better get back, though, before someone notices us. It will give me time to think. You go and—"

"Stop right there," came a voice from behind them.

Henrietta jumped and let out a little scream. She turned to face the intruder, but she was blinded by the beam from a flashlight. Her hand shot up to block her eyes.

"Who are you?" Clive demanded, shielding his eyes as well and stepping awkwardly in front of Henrietta. "Put that thing down!"

The intruder lowered the beam, then, and Henrietta, blinking rapidly, was shocked to see that it was, of all people, Pascal!

"What are you doing up here?" she asked and allowed herself to briefly hope that he was up here merely to romance a girl. She looked beyond him, half expecting a girl to materialize, but it was impossible to see in the darkness.

"That would be a better question for you, madame, no?" He nodded his head toward the painting, thereby instantly dispelling Henrietta's faint hope.

"Look, we're taking this painting," Clive said cautiously. "It's a stolen work of art, and we're returning it to the authorities."

"How . . . how do I know you are not the ones doing the stealing?" he asked timidly. "This is *très suspect.*"

"We're working with the British authorities. This is a very valuable painting, and it's clearly been stolen. This doesn't involve you. Just go back to the main house and forget what you saw."

"No, I . . . I do not think I can do that. I do not work for you," Pascal said carefully. "I must report what I have seen."

Henrietta saw Clive slowly pull out his revolver. "Now, listen, sonny. You're not going to say a word of this. Understand?" Clive said evenly.

Pascal's previously nervous face transformed into one of terror. "*S'il vous plaît, monsieur,*" he said holding up his hands, the beam of the flashlight shooting up to the rafters now. "I mean you no harm. I . . . I can help you."

"How?"

"I can . . . I can help you get it down. You will never manage it alone. Believe me; I am the one who helped to put it up there."

Clive remained silent, considering.

"Yes, yes," Pascal urged, suddenly gaining confidence. "I will help you. And I will only ask for one small thing in *remboursement,*" he added tentatively.

"Repayment?" Clive exclaimed.

"Clive, just listen." Henrietta kept her eyes on Pascal. "What do you mean?"

"Take me with you."

"Take you with us? Where?" Clive asked.

"Back to America. I will help you with that . . . that thing." He looked up briefly. "I will help you to take it to wherever you want. I will never tell. Please," he begged. Henrietta could see that his right leg was trembling. He was clearly terrified.

Clive let out short laugh. "Don't be ridiculous."

Pascal's face looked pale now. "As you wish," he said crisply with a little bow. "Then I will go wake the house. Most interested, the Germans will be. They will rush down here in an instant. They are *très désireux* for this painting, so I am told."

"You wouldn't dare."

"Why would I not? What are you going to do to stop me? Shoot me?"

"Maybe I will." Clive cocked the gun.

"Clive!" Henrietta exclaimed.

"They will hear the shot!" Pascal squeaked.

"There are other ways to silence you, you rat," Clive said, stepping closer. Pascal backed away.

"Please, monsieur! Listen to me. You will never get out of here without my help. I also have all the keys to the cars. Please, take me . . . take me as far as New York, and then I will disappear."

"You little—"

"Clive!" Henrietta said, pulling on his arm now. "Wait. He has a point. We need his help."

"How can we trust him?" he said, quickly glancing at her before returning his eyes to Pascal.

"Well, why shouldn't we? It's in his best interest for us to escape, that way he makes it to America."

"But maybe it's a bluff."

"Yes, but why go to such elaborate lengths to double-cross us? Why not just run back to the house as soon as he saw us up here?"

Clive thought for a moment and then slowly lowered the gun. "All right, kid. But one false move, and it's over. Got that?"

Pascal nodded eagerly. "But first you must promise. Promise to take me back to America with you."

Clive rubbed his brow. "Fine. I'll do what I can."

"What should we do now?" Henrietta asked, looking from one to the other.

"We need to act quickly," Pascal said. "They plan to move it in the morning. We should leave *dès que possible*."

"We can't do it now," Clive grunted. "We've been away from the house for too long already. It'll have to be later. Can you bring a ladder?"

"*Oui,* there is one below."

"And we'll need a car. The biggest car."

"*Oui,* certainly."

"Let's rendezvous here at midnight."

"It will be *risqué*. Mademoiselle Von Harmon is often still awake at that hour, and maybe even later with all the Germans in the house."

Clive rubbed his brow. "We can't wait too long. It's going to take some time to get this down and wrapped." He paused to think. "Okay, you meet me here at midnight," he said to Pascal. "It will be easier for me to sneak out alone than for all of us together. Henrietta, you and Edna be ready by one. Meet us by the upper garage. Got it? And don't pack a lot."

"*Oui,* I understand," Pascal said, and Henrietta merely nodded.

"Come on, then. Let's go."

Chapter 21

I t was nearly one a.m. when Henrietta dared open her bedroom door to peek down the hallway. All was dark and silent, and she began to hope that perhaps everyone had finally gone to bed. "Ready, Edna?" she whispered to the girl behind her, who, at the moment, resembled a small pack horse, loaded down as she was with two hat boxes in one hand, a small valise under that same arm, and a rather large suitcase in her other hand. Henrietta despaired that she was leaving behind a whole trunk of expensive gowns, but there was obviously no choice. She took one of the hatboxes from Edna and added it to the two small cases she herself carried. Edna nodded, but Henrietta could see that the girl was trembling.

"It'll be all right, Edna. Just be quiet and follow me."

They crept out into the hallway, Henrietta pausing at the top of the grand staircase, listening for signs of life below. She could hear nothing, so she took a few tentative steps down, Edna practically on her heels. Henrietta stopped abruptly, however, when she heard male voices coming from somewhere below. Edna collided into her and nearly toppled over, but Henrietta caught and righted her. She strained to hear who was speaking. It was Major Wirnhier and Valentin for sure, and maybe others. Terrified, she frantically gestured for Edna to retreat back up the stairs.

"We'll have to go down the servants' stairs," she whispered to Edna. "Do you think anyone will be in the kitchens?"

"Not at this hour, I don't think," Edna whispered back. "But the scullery maids are up at four to start."

"We'll be well away by then, I hope," she said, hurrying down the hallway to the door at the end that led to the back staircase. Silently, she opened the door, and the two of them tiptoed down until they reached the kitchens, which were thankfully empty, save for a dog sleeping by the hearth. It raised its head and growled softly.

"It's me, Jacques," Edna said, setting down the biggest case and approaching him slowly. "It's just me." She held out her hand for him to sniff, and his ears immediately lowered, his tail thumping loudly now on his cushion. "I've been giving him treats now and then since I got here," she said to a surprised Henrietta. "He's a real good dog." She gave him several generous pets.

Henrietta saw this as her cue to sneak past and try the door. She set down the cases and tried the big iron handle, but the door wouldn't budge. She balanced the hat box on one of the cases and tried again, this time with both hands, her sense of panic rising. *How had Clive gotten out?*

"It's locked!" she hissed to Edna. "I'm sure it's already past one by now. We've got to get to the car! Do you know where the key is?"

"No, miss. I don't," Edna said, standing up straight and looking around fruitlessly in the dark. "It's more than likely on Madame Chauvin's keyring. Or Monsieur Gaspard's."

"Damn! We'll have to go around," Henrietta whispered fiercely.

"Won't that be locked, too?" Edna asked feebly.

"More than likely. But there's probably a bolt we can turn from the inside. You lead the way, Edna. I'm all mixed up."

"Yes, miss," Edna squeaked and led them back through the kitchen, Jacques raising his head and thumping his tail again as they passed. Edna paused for a moment in the main hallway, as if trying to remember the correct way, then turned left and left again down a long narrow corridor. They passed various storerooms and the laundry, but it was too dark for Henrietta to see much. Finally, they reached a small stone spiral staircase.

"I think this is the one, miss," Edna said. Henrietta moved in front of her and picked her way up the narrow pie-wedge steps until she reached a tiny door at the top. Carefully, she cracked it open a sliver and peeked out, rejoicing that they were in the hall's main foyer!

"Well done, Edna!" she whispered behind her. Though her first instinct was to dash across the foyer to the waiting door, she made herself pause to listen. She was eternally grateful that she did, as the sound of Major Wirnhier's laugh could be heard somewhere nearby. Now she could hear Valentin. He was saying something in German. Their voices grew louder, then, and Henrietta realized with horror that they were coming closer.

"Quick," she hissed to Edna and tried to pull the door shut, but it wouldn't close tightly. Henrietta froze, her heart thudding in her chest, as the two men stopped at the bottom of the stairs.

"*Gute Nacht, Monsieur Von Harmon. Es war ein sehr angenehmer Abend. Und ein produktiver*—Good night, Monsieur Von Harmon. It was a most enjoyable evening. And a fruitful one," the major said.

"*Ich bin froh, dass wir uns einigen konnten. Die letzten Details können wir morgen früh besprechen*—I'm glad we could come to an agreement. We can discuss the final details in the morning."

Henrietta held her breath, wishing she could understand what they were saying. Only when she heard footsteps on the staircase did she allow herself to exhale, silently cheering the fact that the two men were dispersing, possibly going to bed. It took her a few moments to realize, however, that there was only one set of footsteps on the stairs. Henrietta put her eye to the crack and saw that it was Valentin ascending. The major was not in her sightline. Before she could think what to do, she heard heavy footsteps coming toward the servant door. It must be him! Her first instinct was to flee down the stairs with Edna, but she feared it would make too much noise, as he was only steps away now. Surely, he would hear them scurrying down the stairs. Instead, she put her finger to her lips, indicating to Edna, who looked about to scream, that she should be quiet.

"What is it?" Valentin suddenly called from the stairs.

The major was so close to them now that Henrietta was sure he would be able to hear the pounding of her heart. She clutched Edna's sleeve and crouched, waiting for him to fling open the door . . . but he did not. Instead, he gave it a shove, shutting it tightly. Henrietta nearly cried out in relief and slapped her hand over her mouth to keep herself from doing so.

"The servants left a door open," Major Wirnhier answered. She could still hear them, faintly, from behind the closed door, and wished, again, that she knew what they were saying.

"Are you not coming?"

"No, I think I will take some air before bed. The gardens perhaps. Clear my head."

"Ah. I see. You are meeting someone, no?" Valentin was silent then for few moments. "Is it Henrietta?"

Henrietta's ears pricked at the sound of her name. What were they saying? Did they know she was on the other side of the door?

Major Wirnhier laughed. "Perhaps."

"I sense you won't get far."

"Perhaps not. But I can be very . . . persuasive, you might say."

"As you wish. I'm going to bed. Good night."

"Good night."

Major Wirnhier remained standing just on the other side of the door for several minutes, as if he knew she was there and was toying with her, allowing her fear to build until she thought she would scream. She could hear his loud breathing. Why didn't he go? Was he waiting for her? Is that what he had been discussing with Valentin just now? As careful as she had been to avoid him after dinner, he had, upon her and Clive's rejoining the party after their jaunt to the stables, managed to find a way to sidle up to her and whisper in her ear that he would wait for her by the fountain. She had given him what she hoped was a convincing nod and a brief smile before retreating up to her room.

Sweat dripped down the back of her neck and under her arms now. Surely Clive and Pascal were waiting, ready, and she prayed Clive would not come back into the house looking for them. She and Edna needed to get out now! They would just have to find a different way. She gestured for Edna to begin creeping back down the stairs, but then held up a finger to halt when she heard the major suddenly walk away. A miracle! For a moment, she rejoiced, until she just as quickly wondered if perhaps he had decided to go looking for her. If that were the case, she despaired, how would they ever make it to the rendezvous point without getting caught? They would have to be fast.

Henrietta waited for several minutes, though it felt like hours, before she finally, her heart racing, pushed open the little door and peeked out.

The major was nowhere in sight. She could see the doors just a few yards away, but maybe, she fretted, they shouldn't chance it. Maybe Wirnhier was just down one of the hallways, waiting in the shadows. But, on the other hand, if they went creeping about looking for an alternate exit, it would take longer and they might run into Wirnhier anyway. No, she decided, looking around the foyer one more time. This seemed the best chance.

Slowly she pushed the door open further, freezing mid-step when it creaked loudly. No one appeared, however, so she emerged fully then, tilting her head at Edna to follow. The two of them half-ran, half-tiptoed across the stone floor and managed to reach the main doors undetected. Henrietta carefully set down her two cases. As she had thought, the door was shut with what looked like an utterly medieval iron bolt strapped across it, but at least there was no key required. She grasped what looked like a small handle and tried to gently push the bolt to the right, but it didn't move. She took a deep breath and pushed harder. This time it moved, but it was accompanied by a loud scraping noise as the metal rubbed on metal and then connected with the metal band at the end with a bang. Both

Henrietta and Edna stood rigidly in place, listening. No sound was heard, so Henrietta proceeded to pull on the heavy door. Wondrously, it made no sound. She poked her head out, but there was no sign of Wirnhier, or anyone else, for that matter. She prayed he had not wandered outside.

"You go through first, Edna," Henrietta whispered, "and I'll close it."

Edna gathered up as many cases and boxes as she could and hurried through, but just as Henrietta, her heart in her throat, was pulling the door closed, she heard a loud cry of "Countess!" coming from the direction of the stairwell. "There you are! Wait!"

Henrietta's head jerked toward the stairs, and she was mortified to see the baron standing there, fully dressed, an old-fashioned traveling cape about his shoulders. She was utterly dumbfounded! She knew she should run, but her legs were paralyzed with shock.

"Countess!" he repeated, hurrying down the last of the stairs and scuttling across the foyer to her. "Finally, you have decided to flee with me!" he continued in French. "I knew this day would come. Let me get my things."

Henrietta hadn't the faintest idea what he was saying, but whatever it was, it was much too loud.

"*Père?*" came Valentin's voice from somewhere above.

Panic overwhelming her, Henrietta's legs finally began to move, and she bolted out the door. "Run!" she called to Edna, who did not need much encouragement. The two of them ran up the drive toward the garage and saw, with relief, that a car, the Bugatti, was waiting, a giant rectangle wrapped in burlap tied to its roof. It looked ridiculously flimsy, but Henrietta couldn't worry about that now. She could see Clive pacing by the car; Pascal was nowhere in sight.

"What's wrong?" Clive called, as he hurried toward the two women. He glanced at the house worriedly.

"The baron saw us! I think he's woken the house," Henrietta cried breathlessly as Clive began grabbing some of the cases from her. "Valentin at least. Also, Wirnhier is wandering around somewhere."

"Get in," Clive ordered. "Give me a hand," he shouted at Pascal, who had since jumped out of the car and hurried around now to relieve Edna of her load. "I told you to pack light!" Clive said incredulously, as he began tossing the cases into the small trunk.

"Countess!" The baron had emerged from the château and stood calling to them. Clive swore when Valentin and Major Wirnhier appeared beside him.

"Come on; we need to go!" Clive shouted.

Henrietta slipped into the back seat beside Edna.

"Give me the keys," Pascal commanded from where he stood now by the driver's side of the car.

"I'm driving," Clive snapped.

"The route is treacherous. I know the way. Give me the keys," Pascal begged, looking nervously back up at the château.

"Stop!" someone shouted. It was Valentin, hurrying down the steps, dressed only in his trousers and his white dress shirt, which flowed out behind him.

"Clive! Come on! Give him the keys!" Henrietta shouted from the back seat.

With one more desperate look at the house, Clive tossed the keys to Pascal and dove into the passenger's seat.

"You can take over later if you wish," Pascal said, his head bent toward the steering wheel as he choked the car into life.

Valentin was running up the drive now, but Pascal expertly threw the car into gear and pulled away, pea gravel spewing from under the car's wheels. Henrietta turned to see the confusion left behind. Servants had appeared now and Valentin was shouting orders. Wirnhier's men could also be seen, and she was horrified to see one of the German cars pull up.

"They've got their car out!" she said to Clive. "I think we're going to be followed."

"Jesus, step on it," Clive shouted. "So much for a stealthy getaway," he muttered bitterly, running his hand angrily through his hair.

"It's my fault, Clive. I'm sorry!"

"No, it's not. How were you to know the baron would be prowling around like some kind of deranged ghost?"

They all slid to the right suddenly as Pascal rounded the Freudeneck Gorge. "Don't look down," he commanded, without letting up on the gas.

"Jesus! Careful, man!"

"Do you want to get away, or no?" Pascal did not look at him, his eyes glued instead to the dark road in front of them.

Henrietta turned around again to check the Germans' progress. Faint headlights appeared behind them. "They're behind us!" she exclaimed, and Edna let out a little cry.

"I know a different route, through the Vosges Mountains, but it is much more treacherous than the main road. It will slow them down."

Clive looked behind them and swore again. "How do we know it's not a trap?" he said, pulling out his revolver now.

"Does this look like a trap?" Pascal asked frantically and took his eyes away from the road for a second to glare at him.

"Fine. Do it," Clive commanded. "But any funny business, and you get it," he said waving the gun toward him.

"Clive!" Henrietta cried as they slid to the right again, Pascal turning down a dark lane. They bounced nearly to the ceiling as he drove through several deep ruts. "Don't be ridiculous!"

"Hold on," Pascal shouted. "This is our best chance. If the Germans are driving, they will not know this route."

"Oh, miss," Edna cried. "Are we going to die?"

"No, of course not, Edna," Henrietta said as she looked behind them again. "They're gaining on us!" she cried.

Pascal increased their speed, if that was possible, and they careened through the dense woods on what Henrietta guessed was some sort of old carriage road or maybe a log-cutting route. Whatever it was used for, it wasn't paved, and she could see by the glow of the headlights that they were following two tracks of dirt. She peered out the side window but could see nothing until the trees suddenly opened up enough for the moonlight to reveal a razor-thin edge of grass to their right, below which was a deep chasm. Henrietta craned her neck to see the bottom, but she could not, whether because of the ravine's extreme depth or perhaps just the darkness. Regardless, she suddenly felt a wave of vertigo and worried that she might vomit. Hurriedly, she looked behind them again. Somehow, the Germans were gaining on them, so much so that she could see the small Nazi flags on either side of the hood flapping wildly, illuminated by the car's headlights.

"Faster, Pascal!" she shouted.

"I am trying, but the panel is slowing us down." Indeed, the panel was vibrating wildly on top of the car, so much so that Henrietta feared the rope would come loose and that the panel would simply fly off.

"Grab hold of that rope," Clive shouted, obviously thinking the same thing. "You, too, Edna. Hold it tight! That's it."

Clive himself was just reaching for the rope that ran above his and Pascal's head when a shot rang through the air. Then another.

"They're shooting at us!" Henrietta exclaimed. Edna screamed and let go of the rope.

"Edna! Keep hold of that!" Clive shouted as he roughly cranked his window down. Henrietta was horrified to see him lean out the window.

"Clive!"

He ignored her, however, and fired. Several shots rang out from behind them, one of them hitting the car, and Henrietta quickly realized that more than one of them had guns. Oh, God! How on earth would they escape?

Clive leaned out the window again and fired. Whether he hit anything or anyone was unknown, but the car continued its chase. They were nearly upon them now.

Clive popped out another time, and this time he hit the German windshield, shattering it. The German car swerved, filling Henrietta with a flicker of hope, before it quickly righted itself and continued its pursuit as if nothing had happened. The Germans began firing in earnest now.

"How much further until we hit the main road?" Clive shouted at Pascal.

"Not too much further. Another few miles, perhaps."

"A few miles? I've only got three shots left!"

Bullets riddled the car now, and Henrietta was sure some damage must have been done.

"Slow down just a little," Clive shouted.

"Slow down?"

"Yes, let me get one good shot. But it's got to be in the right spot. I'll tell you when."

"*Oui.*"

A bullet hit the back window, and Henrietta and Edna both screamed.

"Now!"

Pascal slowed the car, and Clive leaned out the window, firing two shots. Henrietta looked behind and saw the Germans' car again wobble and swerve. This time, however, the car did not right itself. The driver must have been hit. The car veered dangerously close to the edge of the cliff and seemed almost to hover there for a few seconds before it finally plunged headfirst over the side into the black darkness.

"Oh!" Henrietta said, staring at the empty space behind them where, one second ago, a car had been. Sweat was pouring down Henrietta's face, and her hands were raw from holding onto the rope. Pascal stopped, and it seemed like minutes before they heard a horrific crash as the Germans' car hit the bottom of the ravine.

"They went over the edge!" Edna cried.

"Should we go back?" Pascal looked to Clive for direction.

"No! Keep going. We've got to get to Paris before the German authorities discover this."

"We have been hit, I think," Pascal said. "The damage, I am not sure."

"We'll go as far as we can."

Henrietta briefly let go of the rope to look behind them one last time, wondering who was in the car and hoping, wickedly, that it was Wirnhier.

"Oh, miss!" Edna cried, leaning against her shoulder and beginning to cry.

"It'll be okay, Edna. Don't worry."

"I don't ever want to leave home again," she sobbed.

"Yes, I think that's probably a good idea." Henrietta put her arm around the girl and rubbed her shoulder.

As it turned out, the car only made it another hour before puttering out. Pascal rolled the car off the side of the road and switched off the ignition. The engine was smoking, and for the last several miles, he had not been able to shift into high gear. The four of them exited the car and walked around, examining it. The chassis was riddled with bullet holes, and Henrietta could not resist running her fingers along them, amazed that something as small as a bullet could chew through metal with such ease. How much more damage could it do to flesh and bone? She shuddered and led Edna away to the stone fence running along the road and leaned against it. Pascal had popped the hood and was examining the engine, while Clive inspected the panel for damage.

"Is it all right?" Henrietta asked.

"Yes, I think so," Clive grunted. "At least as far as I can tell. What about the car?" He walked toward the front of the car.

"In this dark, it is impossible to see what is the problem," Pascal answered, bent over the engine now, "but we are in desperate need of petrol. The tank was nicked, and it has been leaking slowly. It should not be empty already. Also, we are burning oil."

"Damn it!" Clive rubbed the back of his neck and looked anxiously down the road behind them as if worried that another car of Germans would appear at any moment. "Now what?"

Pascal straightened and looked around the dark. "There," he said, pointing in the direction of a little hill, not five hundred yards from the road. Behind it, they could see a faint tendril of smoke rise.

"There is probably a farm there," he said, wiping his hands on his handkerchief. "I will go and see."

"All right, but hurry!" Clive snapped. Pascal nodded and accordingly set off on a jog. Clive watched him go and then turned toward Henrietta and Edna, still huddled by the fence.

"What now?" Henrietta asked, going to him.

Clive sighed. "I don't know. We're going to have to get this car fixed. That or find some other means of getting to Paris. Maybe this farmer will have something we can borrow." Clive began to pace. "We've got to hurry, though. It's not safe to just sit here. Especially with the panel." He glanced toward the little hill. "Where the bloody hell is he?"

"Well, it *is* the middle of the night, Clive. I'm sure it's taking time to wake them up." She shivered, wishing she had brought a shawl.

"I don't trust him."

"Yes, you've made that very clear. But then again, you don't trust anyone."

"Can you blame me?"

"Darling, if he were going to double-cross us, he would have done it by now. He just drove us to safety after causing a whole car of Germans to career off the side of a cliff. That's not exactly nothing."

Clive looked over at her, his taut face relaxing for a moment. He didn't respond, but merely put his arms around her.

"What is it about him that you don't trust? He seems harmless to me," she said into his chest. "He reminds me of Stan, actually."

Clive grunted. "I don't know. There's just something about him. He took advantage of Edna in the hayloft for one thing. And then he conveniently popped out of the darkness offering to help us just when we needed it? And for what? So that we would take him back to America with us? It just sounds fishy. There's something about it. And then there's the fact that he speaks perfect English. Do you not find that odd? He learned it from a former English stable boy in their employ? It's all terribly hard to believe."

"I suppose you do have a point," she said, a niggle of worry erupting.

"And did you notice that he used to have more of an accent than he does now? He isn't French at all. I think he's an English agent."

"Well, wouldn't he be on our side, then? And why not tell us that?"

"I don't know. Maybe I'm wrong."

Henrietta continued to rest her head on his chest and closed her eyes. Unfortunately, every time she did, she saw the German car go over the side of the cliff. She shuddered and tried to erase it from her mind. "Do you think Valentin was in the car?" she asked softly.

"Probably. I'm sorry, Henrietta."

Henrietta did not respond. She wasn't sure how she felt about Valentin. He was boorish and rude and in league with the Nazis, but he *was* her family. Still, if she were honest, she felt more than a little guilty that she did not feel any sadness whatsoever. Except for how Claudette might take it when she learned of it. She wondered what Claudette's reaction *would* be, after everything she had confided to Henrietta about her feelings toward her brother. She suspected that despite Claudette's lack of feeling toward her brother, she would still be sad. After all, she mused, she herself would be heartbroken if Eugene were killed, even with all of the trouble he had caused them. But then again, maybe Valentin hadn't actually been in the car. Maybe he had stayed behind at the château . . .

"Where the bloody hell is he?" Clive muttered, eventually releasing Henrietta and beginning to pace again. He drew out his pocket watch. "It's been nearly thirty minutes. Something's wrong." He shot Henrietta a worried glance. "I'm going over there. I should never have let him go alone, but I didn't want to abandon you. And Edna," he said, glancing over at the poor girl still huddled by the fence.

"May I sit in the car, sir?" she squeaked, now that she had caught his attention.

"Yes, yes. Go on," he barked. "Why don't you join her," he said to Henrietta, rubbing her upper arms. "You're shivering."

"No, I—"

"Come!" Pascal shouted as if on cue, finally appearing back on the road. "We can stay here for the night! It is a farm, as I thought. An old widow."

"What took you so long?" Clive demanded.

"She is nearly deaf. It was hard to wake her up. I had to knock on her bedroom window. She nearly had a fit."

"What did you tell her?" Clive asked.

"That you are my relatives from America and that we are traveling from Strasbourg to Paris, but our car broke down. She says we can stay the night."

Clive sighed. "That's no good. We need to get back on the road. I suppose it's too much to hope that she has an automobile."

"Yes, I did ask. But she has only an old horse and a cart she takes to town occasionally."

"How far away is the town?"

"About five miles. A place called Saint-Quirin."

Clive paced about, thinking. "Jesus. Five miles?" He rubbed his hand through his hair. "All right. We'll have to bring the panel into the house. Make some excuse. Say that it's a painting we bought. Henrietta and Edna will stay here with it while you and I walk to this Saint-Quirin to try to find another car."

"Do you think that's wise, Clive?" Henrietta asked, suddenly not wanting to separate from him. "Maybe you should wait until morning."

"By morning, they will have discovered the car, if not before. If we all go, we'll have to carry the panel with us, and we'll get nowhere fast. No, we don't have a choice. You and Edna should be safe enough here. Hopefully, we'll be back before the morning is too advanced."

"Why not hide it here and come back for it?" Pascal suggested.

Clive glared at him. "You'd like that wouldn't you? Bump us off and come back and collect it. No, I don't think so. You're coming with me."

"Clive, maybe he's right," Henrietta put in, worried now for his safety, walking alone on a dark road with Pascal. "Maybe he should stay with us. What if the Germans come looking for us here?"

Clive shook his head. "We'll have to take that chance. Come on. Let's get going."

Chapter 22

Pascal led them back to the farmhouse and introduced them to the old woman as his relatives, as if it really mattered. The old woman did not seem to care. Clive attempted to speak to her in French, offering to pay her for the accommodation, but it did not register.

"Eh?" she croaked, holding her hand up to her ear and bending forward slightly. She reminded Henrietta of the witch from Hansel and Gretel, ready to push them into the fire when the time was right.

"We can pay you!" Clive shouted in French.

"Eh?" she said again, absently rubbing several stringy white wisps of hair that hung from her chin, and then looked at Pascal, as if he were the interpreter.

"You see why it took so long?" Pascal grumbled at Clive. "*Nous pouvons vous payer*," Pascal repeated, shouting it into the old woman's ear.

The woman nodded and then spoke. "*Réparez ma clôture à la place*," she said, gesturing toward something in the darkness.

"What did she say? I didn't catch it."

"She doesn't want money. She wants us to fix her fence instead."

Clive pulled at his chin. "Yes, yes. We'll fix the fence. I'll arrange for someone to come back and do it."

The woman was looking hopefully at Pascal, and when he nodded their agreement, she broke into a toothless smile and immediately turned toward the stove. She threw in some wood and filled an old enamel kettle with water from a bucket near the sink.

"Come on," Clive said to Pascal. "We've got to go get the car out of sight."

"What do you mean?" Pascal asked. "It won't budge."

"We're going to put in neutral and roll it behind the barn. We can't leave it on the road. And we need to hitch up the horse to the carriage or the cart—whatever she has out there."

"Should we not ask her first?"

"No, we're taking it no matter what she says, and anyway, we can't waste time trying to get her to understand."

"*Oui, je suppose,*" Pascal said hesitantly.

"Come on; let's go," Clive said gesturing impatiently toward the door. He shot Henrietta a look of exasperation, his eyebrows raised, and followed the young man out.

The old woman took no notice of the men's absence and instead began to shuffle around the kitchen, mumbling endlessly in French. She appeared to be preparing them some food. Henrietta tried to call to her to tell her they weren't hungry, but the woman either did not hear or did not understand, or both. She eventually produced a plate of toasted bread and cheese and some tea, gesturing with her hands that they should eat. Henrietta thought she might be sick if she ate any food at the moment, but, thankfully, Edna began to eat ravenously. Henrietta hoped the old woman would be satisfied with this, but she was not and continued to ramble in French and gesture with her hands until Henrietta finally picked up a piece of toast and bit the corner. Satisfied, the old woman went to the counter and began slicing more bread.

"*Non, madame,*" she began to say, but was interrupted by Clive and Pascal, who had now reappeared. They banged open the door and struggled across the threshold, trying to balance the lost panel between them. "Flip it," Clive called, and they turned it on its side to get it through the small door. Once inside, they gently set it down on the stone floor. Sweat was pouring down their faces.

"What is this?" the woman cackled in French, pointing a gnarled finger at the burlap-covered panel tied up with twine.

"It's a painting," Clive said loudly back in French.

"Eh?"

"A painting!" Pascal shouted directly into her ear.

"Ah!" The woman clapped her hands in delight. "Let me see!"

"In the morning," Pascal shouted, but the woman did not seem to understand and stepped closer to it, her hands outstretched, as if it were a treasure to be unwrapped, her previously cloudy eyes now slightly brighter.

"In the morning," Pascal shouted directly into her ear. "First sleep," he said and gestured toward Henrietta and Edna.

The woman looked over at them as if she had already forgotten they were there. A frown settled on her face, and she despondently pointed to the rickety-looking wooden steps in the corner. "Upstairs. You can sleep upstairs."

"I don't think it's going to fit up there," Pascal said now to Clive in a lower tone.

Clive wiped his brow and looked over his shoulder. "I think you're right, but we've got to try."

With a grunt, Clive picked up his end, Pascal following, and inched backwards and up the stairs until they got to the first turn, which proved to be too narrow for the panel. They set it carefully down and tried flipping it in various positions, but to no avail. There simply was no way to get it up the tiny staircase.

"Damn it," Clive said under his breath. "Go back," he barked at Pascal. "We're going to have to store it down there somewhere."

Pascal, his face beet red, backed down the staircase.

Henrietta looked around for a hiding place, but unfortunately there were not many choices. The cottage was small. Just a front room, a kitchen, a little larder, and what was probably the woman's bedroom.

"Try back there," she suggested, pointing at the larder. "It will be hidden by the curtain," she said, referring to the blue plaid scrap of fabric that hung across the doorway to separate it from the kitchen.

Clive nodded at Pascal, and the two of them shuffled across the room with the panel, Henrietta hurrying ahead to hold the curtain. Though the larder was small, it was tall enough for the panel to stand on end amidst the shelves lined with jars of pickles, cheeses, baskets of root vegetables and apples, and a few hanging sausages. Once on its end, Clive managed to shove it to the back and lodge it between the floor-to-ceiling shelves and an old chopping block. "That ought to do it for now," he said, his hands on his hips as he gave it a final look. "Come on, we've got to get going," he said to Pascal. "Go get Mrs. Howard's case from the car."

"I'll go, too," Edna said. "If that's okay. Make sure it's the right one, an' all."

Clive gave her an absent nod and led Henrietta back toward the stairs. "Listen, be careful," he said in a low voice, as if stealth were necessary with the old woman. "Lock your bedroom door if you can. And make sure this one is locked before you go up. Don't answer the door to anyone. Got it?"

"Yes. We'll be all right."

"Are you afraid?" he asked.

"No," she lied. "Not for me, but for you. What if . . . what if Pascal *is* a double agent? Oh, Clive, be careful."

Clive kissed her on the top of the head. "I will. Don't worry. I'll be fine. I have my revolver. And he knows I have it."

"But what if *he* has a gun?" she whispered frantically. "Hidden somewhere?"

"I don't think so. I sized him up. Darling, don't worry. I've faced much worse than him. And maybe I'm wrong. Maybe he's harmless. A veritable Stan, as you say."

The sudden mention of Stan made her smile. "Just be careful, Inspector," she said, grabbing hold of his lapels and giving him a little shake. "You're not invincible, you know."

"I know. But almost." He winked at her.

Pascal and Edna bustled in, then, each carrying a case. Clive gave her a quick kiss, but paused long enough to look into her eyes. "I'll be back as soon as I can. Be careful."

The upstairs room was horribly musty, and cobwebs hung in the corners of the slanted ceiling. There was only one big feather bed positioned between two dormer windows and a small chair and bureau. Henrietta went to one of the windows and considered opening it. She should probably leave everything locked up tight, but there was no way they could sleep up here without any air, she decided. She picked up the little latch and pushed the frame open just a crack. Immediately, she felt a little breeze.

"That's better, isn't it?" she said, turning around to see Edna just standing forlornly in the middle of the room, gripping the case handle with both hands, as if she were in shock. She seemed to have forgotten her purpose.

"Just set that in the corner, Edna," Henrietta instructed kindly.

Edna shook her head as if in a daze and looked around, blinking her eyes several times. "But won't you be wanting your things, miss?" she finally said slowly, as if coming out of a dream. "Your dressing gown?"

"No, I'm not getting undressed. And if I do need something, I'll get it myself."

"Yes, miss."

Edna dutifully set the case in the corner and then walked back to the bed. She removed the quilt folded neatly at the foot and began to arrange it on the floor beside the bed.

"What on earth are you doing?" Henrietta asked.

"Well, I can't sleep in the bed with you, miss."

"Don't be silly. Of course, you can."

"Oh, I don't think so, miss. What would Mrs. Caldwell say? Or, worse, Mrs. Howard? The other Mrs. Howard, I mean, miss?"

Henrietta laughed. "I can assure you, Edna, neither of them will ever know. We'll swear an oath of secrecy; how about that? And anyway, remember what I told you so long ago about my family? About how we used to sleep three or four to a bed?"

"I figured that was all just a big story you told, miss. I believed you, too," she said with a little pout. "In the beginning, anyway. Then I realized you were just foolin'."

"I wasn't foolin', Edna," she said, amused. "I'm from a very poor family. That's the truth."

"How come you don't sound poor? How come you always sounded so posh, then?"

"I guess I was a good actress. All those Saturdays working at Marshall Fields as a curler girl." She laughed again. "I picked up a lot on how one should speak," she said in a prim and proper voice.

"Oh, miss!" Edna suddenly cried, and Henrietta was surprised to see tears in the girl's eyes. "I do miss home so much. And who knows if we'll ever make it back. I have a terrible bad feeling. I really do."

Henrietta swallowed hard. She had a bad feeling, too, but she didn't dare admit it. "It'll be all right, Edna. You get some sleep. Go on," she urged, nodding toward the bed. "I'll keep watch. Not that there's anything I need to watch for, mind, but I need to be awake in case Mr. Clive comes back."

"Oh, miss, I should be the one to wait up an' all."

"Nonsense. I'm not in the least bit tired. It would be wasted on me. You lie down now. I insist."

"Yes, miss," Edna said tentatively. "If you're sure, like."

"Yes, now go on."

Henrietta watched as Edna crawled, gratefully it seemed, into the bed, careful to take up only a fraction of the whole. It didn't take long before Henrietta heard long, deep breaths coming from the girl. Henrietta picked up the small brass candlestick holder that the old woman had given her and walked back to the window, cupping the flame with her hand so that it wouldn't go out. She could see nothing in the blackness outside. No moon shone now, and even the stars seemed hidden behind invisible clouds. Henrietta paced back and forth, wondering how long it would take for Clive and Pascal to reach Saint-Quirin. She contemplated trying to riffle through her case to find her book but decided against it, as she didn't want to disturb Edna, and, if she were honest, she was too agitated to read. Finally, she sat down on the lone chair in one corner of the room, grateful that it was hard and scratchy, as she was determined to stay alert. The old woman had apparently returned to bed as well, and the house was now utterly quiet.

For a long time, Henrietta's mind raced with the events of the last few days, but the sound of a clock faintly ticking somewhere below eventually lulled her frenzied thoughts, and she finally gave in to her own exhaustion and nodded off, the candle still burning on the little table beside her.

When she startled awake, she had no idea how long she had been asleep. It was still pitch black out, she realized, her eyes darting around the room to get her bearings, so she couldn't have been asleep too long. She had been dreaming about Elsie and, oddly, Eugene. Something had woken her, but she wasn't sure what. She listened carefully, waiting, and then heard the noise again. It was a knock! Could it be Clive, back already?

Henrietta picked up the candle, which had burned down to a mere stub, and hurried down the stairs. There was another knock. It was strong, but not urgent, and it seemed to Henrietta that it was not the knock of a person who intended for the whole house to be woken, which made it seem all the more like it was Clive. As if he knew that only she would hear it.

She crept down the stairs and twisted the bolt. She was about to fling open the door, but instead paused, suddenly cautious for some reason, and peeked out the tiny pane of glass to the right of the door. It was not Clive as she had suspected, but Claudette! *Oh, Claudette!* Henrietta hurried back to the door, opening it wide.

"Oh, Claudette! Come in! How did you find us? I . . . I'm afraid I have some bad news. Here, come in."

Claudette said nothing but stepped quietly into the cottage.

Henrietta shut the door and turned back to embrace the poor woman, frantically trying to decide how she would explain what had happened. She stopped in her tracks, however, when she saw Claudette pull a gun from her coat pocket and point it directly at her. "Yes," she said, stiffly. "I'm afraid I have some bad news, too."

Chapter 23

"Oh, Melody, I'm afraid we won't make it," Elsie moaned. "What if he's already gone?"

"Well, we'll cross that bridge when we come to it, as my pops always says. Or, no use putting the cart before the horse."

"This is no time for jokes, Mel," Elsie said morosely, looking out the cab window at the buildings on Michigan Avenue passing by.

"I wasn't joking. All I'm saying is that you're awfully pessimistic. I've never met such a wet hen as you. But that's why I like you so much. You're a challenge. And I do like a good challenge, as you know."

Elsie sighed. She was tired of being everyone's pet project, but she couldn't worry about that now. She felt the sting, however, in being called pessimistic. *Was she pessimistic?* She didn't think so. In fact, she felt she was the opposite. Too hopeful for her own good.

"Aren't your classes challenge enough?" Elsie asked with just the tiniest trace of peevishness.

"You know those don't count. The only degree I care about getting is an MRS degree."

"MRS?"

"You know. Missus." Melody let out a little laugh.

"Oh, Mel," Elsie said, leaning her head against the window glass.

"All right. Let me get this straight." Melody clasped her hands neatly in her lap, appearing, finally, to be in earnest. "We're rushing to try to stop Gunther from leaving because you're becoming a nun. Do I have it so far?"

"Yes." Elsie fidgeted with her handbag.

"I'm sorry, but I don't quite follow."

"Look, Melody. It's not that difficult to understand. I've decided after all to become a nun, and there's no going back now, so don't even try. It's all arranged with Sister B., and I've written to inform my grandfather."

"Yes, I understand that part."

"Well, don't you see?"

"No, I'm afraid I don't. I suppose the MRS degree doesn't allow for such advanced logic."

Elise let out an exasperated breath and tried to quickly make sense of it herself. "If I disassociate myself from my grandfather and his money," she recited slowly, "then there is no money for Heinrich and Rita to chase after, and therefore they will relinquish their claim on Anna."

"So you hope."

"I'm very sure they're bluffing, to use your own word. Likewise," she went on, "if I become a nun, I won't be forced to marry someone I don't love and won't jeopardize my family's happiness by marrying . . . someone else."

"Meaning Gunther."

"Yes, Gunther," Elsie admitted with a blush.

"I see. So, essentially, you're sacrificing yourself?"

Elsie thought for a moment. "Yes, I suppose I am. What's wrong with that?"

"Hmmm . . . I can't decide if this is *It Happened One Night* or *Romeo and Juliet*."

Elsie rolled her eyes. "I thought you were being serious."

"I *am* serious. Look, Elsie, if you're so decided, then why are we chasing after him? Why not just let him go?"

"Because . . ." Elsie hesitated. "Because he doesn't have to leave because of me! He can stay here, and things can go on as they were for him. I've disrupted his life enough."

"I think he would call you more than a disruption," Melody tinkled. "And anyway, why would he want to stay here? He has a job, yes, and a place to live, but no way to care for Anna. He would have to return her to an orphanage and risk having her be committed to an asylum, or else find a different job where he can keep her with him, which is highly unlikely. What choice does he have? None. His decision to try to find work on a farm makes sense to me. Just let him go."

They had arrived at Union now, and Elsie, her face burning, paid the driver.

"Has it occurred to you that Gunther is trying to sacrifice himself for *you*?"

Elsie was finding it difficult to breathe. So much of what Melody was saying made sense, for once. But it was too late now. Or, was it? Maybe she shouldn't beg him to stay; maybe she should just wish him well on his journey—if they did happen to find him, that is, which was seeming unlikely now that she saw the crowds hurrying to and fro as they stepped inside of Union Station. *How would they ever find him?* Elsie stood in a daze, looking around bewilderedly until Melody took her by the arm, pointing to the sign for tickets.

They weaved their way through the crowd to the ticket booth, Elsie despairing at the sight of the line in front of it. As she waited her turn, she tried to read the big chalkboard behind the counter, searching desperately for a train bound for Nebraska, but not seeing it anywhere. Did that mean it had already left? Her palms felt sweaty by the time she reached the counter.

"Where to, miss?" the clerk asked, his green visor pulled so far down his forehead that Elsie could barely see his eyes.

"I'm looking for a train going to Nebraska."

"Where at in Nebraska?"

"I'm not sure exactly. Omaha maybe?"

"Don't you even know where you're going?" He peered at her suspiciously and then at Melody.

"She's looking to catch someone before he leaves," Melody said over her shoulder. "She forgot to tell him something."

"Like that, is it? Sweethearts, eh?"

"Something like that, yes," Melody answered.

"Ah. Well, I reckon he'd be on the California Zephyr."

Elsie blinked, trying to comprehend this information. "Does it stop in Omaha?"

"Sure does, miss."

"Did it leave already?"

"No, miss." He glanced behind him at the many clocks on the wall. "Leaves in fifty-six minutes."

"Oh!" Elsie cried. "Where would I find someone who was waiting for that train?"

"Now, how would I know that?" He gestured impatiently. "But if it was me, I'd bet on them being in the Great Hall. That way." He pointed.

"Thank you!" Elsie cried, and she and Melody hurried in the direction the clerk had pointed, racing past newspaper boys and carts selling bags of peanuts and pipe tobacco until they reached the Great Hall. Elsie paused for a moment at the edge of it, awed by the hall's majesty and marveling that such beauty had been afforded to what was essentially just a holding place for people traveling through. It was a room made almost entirely of marble, with a domed roof of glass and marble pillars, their Corinthian flourish trimmed in gold, keeping sentinel around the vast perimeter. Long dark mahogany benches ran from one end of the hall to the other, upon which were seated at least a hundred people, dwarfed by the voluminous space above them and waiting to begin a new chapter of their lives. Elsie looked out at the sea of people and wondered how they would ever find Gunther.

"Let's start at one end and make our way," Melody suggested. Elsie nodded and followed her to the left. Quickly, they walked down the rows, sometimes having to step over people who were sleeping on the ground or piles of baggage, looking for a lone man with a little girl.

They passed row after row, Elsie's panic rising with every step, until they finally spotted them on one of the last benches.

"Gunther!" she cried, running to him. "Oh, Gunther, I'm so glad I caught you."

At the sound of his name, Gunther looked up quickly, his face one of curiosity before it evolved into one of joy and then concern. He stood up uneasily. Anna remained sitting on the bench, her little legs dangling and her fingers in her mouth as she watched them. An old suitcase and a seaman's duffel bag were piled beside her.

"What are you doing here?" Gunther asked eagerly. "And you are here, too, Miss Merriweather."

"I think you can call me Melody by now," she said with a little grin.

"Melody," he said then with a little nod, his face grave. "What is it? What is wrong?"

"That depends on whom you ask," Melody added, twirling a lock of her blond hair. "Elsie, here, has something to tell you. Don't you, Els?"

"Melody, perhaps we could have a moment. Alone."

"Oh, sure thing! I'll just wait over there," she said, nodding toward a bench where two soldiers were sitting. She gave Elsie a wink and sauntered slowly away.

"Elsie, why are you here?" Gunther said, looking up at the big clock on the north wall. "I have to go soon."

"Gunther, how could you just run away? Without telling me? Without saying good-bye?"

"Elsie. I hoped to spare you. It is better this way, no?"

"No, of course it isn't!"

"Elsie, we must do this thing. Do not make it harder than it already is. After our talk with Mr. Bennett, I went and spoke to Heinrich. He is ruled by this woman, Rita, and they will not relent. I know it now.

He gave me no hope, though I believe it grieved him to tell me such. He is utterly in her power."

Elsie shook her head dismissively. "We don't need to worry about them anymore. I've . . . I've come to a decision, Gunther," she said steadily. "I . . . I'm entering the convent. Don't say anything!" she blurted, holding up her hand at his immediate facial protest. "I've already spoken to Sister Bernard, and I've also written to my grand-father, renouncing him and his money. I'm going away soon, as a matter of fact. To Dubuque, to the mother house. There I will con-tinue my studies and take my final vows."

"Oh, Elsie. No. This is not the way."

"Gunther, please," she said, trying her best to be calm though her insides were roiling. "You must let me go. I *want* to go."

The look he gave her was filled with so much love that she felt she might burst into tears. She bit the inside of her cheek to steady her-self. "So, you needn't run," she said hoarsely. "You can stay. Heinrich and Rita will soon drop their claim. Don't you see?"

"Oh, Elsie," he repeated. "We have been through all of this before, you and I. You are not meant to be a nun."

"Yes, I am!" she said, tears in her eyes now.

"No, *Liebling*. You were meant to be some good man's wife." He reached out and stroked her cheek. "And I will not be able to be near you when that happens. It is better if I go."

"Oh, Gunther!" Elsie sobbed now, unable to hold in her tears any longer. "*You* are that good man," she said before she could stop herself.

Gunther wrapped his arms around her, holding her as she cried. He kissed her hair and then her cheek and then, before she knew what was happening, he kissed her lips, deeply, tenderly, as she had never been kissed before, and something inside of her snapped. She felt unable to breathe at the thought of not being with him. Of saying good-bye to him and of herself boarding a train in a week to begin a religious life. She felt utterly claustrophobic, as if something inside her was being born and dying at the same time.

"Elsie, it's too late," he said into her hair. "Everything's arranged. I used all of my money for these tickets."

"Gunther, please don't go."

"Elsie," he said, cupping her face in his hands. "I have to go. For Anna's sake. There is nothing here for us. I feel deeply for what you have done for me, but let us finish it. This is what real love looks like. Letting go."

Elsie stared frantically into his deep-blue eyes, her heart pounding. "Take me with you," she said desperately, before she could even think it through. "Please."

"That's impossible," he said, though she saw just a flicker of hope in his eyes before he extinguished it.

"Nothing's impossible." Hesitantly, she brushed back a lock of his hair, and his eyes closed at her tender touch. "'Heart, are you great enough / For a love that never tires?'" she dared to say, quoting the Tennyson poem they had once recited to each other. "'O, heart, are you great enough for love?'"

"Elsie, do not do this," Gunther begged, his voice wavering.

"'I have heard of thorns and briers,'" she went on steadily. "'Over the thorns and briers, / Over the meadows and stiles, / Over the world to the end of it / Flash for a million miles,'" she said in a whisper.

Gunther stared at her, tears welling in his own eyes now. "Oh, Elsie," he said, wrapping his arms around her and drawing her close. "I love you so. God forgive me, I love you."

Chapter 24

"Oh, Claudette! What . . . what are you doing?" Henrietta exclaimed, unable to take her eyes off the gun pointed at her chest.

"Where is it?" Claudette demanded.

"Where is what? Claudette, please." Henrietta tentatively reached out a hand. "You're upset. In shock, maybe."

"Do not move!" Claudette barked. "Stay where you are." Claudette cocked the gun, and Henrietta's pulse jumped. She took a step back.

"I said, where is it? The panel. Where is it?" Her eyes darted briefly around.

"It's . . . it's over there," Henrietta answered with a nod of her head.

Claudette followed Henrietta's nod and then backed slowly across the kitchen, keeping the gun trained on her all the while.

"Good. Do not move," she snapped again and lifted the pantry curtain back to take a quick look. "It is all wrapped perfectly, I see. Good. I will take it from here."

"Claudette," Henrietta said, taking a few tentative steps closer. "I don't understand. What's going on?"

"Of course, you do not. You Americans are so stupid. You could not leave it alone, could you?"

"I thought you didn't have any interest in the panel . . ."

"Well, I lied. Obviously. Again, your stupidity is *incroyable*."

"But . . . but why?" Henrietta tried to stay calm. "You can't possibly be allied with Hitler. . . . Are you?"

"No, of course I am not. I mean to sell it to his henchmen and then escape with the money. You came very close to the truth the other night when you asked me if I did not yearn to get away, to travel, to have a life of my own. But of course, I desire these things, but I cannot have them while under the thumb of Valentin. Instead, I am forced to sit in a moldy château caring for my doddering father, hopelessly lost in his own deluded past. The panel is my only chance to escape."

Henrietta swallowed hard at the mention of Valentin. "Claudette," she faltered, "I think you should know . . . I . . . I think Valentin might very well be dead."

"*Oui*, he is," Claudette said coldly.

Henrietta was stunned by her lack of emotion. "You know?"

"Yes, he was in the car with the Germans. I saw him get in."

"But don't you . . . don't you care?"

Claudette shrugged. "*Un peu, peut-être*. But it is Wirnhier that is the more immediate loss. He was my contact."

"Your contact? I thought he was a friend of Valentin's."

"A friend? *Non*. He was merely a business associate. It was me that negotiated the deal with him regarding the panel. It was me that invited him and his fellow officers."

"*You*? So it's not Valentin who's in league with the Nazis?"

"I'm sure he was in some capacity. He was just as much of a swine as they are. Both of us, it seems, understood good business. Valentin had his own dealings with them, and I found an opportunity as well. Something they couldn't resist. We have been negotiating for months now, and you have made a mess of it."

"So he . . . he didn't know anything about the panel?" she asked, trying to think back through her various conversations with him to see where she and Clive had gone wrong.

"I am fairly certain he did not. When the panel came into my hands some months ago, it took me a while to realize exactly what it was and its immense value, especially to the Reich. But when I did, I hid it before Valentin or anyone else might discover it. That is until this Stafford showed up. That little *épisode* made me see that it was time to get rid of it. I thought I had sufficiently dealt with the problem, but obviously not. Once one rat appears, there are usually more."

Henrietta allowed Claudette's words to sink in and felt slightly sick to her stomach as she realized what she meant. "Did *you* kill Stafford? And Monsieur Bonnet? We thought it was Valentin."

Claudette let out a loud laugh. "Valentin? No, of course it was not him. He did not possess the stomach for such things."

"So, it was you?" Henrietta swallowed hard, realizing that, if this were true, she was in very grave danger.

"Not me exactly, but . . . Come, enough of this. You will help me."

"Help you? You don't mean to just walk out of here with it right now, do you? It's impossible. It's almost too much for two men to lift."

"Oh, help will be along soon."

"Help?" Henrietta's mind darted ahead to who that might be. "Who? The Nazis?"

"No, unfortunately, they were all in the car that went over the cliff. No, it is Pascal, of course. We have been in league from the very beginning, you see. Or did he not mention that?"

Henrietta could feel all the color drain from her face. Clive had been right all along!

"But he's . . ."

"With Clive? *Oui,* but not for long. He will soon take care of him."

"But Clive has a gun . . ." Henrietta croaked.

"So does Pascal, *chérie.* Do you think I am stupid?"

Henrietta's mind raced, thinking quickly back through the events of the night. She was so sure Pascal was on their side. *Oh, what should she do!*

"Pascal should be arriving any time now, and then we will go. Very soon, I suspect the car of overturned Germans will be discovered by some farmhand, and then a whole swarm of them will be upon us.

They will see the panel and take it, not understanding what it is, of course. But it will eventually reach Himmler or Göring. And then I will have lost my chance to profit by it. No, I must find a new contact before that happens."

"But where will you go? With a giant panel in tow?"

"I will worry about that, *chérie*. You should worry about yourself."

"Claudette, you can't give it over to Hitler," Henrietta pleaded. "He's planning on using it for something terrible. Once he has this piece, he'll be able to slot it into the bigger whole and a map of lost weapons will be revealed."

Claudette let out a loud laugh. "You believe this?"

"It doesn't matter if I believe it," Henrietta said, suddenly aware that she was repeating Hartle's own words, "it's if Hitler believes it. Or, better yet, if the German people and the German army believe it. They will think themselves invincible."

"*Chérie*, you are entirely influenced by too many fairy stories. I care not what Hitler does with this panel."

"But there might be a war!"

"Of course, there will be a war. Like all men, Monsieur Hitler will play his part in history, grand or small, and then fade away. It is the women who endure. Remember that, *chérie*, and do not be so very dependent on men. It is a very bad habit you seem to have."

Henrietta's face flushed. "How dare you lecture me! You're nothing but a common thief."

"No, *chérie*, not common. That is you, I think."

Henrietta was about to throw out another retort, but before she could, both she and Claudette froze when a squeaky "Miss?" was heard from the top of the stairs. With horror, Henrietta realized that Edna was awake and about to come down. "Is that you? Is Mr. Clive back?"

Claudette shot Henrietta a look of not exactly panic, but of suspicious concern, and put her finger to her lips, indicating that Henrietta should be quiet. Henrietta's heart was racing. "Don't come down, Edna!" she shouted, but it was too late. Edna's bare feet appeared on the upper steps, followed by the girl herself, her thick brown hair loose and flowing down her back. "Miss?" she called uneasily.

"Edna!" Henrietta shouted, trying to warn the girl to retreat, but just then, the door behind them burst open. It was Pascal, himself holding a gun. Startled, Claudette lurched to the side, but as she did so, her gun fired. Henrietta screamed when she saw Edna fall down the stairs.

"Edna!" Henrietta cried and rushed to her, falling to her knees beside the unconscious girl. She could see blood already beginning to seep through Edna's dress near her shoulder, and Henrietta let out another cry of panic. "Oh, God! Edna!" She lifted the girl's upper body off the ground and cradled her. Only then did she look behind her and was surprised to see a horrified Pascal, his hands shaking uncontrollably as he held the gun. For a moment, she was afraid he would turn the gun on her, but she quickly realized by the look of shock on his face that he was paralyzed by fear. Claudette, however, if she was at all shaken by accidently shooting a young girl, did not show it.

"Come, Pascal," she commanded. "Tie them up and get the panel."

Pascal continued to stare at Edna, awkwardly wrapped in Henrietta's arms now, as if he hadn't heard Claudette.

"Pascal!"

He slowly turned his gaze on her. "No," he said finally. "No, I am not going with you." He turned the gun on her. "I am going to America. With them."

Claudette's face changed from one of mild irritation to one of anger. She cocked the gun and pointed it at him. "Get the panel. Now!" she shouted.

Henrietta gripped Edna tighter and braced herself for whatever was coming next. Pascal, however, did not move, and Henrietta saw his eyes grow suddenly big, as if he were seeing a ghost. She followed his gaze and stifled a cry to see that Clive had suddenly appeared in the doorway, hovering directly behind Claudette. Without waiting a second, Clive grabbed Claudette swiftly, wrapping his arms around her from behind and trying to disarm her. She fought valiantly, trying to wriggle free, but he easily overpowered her and the gun dropped from her hand, but not before again discharging.

Henrietta screamed at the sight of Pascal dropping to the ground, but Clive did not release his grip on Claudette, who continued to struggle violently to escape. He eventually twisted her arms behind her back and pulled her to the kitchen. "Let me go!" she yelled.

"Henrietta, help me," he called.

"I can't leave Edna, Clive; she's bleeding!"

"God damn it" he muttered, his face beet red now as he fumbled to undo his necktie with one hand and roughly yanked it from his neck. He thrust Claudette into a chair and tied her hands behind it.

"Let me go, you bastard pig!" she shouted in French.

Clive ignored her and hurried to Pascal, bending down to feel his neck for a pulse and quickly examining him. "He's all right. I think he fainted." He straightened and strode quickly over to Henrietta. "Here," he said, taking hold of Edna, "lay her down."

Henrietta released her grip on Edna and watched as Clive carefully peeled back the fabric of Edna's dress near the hole—*the hole!*—where the bullet had entered. "It's just a graze. She'll be fine. Here," he said, fishing for his handkerchief and placing it on the wound. Edna moaned. "Hold this tight," he instructed Henrietta.

"What is this?" called a raspy voice in French, and both Clive and Henrietta jumped. It was the old woman standing in the doorway of her bedroom, dressed in an old-fashioned white nightgown, her gray hair hanging down over her chest in one long plait. Henrietta had forgotten all about her! The woman looked confusedly at the scene in front of her and put her wrinkled hand to her mouth in horror. "What is this?" she repeated. "God have mercy."

"Madame!" Claudette called to her in French. "Help me! They are robbers. I am Claudette Von Harmon of Château du Freudeneck! They have stolen a very valuable painting and are trying to make off with it. See? They have tied me up. Help me."

Clive stood up and walked closer to them. "Believe no such thing, madame!" he also shouted in French. "This woman is an imposter; she is working with the Nazis. She is lying!"

The woman looked from one to the other as if trying to decide who to believe, though Henrietta wasn't convinced she had really heard either one of them.

"Clive, forget it. We need to get out of here!" Henrietta hissed.

Clive looked back at her and the unconscious Edna. "Yes, you're right. Come on," he said, giving Pascal a little kick before stepping over him. The woman gave Clive a feeble punch on the arm as he passed by her, but Clive ignored it.

Pascal groaned and stirred.

"Get up. Come on, hurry." Clive shouted. Pascal slowly raised himself up on one arm and looked dazedly around the room. He got to his feet and held his head.

"Come on," Clive called from inside the larder. "We've got to move this. Now!"

Henrietta watched intently as Pascal stood there, hesitating.

"Do not desert me, Pascal," Claudette said urgently. "I will reward you. Handsomely. Then you can go to America on your own if that is what you wish. Do not help them."

Pascal wavered for only a few seconds more, before turning his gaze from Claudette and running back to the larder. "*Non, je ne te fais pas confiance*—No, I do not trust you."

Pascal's defection seemed to ignite a hidden fury within Claudette. "Untie me!" she shouted at the old woman as she tried to lurch the chair toward her. Whether she could hear her or not, the woman seemed to understand Claudette's meaning nonetheless and hobbled forward, muttering in French what sounded like prayers. She went around the back of the chair to try to undo Clive's knot, but before she could do anything, Clive and Pascal appeared back in the room, heaving the panel between them. The woman paid them no attention, however, and continued to try to untie Claudette.

"Clive!" Henrietta shouted. "The old woman."

"Get the guns," Clive grunted as he and Pascal passed through the doorway.

"I can't leave Edna!" Henrietta cried.

"Get the guns!" Clive shouted more urgently this time, now outside.

Henrietta briefly lifted the towel she was holding against Edna's wound and nearly vomited when she saw the blood still gurgling. She pressed the towel back into place and closed her eyes, trying to control her panic. She took a deep breath, hurried to where Pascal had dropped his gun, and gingerly picked it up. Then she picked up Claudette's and carried them back to where Edna lay sprawled on the ground, carefully setting them down beside her. The old woman was still fumbling with Clive's knot.

"Get a knife!" Claudette shouted, but the old woman did not stop in her efforts. "Get a knife!" Claudette shouted again, this time hopping a little in the chair to get the woman's attention. The woman stopped, perplexed.

"Get a knife!"

The woman seemed to understand this time and nodded eagerly before hobbling to the kitchen.

"Clive!" Henrietta shouted, but there was no response. *Oh, God!* "Clive!" she shouted again. The woman had procured a paring knife now and was shuffling back toward Claudette.

Henrietta reached for Clive's revolver and stood up. "Stop right there!" she called, making her way over to the two of them. Claudette's face was flushed and perspiring. "Stop or I'll shoot!" she warbled, standing dangerously near Claudette now. The old woman seemed unaware of her presence and continued on in her task.

"You would not dare," Claudette spewed.

"Claudette, it's over. Give up. I . . . I don't want to hurt you."

"Ha. You do not have it in you."

Privately Henrietta suspected this to be true, but before she had to put her words to the test, Clive miraculously appeared.

"She's got a knife!" Henrietta called, nodding at the old woman.

Clive held up his hands, indicating that Henrietta should throw him the gun. Henrietta tossed it. Clive easily caught it and pointed it at Claudette in one swift movement. "Pascal!" he called.

Within moments, the young servant appeared in the doorway, completely out of breath.

"Get them to the car!" he commanded, and Pascal hurried over to where Edna lay, sprawled out and bleeding.

"*Mon Dieu!*" he muttered and scooped her up tenderly. Henrietta gathered the remaining gun and followed him, giving Claudette one last look.

Claudette, however, was not looking at her but at Clive, a small grin on her face again.

Henrietta followed Pascal outside to a battered old Renault, which was much smaller than the Bugatti had been, and helped him gingerly place Edna into the back seat. She was just hurrying around to the other side when she heard a gunshot and winced.

Clive came hurrying out of the cottage, then, and jumped into the passenger's seat, just as Pascal slid into the driver's.

"Clive!" Henrietta cried. "You didn't shoot her, did you?"

Clive did not answer. "Let's go," he said grimly to Pascal. "Now!"

Chapter 25

"As much as I hate to break up this touching scene," Melody chirped, interrupting Gunther and Elsie's long embrace, "you really should go soon, Gunther. The train leaves in sixteen minutes."

Gunther and Elsie broke apart, but Gunther continued to hold one of her hands, giving Melody only a quick glance before returning his gaze to Elsie.

"Melody, I'm . . . I'm going with him," Elsie said, though her eyes remained locked with Gunther's as she spoke.

Melody positively squealed. "I knew it! I knew you wouldn't be able to let him go! But what do you mean you're going with him? You mean now?"

Elsie nodded.

"No! How positively romantic! I knew you were a dark horse, Els!"

Elsie gave Gunther's calloused hand a squeeze and then released it. "Give me a moment," she said quietly to him.

"Yes, but if you mean to do this, we must hurry," Gunther said gently.

Elsie gave him a nod, looped her arm through Melody's, and walked a few steps away as Gunther began to gather his things and help Anna off the bench. "Melody," Elsie said glancing behind her for a moment, "will you help us?"

"Of course, I will! I'll play the role of the Nurse in *Romeo and Juliet*, only I won't inadvertently cause your deaths. Believe me! What should I do? I suppose you want me to cover for you with Sister Bernard?"

"Yes, but I don't know how. Tell her . . . tell her that I'm ill. And that I went back home. I'll write her a letter eventually and explain everything."

"Don't you think she'll be disappointed?"

"I'm sure she will, but probably not surprised."

"But what about your grandfather and this Heinrich business and all of that? Isn't that why you were proposing to become a nun in the first place?"

"I don't know, Melody!" Elsie groaned. "Maybe he won't find out that I defected? Maybe he'll just assume I'm off in some convent somewhere."

"What if Sister Bernard writes to him?"

"Oh! I hadn't thought of that!" Elsie's mouth twisted in despair.

Melody was quiet several moments, thinking, before her face erupted with a sly grin. "I've got it!"

Elsie looked at her hopefully.

"Maybe neither of them have to find out."

"What do you mean?"

"Listen, you're supposed to be in Dubuque next week, right?

"Yes," Elsie said tentatively.

"So . . . I'll go in your place! That will buy you some time."

"What do you mean you'll go in my place? That's ludicrous!"

Melody gave a little laugh, clearly pleased with herself. "No, it's not; it's brilliant. Listen," she said leaning closer, "the nuns in Dubuque don't know what you look like, do they? So, I'll go in your place, pretend to be you for a few weeks."

"Well, how will you explain your own absence?"

"My summer class is over next week. So, instead of going home to Wisconsin, I'll board a train for Dubuque."

"But what about your family? Won't they be expecting you?

"I'll say I didn't pass yet again and have to stay a few extra weeks for tutoring."

"And they'll believe that?"

"Probably. As long as I'm back for my cousin's wedding, they won't care."

"Oh, Melody, I don't know. This seems risky. And how will you get away from Dubuque?"

"Well, I'll eventually have to confess, of course, but it will be deliciously fun when I do. And in the meantime, you'll have time to get settled. Perhaps married in some city clerk's office," she added with a little wink.

The thought of not getting married in a church terrified Elsie, but she pushed it away. "I don't know, Melody. This is sounding more and more deceitful. Perhaps I should just write to Sister Bernard right away and tell her the truth. I'll write it now, if I can find a scrap of paper, and you can deliver it for me."

"No, you can't risk it. This will give you time. Believe me, I'm a terrific actress; no one will ever suspect. I can be very devout, you know, when I want to be."

"No, I can't lie to Sister Bernard," Elsie said, deciding that it might be bad luck to start her new life on a false note. "Here," she said, rummaging in her handbag and pulling out a scrap of paper. It was an old note that Gunther had written to her a long time ago—*To Elsie, with many thanks.—G.* It was nothing terribly touching or romantic, yet it had been the first thing he had ever written for her. It was the note he had attached to the tattered copy of *Family Happiness* that he had left outside her room. She couldn't possibly use it now, especially for something so formal as a resignation letter of sorts to Sr. Bernard, but she couldn't find anything else. A train whistle sounding in the background helped her to make her decision. She sat down on the nearest bench and dug for the stub of a pencil she always kept in her pocket, then began hurriedly writing, using her handbag as sort of desk. She wrote only the briefest of notes, saying that she had again changed her mind and that she would explain all in a letter later on. She closed it by begging for forgiveness.

"Elsie," Gunther called. "Come, we need to go."

Elsie stood up and handed the folded note to Melody. "See that she gets this, will you?"

Melody nodded quickly and wrapped her arms around Elsie. "This is it, I suppose," she whispered, hugging her tight. "Are you sure?"

Elsie could hear, finally, some real concern in her friend's voice. "You'll be okay?"

Elsie nodded. She didn't need to think it through. It all made perfect sense now. No one needed her as much as this man and this child did, and Elsie, for better or worse, needed to be needed. She had already reconciled having to leave her family when she thought she was to enter the convent, so she didn't need to work through all of that again. She did pause, however, at the thought of leaving Sr. Bernard herself, the woman who had strangely become a sort of surrogate mother to her. Well, she would have to. Perhaps she could write to her from time to time. And Sr. Bernard, she knew, while perhaps momentarily sad at the loss of Elsie, would not be devastated. For one thing, Elsie was not fool enough to regard herself that highly. And for another, wasn't this the essence of a nun's life? To not become attached to the people, or the things, of this world, to blindly go and serve where bidden? Hundreds of girls would come and go through Mundelein, and Sr. Bernard could shepherd *them*. The loss of one, surely, was not so very great.

"Yes, I'm sure," she said quietly and gave Melody a final squeeze. "Take care of yourself." She released her. "I'll write soon. When we get settled." She looked at Gunther shyly. He was holding Anna in one arm and carrying a suitcase in his other. Elsie went and picked up the duffel bag, which clanked, as if it held cookware.

"Thank you, Miss Merriweather," Gunther said earnestly. "I am in your debt. Thank you for bringing her to me."

"Go on!" Melody chirped. "You're going to miss your train!"

Gunther gave her a final nod and turned away, beginning to walk quickly across the Great Hall. Elsie followed. She gave one last look over her shoulder. "Good-bye, Melody!"

"Good-bye!" Melody called back, waving frantically. "Be happy!"

Melody continued waving until the new little family was out of sight before crumpling Elsie's note to Sr. Bernard and tossing it in the nearest garbage can.

Chapter 26

I f his calculations were correct, they should reach Paris by nine a.m. Clive had commandeered the old Renault now with Pascal beside him and Henrietta and Edna in the back. Edna had only once or twice gained consciousness, and though Clive assured all of them that her injury was negligible, he was, in truth, worried that the girl might be going into shock or that the wound would become infected if not treated soon. He had been driving for nearly two hours in the pitch black, the French countryside invisibly rolling along beside them. They needed food and water and also something to help Edna, but it was no use stopping in any of the villages they rumbled through, as everything was dark and shut up tight for the night.

The sun was just cresting the horizon when they rolled into a little town by the name of Châtillon-sur-Morin. It was just a small little hamlet, but Clive could see various merchants drawing open their shutters and shop boys wheeling out carts of wares and setting up pavement signs.

He drove the length of the high street and then pulled the car off the road near an old stone church. For what seemed the hundredth time, he looked behind him to see if they were being followed, but saw nothing. He had not, as Henrietta had feared, shot Claudette, or the old woman, for that matter, when exiting the cottage. He had intended to, though. Not to kill her, but to injure her enough to not be able to follow. He had aimed the gun at her foot, but at the last minute, he had shot the floor beside her instead. Quickly, he had tied up the old woman in a kitchen chair and thrown all the knives he could find out the back door and into the garden. Still, he knew it was only a matter of time before Claudette got free and either made haste to follow them or to return to the château and alert either the French authorities or some other German connection. The sooner they got to Paris and were rid of the bloody panel, the better, he thought bitterly as he turned off the car's ignition.

"You go see if you can find some food and water. Maybe some wine," he said to Pascal and tossed him some Francs as the two climbed out of the car. "Also some vodka, if you can find it."

"Vodka?" Pascal asked, his voice hoarse from lack of use.

"For her shoulder," he said, nodding toward the car. "Unless there's a *pharmacie* open somewhere, vodka will have to do."

Pascal nodded and hurried off. Clive opened the back door of the car and observed the girl. Henrietta had wedged herself at the very edge of the seat so that Edna could lie as flat as possible, her head resting on her mistress's lap.

"What do you think?" Henrietta asked as he felt Edna's forehead.

"She's a little warm, which isn't good. Has she woken at all?"

Henrietta shook her head. "Not really."

Clive swore internally. That wasn't a good sign. If it was just a graze, she should have gained consciousness by now. Maybe there *was* still a bullet lodged there.

"Here, let's try to get her coat off so I can see better," he said and balanced one knee on the seat while he gently lifted the girl's torso. "You pull the coat," he huffed.

Henrietta began to tug at the coat and was able to get the girl's good arm free. When she pulled at the other sleeve, however, Edna let out a long moan. Henrietta looked at him as if for instruction, and he nodded. She pulled harder and the coat came off, though Edna let out an actual shriek as she did so. Clive saw Henrietta blanche at the sight of the girl's dress soaked in blood and suddenly feared she might faint herself.

"You all right?" he asked her gently. "It's not as bad as it looks," he said, hoping it wasn't a fib. "I've seen worse."

"Yes, I'm fine, darling," Henrietta said, but he could see she was struggling.

"Hold on a minute." Clive reached inside his jacket pocket for his flask. "Here you go," he said, unscrewing the cap and holding it out to Henrietta.

"No!" she protested. "Give it to Edna. I'm perfectly fine," she insisted.

"Doctor's orders," Clive commanded. "You're no good to Edna if you pass out as well. Nor to me; I need you to help."

"So, the truth comes out, I see. This is really just about you, isn't it?"

"Well, I can't do this alone," he said with a small grin.

Henrietta took a longish drink and gasped. "That's very strong, even for you, you naughty thing!"

Clive merely raised an eyebrow. "I need to get a look at that wound. Do you think you can slide out from under her so that she's lying flat? Yes, that's it," he said, as Henrietta squeezed out from under Enda's head, her back against the front seat. "Here, climb out," Clive said, backing out and holding his hand out to her. "That's it. Steady," he said, and watched as she stretched her back and took a few wobbly steps.

"What should I do?" she asked, tenting her eyes against the rising sun and looking around.

"Look for something I can use for a bandage," he said, nodding toward the trunk. "A scarf or something."

Clive leaned back into the car, again balancing on the seat with his knee. He grabbed hold of the girl's collar and ripped it. Gently he pulled the fabric back to reveal her bare shoulder, save for her the strap of her shift, which itself had been torn by the bullet. The bleeding had stopped somewhat, but the wound looked angry. It was already beginning to fester and ooze. He was tempted to poke at it, to

determine if there was still a bullet lodged there, but he didn't want
to proceed without an antiseptic. Without any sort of warning, then,
he was suddenly overcome with memories of the war, and he felt he
might be sick. His hands began to tremble, and he shut his eyes tight,
trying to control the "fit," as he called these episodes, before it got out
of hand. He hated succumbing to this weakness, and he desperately
did not want Henrietta to see him in the throes of it.

"Here you go," called Pascal, interrupting Clive's concentration by
thrusting a bottle at him. He had somehow appeared by the side of
the car. Clive made himself open his eyes and unclench his fists to
grasp the bottle.

"It's gin. They didn't have any vodka. It'll have to do because they
didn't even want to sell me this, being so early in the morning," Pascal
chattered. "How is she?" He peered into the car.

"Not good," Clive muttered, unscrewing the cap and taking a swig.
The feeling of gin hitting his empty stomach served to distract him
from his panic, even more than the presence of Pascal had. "We need
to get going," he muttered, look down the street behind them again.
"Go around the other side and hold her. This is going to hurt."

Pascal jogged to the other side of the car and opened the door.
Tentatively, he put his hands on the girl's chest. "Like this?"

Clive nodded. "Hold tight." He pulled back the fabric again and
poured the gin onto the wound, which caused Edna's eyes to open
wide as she let out a loud scream.

"Clive!" shouted Henrietta, coming around behind him now.
"What are you doing?"

"I've got to clean the wound," he shouted over Edna's screams.
"Edna!" he commanded. "Stop! You must stop screaming! Oh, bloody
hell," he mumbled. "Give me the scarf!"

Henrietta handed it to him quickly. "Edna," she called from
behind him. "You're going to be all right. You're all right."

Edna, however, was hysterical now, thrashing about despite
Pascal's attempts to hold her. She screamed again. Clive clapped
his hand across her mouth, and her eyes grew wide with additional

terror. "Edna! Stop! You must stop screaming. You'll get us all killed. Do you understand?" he asked. Edna finally stopped wailing, seeming to comprehend Clive's words and slowly nodded. Clive released his hand and held a finger to his lips. "Shhh," he said and then quickly finished bandaging the girl's shoulder. By the time he climbed out of the car, her eyes were already closing again. She desperately needed medical attention, and yet he dared not delay here any longer. He looked at his wristwatch. If they didn't stop, they could probably make Paris in a couple of hours, he guessed. But Edna was already feverish and probably would get worse.

Damn it! Well, they would have to risk it, he decided. They couldn't just sit in this little village waiting for Edna to get better until the Germans found them. Besides, he argued with himself, it would be better for the girl to be in a real hospital in Paris, not attended by a local quack. "Get in!" he commanded Pascal and Henrietta. "We need to get back on the road."

"Clive," Henrietta said from beside him. "How is she?" He could see the fear in her eyes.

"Not good, I'm afraid. But she's young and strong; I'm sure she'll be fine. But the sooner we get to Paris the better. Sit with her and try to keep her calm."

"Yes, all right," Henrietta said, climbing into the back seat and lifting Edna's head back into her lap.

"Here, cover her with her coat. That's it," Clive said and slid into the driver's seat and started the car. He prayed that Hartle had gotten his message to meet him there. Otherwise, they were just sitting ducks.

"Sure you don't want me to take a turn?" Pascal asked, crossing his arms.

"No." Clive smoothly shifted the car into gear and sped up. Pascal was another problem he didn't have time for. He still didn't trust him, especially after Henrietta had hurriedly whispered to him what Claudette said about them being in league from the beginning. He thought it rather honorable of Henrietta to relate this damaging information, considering that she felt he was, even now, innocent.

Clive tried to observe him out of the corner of his eye. He seemed innocent enough, but what had Claudette meant? How exactly would they have been in league beyond having him hide the painting in the stables? He looked in the tiny rearview mirror and saw that Henrietta's eyes were already closed.

"How long have you worked at Château du Freudeneck?" he asked softly, careful not to wake Henrietta.

"About eight years," Pascal said absently. "I started when I was a boy."

"How well do you know Claudette?"

Pascal shrugged. "Not very, I suppose you would say."

Clive sighed. "Listen, Claudette told Henrietta that you were in league with her from the very beginning. What the hell does that mean?" He looked at him directly.

Pascal's eyes grew big. "I . . . I do not know."

"Cut the bullshit. What's going on?"

"I do not know. Honestly. She never singled me out before this . . . this incident with the panel. Perhaps that is why she asked me to escort Edna into town. I am not the only servant at the château to speak English, and yet she asked me. Asked me to be friendly with her."

"Friendly? Is that what you call it?" He shifted into a higher gear.

"I . . . you know, for what it is worth, I actually care for Edna."

"Like I said, cut the crap, kid."

"Look, I do not know what you wish for me to say. A couple of days ago, she summoned me and asked if I knew anything about you. If Edna had said anything. She said you might be looking for the panel that she had me hide in the stables. That I should keep an eye open in case there was trouble."

"What kind of trouble?" He glanced at the rearview mirror again.

"I do not know! I asked the same thing, and she told me to shut up and be ready."

"And you had no idea what she was talking about? About the German transfer?"

"No!"

"And you didn't think it was odd that you were asked to hide a painting in the stables in the first place?"

"I . . . I do not know. I do as I am bid." Pascal crossed his arms and looked out the side window.

"And you did not think it was odd that the mistress of the house gave the stable boy a gun?"

"Yes, I did. I tried to refuse, but she insisted," he said, looking back at Clive now. "There are many things about the Von Harmons that are odd, as you say."

Clive reflected that this was true, in more ways than one. He let out a deep breath. "How come you didn't use it on me? Wasn't that your instruction? And didn't you just say that you do as you are bid?"

"I . . ." Pascal fell silent, thinking. "Why should I have killed you?" he blurted.

"Shh!" Clive warned, looking nervously in the mirror again.

"For what?" Pascal asked in a quieter voice, himself looking over his shoulder at the two women in the back. Edna let out a little moan. "For a painting? For the Germans? I think not," he said bitterly.

Clive looked over at the young man, surprised by this new expression of emotion. Perhaps he *was* innocent, he mused, and decided to let the conversation drop. Whatever the case, he couldn't waste any more time at the moment trying to figure it out; there were too many other things to consider, such as how he was going to find Hartle in the huge city they were speeding toward.

It was just before nine when they reached the outskirts of Paris. The streets were becoming more crowded now and narrower. Clive was at first disoriented, not being as familiar with the southeast side of Paris, but as soon as they crossed the Marne river he began to recognize where he was. In fact, as he drove closer to the city center, he was amazed that it looked much the same as when he had marched through with the Second Calvary. A flood of memories washed over him, and he glanced in the mirror to see if Henrietta was awake yet.

He had been so eager to show her Paris, but, as usual, circumstances had intervened. *Why did nothing ever go according to plan?* He let out a frustrated sigh and pulled the car to the side of the road at the sight of a telephone box ahead. He could see Château de Vincennes in the distance.

"Are we here? In Paris?" Henrietta asked groggily from the backseat.

"Yes, I'm going to try to telephone Hartle. You three wait here." He shot Pascal a warning scowl.

Clive gave the car a backward glance as he strode down Rue de la Pyramide, then pulled open the tiny black door of the phone box and eased himself inside. The person before him must have been smoking because the booth was still cloudy with the scent of cheap French cigarettes. Clive rang the operator and waited several minutes for the call to be put through to the number Hartle had given him. He prayed that Hartle himself would answer instead of his assistant.

"Roberts here," came the voice over the line. Clive silently swore. It was Hartle's sergeant.

"Roberts, it's Howard. I'm in Paris. I've got the panel."

"*Well* done." Roberts's voice was professional, yet Clive could hear the excitement underneath. "Inspector Hartle left London yesterday. His instructions are for you to rendezvous with him at the Hotel Montmartre, near Sacré-Cœur. Rue de la Bonne. Twelve noon."

"The Hotel Montmartre? Got it," Clive said, looking at his wristwatch. It was already nearly ten. He would have to hurry.

"But, Howard? Be careful, there are spying eyes everywhere."

"Confirmed," Clive answered and hung up. He stepped out of the telephone box and looked up and down the street. Nothing seemed unusual. He hurried back to the car and slid into the front seat.

"Did you reach him?" Henrietta asked, looking curiously out the windows as best she could with Edna's head in her lap.

"More or less," he said as he pulled the car's ignition lever. "I've got to meet him at noon." He looked over his shoulder, and, seeing that nothing was coming, pulled back into the street.

"Noon? What about Edna?"

"Yes, I know," he said, shifting. "I'm going to take care of that first."

"What do you mean?"

"I'm taking her to a hospital. Hold on," he said and began dodging and weaving through the traffic as fast as he dared.

Fortunately, the attending staff at Lariboisière Hospital responded quickly upon seeing Clive carrying the senseless Edna through the front doors and immediately whisked her away into an exam room. The person behind the desk, however, a very rigid young man wearing a white coat, though the embroidery above his pocket did not designate him as a doctor, but rather a monsieur someone or other, acted with much more deliberation and careful attention to detail. He was rather dubious, for example, regarding Clive's elaborate explanation as to the cause of Edna's gunshot wound— something to do with an accidental shot aimed at a rat or maybe it was an owl. The man looked at Clive disbelievingly, one eyebrow raised suspiciously.

"You were shooting an owl?" he asked again in French. "In a barn, did you say?"

"Yes, that's right," Clive answered impatiently.

"And the bullet ricocheted off of solid wood?"

"No, I've explained this already. The bullet hit a piece of metal, a door hinge maybe, and bounced back."

"And who else was there? All of you?" The man looked at Henrietta now.

"Look, we need to go. We have urgent business, but we'll return shortly."

The man clicked his tongue against the roof of his mouth in disapproval. "I'm afraid not, monsieur. A gunshot wound requires us to inform the police. Even if the event was, as you say, accidental." He said the last word with deliberate emphasis. "There will have to be a thorough investigation."

"God damn it," Clive muttered, rubbing his eyes with one hand. "Look. We're leaving."

"Then I have no choice but to telephone the authorities at once," he said, picking up the receiver of the big black telephone on his desk.

"What is he saying?" Henrietta asked.

"He's not letting us leave. He says we have to wait for the police to come and question us because of the nature of the wound."

"Tell him I'll stay."

Clive searched her eyes, surprised that she would willingly volunteer to stay behind. "Are you sure?"

"Well, it's the thing that makes the most sense. You need Pascal with you to lift the panel, and, anyway, I should probably be here when Edna wakes up. She's sure to be terrified, poor thing."

Clive considered this plan. He didn't like the idea of splitting up again, but she did have a point. "But you're no good to the police; you can't speak French."

Henrietta shrugged her shoulders and gave a little grin. "Yes, that's unfortunate isn't it?"

Clive bit back his own smile and gave her a quick kiss on the cheek.

"My wife will stay behind," Clive said to the man. "We'll be back soon." Clive looked at Pascal and nodded at the front doors. Pascal obediently began a little jog toward them.

"Oh, no! None of you can go! I insist you remain!" the man squeaked, balancing the receiver between his cheek and his shoulder.

"Take it or leave it," Clive retorted and pulled Henrietta off to the side while the man began to furiously dial. "I'll try to be back as soon as I can," he said to her.

"What if the Germans turn up?"

"I highly doubt it. It's the panel they're after, not you and Edna. But, even if they do, you'll be safe here," he said, looking around at the staff hurrying to and fro.

"But will you be?"

"Course I will. We've got a substantial head start. If Hartle really makes it to the hotel by noon, this shouldn't take long. I'm well ready to be rid of this thing."

"I did so want see his expression when we handed it back."

"I'll make sure you get the credit," he said with a small grin.

"Beast! That's not what I meant, and you know it!" she said, pinching his arm.

"Ow!" He kissed her quickly. "I'll be back soon."

The Hotel Montmartre was a typical small establishment that looked centuries old, perched not far from Sacré-Cœur Basilica. Clive quickly assessed it, though it wasn't the peeling mustard-yellow paint on the inn's stucco exterior, the charming pots of flowers just outside the front doors, or the French flag snapping in the breeze to which he was paying attention, but rather how many doors there were and if the windows were accessible.

He pulled the car off the main street and into the tiny circle in front of the hotel and hesitated about what to do next. Roberts hadn't specified whether they were to meet inside or out. Clive slowly got out of the car, motioning with a finger that Pascal should remain where he was. Clive stood by the car and studied the streets surrounding, but saw no sign of Hartle. It would take a lot to transfer the panel up to a room, only to have it carried down again in what he assumed would be a matter of minutes, but, on the other hand, it seemed risky to just wait here with it in plain sight. Finally, at 12:05 and still no Hartle, he put his head back through the open car window. "I'm going in. Stay here," he said and pulled the keys from the ignition and safely deposited them in his pocket.

Clive stepped inside the foyer, immediately noting the delightfully perfumed air, a sharp contrast to the smell of diesel outside.

"May I help you, monsieur?" a clerk asked him in French.

"Yes, I'm Mr. Clive Howard," Clive responded, also in French. "I'm looking for—"

"Ah. Mr. Howard. Your party has already checked in. Mr. Hartle and associate, I believe," he said, running his finger along the guest book. "Room 201," the clerk said. "Shall I call the porter?"

"No," Clive answered slowly, relief flooding him that he had already arrived. He looked out through the doorway at Pascal, waiting patiently in the car. Maybe he should wait by the panel and send Pascal up with a message. No, he decided; he would run up quickly himself.

Rather than take the tiny, antiquated elevator sitting open at the right of the desk, Clive ran up the stairs to the second floor and strode quickly down the hallway until he reached Room 201. He looked up and down the hallway and then knocked quickly. "Hartle? It's me, Clive Howard."

A young man dressed in plain clothes opened the door and gestured Clive in. Hartle was standing over a table, examining a map of Paris.

"Howard, thank God you made it." Hartle said, holding his hand out to him and shaking it firmly. "Well done on retrieving the panel, old man!" His eyes darted beyond Clive toward the hallway. "But where is it?" he asked worriedly.

"It's down below, but we probably shouldn't just leave it down there. Have you brought some sort of truck? How are you going to transport it?"

"Yes, don't worry about that. I have it all arranged." He nodded at the man who had opened the door, and who now accordingly disappeared.

"Look, Hartle, you should know, we had some trouble getting out of Strasbourg. We were followed. Seems the Von Harmons do have Nazi connections. How deep I can't say."

"Just as I thought." Hartle began to pace a little. "You were followed?"

"Yes. A whole car of Nazis. We managed to evade them on a tricky pass just outside of Strasbourg."

"How?"

"There was an exchange of fire, and their car went over the side. I'm sure it's been discovered by now." Clive put his hand behind his neck. "And I'm pretty sure Valentin Von Harmon was among them."

"Jesus. Are you sure?" Hartle's gray eyes grew wide.

"Yes, his sister, Claudette, confirmed it. However, it seems that it was *she* who was the real mastermind behind the procurement and hiding of the panel. She meant to sell it to the Germans the night we escaped with it."

"Hence the chase."

"Yes."

"Where is she now?"

"I left her tied up in some cottage near Saint-Quirin, but she won't remain there long. I'm sure she's in pursuit." Clive walked to the open window and looked down at the car. He could see Pascal, outside of the car now and arguing with Hartle's man. "Listen, we need to get down there. Pascal doesn't know your man from Adam, and from the looks of it, he's going to get himself punched in the face."

"Whitfield has had worse."

"Still—" Clive broke off. His eye had caught sight of a car flying Nazi motor flags turn onto the Rue de la Bonne. "Jesus Christ!"

"What?" Hartle quickly joined him at the window.

"The Germans have arrived," Clive said hurriedly. "Seems they weren't all that far behind us after all."

"Shit!" Hartle said, letting the curtain panel he was holding drop back into place.

"You stay here and cover me; I'll go down," Clive said, striding quickly toward the door.

"Right." Hartle drew a pistol from his inside jacket pocket. "Whitfield is armed as well," he called to Clive.

Clive flew down the stairs two at a time, pulling out his revolver as he did so and trying to control the wild beating of his heart. This was quickly dissolving into a nightmare situation. He wasn't sure he could endure another shootout with the German army after St. Mihiel, where the war had ended for him when he had taken a bullet in the shoulder.

Clive looked quickly around the lobby for the desk clerk, but he had conveniently disappeared. *Well, one less thing to deal with.* Clive held the gun upright in front of his face, sidled up to the window, and cautiously peered out. The German car had pulled into the circle as well and was parked at an angle, so that there was no way the Renault with the panel affixed could drive around it. Clive saw that Pascal was cleverly crouching behind the car in an attempt to hide himself. Whitfield was not in sight. Clive arched his neck to try to see how many Germans were in the car that had just pulled up, but it was impossible to tell. At least two, for sure. But why did they just sit there?

Clive inched closer to the door, trying to decide what his plan of attack should be, when the door opened, startling him. He whipped his gun at the person entering and was shocked to see that it was, of all people, Claudette.

"Ah. Monsieur Howard. We meet again," she said calmly, also pointing a gun at him.

"Claudette?"

"I have new friends, you see. They are waiting in the car. In but a few moments, they will emerge and take the panel, which you have so kindly left for us."

"Put the gun down, Claudette," Clive said steadily, his heart pounding. "Before one of us gets hurt."

Claudette laughed. "Well, it will not be me, *chéri*. I should have shot you already, but I owe you one chance. I'm grateful that you did not shoot me in the cottage, though you really should have." She patted his cheek. "That was bad judgement on your part."

Clive swallowed hard. "How did you know we would be here?"

"I have my sources."

"Like who?"

"That is not important, *chéri*."

Clive watched her as she slowly backed up and waved her hand out the door, clearly a signal. He could hear orders being barked in German, and a young lieutenant approached.

"If there is any resistance from your friends outside," Claudette went on, "or upstairs, I suspect,"—her eyes briefly raised to the ceiling—"they will be shot."

"Claudette, there's no way out of this," Clive fibbed. "There's still time for you to get away."

Claudette laughed loudly. "No, *chéri*, there is still time for *you* to get away. If you hurry that is." She inclined her head. "Go on, out the back." A sly smile hovered on her lips.

"Don't be ridiculous."

"Have it your way, then," Claudette said, cocking the gun. "Come, come. Call off your lackeys. I cannot hold the German dogs from their prize forever. I must deliver what they have paid me for, but I cannot be responsible if you get caught in the middle. It would be a shame to kill you, but that is your choice."

Clive glanced at the stairs. Where the hell was Hartle?

Claudette took a step closer.

Out of the corner of his eye, he could see the German lieutenant open the car door and look inside. *Fuck!* The German pulled his head out and began to slowly walk around the car. Any second, he would practically trip over Pascal.

"Now!" Claudette commanded.

Clive raised his hands in submission, his revolver still in one of them, and shouted "Pascal! Back away from the car!"

"And the other one," Claudette ordered.

"I don't know where he is."

"Just do it!"

"Whitfield, don't shoot!" he called. The next thing he heard, however, was a shot ring out, and he was surprised to see the lieutenant fall. He had no idea if the shot had come from Whitfield or from Hartle, but he took advantage of Claudette's momentary distraction to knock the gun from her hands and kick it across the floor. More shots were being fired now. *Jesus, what was Hartle thinking?*

While Claudette ran to retrieve her gun, Clive hurried to the door and poked his head out, trying to assess the enemy's strength. Two, including the lieutenant, lie dead, and from what he could count, there were only four of them left, but they were positioned well. From behind one of the hotel columns, Whitfield gave him a quick nod.

"Cover me!" Clive called to him. He made a dash for the car and dodged behind it, where Pascal was kneeling prostrate, his hands over his head.

Clive waited for a break in the bullets whizzing by to poke his head around the edge of the car and fire. Another German went down. Both Hartle and Whitfield were firing wildly, but the Germans were too well covered. The return fire was intense, and Clive's gut wrenched when he saw Whitfield go down.

"Give me a gun!" Pascal shouted. "I know you have an extra. Give me the gun Claudette gave me before!" he insisted, his voice one of terror. "Now!"

Clive ignored him and fired again but missed. "Shit," he cursed, slumping back behind the car and breathing heavily. He was a sitting duck without Whitfield, but he was reluctant to give up his spare, and to Pascal, at that; but neither could he just leave him defenseless. He reluctantly groped his pocket for the small Luger and tossed it to him. "On my count," he commanded. "You shoot left, and I'll go right."

Clive waited for Pascal to creep into position and then quietly counted, "One, two, three—"

Both of them popped up, then, and began firing, and at least one German dropped. More shots were heard, then, and Clive realized that Whitfield was still alive and shooting from where he lay. Clive continued to shoot until he was out of bullets, cursing under his breath. All of his extras were in his case. Pascal seemed out, too. The two remaining Germans fired, and with no resistance, grew bolder and began to gingerly advance. No more shots came from above, and Clive feared that Hartle had been hit. He glanced up at the window, but his attention was immediately drawn back to the street when more shots rang out. Whitfield, apparently not yet dead, had managed to shoot one of them from where he lay, but Claudette emerged from the hotel now and, standing over him, shot Whitfield point blank.

"Shit!" Clive cursed. He had almost forgotten about Claudette.

Why hadn't he knocked her out when he had had the chance just now in the hotel? What was wrong with him?

He poked his head around the edge of the car again and was pretty sure it was just her and one German soldier left. If he could just sneak around behind them . . .

Clive looked over at Pascal, who seemed to have the same idea by the way he was tilting his head to the side and pointing, trying to get Clive to understand his plan. Clive looked desperately around for something to throw as a distraction, but could find nothing, not even a rock. Miraculously, Pascal seemed to understand and, after rummaging for a moment or two in his coat pocket, pulled out the bottle of gin he had purchased that morning in Saint-Quirin. He stretched and handed it silently to Clive, who gave him a nod. Balancing on the balls of his feet, Clive arched his arm behind him and threw the bottle as hard as he could toward the German soldier. He heard it shatter on the pavement, and while that meant it had not connected with the man, it had been enough, Clive knew by the rapid stream of fire now in his direction, to distract him from Pascal's quick dodge to an automobile parked nearby. Clive again looked around for something to throw but stopped when he heard Claudette's voice call out.

"You've resorted to throwing bottles of alcohol now? Come, *chéri*, we both know that it is over. We are done with silly games, and you are at my mercy. Step away from the car and let me have the panel. Neither of us really want it, but there are those that do, like Mr. Hitler and your poor Mr. Hartle." Something pinged in the back of Clive's mind. How did she know Hartle's name? "Since Mr. Hartle seems to be no more, let us let Mr. Hitler have it, shall we? I will allow you and your pretty wife, the countess, to leave quietly. All you have to do is walk away. I will sail to Costa Rica and never be heard from again. It is simple."

Sweat was pouring down the back of Clive's neck as he quickly assessed the situation. Calculating that it would be better to face her standing than to have her tower over him with a gun while he crouched behind a car, and banking on the fact that it would distract both her and the soldier from Pascal's movements, Clive decided to slowly stand up with his hands raised.

"Ah. There you are. It is always better to face one's executioner, is it not?"

"Claudette, listen," Clive pleaded, quickly taking in the scene in front of him. Claudette was not more than ten feet away. The German soldier, his machine gun trained on him, stood further back. Out of the corner of his eye, Clive could see Pascal creeping closer and closer, which, rather than filling him with relief, was now suddenly filling him with panic as he realized the improbability of a young servant successfully overtaking a trained soldier of the Reich. More than likely, Pascal would get himself killed, adding yet another senseless death to this fiasco. Maybe he should just let Claudette have the panel, Clive quickly bargained. What would it matter in the long run? It wasn't worth getting killed for, especially something that was so ludicrous in the first place, but it was so damned difficult to just walk away.

"*Oui, chéri?*" she called out, amused. "What do you possibly have to say to me?"

"Claudette, you're deluded. You mustn't give this to the Germans. It will be a powerful tool in Hitler's hands. It would be a tragedy."

"A tragedy? What do you Americans know of tragedy?" she scoffed. "And it is you who are deluded. You play the part of the upstanding detective very well, *Inspector* Howard, but something darker lies deep in your heart, does it not?"

Clive bit the inside of his cheek.

"You know that the world does not play fair. That justice is not always served. Great atrocities go unpunished."

Out of the corner of his eye, he could see that Pascal was nearly upon the German now, and Clive mentally tried to will him to advance no further.

"But you should know, *chéri*, that things aren't always as they seem. Take for example your pretty wife, or even your Mr. Hartle—"

There was a strangled cry, then, from the German, his gun firing aimlessly into the air as Pascal grabbed him and wrapped his arms tightly around the man's neck in an apparent attempt to strangle him. Startled, Claudette turned and aimed her gun at Pascal, and Clive started forward to stop her. Before he could reach her, however, a shot rang out and Claudette fell at his feet. Clive stood, incredulous, his heart pounding as he stared at her lifeless body. His first thought was that it was the German who might have accidentally shot her while wrangling with Pascal, but then another shot rang out and the German fell, too.

Clive looked at the upper window and saw that it was Hartle, still very much alive and well. Hartle grimly waved his hand and then disappeared inside.

In a daze, Clive looked back at Pascal, who stood beside the dead German, his chest heaving. Pascal looked as if he was about to be sick, or at least cry. In a state of shock himself, Clive dropped to the ground and felt Claudette's neck for a pulse, though by the size of the hole in her chest, he knew it was pointless. As predicted, he could feel no pulse and instead felt a wave of grief overcome him. It was the same as he had felt during the war and for months after, when he lay convalescing outside of London. The horrible waste of life. He closed his eyes and tried to steady himself. Maybe he wasn't cut out for this type of work anymore. He felt a hand on his shoulder.

"I'm sorry, Clive. But it couldn't be helped."

Clive stood up, his chest tight with anger. "Why did you shoot her?" he demanded. "It wasn't necessary!"

Hartle looked at him, incredulous. "Not necessary? Are you blind, man? She was coming toward you with a gun pointed straight at you. You were unarmed, as was your man, who looked to be in a deadly struggle with the enemy and a shot went off." Hartle's brow was deeply wrinkled. "I'd say that was grounds for shooting. Look, I'm sorry that she was family, but she was colluding with the enemy. I didn't have a choice."

Clive didn't respond, trying for a moment to take in the scene from Hartle's point of view. He gave a slow nod and then rubbed his eyes with one hand. Hartle patted him on the shoulder.

"Come on," Hartle urged quietly. "We've got to get going."

Clive let out a long, deep sigh. He looked over at Pascal, who was sitting on the ground now. His hands were bloody, and he thought he saw actual tears in his eyes. He knew he should probably go over to him, but now was not the time.

"Come on," Hartle repeated. "We've got to get this panel hidden. Let's go. Before the French authorities show up." Even now, Clive could hear the familiar drone of a French police siren in the distance. "There's a truck in the alley. Behind the hotel. Let's go."

Clive gave a whistle in Pascal's direction, and he looked up blearily. "Come on, Pascal," Clive said, suddenly realizing that it was the first time he had actually ever used the boy's name. "We need to hurry. Get inside and cut the ropes," he said, tossing him a pocketknife. "No time to untie them."

Pascal caught the knife midair and climbed into the car. Within seconds, he had cut the ropes, and Hartle and Clive slid the panel, still wrapped in burlap, from the top of the car. Pascal came around and took one corner, and together the three of them lugged it down the alley beside the hotel until they reached a small black French lorry parked between some trash cans and old wooden crates. It looked like something from the war, too small to be a troop truck, but maybe munitions. "Set it down," Hartle grunted and then climbed up on the truck and untied the canvas cover. He hopped back down and again lifted his side of the panel. "Steady now. Easy does it," he instructed as the three of them managed to slide it into the truck. "Get up there, lad," he said to Pascal, who jumped up and took hold of it. Hartle climbed back up. "That's it. Now, lay it flat," he instructed, helping him to carefully lower it. "Good."

Pascal looked down at Clive as if waiting for the next instruction. Clive indicated with his head that he should jump down. The sirens were growing louder now.

"Howard, I must go. You'll deal with the police?"

"Do I have a choice?"

"Don't worry. MI5 will be involved. You've done your country and your father's country a great service."

Clive grimaced, remembering how many times he himself had written that to the parents of his men who had perished in the trenches. "I'm sorry about Whitfield."

"Yes, he was a good man. The best."

Hartle's eyes looked haggard as he climbed into the truck and bent to pull the choke. "Where will you take it?" Clive asked, nodding toward the back of the truck as it coughed into life.

"I can't say. I need to take it to my superiors. No doubt, it will go into deep storage somewhere. Best if you don't know. Thank you again," he said as he ground the truck into gear.

"Good luck," Clive called, just as two policemen rounded the corner of the hotel.

"*Arrête toi là!*" they shouted.

Clive put his hands up and let out a deep sigh. "Come on," he said to Pascal. "This isn't going to be pleasant."

Chapter 27

"Can't you just be pleasant for one evening?" Julia implored, turning on her tufted vanity seat to address Randolph, who had barged, unbidden, into her bedroom sanctuary.

"Pleasant? Of course, I can be pleasant." He stood behind her, bending to look into her mirror and straightening his tie. "When the situation calls for it." He stood up. "But this is not necessarily it. Your mother has really gone too far this time."

"For heaven's sake, Randolph." Julia leaned away from him and adjusted her earrings in the mirror. "It's just a small dinner party."

"Even so. It's unheard of for a widow to entertain before a year is up. Antonia Howard, of all people, breaking with etiquette? It's outrageous."

Julia gritted her teeth and stood up, swishing the tail of her claret Chanel gown behind her. "Well, she has already broken with convention in having the garden party, so perhaps she doesn't think it matters. And it's only us, really."

"And Agatha and John. And that grasping lawyer. Something's going on there; I swear, Julia. I think he's trying to take advantage while Clive's away." Randolph inserted the fingertips of his right hand stiffly into the front pocket of his tuxedo jacket. "I never did like him. Time and again, I tried to warn Alcott, but he wouldn't listen. Had the audacity to tell me—me!—to mind my own business."

Randolph wandered to the mantel and moved a small statuette of a cat, a gift from Randolph Jr. to Julia on her birthday last, to the right a fraction of an inch. "Personally, I think this Mr. Bennett is trying to wrest control of Linley Standard away from Clive, and he seeks to do it through Antonia. It's obvious, but she's too blind to see it."

Julia bit her lip. If only he knew.

"Well, all the more reason for us to be present, wouldn't you agree?" she said smoothly, thinking of Antonia's telephone call to her last week in which she asked if somehow just *she* could come to a dinner at Highbury and leave Randolph behind. The fact that her mother had so little love for Randolph was the source of extreme sadness, nearly despair, for Julia. She couldn't care less if her mother enjoyed Randolph's company—who did?—but it was the fact that her parents, mostly her mother, had practically pushed her into this marriage, which made her at times furious and at other times overcome with depression and regret. She had done what everyone had wanted her to do, what everyone expected, and now she was the one paying the price. It was so horribly unfair; she wanted to weep.

"No, Mother," Julia had said quietly into the telephone receiver in response to her mother's request, a small part of her brain privately worrying that her mother would even suggest such a thing—she who had relentlessly schooled Julia in every aspect, every tendril, of correct behavior. Maybe Bennett *was* having a bad influence on her. "I can't attend without Randolph. You know that. It would be unseemly. And anyway, he would be highly offended."

Antonia had sighed. "I know that, darling, but he can be so very disagreeable."

"Yes, well, you should have thought of that before you forced me to marry him," she retorted before she could stop it.

"Julia! How can you suggest such a thing?"

"Well, didn't you?"

"Of course, we didn't! You had your choice. You chose him, and your father and I approved. It was more of a choice than either of us had, as I've already revealed to you. I would have thought you would have taken that confession quite to heart," Antonia sniffed with the slightly wounded air.

Julia had not continued the argument, knowing that it would solve nothing and go nowhere except to cause hurt feelings. While it was true, in essence, that she had chosen Randolph Cunningham, she had *not*, at least in her mind, been given much of a choice. She sighed to think of how many young men had trailed after her, how much fun she had had drinking and dancing with them in speakeasies in the city and over wild weekends at various estates on the North Shore. She had never considered any of them, however, as genuine contenders for her hand, though at least a few of them were sons of wealthy families. She could have had any pick from the men that surrounded her, but somehow it had been Randolph Cunningham who had managed to charm her in the end.

Randolph Cunningham had cut a dashing figure in those days, lean and angular, but it wasn't his looks she had been necessarily attracted to—it was his commanding presence. He was several years older than her, and he had a steadying hand, something Julia, at that time, was rather in need of. He had been a bit of an enigma at first in that she felt safe with him for the most part, but then sometimes not. And it was this "sometimes not" part that had intrigued her. She should have noticed, though, she had reflected many times since, when they had gone riding on one particular fall afternoon early on in their courtship, how rough he had been with his horse and how frequently he had used his whip on the poor beast. At the time, it had caused a small ripple of alarm to niggle at the back of her mind, but she had stupidly put it aside, charmed by his deference to her and his many gifts, which grew more and more expensive as the months progressed, until he finally presented her with a fourteen-carat diamond ring and the request that she become his wife.

Julia had been taken off her guard. It was true that she very much enjoyed his company, in a certain way, but she was not so sure she

was quite ready to be married. Randolph had already spoken to
Alcott, however, who had readily accepted his offer, dependent, of
course, upon Julia's acceptance. Julia, on her part, decided that while
she was flattered by his offer, she would need some time to think.
Eventually, however, she had given in, hounded as she had been by
Antonia, who, though not entirely satisfied that her beautiful daughter should end up with merely a Cunningham, had thought it best
for Julia to settle down before some sort of scandal arose, as it was
bound to do if Julia kept up her wild ways.

For a long, long time after the wedding ceremony—and the
unexpectedly violent honeymoon night—Julia blamed her mother
for the shipwreck she found herself in before ultimately turning the
blame upon herself. She should have been stronger, should have
held out, should have resisted. But she had not. She had instead
convinced herself that marrying Randolph, as everyone had advised,
would be the best thing for her, though she was only twenty-two at
the time.

"Are you ready yet?" Randolph snapped. "My God, you take your
time. What are you worried about if it's only Agatha and John?"

Julia did not respond but wearily picked up her gloves and moved
toward the door.

"I hope that cowboy isn't going to be there," Randolph said, holding the door for her. "What's his name again?"

"Glenn Forbes," Julia said lightly without looking at him.

"Yes, that's it. Forbes. Well, is he?"

Julia made a show of looking around for her handbag. "I wouldn't
know, Randolph. Mother did not mention him."

"I find that hard to believe. Antonia tells you everything."

"Well, she didn't this time."

"If he is, by God, behave yourself. Don't make a fool of me by
throwing yourself at him."

"Randolph!"

Randolph sidled up to her and grasped her upper arm tightly. "You
know what I'm referring to, so don't play the innocent," he hissed, his

face so close to hers that she could feel his hot breath. "If you do, I'll send the boys so far away from you that you'll never see them again."

"Don't be ridiculous," she spat at him, pulling herself away. Would he never stop referring to her acquaintance with Dennis Braithewaite, Victoria Braithewaite's son, of all people, whom she had befriended last summer at the club's annual ice cream social? The poor young man had been born with a twisted foot, and Julia had taken pity on him that day and sat with him. She had never paid him much attention before, but on that particular day, she had been drawn to him, sitting alone in the shade of a poplar tree. She had found him to be surprisingly intelligent and kind, and he was someone, she decided, the more she sat talking with him, who would be perfect for someone like Elsie. While she listened to him talk about his studies at the University of Chicago, she was actually considering how to arrange an introduction when Randolph had come upon them unexpectedly. He had, of course, thought the worst, despite her protestations, and had predictably taken out his anger on her that night. Since then, unfortunately, this cancerous fantasy in his mind had seemed to grow in elaborateness to the point that he now suspected she meant to flee with Dennis Braithewaite at any moment.

Julia maintained a calm exterior as she marched down the main staircase, Randolph following closely behind, but her heart was beating hard against her chest. She could endure his rough treatment of her, but of late, Randolph was using the boys more and more in his attempts to bully her, and it was working. Each time, she tried not to react, as she didn't want him to know how much it would utterly destroy her to have the boys taken permanently from her. At first, she thought he must be cruelly teasing her, but with each passing week, she began to believe that he really might do it.

As they rode in silence to Winnetka, Julia made a point of staring out the window at the darkness, knowing that Glenn Forbes would indeed be at Highbury tonight. In fact, it was the whole point of the dinner party, but she dared not tell that to Randolph.

During the telephone call last week with her mother, Antonia had reported that she had received yet another letter from Mr. Forbes, *tripling* his offer for the painting.

"I simply don't know what to do," she had complained to Julia.

Julia had rolled her eyes and twisted the cloth telephone cord. "Why don't you consult with Mr. Bennett?" she offered, knowing that stating her own opinion would be utterly useless. No one thought her opinion to be worth anything.

"I have! He advocates for selling it, saying that the estate could use the ready cash, an answer I find most indelicate, by the way, but he won't say much more than that, claiming that, being Mr. Forbes's uncle, his opinion could be construed as biased."

"Well, that's noble of him." Julia leaned against the big picture window near Randolph's desk where the telephone was perched.

"But that doesn't help me in the slightest, does it? *And* he's asking if Mr. Forbes might come over one more time to see the painting before he returns to Texas."

"He's returning to Texas?" Julia asked quietly, standing up a little straighter now.

"Well, he can't stay here indefinitely, can he? I assume he has to get back to his ranch or whatever it is. It's monstrous to think of one of your father's paintings hanging in what is probably nothing more than a barn. Or a shed of sorts."

"Mother, I'm sure Mr. Forbes's home is more than that."

"Be that as it may, I'll not be badgered. I'll allow him to see the painting one last time, as a favor to Sidney, but I'll make a dinner party of it to prevent any chance of a last grasping effort on the part of Mr. Forbes."

Julia twisted the telephone cord so tightly around her pinky that it began to feel numb.

"Do you think a dinner party is wise, Mother?" she asked, knowing what Randolph would say, and probably any number of ladies at the club, should they hear of it.

"Nonsense! It's just John and Agatha. And you—and Randolph, if he must."

Julia let out a silent deep breath, knowing how unpleasant it would be to spend an evening in the same room with Glenn under Randolph's watchful eyes, but she pushed this away for the moment. "Mother, have you considered the fact that perhaps you *should* sell it? It's just one painting. After all, Father occasionally bought and sold some of them, didn't he? I'm fairly certain that if he had been offered fifteen thousand dollars for a Frederic Church painting, he would have sold it. It's not as if it's a European masterpiece, you know."

"Whose side are you on?" Antonia had snipped.

"It's not a matter of being on sides, Mother," Julia said, quickly losing patience with this conversation. "But sometimes we have to look at things more practically than through sentiment. I know you've been through a lot these past months, but honestly, it might make sense. Or maybe it will make sense at a later time. Perhaps tell Mr. Forbes you'll think about it as a way to put him off."

"He's the type that, if you give him an inch, he'll take a mile. He's relentless, you know."

"Yes, I've observed."

"Oh, do say you'll come, Julia. I'll feel positively outnumbered if you're not there."

"Yes, of course, I will, Mother," she had answered with yet another sigh.

"Splendid," Antonia said and hung up the phone.

Upon entering Highbury, Julia was not surprised, then, to hear Glenn's deep laugh echoing all the way from the drawing room as Billings took her wrap. She felt her stomach nervously roil as she glanced at Randolph, and she suddenly had a very bad feeling about the evening. Perhaps it had been a mistake to come, after all.

"So, he *is* here," Randolph said under his breath to her and shot her an irritated look, as if it were her fault that he had been invited. She prayed nothing controversial would arise. Randolph was already in a foul mood, and any little thing threatened to set him off.

As they entered the drawing room, she immediately felt Glenn's eyes on her, but she avoided looking at him and instead made much of Agatha Exley, perched on the sofa next to Antonia.

"Here you are!" Antonia said. "We'd nearly given you up. There's barely time for you to have a sherry at all."

"I apologize, Antonia," Randolph said bluntly, straightening his cufflinks. "I must blame your daughter. She took hours to get ready."

"How very ungallant!" Agatha twittered, throwing him a scolding look, before taking Julia's hand. "Well, the result is stupendous. You look lovely, as always, my dear."

"Thank you, Agatha," she said with a false little laugh, though her face, she knew, was flushed. She chanced a glance at Glenn and found him still looking at her, so she looked quickly away. *Why was he always staring at her?*

Billings appeared in the doorway, then. "Dinner is served, madame, or shall I delay?"

"No, we'll come through now, Billings. You don't mind do you?" she asked, looking at Julia and then Randolph.

"Of course not," Julia answered. Randolph scowled at her but did not respond beyond a curt nod. Julia knew how much he preferred several gins before dinner, but it would be monstrous to hold dinner off for that reason.

The little party preceded through to the dining room, where Randolph, with irritating assumption, took the seat opposite Antonia at the head of the table. Julia was disappointed to see that she was seated between Glenn and Agatha, and determined, as a footman Julia didn't recognize held the chair for her, to make sure she spent the evening talking with Agatha.

"So, Mr. Forbes," Randolph said as another footman began setting the first course of smoked salmon in front of each of them, "when do you return to Texas? It's been a long time to be here for . . . what was it? Railroad contracts?"

"Tomorrow, as it happens."

"I thought you were here indefinitely," Julia said and hoped no one else had caught the unmistakable eagerness in her voice. *What was wrong with her?* She chanced a glance at Randolph, but he was absorbed with scraping the dill from his salmon.

"Not indefinitely. I've enjoyed my time with Uncle Sid, but I really do need to be getting back. Duty calls."

"What's this about railroad contracts?" John Exley asked, his thick bushy eyebrows knitted together.

"Union Pacific is wanting to lay track through the northern part of our ranch," Glenn said to him directly. "Uncle Sid, here, is helping me look over the contracts."

"I see. Very interesting," John replied, taking a bite of his salmon. "The railroads seem to be taking over everything these days."

"It would seem. But we do need progress. It's difficult, isn't it?"

"In what way, Mr. Forbes?" Agatha inquired.

"Well, just that it's hard to balance tradition and old-fashioned sentiment with business opportunities. Progress. Change. That's important, too. That's the future."

Julia's heart skipped a little beat that he so nearly echoed her previous words to Antonia.

"Well, I, for one, am not in favor of progress, as you say," Agatha said, taking a small drink of her wine. "Heaven knows that all of the old standards are falling by the wayside. Don't you agree, Antonia?"

Julia thought she perceived her mother glance briefly at Bennett before she answered, "Well, yes, in a way. You should see what some of the young girls are wearing to the club these days." She gave a nervous little laugh. "I don't know where they're getting their fashion sense from. I nearly said something to Victoria Braithewaite just the other day about her niece. But I do understand you're meaning, Mr. Forbes."

"Doubtless, you're not used to formality where you come from," Randolph said condescendingly. "But it's different here in the north."

Julia saw Glenn bristle slightly. "There certainly are a great many things that are different, Mr. Cunningham," he said stiffly. "Civility being one of them."

"What did you say was the name of your law firm, Mr. Forbes?" Julia interrupted, trying to stave off a disagreeable conversation. As Randolph's wife, it was a skill she had regrettably perfected. "It's in Austin, correct?" She could feel Randolph again scowling at her, but she ignored it.

"I didn't say, ma'am, but it's Forbes and McCallahan."

"You're a partner, then?" Antonia asked, clearly impressed.

"Yes, as a matter of fact, I am."

"When do you have time to rustle up the cattle?" Randolph scoffed. "Isn't that what you do on a ranch?"

Julia's insides twisted as she looked down at her as yet untouched plate. She barely ate anything these days.

"My brother, Edward, is the executive director of the ranch and all its holdings, actually. I myself live in Austin."

"And are you married, Mr. Forbes?" Agatha asked.

"I am not, ma'am. Haven't yet found the right one," he said with what Julia swore was a trace of amusement.

"How very peculiar," Agatha murmured. "I'm sure you're very much sought after in Texan society."

Glenn laughed. "I wouldn't know, Mrs. Exley. I'm rather committed to my work just at the moment."

"Speaking of brothers, Mother," Julia interjected smoothly, "have you had any letters from Clive?"

"Why, yes, I have." Antonia gave her a grateful look while the servants stepped forward to clear the first course dishes and began delivering the second.

"Have they reached Lucerne yet?"

"No, they've been delayed in Alsace, it seems. Something about a missing painting," she said, throwing Glenn a quick glance. "It seems to be the topic of the month, does it not?" She took a drink of her wine. "I don't know why Clive continually finds himself wrapped up in one mystery after another. And he drags poor Henrietta into it. I don't know why he does it."

Julia was about to answer but thought better of it, not wanting to broach yet another possibly difficult topic, knowing, as she did, that her mother refused to acknowledge Clive and Henrietta's fledgling detective agency.

"I don't know," John blustered. "I should think it would be very stimulating. Good for the digestion," he said, as one of the footmen placed a fillet of lamb before him.

"What? Detective work?" Antonia asked, the annoyance in her voice obvious.

"Yes, yes. All that running about. Employing your mental powers on solving what is essentially a large puzzle. Wouldn't mind doing it myself, if I were a younger man." He took a bite of his whipped potatoes and nodded his head appreciatively.

"Well, perhaps," Antonia said dismissively, "but it is absolutely inappropriate for a woman to tag along. I'm sure I don't know *what* has gotten into Henrietta's mind. Do you know," she said directly to Agatha, "I asked her to run for secretary of the Women's Club League, and she said she didn't have time! Can you imagine!"

"Mother, really," Julia added. "Remember what the doctor said? That she's to find rest and a hobby?"

"Exactly my point! Running about looking for a missing painting is neither restful nor a hobby!"

Julia bit her lip at the second mention of a painting and prayed that Glenn would not take this as a segue into another plea for the Church painting. She chanced a glance at him, and he utterly shocked her by throwing her a wink. She flushed and immediately looked at Randolph, who had thankfully not noticed.

"So, John," Randolph announced, "did you read this morning's stock report? How do you interpret it?"

"Not good, I'm afraid, not good," the older man chortled. "Though I daresay if there is a war, that will pick things up a bit."

"You would be wise to look to Lockheed," Randolph suggested.

"Indeed, I was just telling Father that—"

Glenn took the opportunity of the two men chatting—Randolph's slight in not including him in the ensuing business conversation horribly obvious—to lean close to Julia, so close that she could smell his cologne. She dared not look at him, however, and kept her eyes fixed on his gold wristwatch. "Speaking of detective work," he whispered, "I've a bit of news."

"Oh?" Julia murmured, wiping the already clean corner of her mouth with her napkin. She forced herself not to look instinctively at Randolph, as if every movement needed to be sanctioned by him lest he erupt. Fortunately, he was still droning on to John Exley.

"It involves Mr. Stockel's case," Glenn whispered again. "There have been some developments, you might say."

"Oh, do tell," she said, hoping that it was some good news. Elsie had much been on her mind these past weeks, and though she had written several letters to the girl, she had not received a reply, which had worried her greatly.

"Yes, it seems that our friend Heinrich has been duped."

Julia's brow creased, and she finally allowed herself to look up into Glenn's gray-green eyes. "What do you mean?"

"Just that his wife, Rita Meyer, who is his *legal* wife, I discovered, is also at this very moment also the *legal* wife of one Lee Gilroy of Kansas City, Missouri."

Julia fingered her glass of wine as she took in this information. "She's . . . she's a bigamist?" She looked up at him again.

"So it would seem."

"Oh, my!" Julia thought for a moment. "That means that . . . that they have no case, no hope to extort money from the . . ." she had been about to say "Exleys" but stopped herself before it was too late and nervously looked down the table at John.

"Yes, I'm quite certain that any judge would laugh this out of court," Glenn said in a low voice.

"Thank goodness." Julia let out a deep sigh of relief. She had been terribly worried that Elsie and Gunther might do something rash, but now they wouldn't have to. She had been successful once before in preventing a hasty marriage on Elsie's part, and she briefly allowed herself to feel the credit once again, if only partly. It was certainly a letter to Henrietta she would not have relished, telling her that Elsie had slipped through her fingers after all. "Do they know? Elsie and Gunther, that is?"

"No, I just received a letter confirming Rita's status before I came out. I haven't even had a chance to tell Uncle Sid. We came separately."

"I see. Poor Elsie. She'll be so relieved."

"Pardon me," Agatha twittered from her other side. "I don't mean to eavesdrop, but are you perhaps discussing Elsie Von Harmon?"

"Yes, I was, Mrs. Exley," Glenn answered. "I must beg your pardon for speaking freely." He glanced at Bennett. "I'd forgotten she was your niece."

"Well, it sounded rather serious. I do hope nothing is amiss . . ." Agatha chirped.

"Yes, just exactly what were you discussing?" Randolph added sharply from his end of the table.

Glenn glared at him. "Mrs. Cunningham and I were discussing a private matter between Miss Von Harmon and her friend, Mr. Stockel," Glenn answered steadily. "I was clearly out of order. It is hardly dinner conversation. I apologize," he said to Antonia.

"Is Elsie in some sort of trouble?" Antonia asked.

"Not exactly. It is actually more Mr. Stockel's problem. It seems he has found himself in a bit of compromising situation."

"And Elsie is involved?" With a quick wave of her hand, Antonia signaled the servants to begin clearing. "Well, I can't say I'm surprised. Both of those Von Harmon girls are terribly willful, not to mention unpredictable."

"Mother! That's untrue," Julia exclaimed, unable to keep silent. "And most unfair, especially of Henrietta."

"I beg your pardon!" Antonia snapped.

"If everyone would please calm down, I'll explain the whole situation," Bennett said loudly. He drained his wine and waited until everyone was silent while the servants cleared. "Miss Von Harmon went to Julia for advice about a very delicate matter, one which—"

"Elsie sought your advice?" Agatha asked Julia in a strained voice.

"Yes," Bennett answered for her. "And Julia, very correctly, brought Miss Von Harmon and Mr. Stockel to me for legal advice."

"Why Bennett?" Randolph barked at Julia, as if she were a naughty child.

"Well, because it seemed a legal matter," she said, emphasizing the word *legal*, "and Mr. Bennett is the only lawyer I know personally."

"You might have asked me."

"Randolph, you're making a scene! Let Mr. Bennett continue," she urged.

"I'll thank you to keep quiet, madame," Randolph growled.

"Randolph!" Mortified, Julia dropped her eyes into her lap.

"As I was saying," Bennett continued, shooting Randolph a dagger, "I consulted with Glenn—"

"You were there, too?" Randolph interrupted, looking at Glenn.

"I asked his counsel, yes," Bennett said evenly, "as his specialty is family law."

"Family?" Antonia asked.

"Yes, Gunther is caring for an orphaned girl," Bennett said with a deep sigh. "If you'll please just let me explain."

For the second time, everyone quieted. Bennett cleared his throat, then, and Julia's heart suddenly began to race in anticipation of what Bennett might accidentally reveal. Much of Gunther's woes stemmed from his desire to marry Elsie and the subsequent threat of extortion, which should in no way be told in present company. Julia held her breath, as the servants began depositing thin slices of almond-and-strawberry cake in front of each of them, and hoped that Bennett would remember.

As it turned out, there was no cause for worry. Bennett shrewdly related the situation in the simplest of terms, spinning it as a custody case more than anything else. Glenn, too, was careful in what he said, finishing Bennett's tale with the report of Rita's bigamy, which caused more than just Bennett's eyebrows to rise in dismay.

"How extraordinary!" Antonia said finally. "I find the whole situation distasteful in the extreme."

"Well, I find it rather intriguing," Randolph scoffed with derision. "Two lawyers and two society women, if you can call Elsie Von Harmon a woman of society, that is, to resolve this affair. Who is this esteemed Mr. Stockel anyway?"

"I believe he is the custodian at Mundelein College, where Elsie attends," Glenn answered stiffly when no one else spoke.

Randolph let out a rare short burst of a laugh and finished off his fourth glass of wine, if Julia was counting correctly. "The custodian? I must say, I'm quite relieved." He tossed his napkin onto the table. "For a moment I thought this was going to involve something on the level of international intrigue. I'm very happy to have been disappointed."

"Oh, dear," Agatha said, rising now, a handkerchief at her eye. "You must excuse me for a moment," she whimpered and hurried from the room.

"I think this is our cue to retire," Antonia said as she stood, all of the men rising, too. "We'll leave you to your port," she said, giving Bennett an unintelligible look, at least from Julia's perspective.

Agatha having already absented herself, Julia alone rose and followed her mother into the drawing room, where she sluggishly took a seat at the piano. She felt sad and defeated somehow, which she couldn't understand. Shouldn't she feel happy? Absently, she played a few notes.

"Julia, for heaven's sake, what on earth are you playing?"

"I'm attempting to play 'Miss Otis Regrets.' It's Cole Porter."

"Well, stop it. It's awful. If you must play something, play something classical. How about Handel?"

"I don't feel like playing Handel," Julia said, rising from the piano and walking toward the window.

"My, everyone is in a mood tonight. I can't imagine what's gotten into you."

Julia wanted to pour out her heart to her mother, as she had wanted to do so many times before, but she knew her sorrows would fall on deaf ears. She looked out at the darkness beyond.

"Ah, Agatha!" Antonia exclaimed now as her friend shuffled in. "Are you quite all right? Come in, you poor dear. Here. Sit here with me on the sofa. That's it," she said, urging her friend to a place by the fire.

"I'm terribly sorry. I just needed to freshen up," Agatha said with a weary smile.

"You mustn't worry about Elsie," Antonia said, patting Agatha's hand. "She'll be fine. She's come such a long way as your protégé."

"I'm not so sure. She refused to go to Miami with me and John in the spring. I thought it was her studies that kept her, that's what she told me, anyway, but maybe it was *this* business that kept her. Oldrich will be furious if he finds out."

"But why, Agatha? Nothing has happened," Julia said, abandoning her post by the window.

"Yes, and it isn't your fault the girl goes and gets herself in these scrapes," Antonia added. "As I said, the Von Harmon girls are terribly willful. You did your best. No one can fault you there. If you ask my opinion, you were given a nearly impossible task."

"She hasn't been taking my telephone calls lately," Agatha said, resurrecting her handkerchief now from inside her handbag. "And no wonder Oldrich has been acting so strangely. He telephoned me just this morning to ask if I had heard from Elsie lately. Said he received a rather disturbing letter from her."

A warning bell went off in Julia's head, and she stopped examining the figurines on the mantel and turned to look more carefully at Agatha.

"Did he say what it was about?"

"No, I asked him, but he was silent on the matter. Said he would get back to me. Oh," Agatha groaned, "this is all my fault. I should never have—"

She was interrupted, then, by the entrance of the men.

"That was quite fast," Antonia declared, looking curiously at Bennett.

"No one was in a drinking mood," he responded tightly, throwing a scowl at Randolph.

"I am," Randolph slurred, picking up one of the decanters on the mahogany drinks cart.

"Randolph," Julia suggested quietly, "perhaps you've had enough."

"Don't you dare tell me what to do," he said loudly, pointing a finger at her with the hand that now held a crystal glass of scotch.

"Perhaps I might be allowed to see the gallery one more time, Mrs. Howard," Glenn said stiffly, his eyes darting from Randolph to his hostess.

"Certainly, Mr. Forbes. Why don't you escort him again, Julia?"

"I'll be damned if you're going upstairs with *him*," Randolph said, slightly swaying. "Alone!"

"Randolph!" Antonia admonished. "How dare you use such language!"

"I apologize," he said, bowing slightly. "How terribly rude of me. Come on, Forbes," he said, stumbling toward him. "Let's go."

"As you wish," Glenn said with a tilt of his head and then threw Julia a look of pity.

Julia turned away and sat back down at the piano, trying to fight back her tears. This evening was turning out even more horribly than she had predicted. She began playing a few chords of Debussy.

She hadn't gotten very far, however, when Bennett appeared beside her. "Mind if I sit down?"

Julia was taken off guard. "No, of course not," she said politely, though she was surprised by his request. He had yet to ever single her out for conversation beyond offering his condolences at her father's funeral, and she hardly counted their interaction in his study regarding Elsie as such.

He took a seat gently beside her, while she continued to play. All of Bennett's movements were always slow and gentle, she realized.

He was not a fool, and he was certainly a man of integrity. She could see why her mother was attracted to him. Bennett watched her for a few moments, and she expected that he would offer a compliment, but he did not. He merely sat with his hands in his lap. Julia could see the curled gray hair on the backs of his hands. So different from her father's . . .

"I thought I should tell you," he finally said in a low voice and leaning slightly toward her, "I received a letter from Mr. Stockel just this morning."

"You did?" She stopped playing.

He nodded his head at the keys. She took his meaning and absently played a few more chords.

"What did he say?" she whispered.

"Glenn just told me about Rita's bigamy, but it seems the discovery came too late." He paused. "There's no easy way to say this, but Gunther and Elise have married."

Married? Julia abruptly stopped playing and felt she might be sick. "What do you mean? Are you sure?" she hissed.

"Yes, they ran off together. With Anna. Obviously, they still think themselves in a desperate situation. They married in Omaha."

"Omaha!"

"Yes, they've found work on a farm near there, apparently. Gunther only wrote, he said, in hopes that it would help his case. He begged me not to tell anyone, however, for obvious reasons." He looked up briefly at Antonia and the Exleys, who were still in a deep conversation by the fire. "It's why I couldn't speak fully at dinner, especially with the Exleys present. I thought you should know, though."

"Oh, God!" Julia couldn't think straight. *Elsie married!* And working on a farm! Oh, what would she tell Henrietta? She groaned and rubbed her brow.

"Everything all right?" Antonia called. Her face was one of concern as she looked from Julia to Bennett.

"Yes," Julia said, slipping out from behind the piano bench. "I think I just need some air." She turned her head slightly so that her mother wouldn't see her tears. "Does Glenn know?" she whispered, turning slightly back toward Bennett, who still remained calmly seated at the piano.

"I just told him as we came through."

"Are you all right, Julia?" Antonia asked. "You're not ill, are you?"

"No, Mother. I simply need a little air. I find the room very close, do you not?"

"Well, take a shawl," she instructed, but Julia did not respond. As she passed out of the room, she could hear her mother address Bennett. "Whatever did you say to her?"

Julia wandered out onto the flagstone terrace and leaned her hands against the rough stone wall running around the perimeter. There was a breeze coming in off the lake, but unfortunately it was not cool, but warm. She closed her eyes and tried to think, though all she could hear was the sound of the waves hitting the beach further down the property. The moon was out, and Julia stared at its reflection on the surface of Lake Michigan. The lake seemed so peaceful, but she knew its extreme depth. Thinking of it had terrified her as a little girl and still did, truthfully.

Oh, how could this have happened? She thought through the whole situation again, wondering how she could have prevented it, and began walking along the terrace wall, allowing her fingers to trail over the rough stones. She wondered if Elsie was happy, hoping desperately that she was. After all, wasn't this ultimately what the girl had wanted? To be married to Gunther? *But how could she be?* Julia despaired. Married to a farmhand, caring for an epileptic child that was not their own? It sounded horribly tragic to Julia. And what about the wedding itself? In some dirty registrar's office in Omaha? And to think that barely a year ago, they had all been gathered at Sacred Heart in Winnetka for Henrietta and Clive's glittering wedding and the stupendous reception at the yacht club afterward. Julia again despaired for Elsie and the raw deal she had been handed.

"You okay?" came a voice from behind her, and she jumped. She turned to see Glenn approaching. "Your mother said I'd find you out here." He held out a black lace shawl. "She said to bring you this."

Julia turned from him to quickly wipe her eyes and then obediently took the shawl, not looking at him. Irritated with her mother, she refused to put it on and instead tossed it on the stone wall in front of her.

"Where's Randolph?" she asked nervously, looking back toward the drawing room doors.

"Uncle Sid has engaged him in a rather detailed discussion about prospective stocks."

"So that you could slip away?"

"Maybe," he said with a little wink.

Julia looked back at the lake, her insides again roiling.

"Quite a shock about Elsie and Gunther," he said, following her gaze. "The whole thing has obviously upset you. I didn't realize you would be so affected by the news. I apologize."

The fact that it was almost a perfect stranger out here comforting her rather than her husband grieved Julia so much she could barely speak. Her throat was thick with tears. All she could do was nod the tiniest bit.

"Hey," Glenn said, touching her shoulder and sending an electric current of . . . of what? . . . down her arm. "Are you all right?"

Julia cleared her throat. "Yes, certainly," she managed to say, trying her best to pull herself together. "I suppose I should thank you."

"Thank me?"

"For finding out the truth about Heinrich and Rita. If they had only waited a little longer, they would have had more choices."

"You mean Elsie and Gunther?"

Julia nodded.

"Is it so very terrible that they ran off and got married?" he asked softly.

Julia swallowed hard. It was the question she herself was asking. *Was it so terrible?* The gossips at the club would make a heyday of it when they heard, but what did it matter? What did any of it matter in the face of love? She had seen the way Gunther looked at Elsie in Bennett's study, and she knew the truth. That they were meant to be together. So what if they had to toil on a farm that wasn't theirs for the rest of their lives? At least they had each other and their love.

"I don't know anymore," Julia said with a sigh. "I feel responsible."

"Responsible for two people falling in love and pledging their lives together, no matter what the cost?"

"Sometimes the cost is too high, Glenn."

"I don't think so."

Julia looked back out over the lake. She was pretty sure he was still staring at her.

"I'm sorry Mother won't sell you the painting," she said abruptly. She plucked up her courage and turned to him. She could no longer deny what she knew she was feeling for him, though she knew it was wrong. Suddenly, she felt very sad. Sad because she could have so easily fallen in love with the man standing beside her. It made her want to weep.

"No matter. I'll try again. It was too soon after your father's death. I see that now."

"Yes, she might come round." She forced her voice to be steady. "I'll mention it to Clive when he gets home. I'm sorry you wasted your time."

"Oh, it wasn't wasted," he said seriously, his eyes searching hers. "I found something infinitely more valuable."

She shivered and looked away.

"You're cold," he said, reaching for the shawl. Rather than simply hand it to her, he took the liberty of draping it gently around her shoulders. Her heart was beginning to race alarmingly, and she hoped he could not see her chest heaving.

"Can you not guess the real reason I stayed so long?" he asked gently. "Why I'm here tonight?" He paused as if he expected her to answer. "It certainly wasn't to see the painting one last time."

She lifted her eyes to his. "So, under false pretenses yet again?" She managed a small smile.

"Julia," he said, his voice breaking slightly, "you must know that I care for you. Deeply."

Julia bit her lip. "Glenn—"

"I'm not a man to take another man's wife, but I don't look at him as a man." He nodded toward the house. "Not a real man. Julia, I know what I'm asking is a lot, but I want you to come with me. Come to Texas."

"Oh, Glenn!" Tears blurred her eyes. "I . . . don't ask me that. You know that's not possible." She suddenly felt panicked, uneasy, as if she were in a ship on the lake, and it was capsizing.

"Anything is possible, Julia."

Julia's thoughts raced; she was thrilled by the prospect, yet utterly terrified—not just of going through with it, but of the fact that she was even contemplating it. A fleeting image of poor Dennis Braithewaite sailed through her mind, and she almost laughed at the absurdity of the question before her. "I can't . . . I can't just leave," she said feebly.

"Yes, you can." He reached out and cupped her cheek in his big hand. "Julia, I'm in love with you. Please," he said huskily.

She closed her eyes at his touch, trying desperately to be strong, to resist, but she could not help leaning into his hand just a little.

"Julia," he whispered and brushed his lips against hers, sending a shock so strong through her that she felt her legs might buckle. She pulled back.

"No, Glenn! I . . . I can't."

"Why? Because of what everyone will say? I know for certain you don't care what the devil your mother's bridge club might say. You agreed with me in there. That things are changing. The old standards are falling. Julia, don't make the same mistake twice. This time follow your heart."

Julia fought desperately to hold back her tears, causing her throat to ache. "I took a vow, Glenn," she said hoarsely.

"And *he* took a vow to love and cherish you. Which he does not. He has broken his vow. Cruelly. He doesn't deserve you."

Julia stared into his eyes, suddenly daring to allow herself to consider what she now realized she had been longing for all these lonely years: to escape. The conscious thought of it, however, made the chain chafe all the more. "He'll never let me go, Glenn." She turned her head away.

Gently he cradled her face and turned it back to him. "Julia, I'll protect you. If you'll let me."

She stared up into his eyes, wanting desperately to believe him. "I can't, Glenn," she said hoarsely, barely above a whisper. "He'll take the boys from me."

"Not if we take them first."

Two tears rolled down her cheeks.

"Just answer one question." He brushed back a tendril of her hair as gently as he would do to a child. "Do you trust me?"

Julia's stomach clenched. Up until this moment, she hadn't allowed even herself to consider such a thing, but as she stood here now by the lake, the waves softly crashing, she knew the answer without thinking. Slowly she nodded her head. "Of course, I do," she said, tightly grasping the lapels of his suit coat. "Of course, I trust you."

Chapter 28

Henrietta again grasped Edna's hand as the poor girl lay, sleeping now, on the third floor of the Lariboisière Hospital. Desperately, she tried not to give in to her increasing fear. *Where was Clive? What could possibly be taking him so long?* With every passing hour, she grew more and more worried, convincing herself that something must have gone horribly wrong, that perhaps the Germans had caught up with them after all. She took to pacing up and down the ward, trying to observe the other patients as a way to distract herself, and even at one point considering fleeing the hospital to find Clive, but where would she go? And she couldn't leave Edna, of course, who was still in critical condition.

Earlier in the day, the doctors had removed a small trace of shrapnel from the girl's shoulder. There was one nurse who spoke enough broken English to let Henrietta know that the patient was doing well and that she should make a good recovery. Still, Henrietta blamed herself for getting poor Edna involved in the first place. Now she knew for sure that she should have left her at home, and yet, if it hadn't been for Edna, they would never have found the missing panel. Gently, Henrietta rubbed her the girl's hand as she gazed down the long ward to the window at the very end. It was beginning to grow dark.

Where was Clive? she fretted for the hundredth time and was about to begin another round of pacing, when Pascal miraculously slipped through the swinging ward door.

"Pascal!" she cried, jumping up. "Where's Clive?"

"All is well with Monsieur Howard, madame," Pascal answered quickly. "Do not worry about him. How is . . . how is Edna?" He looked beyond Henrietta toward the row of beds in the dim room. His face was one of fear.

"She's fine. She's going to be okay," Henrietta said hurriedly. "But what happened? Where's Clive?"

"Come, I will tell you, but not in here." He nodded toward the hallway and pushed open the door for her to pass through. Henrietta stepped outside into the brightly lit ward and braced herself, her hands gripped tightly, to hear Pascal's report of the day's events. Quickly, he related what had happened at the little inn, and that, with Hartle's help, they had managed to defeat the Germans who had indeed turned up. He also related, solemnly, the fact that Claudette had been shot dead.

"Claudette? She was there, too?" Henrietta asked, unsure of how to feel.

"*Oui*, I am sorry, madame. *C'est une tragédie, non?*"

"Oh, God," she murmured, rubbing her forehead. "Where's Clive now? Is he coming?"

"*Non*, he is still with the police. He sent me ahead to relieve you. You are to meet him at the Ritz where he is taking rooms."

"The Ritz?" Henrietta looked worriedly back through the little round window in the ward door. "But I can't possibly leave Edna. What if she wakes up, and I'm not here?"

"Go, madame. She is quite safe with me."

Henrietta turned this over in her mind. She was loathe to leave, but she knew she needed to get to Clive. Pascal had assured her that he was in perfect form, but Henrietta wasn't convinced. She tiptoed back into the ward, Pascal following, and felt Edna's forehead. Still warm. She let out a deep breath, knowing she didn't really have a choice, and gathered up her handbag from where she had stored it under the bed. "You must not leave," she instructed Pascal sternly.

"No, I will not. Of course not." He smiled tiredly and sat down on the chair beside the bed.

"And you must telephone if there is any change. Or if the doctors give any more information." She bit her lip. "Or if the police show up. Or if she wakes up. Or if she asks for me. Or—"

"Madame," Pascal interrupted. "Do not worry. I will guard her with my life."

The seriousness with which he said these words gave Henrietta pause, and she looked into his eyes for any trace of sarcasm. Finding none, she patted Edna's hand and, giving Pascal one last look, hurried out.

A little over a half an hour later, she found Clive waiting for her in a luxurious suite on the fourth floor of the Ritz, a large cognac in his hand.

"Darling," she cried, rushing to him, "you could have been killed."

Clive kissed her and put his arms around her. "Well, yes, that *is* the nature of detective work, as I keep trying to explain to you."

"Tell me everything," she said, tossing her coat on the back of an exquisite white sofa.

"Sherry?" he asked, walking to a Louis XIV-style sideboard where an array of bottles were displayed.

"No, something stronger," she said.

He tilted his head in acknowledgement and poured her a cognac. She eagerly took it. "Well, tell me!" she said, taking a seat on the elegant sofa.

"First, how is Edna?" he asked, joining her.

Henrietta sighed. "There was a fragment, a piece of shrapnel caught in the shoulder. They have removed it, of course, but it was apparently very difficult. She's still feverish. They say she will recover, but it will take time."

"Thank God," he said, taking a drink.

"Do I detect a trace of fondness, finally, for poor Edna?" She couldn't resist a small smile.

"Darling, I was never *not* fond of Edna. On the contrary, it has been quite the other way around. But, yes, I'm very sorry for the poor girl. We'll have to do something for her when we get home."

"Oh, yes! I'm so glad you think so, too. If we ever get home," she said and took a sip of her cognac. "Oh, Clive! I was so terribly worried. It was good of you to send Pascal, but I'm not sure he's up to spending the night after the ordeal you two have been through."

"He told you, then?" He looked at her, and then looked away. "No, he probably isn't. I assume he'll fall asleep by her bedside, but he insisted on going."

"Was it very terrible, Clive?" she asked in a softer tone now. "I can't imagine." There was a tiny part of her that wished she had been part of the action, but she was realistic enough to know she would have been no help in a shootout with Nazi soldiers.

"Yes, it was," Clive said stiffly, swirling the contents of his glass and then taking a large drink.

"Did you . . . did it remind you of the war?"

"Yes, but let's not talk about it."

Henrietta wasn't sure what to say to this. She had tried on several different occasions to elicit stories or memories from Clive about his days in the war, if not from general curiosity, then from a hope that doing so might genuinely help him, but he always declined, saying, "Those days are in the past. Best leave them there."

"I'm sorry about Claudette. And Valentin, for that matter," he said, looking at her apprehensively.

"Yes, it's so awfully tragic, isn't it? A brother and a sister both gone." Henrietta, in truth, still did not feel much sadness over Valentin's death, but she did regarding Claudette's. She felt that, despite Claudette's deviousness and her involvement with the Nazis, her cousin—or whatever she was—had been dealt a bad hand and had simply done what she thought best to escape it. She was a tragic figure, another woman with very few choices in life despite the fact that she lived in a château in such a beautiful part of the world. Henrietta wondered what would happen to the poor baron now. He was the one she actually felt most sorry for, both children dead and nothing left but the ghost of the countess to fill his empty head.

"Who shot her?" Henrietta asked quietly, tucking her arms across her chest and bracing herself should Clive himself admit to it.

"It was Hartle. The shot came from above, and he was the only one up there."

Henrietta let out a little breath and tried to envision it.

"What did the French police say?"

Clive let out a deep breath. "It was the usual malarky. I'm not sure how much Pascal told you, but they held us for hours. Eventually, two of the Deuxième Bureau showed up to interrogate us, I'm assuming because of the Nazi presence. This isn't going to do much for international relations."

"What's the *Deuxième Bureau*?"

"The French version of MI5."

"Ah. Well, what did they say about the panel?"

"They have heard of it, of course, but they seemed very incredulous that it had been hidden here under their bloody noses all this time."

"Well, we don't know that for sure."

"All right, then, for several months. They insist that if the panel had been on French soil, their spies would have known about it."

"So they weren't in communication with MI5?"

"Apparently not. At least not recently on the matter of this art theft. And definitely not in regards to how it relates to the Nazis."

"Maybe Hartle was wrong."

"As crazy as it sounds, I trust Hartle more than I trust the Deuxième Bureau. They definitely have their heads in the wrong place, and I think you know what I mean, to coin a vulgar phrase."

"So now what? They obviously let you go."

"Yes, for now. I've been charged with firing a weapon in a public square, at the very least, and ordered not to leave Paris until further notice."

"That's ridiculous!"

Clive waved a hand in futility. "I'm fairly certain MI5 will turn up tomorrow or the next day. Until then, we wait. Hope that Edna gets better." He stood up wearily and offered his hand, which she took, allowing him to pull her to him. He wrapped his arms around her.

"I'm sorry this is your first taste of Paris, darling. I wanted it to be different."

"I don't mind," she said, looking approvingly around the room, which was exquisite. It consisted of all white furniture trimmed in gold, and even the walls and all of the doors were white with gold hardware. It was stunningly beautiful, as if they were in a museum, and Henrietta, for just one brief second, had a memory of their shabby old apartment on Armitage and smiled to herself. "But what do we do?" she asked, turning back to Clive.

"Do what everyone does in Paris. We make love." He kissed her neck.

"Clive, I hardly think this is the time, considering everything . . ."

Clive continued to kiss her. "Henrietta, please, I need you right now." She could hear the tremble in his voice, which alarmed her.

"Come on, then, Inspector," she said with a smile, slipping out of his arms and taking hold of his hand. He followed her to the bedroom, and she had barely time to undress before he pulled her to the bed. He proceeded to make love to her with an urgency she had not felt since their first nights together, and she knew, as her body responded to his touch, that he was deeply distressed.

They had barely finished breakfast the following morning, Clive insisting on ordering room service, when the telephone rang in the sitting room. Henrietta rose from the little table by the window and went to answer it.

"Hello? Yes, of course. Yes, that's fine. Thank you." Henrietta gently placed the ornate white receiver back into its gold-trimmed cradle.

"A Mr. Morris is downstairs," she called across to Clive. "He's coming up."

"That'll be MI5," Clive said, setting down the morning paper. He had been most intent on looking for any report of yesterday's shoot-out near Sacré-Cœur. He had so far found nothing, however, a fact, he had said aloud to Henrietta, that he found most telling.

"Shall I step into the other room?" she asked, watching him adjust his tie in the gold mirror above the fireplace.

"Darling, don't be silly. You needn't ask that anymore. You are my partner," he said, coming over and taking her hand. "Let's get this over with and then go see Edna."

He was in a much better mood this morning, though he had still not slept deeply. After he had exhausted himself on top of her, he had fallen into a sleep, but it was restless and agitated. Several times he called out, names she didn't recognize. She wondered if perhaps they had been his comrades in the war.

There was a sharp rap on the door, then, and Henrietta jumped despite the warning telephone call from reception just a few moments ago. Clive went to answer it.

"Mr. Howard?" asked the man standing in the hall. "I'm Inspector Morris, and this is my sergeant, Detective Ayers. We just arrived from London this morning. May we come in?"

"Yes, of course," Clive said, gesturing them in. "Allow me to introduce my wife, Henrietta Howard."

"Mrs. Howard," they each said with a tilt of their head. "May we sit down?" Morris asked Clive.

"Please," he said, waving toward the sitting area. "Tea?"

"No, this isn't a social call, as I'm sure you're aware." The two men sat in the white French Napoleonic cane chairs near the fireplace, and Clive and Henrietta sat together on the silk sofa.

"Messy business, this."

"Yes," Clive answered, crossing his legs smoothly.

"Look, we've a number of questions."

"I expect you do."

"Let's get down to it, then, shall we?"

Clive inclined his head.

"I know you've been through this a number of times now, but would you explain it again?" Morris asked, leaning forward now, his arms on his knees. "How you happened to come upon the panel in the first place?"

Clive let out a deep breath and proceeded to relate the whole story one more time, with Henrietta occasionally adding a detail or two, ending with how they had delivered the panel, as instructed, to Inspector Hartle. "So that's it," Clive said, sitting back in his chair. "I'm assuming the authorities will store it somewhere safe and out of Hitler's clutches. Are we allowed to know where?" he asked, throwing a quick glance at Henrietta. "I'm assuming not."

Morris did not answer but continued to study Clive, and Henrietta detected that they were still not satisfied with the story. Morris stood abruptly, his hands on his hips. "No, you may not," he said, beginning to pace a little now. "Because the panel is still at large."

"What do you mean?" Clive asked, sitting up a little straighter.

"Just what I said. The panel is gone. And, worse yet, there is no Inspector Hartle." He glared at Clive. "Not with MI5, anyway."

Clive took a moment to understand what Morris had just said. "What do you mean there's no Inspector Hartle? He works for you," Clive said, his brow furrowed. He cast Henrietta a quick worried look.

"No, I'm afraid he doesn't."

"That isn't possible," Clive muttered as Morris's words sunk in. "We worked on a case in Derbyshire together. I know the man!"

"Or you *thought* you knew him. We've done some investigating. It seems this John Hartle, former Inspector with the Derbyshire Constabulary, retired from the force some five months ago and moved to London. No family, not many friends. Not any that could give an account of him in recent months, that is."

"That can't possibly be true! He . . . he gave us so much information on this case. About the panel itself, the contact in Strasbourg, about Richard Stafford," Clive added quickly. "That he was a missing MI5 agent."

"So he did, which is worrying. Somehow Hartle infiltrated our intelligence. Or knows someone that did."

"Jesus Christ!" Clive exclaimed, running his hand roughly through his hair.

"When did you first come in contact with him?" Ayers asked.

"Last October. We were staying at Castle Linley. My uncle is Lord Linley. There was a murder in the village of Cromford in Derbyshire. We helped him to solve it. He was as solid as could be. This is simply unbelievable."

"He really didn't seem the type to be a spy," Henrietta added. She felt suddenly nauseous, betrayed by the fact that they really had been on a wild goose chase and that two of her relatives had died because of it, not to mention Edna's critical condition.

"Those are the type that make the best spies," Ayers said, taking a cigarette from a silver case in his jacket pocket and lighting it. "Like you two," he said, jabbing it at them.

"Don't be ridiculous," Clive snapped.

"How do we know you two aren't in league with this Hartle character?"

"Because we're not. That should be fairly obvious."

"Oh, I don't know." Ayers eyed him carefully. "Your cousin, Wallace, seems rather fond of the Socialists, is he not?"

"What's that got to do with anything?"

"Are you suggesting that Mr. Hartle is involved with the Russians, Mr. Ayers?" Henrietta asked, bewildered. This was all unraveling too quickly, and definitely in the wrong direction.

"I'm not suggesting anything," Ayers said slowly and then inhaled deeply. "Exactly when did you make contact with him in London? Retrace your steps."

"We've already been through this!" Clive exclaimed.

"Well, tell us again. You know how this works, Howard."

Clive scowled at him. "Look, we're wasting valuable time. We should be out hunting him down, not sitting around here having a chat. You *know* I'm not involved, so let's get on with it!"

"Just answer the question, Howard," Morris said quietly, shooting Ayers a look.

Clive sighed. "We arrived on the Queen Mary on the eighteenth. We took a cab to my family's London home," Clive recited.

"Anyone there?" Morris interrupted.

"What do you mean? From the family?"

"Yes, any family?"

"No, just us."

"And my maid," Henrietta put in.

"May we speak with her?" Ayers asked, his eyes darting toward the doors at the other end of the room.

"She was shot, actually, by Claudette Von Harmon, and is in critical condition in Lariboisière hospital," Clive said irritably. "So, no, you cannot."

"Okay, so you got to your family's digs. Then what?" asked Ayers.

"We did some shopping at Harrods," Henrietta chimed in, "and then we attended the Duke of Buckingham's ball in the evening."

Ayers quickly glanced at Morris, who gave a slight nod. "That adds up."

"What does that mean?" Clive looked at each of them.

"It's not important right now." Morris crossed his arms and leaned a shoulder against the mantle. "Then what?"

"Nothing, really. The next day, we were packing to catch our train to Strasbourg when Hartle turned up. Gave us a long song and dance about this missing panel, how it fit into the Nazi equation, how dangerous it could be should it fall into German hands. He implored us to look for it at Château du Freudeneck and said that we should contact a Monsieur Bonnet. He also knew that Stafford was missing."

"And you believed all this?"

Clive stood up angrily and marched to the window. "Why shouldn't I have?" he said loudly, turning to them now. "I trusted the man!" He began to pace. "I was skeptical of the Nazi theory that the Ghent Altarpiece contained some sort of hidden map, and I said as much, but I was genuinely worried about the missing agent."

"You didn't think that we would go in after him?"

"Yes, I did! I said the same, but Hartle said the plan had changed. That two Americans on holiday in Strasbourg was too perfect a cover. He was convinced we would succeed better than an agent, especially as we had access to Château du Freudeneck. That fucking bastard!" Clive slammed his hand down on a little desk by the window.

"Clive!" Henrietta exclaimed.

"Did he actually say he worked for MI5?" Morris asked.

Clive thought for a moment. "I believe so."

"No, he didn't," Henrietta interrupted with a snap of her fingers. "You alluded to him working for MI5, and he didn't really answer, just smiled. I remember now because I thought it very odd at the time."

"Yes, you're right," mused Clive, pulling at his chin. "Well, who the hell is he working for? The Russians?"

"You tell us," Ayers said coolly, exhaling a cloud of smoke.

"Fuck off, Ayers!"

Morris finally uncrossed his arms and stood up straight. "We don't know. It could be a government, or maybe some eccentric group within a government. Maybe even a private collector."

"Or someone like the Duke of Buckingham?"

Morris tilted his head in acknowledgement. "Perhaps. We've long suspected the duke of having Nazi sentiments."

"What about the Von Harmons?" Clive asked, throwing Henrietta a glance. She had been wondering the same thing, actually . . . "How do they fit in?"

"Good question. I'm not sure Valentin was really involved at all. Further investigation will be forthcoming, but if I had to venture a guess, I'd say that Claudette was little more than a petty art thief."

"But she said she had sources, that she knew where we were going to be. That implies much."

"Yes," Henrietta agreed enthusiastically. "And she basically admitted to having Stafford and Bonnet killed." She looked over at Clive now. "*And* she said she knew the Duke of Buckingham. Do you think she could have been working with Hartle?"

"I don't think so," Clive mused. "It doesn't make sense. If she was, then why send us in to cock it all up?"

"So, there's obviously more than one party involved—"

"The key to this is obviously Hartle," Clive said, looking at Morris now. "We need to go after him! He couldn't have disappeared this quickly."

"Yes, Hartle *is* the key, but it's us who will be doing the pursuing, not you. We'll take it from here."

"But that's ridiculous! We're too involved to stop now. And besides, he doesn't know we know. We could set up a sting," Clive suggested eagerly.

"Look, Mr. and Mrs. Howard," Morris interrupted, "we appreciate what you've done, but we really must insist that you cease any further attempts to unravel this or to locate Hartle. Or the panel, for that matter."

"You can't stop us," Clive snapped.

"Yes, in fact, we can. We can make things very difficult for you. The French police, for example, would love to make an example of you. Hold you indefinitely. You'd have to wait for your lawyers to get here, or trust yourself to someone here, assigned to the case."

"For illegally discharging a firearm?"

"For murder and for aiding and abetting an international art thief."

"Are you threatening me?"

"Not at all. Just explaining the situation."

"Piss off."

"Look, Mr. Howard, the panel has eluded the best intelligence officers and multiple police forces, detectives, and even psychics for years. The fact that a private citizen, *two* private citizens," he said with a nod toward Henrietta, "were able to locate it, fend off several German officers, and transport it to Paris is a feat of great accomplishment. A grateful nation thanks you."

"Funny, that's what Hartle said to me as he drove away with the bloody panel."

"Look, it's over. Forget about it. Count yourselves lucky that it didn't go worse."

Morris stood up, fastening his jacket as he did so. "Look, I know it's difficult, Howard, but you have to let it lie. You understand, don't you? You'll need to come down to the morgue and identify Claudette and Valentin Von Harmon, and you might be needed at the inquest. So don't leave town. Got it?"

"Yes," Clive said with a heavy sigh. "I understand."

"In the meantime, if there's anything we can do for you, let us know—besides clearing everything up with the French police, that is. Where will you go from here?"

"We hadn't fully discussed it. I suppose we'll have to go back to Strasbourg to . . . to make arrangements. I'm assuming there will be funerals." He glanced at Henrietta.

"Well, if there's anything we can do."

"Forget it."

"Actually, there is something," Henrietta suggested tentatively. Clive shot her a confused look.

"What is that, Mrs. Howard?"

"There was a young man assisting us. A servant at the château. He's been of tremendous service to us, and I believe he helped to save my husband's life. We wish to take him back to America with us. But he needs a passport or papers of some sort. Can that be arranged?"

"Henrietta!"

"What's his name?"

"Pascal Tremblay, I believe."

"I'll look into him. I'll see what I can do."

"Thank you, Inspector."

"We'll leave you, then," Morris said, tilting his head toward the door. Ayers dutifully rose. "Do we have an agreement?" Morris asked, holding his hand out to Clive.

Clive let out a deep sigh and shook the man's hand. "Yes, fine. You won't see us again—after the inquest, that is."

"I have your word?"

"Yes, you have my word."

"Thank you. Mrs. Howard," he said with a small smile, "it's been a pleasure. Enjoy the rest of your honeymoon."

The two agents exited the suite then, and Henrietta and Clive were left alone, despondently looking at each other. Henrietta desperately wanted to say something, but she wasn't sure what, predicting that whatever she did say would cause some sort of angry retort from Clive.

Clive walked to the window and looked out. Henrietta quietly took a seat on the sofa and watched him. He remained in that position for nearly ten minutes before he finally spoke.

"Well, I guess I've been had." He said it bitterly as he put one hand on his hip and rubbed the other through his hair.

"*We've* been had. Anyway, how were we to know?" she offered as gently as she could.

"I just don't understand it, Henrietta. Something isn't sitting well with this."

"Yes, I know."

"Do you really think Hartle was capable of this kind of thing? I can hardly believe it."

"I guess everyone is capable of anything," she said, standing up and going to him.

"He's just not the type."

"Well, something must have happened to make him . . . well, to make him abandon ship. Maybe his wife died? Or a child? Was he married?"

Clive let out a sigh. "I have no idea. But maybe we should find out. Travel to Derby and begin to investigate. See what we can find."

"Clive," she cautioned, "let's not." For once she was not eager to pursue a case. "What was it you said about one getting away every once in a while? What were the chief's words? 'Try your best and move on. Catch the next one.'?"

"That's hardly fair, Henrietta," he said bitterly.

"Clive, you were right to begin with," she said softly, running her hand down his arm. "This is bigger than us. International espionage.

And as exciting as it sounds, we can't really travel across Europe looking for a panel that reveals a treasure map to a polar gateway to mystical beings and weapons of mass destruction. As you said, let them scurry around looking for it. It distracts them from the business of war. And you gave your word, or does that not mean anything?"

"I'm surprised at you," he said, looking at her curiously. "Any other time, you'd be urging us on."

"Not this time, Clive," she said, taking his hand. "There is a war coming. I can feel it. We need to get back. If nothing else, for Edna's sake. How can we possibly carry on with the rest of the trip?" In truth, she was utterly crushed to give up their lovely trip, but she didn't want Clive to know. It would only make it all the harder to get him to drop the case.

Clive sighed. "I suppose you're right. But are we doomed never to have a honeymoon?"

"Well, we've had more than most people get. Some people simply run off and get married, and that's it. And, anyway, I just have this feeling that we need to get back. I've had barely any letters from Elsie. Something's not right there."

"Darling, no letters from Elsie in crisis is a good thing."

"I suppose . . ."

"And what on earth were you thinking by asking MI5 to help with Pascal?" he asked disgustedly as he strode to the sideboard and poured himself a drink.

"What do you mean? Darling, we did promise to take him to America with us."

"We're not really going through with that, are we?"

"Yes, of course, we are. We promised." She crossed her arms. "Any other promises you want to try to wiggle out of?" She gave him her most severe look.

He let out a deep sigh. "Well, what on earth will we do with him?"

"He says he simply wants passage to New York." She joined him at the sideboard. "Unless you want to give him a job at Highbury. He could be a junior footman. Or he could be your valet," she suggested eagerly.

"You can't possibly be serious. You are teasing, aren't you?"

"Well, it's not really a bad idea."

"I can think of a number of reasons why it is most certainly a bad idea."

"Such as?"

"Well, for one thing, I still don't trust him."

"After he killed at least a few of the German soldiers firing at you? I don't know what else you expect him to do to prove his loyalty."

Clive sighed. "Oh, all right. I don't care anymore." He took a long drink. "This whole thing has turned into a disaster anyway. Why not complete it with one?"

"Now you're cross."

"Yes, I suppose I am," Clive said bitterly. "We're stuck here until after the inquest and then we'll have to return to Strasbourg. Help with the arrangements, I suppose. Hopefully, the baron will be lucid enough to inform the rest of the family. Who knows who the next of kin are?"

"The poor baron. What will happen to him?"

"I'm not sure." He groaned and put his hands over his face.

Henrietta kissed the back of one of his hands, and he lowered them. He looked dreadfully haggard. "Listen, Inspector," she said, putting her arms around him now. "It will be some time yet before we need to leave and before Edna is well enough to travel. And I would dearly love to see Paris. You did promise to show me. Remember?" She kissed his lips now. "Please?"

She could feel the tension in his shoulders release as he put his arms around her in kind.

"I'm not sure I have it in me."

"Of course, you do. We can't just mope around a hotel room." She kissed his lips.

"Are you attempting to seduce me?"

"Perhaps."

She saw his eyes flicker with interest. "How very naughty of you, Minx." He kissed her deeply. "All right, you win," he whispered and leaned his forehead against hers. "But don't think you're always going to get your way."

"Of course not, Inspector," she said. "But I would prefer it if you called me Countess."

Clive laughed out loud. "Not a chance. Once a minx, always a minx."

"Have it your way, then." She smiled at him, relieved that she had averted his foul mood, at least for now.

"Let's go see Edna, and then I have some things to show you."

She put her finger to his lips, and he kissed it.

"I love you, you know," he said gruffly.

"Yes, I love you, too. I'll just get my hat."

Epilogue

Melody Merriweather adjusted her hat and stepped out of the train carriage in Galena, Illinois. It was just across the Mississippi River from Dubuque, the farthest the train went. She looked around eagerly, taking in all of the old-fashioned buildings on the main street, and felt as though she had marvelously stepped into the 1800s.

"Miss Von Harmon?" someone called to her from the far end of the platform. Melody squinted and saw that it was a nun, dressed all in black except for the white lining of her veil and the wimple that framed her face. Melody grasped her suitcase and walked toward her. It was impossible to tell the woman's age, though the fact that her face had no wrinkles suggested that she was young. She was wearing an old-fashioned driving duster and black driving gloves.

"Miss Von Harmon?" the nun repeated.

"Yes," Melody answered with a small smile. "I'm Miss Von Harmon. But you can call me Elsie."

Author's Note

*T*he *Ghent Altarpiece* is a real work of art painted in 1432 by Jan and Hubert van Eyck, and one of its panels, "The Just Judges," really was stolen from St. Bavo's Cathedral, Belgium on April 10, 1934. The supposed thief, one Arsène Goedertier, was caught seven months later. The panel, however, was never recovered. It remains missing to this day.

Considered one of Europe's masterpieces and a world treasure, the altarpiece, also known as *The Adoration of the Mystic Lamb*, was revolutionary in its content and artistic technique. It was the first major work to be done in oils, marking the transition between Middle Age and Renaissance art, and is considered a forerunner to artistic realism.

The altarpiece is also one of the world's most storied works of art, having been the target of some thirteen crimes throughout the centuries, including having been stolen—in part or as a whole—six different times. Napoleon, Kaiser Wilhelm, and Adolph Hitler were just a few of the notorious men who coveted it. It was one of only four items of cultural heritage listed in the Treaty of Versailles, which dictated that it be returned to Ghent after its appropriation and display in Berlin by Kaiser Wilhelm during World War I.

As described in *A Spying Eye*, Arsène Goedertier actually stole *two* panels ("The Just Judges" and "St. John the Baptist") in 1934 and sent to the Bishop of Ghent a series of letters containing clues as to the hidden location of the panels in exchange for a ransom. Following the clues laid out, the authorities were able to recover the panel of St. John the Baptist in a luggage office in Brussels, which Goedertier had revealed as a measure of good faith. The location of "The Just Judges," however, was never given. On his deathbed, Goedertier confessed, "I alone know where *The Mystic Lamb* is. It rests in a place where neither I, nor anybody else, can take it away without arousing the attention of the public."

There are many theories regarding the whereabouts of the panel. One is that it is hidden somewhere inside St. Bavo's Cathedral itself. Another is that a group of church members, Goedertier among them, were involved in a failed investment scheme that lost the church money, and therefore stole the panel to recover their losses. Other theories are that a wealthy Ghent family came into possession of the panel and have not revealed its whereabouts for fear of scandal, or that it is buried in the crypt of the Belgian Royal Family.

One of the most popular theories, however, and the one I decided to explore for the purposes of this book, is that the panel was purposely stolen by an entity bent on preventing Hitler from eventually possessing the whole altarpiece. Given the altarpiece's history of being stolen, particularly during wartimes by notorious enemy leaders, it was assumed that it was only a matter of time before Hitler turned his eye upon it. Therefore, so the theory goes, a part of it was taken ahead of time and hidden so that Hitler would never be able to have the altarpiece in its entirety.

Whether or not the panel disappeared for this reason, the prediction regarding the Nazis' attention proved correct. The Nazis did indeed seize *The Ghent Altarpiece* in 1940 while it was en route to the Vatican, where the Allies had hoped to safely store it. For a short time, the Nazis kept it in a museum in Pau, France. In 1942, however, Hitler ordered it to be moved to Schloss Neuschwanstein in Bavaria, and from there to the Altaussee salt mines, where seven thousand other works of the world's art were being hoarded by the Nazis for the duration of the war.

When the panel was taken, Hitler, not to be foiled, sent one Heinrich Kohn, an art detective, to Ghent to look for it. At the same time various top Nazi officials, such as Heinrich Himmler and Hermann Göring, were also frantically scouring the planet looking for the panel, hoping to present it to Hitler for his birthday.

Why the obsession with the panel?

Besides wanting to possess the whole of one of the world's masterpieces, Hitler viewed its repatriation from Berlin to Belgium after the loss of WWI as a bitter humiliation for Germany. He sought to build a super museum in Berlin after the war where he could display the massive collection he was hoarding, and where *The Ghent Altarpiece* would be featured as a central figure.

Besides these relatively obvious reasons for wanting to possess it, however, there was a more insidious one.

Hitler believed that *The Ghent Altarpiece* contained a hidden map of the location of the Arma Christi, the instruments of Christ's passion, which would give him unlimited power to rule the world. He also believed that the map would lead him to Thule, the mythical birthplace of the Aryan super-race—which, once found, would grant him and his army supernatural powers such as flight, telekinesis, and telepathy. But he was convinced that he needed all of the panels in order to decipher the map.

As mentioned in *A Spying Eye*, Hitler was obsessed with the occult. He regularly consulted with sorceresses and also believed in werewolves and witches. Likewise, Heinrich Himmler really did create a German think tank, the Ahnenerbe, which sent expeditions all over the world to search for ancient relics such as Thor's hammer, the Holy Grail, and the Ark of the Covenant, as well as for proof of Aryan superiority.

Obviously, Hitler never found the panel. *The Ghent Altarpiece* and all of the other works of art in the Altaussee salt mines were ultimately recovered, having been saved from destruction by the

"Monuments Men," as depicted in the Hollywood film by the same name. When the war finally ended, the altarpiece was removed and painstakingly restored, including a replica of "The Just Judges" panel painted by master art historian Jef Van der Veken. Today, the whole piece can be viewed back in St. Bavo's Cathedral.

The theft of "The Just Judges" remains an open case, and to this day, the bishopric of Ghent still receives several tips a year as to its location, a few of which they follow up on before passing the rest along to the Ghent police department, which still maintains an officer in charge of this long-cold case.

It is impossible to know how many hands "The Just Judges" might have passed through and where it now resides (if it hasn't been destroyed), but it was fun to imagine that, for a very short time, anyway, it passed through the hands of our hero and heroine on their journey through Strasbourg.

The history of *The Ghent Altarpiece* is fascinating, and a whole mystery novel could be written just about the 1934 theft. The above is merely a brief retelling of the simplest of facts. The entire story is very intriguing, and I encourage you to read about it yourself (a list of sources I found useful appears after this section).

The other painting in our story, *El Rio de Luz* by Frederic Edwin Church, plays a smaller part but is not any less real. Church was a central figure in the Hudson River School and is best known for painting large landscapes. In his prime, he was one of the most famous painters in the United States.

Other real places that figure into the story are, of course, Sacré-Cœur Basilica, Lariboisière Hospital, and the Ritz in Paris, and even Château du Freudeneck, though in reality it is now a ruin. Also real are Mundelein College in Chicago, Illinois, and Clark College in Dubuque, Iowa, which truly are sister schools and were both founded by the Sisters of the Order of the Blessed Virgin Mary.

Sources

Charney, Noah. "Hitler's Hunt for the Holy Grail and the Ghent Altarpiece." *The Daily Beast*. Last modified July 11, 2017. https://www.thedailybeast.com/hitlers-hunt-for-the-holy-grail-and-the-ghent-altarpiece.

Charney, Noah. "Lost art: chasing the elusive Ghent Altarpiece panel." *The Art Newspaper*. Last modified August 22, 2018. https://www.theartnewspaper.com/2018/08/22/lost-art-chasing-the-elusive-ghent-altarpiece-panel.

Charney, Noah. *Stealing the Mystic Lamb: The True Story of the World's Most Coveted Masterpiece*. New York: PublicAffairs, 2010.

Lost Treasures of History. "The Just Judges." Last modified May 28, 2008. https://losttreasuresofhistory.wordpress.com/2018/05/28/the-just-judges.

NPR. "Is This The World's Most Coveted Painting?" Last modified December 23, 2010. https://www.npr.org/2010/12/25/132283848/is-this-the-worlds-most-coveted-painting.

Pitogo, Heziel. "Hitler, the Ghent Altarpiece and the Holy Grail." War History Online. Last modified December 27, 2013. https://www.warhistoryonline.com/war-articles/hitler-ghent-altarpiece-holy-grail.html?chrome=1&A1c=1.

sky HISTORY. "The Nazi Hunt for Holy Treasure from Thor's Hammer to the Holy Grail." Accessed March 4, 2022. https://www.history.co.uk/shows/lost-relics-of-the-knights-templar/the-nazi-hunt-for-holy-treasure-from-thor-s-hammer-to-the-holy-grail.

Tikkanen, Amy. "The Most Stolen Work of Art." *Encyclopedia Britannica.* Accessed March 4, 2022. https://www.britannica.com/story/the-most-stolen-work-of-art.

Wikipedia. "Just Judges and the Knights of Christ." Ghent Altarpiece. Last modified February 21, 2022. https://en.wikipedia.org/wiki/Ghent_Altarpiece#Just_Judges_and_the_Knights_of_Christ.

Acknowledgments

First and foremost I'd like to again thank Brooke Warner of She Writes Press for shepherding me through my publishing options and for welcoming me back to She Writes Press. I am fortunate to have had access to your wisdom and foresight these many years. Thanks, in fact, to the whole team at She Writes Press for the magic you do in bringing stellar books into the world and especially for championing women writers. To be counted in your number is indeed quite a special thing.

Thanks specifically to Julie Metz for yet another beautiful cover, and to my project manager, Lauren Wise Wait, who makes her very complex job look effortless. Thank you, Lauren, for your untiring support and guidance. I'd also like to thank my copyeditor, Susie Chinisci, who not only did an amazing job editing this book (and under the pressure of a looming deadline, I might add), but who has also created a character chart for me of the whole series—something I've sadly been in need of for a very long time. I should have started one at the very beginning of the series, but, alas, I didn't realize while writing Book 1 that Henrietta and Clive would convince me to write them into a next book, and a next, and a next. Now, thanks to Susie, if I need to reference, say, a specific car from Alcott's collection or remember the color of Mrs. Hennessey's eyes, I will have those details at my fingertips instead of having to search endlessly through Word docs looking for it.

And speaking of searching through Word docs, I'd like to again thank my beta readers—Otto, Margaret, Susan, Marcy, Ruth, Phil, and Amy—for quickly reading through the manuscript even as it was being edited!! As always, I treasure your insight, first comments, and suggestions about how to make the story stronger.

But most importantly, I'd like to thank all of YOU for being so patient while you waited a whole extra year for this latest installment to be released. Your emails and encouraging comments spurred me on to continue the series, even while I was working on other projects. It means the world to me that you love Henrietta and Clive and the whole gang as much as I do. Thank you for being so loyal during such a tumultuous couple of years. You are the reason I keep doing this—honestly. More than I can say, I appreciate every like or comment you make on a post, every time you open the newsletter, and every message or email you send to me. They definitely keep the home fires burning.

Lastly, I'd like to thank my family for again giving me the space to write, though it has certainly been challenging to weed this time out with everyone in the house Zooming to learn and work and be social in brave new ways. Somehow we all made it through, and, I believe, are closer for it. Thank you to my three children—Nathaniel, Owen, and Ellie—for picking up the slack around the house (sometimes) and for playing board games with me (sometimes) to help me clear my mind.

And of course, thank you to my lovely husband, Phil, who makes all of this possible and who has always been my number one supporter. Without you, this book would not be—so thank you, again, my love, for the gift. You to me are everything.

About the Author

© Cliento Photography

Michelle Cox is the author of the Henrietta and Inspector Howard series, a mystery/romance saga set in the 1930s Chicago often described as "*Downton Abbey* meets Miss Fisher's Murder Mysteries." To date, the series has won over fifty international awards and has received positive reviews from *Library Journal* (starred), *Booklist* (starred), *Publishers Weekly, Kirkus,* and various media outlets, such as Popsugar, Buzzfeed, *Redbook, Elle,* Brit&Co., *Bustle,* Culturalist, *Working Mother,* and many others.

Cox also pens the wildly popular *Novel Notes of Local Lore,* a weekly blog chronically the lives of Chicago's forgotten residents. She lives in the northern suburbs of Chicago with her husband and three children and is hard at work on her next novel.

SELECTED TITLES FROM SHE WRITES PRESS

She Writes Press is an independent publishing company founded to serve women writers everywhere. Visit us at www.shewritespress.com.

A Child Lost: A Henrietta and Inspector Howard Novel by Michelle Cox
$16.95, 978-1-63152-836-1
Clive and Henrietta are confronted with two cases: a spiritualist woman operating on the edge of town who's been accused of robbing people, and an German immigrant woman who's been lost in the halls of Dunning, the infamous Chicago insane asylum. When a little girl is also mistakenly taken there, the Howards rush to find her, suspecting something darker may be happening . . .

A Girl Like You: A Henrietta and Inspector Howard Novel by Michelle Cox
$16.95, 978-1-63152-016-7
When the floor matron at the dance hall where Henrietta works as a taxi dancer turns up dead, aloof Inspector Clive Howard appears on the scene—and convinces Henrietta to go undercover for him, plunging her into Chicago's gritty underworld.

A Promise Given: A Henrietta and Inspector Howard Novel by Michelle Cox
$16.95, 978-1-63152-373-1
The third installment of the Henrietta and Inspector Howard series unveils the long-awaited wedding of Henrietta and Clive—but murder is never far from this sizzling couple, and when a man is killed on the night of a house party at Clive's ancestral English estate, they are both drawn into the case.

A Ring of Truth: A Henrietta and Inspector Howard Novel by Michelle Cox
$16.95, 978-1-63152-196-6
The next exciting installment of the Henrietta and Inspector Clive series, in which Clive reveals that he is actually the heir of the Howard estate and fortune, Henrietta discovers she may not be who she thought she was—and both must decide if they are really meant for each other.

A Veil Removed: A Henrietta and Inspector Howard Novel by Michelle Cox
$16.95, 978-1-63152-503-2
In this fourth installment of the Henrietta and Inspector Howard series, Clive and Henrietta are once again pitted against their evil nemesis, Neptune, as they delve deeper into Alcott Howard's secret life and apparent murder.

In the Shadow of Lies: A Mystery Novel by M. A. Adler
$16.95, 978-1-93831-482-7
As World War II comes to a close, homicide detective Oliver Wright returns home—only to find himself caught up in the investigation of a complicated murder case rife with racial tensions.